the elm stone saga

# unbidden

# shayla morgansen

Unbidden

ISBN: 978-0-9945897-6-7 (pbk.)

Published by Ouroborus Book Services
www.ouroborusbooks.com

# Contents

# prologue

*1958 – New York*

The basement was spacious, but it was always cold, and piles of useless items lined the walls. One of the pipes on the ceiling always dripped, and the two lights seemed to take turns flickering. It was not a place that an average citizen would spend much time in. Cassán Ó Grádaigh had been here twice before, briefly, didn't like it at all, and was beginning to wonder why he had bothered to come tonight.

Of the other three men present he knew one, and only very superficially. Younger than he, Mánus Morrissey was a fellow Irishman and came from an extremely powerful and influential family. Cassán had met him several years before at a distant relative's wedding – he was a difficult man to forget. Mánus reminded Cassán of a vampire, darkly handsome with his clichéd jawline, jet black hair and odd violet eyes, almost supernaturally intense. He was the sort of man people glanced at twice.

The other two men in the basement were strangers to Cassán, and apparently to one another too, because they (like Cassán and Mánus) stood alone in their own corners without making eye contact with anyone else. They were extremely powerful witches, Cassán sensed. Were he not so curious about the reason why they had all been brought together, he would have left already. The basement was a dank and uncomfortable place to gather.

All eyes turned to the stairs as the fifth of their number arrived. Cassán knew Moira Dawes from the local witchcraft scene. A well-read and enthusiastic young sorceress of deep personal power and wide knowledge, she frequented the occult bookstores, where he'd met her a number of times and fallen into hours of serious conversation about the nature of magic. Amongst the shelves she came across as bookish, deep and studious, but then other times he'd looked up from his morning coffee at a café on the main street to see a band of angry young people marching with Moira Dawes at the lead, protesting the construction of a new department store on the site of a Native American burial ground. She was as likely to be found studying as she was to be found in the back of a police car. Tonight she took the steps two-at-a-time and bounded into the middle of the group with the cheerful energy of a puppy. She looked around at them all, smiling her charmingly lopsided smile.

'Welcome,' she said, turning in a lively circle to meet everyone's eyes. 'I'm very glad you could all make it tonight. I'm sorry for all the secrecy but it was so important that nobody else know about this. I've just finished another layer of silence wards, in case anyone is watching us. Being underground should also help.'

The gathered men said nothing, but Cassán felt their collective interest and curiosity increase.

'As you know,' Moira said, still turning slowly as she spoke, 'the White Elm has just passed a new set of laws regarding the possession of information. According to this amendment, we're not only prohibited from practising, we're no longer allowed to even own books that mention any of the following...' Her energy darkened as she pulled a hastily folded set of papers from the pocket of her dress. "As of August twentieth, all materials that discuss or instruct the reader in illegal magic are banned from use and possession. A full list of illegal branches of magic is included in appendix A. Please destroy all offensive texts or contact the White Elm Council for clarification on uncertain titles or requisition of large collections. Failure to cooperate may result in confiscation of material and disciplinary action'.'

Obviously disgusted, Moira threw the first sheet onto the cold cement floor. She held the second page at eye level and continued reading, her voice rising with hardly controlled anger. The bookish scholar becomes the heated political activist.

"Appendix A: Illegal branches of magic. The following activities are henceforth banned from use, and any materials discussing or instructing the reader in the use of the following activities are henceforth also banned from possession'.' Moira looked up from the correspondence momentarily to make sure they were all listening. They'd all read the notice they'd received in the mail, too, but her passionate oration made it riveting. 'Active scrying-slash-Haunting, sacrificial magic – all forms, weather-slash-season manipulation, human possession, animal possession, *spell crafting*...' She threw that sheet away, too, without finishing it and began on the next one. 'The list goes on: human transformation magic, animal transformation magic, summoning... At the bottom of the page it adds that any magic done with a negative intent should be recognised as dark magic and must be avoided.'

Moira dropped that page, too, and stared down at the small pile of litter she had created. She was seething.

'They've gone one step too far this time,' she said quietly. 'It's fair of them to say magic with a negative intent shouldn't be allowed. I agreed with them when they first said that in '52. But this time, they've outlawed *knowledge*. They've asked us to *burn* our books. Nearly every book in my house infringes this law, so I'm expected to destroy them? *My books*? Knowledge is harmless – it's precious – but they've decided that it's evil and should be destroyed. Hundreds of years of work, up in smoke! Who are they to censor what information we have access to? I read those books; I practise the magic they talk about. It doesn't make *me* evil!'

That, Cassán thought, was a matter of opinion – he'd spell-crafted with her twice before, and she was *intense* – but otherwise he agreed with her. A Crafter, he manipulated magic on a daily basis, and was in the process of writing a book to help practitioners in refining their techniques to re-craft conventional magic to suit modern needs. He had been very annoyed, to put it nicely, to receive the notice from the White Elm that outlawed his book's content before he even went to print. But what they said went.

'They say that magic intended to harm is dark magic – as if that weren't obvious,' Moira carried on. 'That should have been the extent of the letter! *Do no harm.* What about those of us who read these books and perform this magic to expand ourselves as sorcerers? Our world's academics and historians will be out of work, and their libraries will be emptied, nothing but ash! What about those sorcerers who Haunt their friends or family members to protect them when they might be in danger? Since when can possession of animals or transformation into animal form be considered dangerous or harmful? Anyone who has ever lived a day as a bird or wildcat knows what an intense, spiritually expanding journey it is. And no more sacrificial magic?' She scoffed, almost ready to laugh at the ridiculousness. 'Everything good in life comes with sacrifices. Everything has a cost. A nice meal costs money. A wonderful night out costs a good night's sleep. A good spell costs some energy, or maybe a fingernail.'

'*Maybe* some blood,' one of the other men agreed cautiously, tossing dark red hair out of his eyes, 'maybe something more, but no one's using anything that wasn't already dead, already redundant, so long as the market's alive and flourishing. These laws threaten that whole trade. Tresaigh and Ellis are both struggling to maintain things now that the Elm has blocked their channels. It's forcing them underground. No one knows where we'll get supplies from if those two are shut down.' He paused. 'And did you hear about the O'Malleys?'

He directed the question at Mánus, whose face did not even twitch. Of course he'd heard about the O'Malleys. He said nothing. Moira picked up where she'd left off, impassioned.

'Exactly. Our way of life is under threat from this amendment. This letter,' she gestured at the paper at her feet, 'has such huge implications, and no one is arguing with them. This law, passed without so much as a vote, takes magic out of the hands of the people and places it firmly in the control of the White Elm. Take away all the old forms – sacrifice, song, earth magic – and what are we left with? *Their* magic. Their clean, white, controlled magic. My point is that magic is all of ours, not just theirs. My point is that magic comes to us all as naturally as it does them, and our cultural form should not fall to them to choose. My *point* is that it is up to the individual to evaluate the cost and decide whether it is worthwhile. It is *not* the White Elm's job to choose for us. These are our civil liberties I'm talking about here, our rights to choose and think for ourselves. We're losing them.'

Cassán folded his arms, wishing her words weren't hitting home as precisely as they were. Moira was an absurdly persuasive woman, so charismatic and well-spoken. Her bronze-brown eyes glowed with a contagious fire. Cassán knew that wherever this was going, he was going to have a hard time saying no.

'The White Elm searched my house this morning,' the stranger with the dark red hair said darkly. His English accent was thickened with a heavy suggestion of Scottish. 'They spent hours picking the place apart, and left with a stack of old books each and a few family heirlooms. Looters, I say. Aside from getting the important stuff out of the house ahead of time, there was nothing I could do about it. I know what I *wanted* to do, but…'

'Did they at least tell you they were coming?' Mánus asked sharply. Worriedly, Cassán was sure. The Morrisseys no doubt had more than a couple of stacks of books and a few family heirlooms in their stately mansion the White Elm would like to take a look at. The English stranger shook his head.

'Not a word of warning, but I did foresee it,' he said. 'They just turned up on the doorstep, quoted a bunch of legal rubbish at me and let themselves in. I need some better wards on my place, something to deter them next time.' He paused, looking over Mánus's aura, sizing him up. He extended a hand. 'Andrew Hawke.'

'Mánus Morrissey,' the Irish millionaire answered, accepting the handshake. 'I might be able to help you out with those wards.'

'Mánus is an expert at keeping people out,' Moira cooed, leaning close and pressing a cheek affectionately against his shoulder. Cassán gathered that there was more to her comment than just an allusion to the Irishman's fortified home, but also knew that Mánus was happily married to a ridiculously beautiful heiress. Moira stood no chance. She must have known this, because she turned her attention to Andrew. 'Mánus, Andrew is my favourite Seer – so much better than those new "ethical Seers" you find everywhere. He's just a wealth of information. Whatever you need to know, Andrew can tell you. He's *amazing*. He even told me I would hold this meeting.' She giggled girlishly. 'Andrew's always right.'

'A rebel Seer,' Mánus commented. 'You believe in sharing people's futures with them?'

'I believe in freedom of information,' Andrew answered. 'If I know and you want to know, who am I to decide whether you should have access to it?'

'Doesn't Fate decide that by giving the information to you and not him?' Cassán asked before he could stop himself. He'd researched the concept of Fate very deeply in his studies of the essence of magic itself. The two were tightly entwined, and one could not be twisted without affecting the other. He'd written extensively on the topic, and felt quite strongly about it as a result.

'Ah, Cassán, my celebrity guest,' Moira said warmly, deftly interrupting before a debate of ethics and philosophy could begin. 'I'm sure you're all familiar with the writings of my friend Cassán Ó Grádaigh?'

'Certainly,' Andrew agreed, offering his hand again, now to Cassán. 'Beautiful work.'

'But not something Mister Hawke agrees with,' the remaining stranger spoke up coyly. Andrew's pleasant expression slipped slightly. 'One doesn't have to agree with what he's reading in order to appreciate its reasonableness and compare its merits with his own beliefs, of course, but it does help,' the stranger continued. His accent was American, Southern. 'Regretfully I must admit I'm the only one present who hasn't read your work, but meeting you tonight has prompted me to do so. I like the way you think; I imagine I'd like your writing.'

'Eh, I'll, uh… I'll send you a copy of my last book,' Cassán said, mildly disarmed by the stranger's openness. Moira smiled and tucked her hands into her pockets.

'Eugene Dubois is a private investigator – the most talented Telepath I've ever known. Watch your thoughts around him.'

Eugene was chubbier and shorter than the other men. He had a full and stubbly face with round, friendly eyes. He was unremarkable and would easily slip into any crowd.

'Makes the job easier,' Eugene said, still watching Cassán. Nobody had spoken so Cassán assumed he was responding to his thoughts. 'Yes, that's right.' For real? 'Yes. Neat, don't you think?' Cassán worked to build denser wards around his mind, mildly annoyed by the intrusion. 'No point.' He'd never met anybody whose gift transcended the normal laws of telepathy. 'Am I making you uncomfortable?'

'Yes, you are,' Cassán agreed, and Eugene smiled. He was something special and he knew it. No wonder Moira had picked him out and asked him here tonight to join this strange circle of… what, exactly? Magical misfits? A writer, a telepathic private investigator, a rebellious Seer, a millionaire scrier and the troublemaker that was Moira Dawes had nothing obvious in common.

'You don't think so?' Eugene asked of Cassán. He smirked at Moira. 'Your friend thinks the five of us share nothing in common.'

'I'm inclined to agree,' Mánus commented. He paused. 'No offence intended, of course.'

'Oh, but Mánus,' Moira sang, grabbing his hand and swinging it playfully. 'How can you not see what I've brought us together for? How can you not see that we are all brothers and sisters in the same fight?'

Cassán folded his arms, waiting for the explanation.

'What fight?' Mánus asked, and took back his hand. Moira just smiled.

'The fight for our right to information,' Andrew said, as if it were obvious. 'We have a right to know what we know and learn what we want. It's *our* responsibility to use it sensibly, not the White Elm's job to bury it all.'

'Sorcery has progressed perfectly well for thousands of years without this kind of interference. Who are they to decide to take this sort of action now?' Eugene shook his head and sat down on a pile of boxes. 'Our culture, our mythology, our people's history, is built on great acts of magic like transformations and possessions.'

'Without the books and without the masters passing on the skills, those kinds of spells would be lost within a generation,' Mánus realised.

'They're going to kill centuries of magic through this one stupid law,' Moira added.

'We don't have to let them,' Eugene interjected. 'We don't have to stand back and let them pull our society apart.'

'We kind of do,' Cassán disagreed. 'They're in charge.'

'They're in charge because the people allow them to be,' Moira said simply. 'Perhaps we oughtn't allow them to be.'

'How? An uprising of five?' Mánus asked incredulously.

'Most people are going to fold and do what they ask,' Cassán warned the others. 'You're not really suggesting we take on the White Elm council, are you?'

'No, Cassán, nobody is suggesting marring your famous little name,' Moira laughed. 'Not everyone is going to agree with us, just as we don't agree with the council. This is about *me*, and *you*, and *us*. The *people* can do what they like, but *I* intend to keep my books and continue with my study. Perhaps with some help.'

'Out with it, Moira. Why are we here?' Mánus asked. Moira sighed and folded her arms.

'Book club.'

'Excuse me?'

'Book club.' She grinned. 'Once a week we meet and we share. New magic will be hard to come by very soon and harder still to ask for. I've brought you all here tonight to ensure we have a network,' she gestured to the men around her, 'to turn to when we are working. I know each of us to be academics of the magical arts and I will not have our studies interrupted or ceased by the forsaken White Elm. They do not own magic, and they do not own us.'

The four men around her stood in total silence for a very long, still moment.

'That's it?' Andrew asked. 'That's all you want? A professional friendship?'

'I want your secrecy,' Moira corrected. 'I want your promise that you will never bend to the council the way the rest of the world will. I want the knowledge in you to be free to me, the way the knowledge in me is free to you. And yes,' she added with the kind of charming smile no man refuses, 'your friendship would be lovely.'

There was another silence as everyone considered the proposition. Then Moira Dawes extended her hand, and Eugene Dubois took it. The two stared at their joined hands. Andrew Hawke stepped forth and clapped his hand atop theirs with an agreeable nod.

Cassán knew that this was a pact he was being asked to make, bigger than what it sounded like, and that he'd be held to it by these most gifted and resourceful of sorcerers. In principle he agreed with their words, so why was he hesitating? He wasn't the only one. Mánus Morrissey, beside him, cast him a doubtful sidelong glance.

'Come on, Mánus,' Moira called. 'What's the worst that can happen?'

The Morrissey heir almost smiled as he reluctantly approached the trio.

'A wiser man would stop to think of an answer to that question,' he said, resting his palm over Andrew's knuckles. 'But I can only think, screw the White Elm.'

Now was the time to leave if he was ever going to. Cassán looked at the dusty stairs leading out of the basement and *knew* he should take them and get away from these people. Their words were pretty but they were eccentrics and extremists and he could do without them. They wanted him to break laws with them.

This was bad news.

There was no changing his mind after his next decision.

It was time to go.

But instead he grasped their collective hands in both of his and channelled the power through them to cement the pact. The gaps between their fingers glowed briefly as though they were holding a ball of light, and then it went out and they were just five people standing together in a dank, dirty basement, holding hands. Everyone was staring at Cassán.

'Screw the White Elm,' he agreed.

# chapter one

There was a loud snap as a door shut, and I woke suddenly. For a moment I didn't know where I was, parts of my mind still fuzzy and trying to focus on the frayed ends of my dream. I blinked, and recognised my surroundings as Renatus's office. I must have fallen asleep in this armchair.

Emmanuelle, my favourite White Elm councillor and my informal guardian, had just entered the office, looking worn and stressed. When I hurriedly sat up and rubbed my tired eyes, though, her tight expression softened.

'Sorry to wake you, Aristea,' she said. 'Sometimes a healing can be as tiring for the patient as for the Healer.'

Earlier in the night, I'd suffered horrific burns across my arm and neck and broken my shoulder. The harsh memory of the blistered flesh that was my arm only a few hours ago still made me feel unwell. Because of Emmanuelle's incredible gift of healing, I was as good as new, with not a scratch on me. Except for the jacket that had been disintegrated in the process, you would never have guessed from looking at me the trauma I'd experienced.

'I'm okay,' I assured her, trying to smile. I wanted her to believe everything was alright – before she'd healed me, our friendship had taken a severe beating when I'd suspected her of betraying me. Thankfully I was mistaken, but I could tell from her eyes that she was worried I might still harbour resentment for the act she'd played out. 'I was just dreaming.'

'No, you weren't.'

I looked over at the beautiful oak desk in front of the room's stately arched window. My master, Renatus, was bent over an old list, as he had been for hours. Now he was looking up at me, his intense violet eyes bright and revealing none of the exhaustion I knew he must be feeling.

'You weren't dreaming,' he clarified. 'It's not possible. You can't dream here.'

I'd forgotten about that. Ever since coming to stay at Morrissey House two months ago my nights, once plagued with nightmares, had been totally dreamless. For reasons I didn't know, enchantments on the house prevented anyone inside it from dreaming. Until tonight.

'I was dreaming,' I insisted. I grasped at the details that were quickly fading from my memory. 'I saw five people, talking about magic-'

'You were scrying,' Renatus interrupted, referring to our special ability to remotely observe past and present events with the power of our minds. I'd only learnt to do this in recent weeks, and only once before done it in my sleep. 'You're starting to tap into events pertaining to others rather than just yourself. It's a natural progression of your gift. It's probably something happening nearby, with little relevance to you-'

'It was my grandfather, in the United States in 1958,' I said firmly, remembering at least these little details. Renatus frowned; he looked like he was going to say something, but he was cut off by a sharp knock at the door. He flicked his wrist towards it and it swung open for the rest of the White Elm.

Usually made up of thirteen super-powerful international sorcerers, the White Elm council governed and protected most of the world's magical community. Needless to say, they were a very impressive bunch, even in their current defeated and exhausted state. The leader, Lord Gawain, headed the group as they filed into Renatus's office.

2

'Where are we up to with the gates?' he asked. The old Welshman looked more tired than anyone else present. Under the stubble, his face looked drawn and pale.

'We did everything we knew of,' Renatus answered. 'Aubrey's never getting back onto these grounds.'

Upon our hasty return to the house a few hours ago, the first task allocated to Renatus, Emmanuelle and I had been to fortify the estate's magical barriers against the return of Aubrey, a member of the White Elm until tonight when he'd tried to fake his own death as part of his shock betrayal and departure from the council. I'd never made wards that big before but both Renatus and Emmanuelle had assured me I'd done a good job.

'Now that we're all here, can someone please tell me about Teresa?' Jadon asked, pushing the door closed behind him. The youngest councillor on the White Elm, Jadon had probably had an even worse night than mine. What had started off as a mission to rescue his two closest friends, Aubrey and Teresa, had ended in Aubrey's apparent death, the realisation that he was in fact alive and working for the other side, and the discovery of the newly rescued Teresa, unconscious and left for dead, drained of all energy by Aubrey. Jadon was handling it quite well, I thought, for someone normally quick to anger.

Lady Miranda, the co-leader and a powerful Healer more gifted even than Emmanuelle, sighed and sat down in the armchair opposite mine. Black and silver curls hung limply around her face. Everyone listened attentively; they were all worried about fragile Teresa, and with good reason, if our understanding of her treatment in captivity was correct.

'She's... We've erased every physical injury,' Lady Miranda said finally, her gaze fixed firmly on Emmanuelle. After helping us with the gates, Emmanuelle had left Renatus and me to assist Lady Miranda in counselling the stirring Teresa. The two Healers were emanating a reluctance only I could really feel.

'Do you know what happened to her?' Jadon asked, genuinely worried, but Emmanuelle refused to look at him. Eye contact gave Telepaths easy access to the mind, and she wasn't giving him anything.

'The physical recovery is complete but the emotional healing is Teresa's journey,' Lady Miranda explained. She looked up at Elijah, the best man in the world if you wanted something teleported. 'Any trace of Aubrey?'

'Nothing,' Elijah reported, clearly annoyed with himself. I knew that he possessed the ability to actually sense anomalies in the Fabric of space where someone had teleported, and follow the wormhole left behind. Aubrey, however, was clever and talented and had neatly covered his tracks. 'Nor of the boys.'

'Anyone else missing?' Lord Gawain asked the rest of the council. They all shook their heads. They were all responsible for mentoring one dorm room of students at Morrissey House, and had all checked on their students immediately upon returning to the estate. Aubrey had disappeared with the four students who trusted him the most, taking them straight to Lisandro.

I stood suddenly, because even the thought of the White Elm's enemy and former member disturbed me more deeply than I was ready to admit. Before this night, he'd just been the bad guy, an elusive and distant threat I had no real understanding of. He'd killed some people – that was mean – and he'd kidnapped two of the White Elm's youngest councillors, which was also quite nasty but had created the catalyst for my selection as Renatus's apprentice, so it was difficult for me to view that event as totally bad. On this night, however, Lisandro had kidnapped *me*, forced the White Elm to hand over to him a source of incredible power and disappeared, but not before revealing – accidentally – his most horrifying secret.

Lisandro was the killer of my parents and brother. He'd murdered them, without a care. He'd even told me that it hadn't hurt to do it. He'd destroyed my family, leaving me

4

and my sister orphans, all because it suited his sick, twisted purpose.

I still wasn't sure how it made me feel. Sad? Not quite, as I'd already had over three years to grieve for their loss. Angry? Yeah, kind of, although how angry? Confused? Definitely, because I'd always believed their deaths to be accidents, but now I knew different.

Turbulent. That's how it made me feel.

'They were your friends,' Lord Gawain guessed, trying to be kind. I blinked, then realised that he was referring back to the conversation my mind had strayed so far from, and the way I'd suddenly jumped up and begun to pace agitatedly.

'Aye, sort of,' I agreed, forcing myself to reflect on the four missing students. Tyson and Enrico had never really spoken to me, except maybe to make fun of me at some point, but Joshua and Garrett were both nice enough. My stomach tightened a little at the thought of Garrett and his newfound relationship with Hiroko, my best friend. Who was going to tell her that her sweetheart was missing? It made little enough sense to me. How was anyone going to make Hiroko understand?

'We have to assume that they are safe,' Lord Gawain reminded me. 'Aubrey and Lisandro have no good reason to hurt any of the boys. It makes more sense that they are trying to win their allegiance than use them as hostages.'

I nodded as though this made me feel better, although I was finding it difficult to feel the urgency others were feeling about my peers and their disappearance. According to my recent experiences with Lisandro, when he made someone disappear, they were pretty well gone until such time as he chose to make them reappear or the hostage managed to escape. I'd been lucky enough to get away, although in retrospect I could see that he'd known I would. He'd expected it, and hadn't made it too hard for me, except to throw a few bolts of lightning at me. All fun and games in the mind of a supernatural serial killer. I'd believed at the time that I was going to die, but I could see now that once

Lisandro had what he'd wanted – the ring – I'd been in no further danger. Killing me would have been so easy for him if he'd meant to, which left me with one fact: I was alive because Lisandro intended it. Which made life feel pretty redundant, if someone else got to call shots like that.

Renatus was watching me closely. Since our bonding ceremony as master and apprentice, only two weeks ago tonight, we'd enjoyed, or perhaps put up with, a strong new link between our minds. Whatever I thought, he could know; whatever he remembered, I could feel. We'd quickly learnt how to section off various parts to maintain our privacy and our sense of individualism, but right now, he knew exactly what was going through my head. It was exactly what was going through his.

Four years before the deaths in my family, a storm had ripped through Morrissey Estate and wiped out the whole Morrissey family, leaving only Renatus, then a teenager. I was hurting, but really, his situation was so much worse, because he'd been left all alone in the world except for one person: his godfather, Lisandro himself.

Lisandro had admitted to murdering *both of our families*. Even thinking it sounded numbly, dumbly melodramatic. Ridiculous, laughable. And no one else even knew, bar Emmanuelle and Lord Gawain, who'd overheard. I was fading in and out of the conversations but I'd distinctly noticed that this topic had not been broached. For that I was glad. I didn't know what I'd do if someone brought it up now. Cry? Laugh? Scream? Run out of the room, most likely.

If I was struggling to know how to feel about the fact that Lisandro had killed my parents and big brother, Renatus had every right to completely fall to pieces. But he wouldn't. He would keep it inside and let it stew, like the silent brooding type he was. That dark, tortured aura was part of his appeal, I knew, that drove girls and women to throw themselves at his feet and act like complete idiots whenever they saw him.

'I've already sent for the families,' Qasim said. 'Two are awake and preparing to be collected.'

Like me and like Renatus, Qasim was a scrier. In fact, he was *the* Scrier for the White Elm, probably the most skilled scrier in the world today. I'd had more than my share of run-ins with him, and I was pretty sure that Renatus and I were his least favourite people ever, but I still found that I deeply admired Qasim and wanted, almost more than anything else, to be just like him.

'This conversation will be unpleasant,' Susannah murmured. She and Lord Gawain were both Seers, with the challenging and incredible gift of being able to foresee how actions in the present affected potential futures. It made them both very influential people, but I'd long since guessed that, despite popular belief, Susannah was the more powerful of the two.

'Aristea, you're not to rejoin the student body until we've announced the bad news,' Lady Miranda said to me in her firm tone as she got heavily, tiredly to her feet. 'I'm sure you have friends you want to share with and comfort, but they'll all find out at the same time this way. We don't want miscommunications. You can stay with Renatus until after the announcement.'

I nodded, fiddling with the ring on my pinkie finger. Before I'd left last night, Hiroko had given me the little ring to match hers, a symbol of our friendship. Was I any kind of friend if I stood idly by and let her find out from our teachers, in front of everybody, that her almost-boyfriend was missing? Shouldn't it be me that told her, before the announcement, so she would have a chance to react without everyone watching her? Last night at dinner, in quite possibly the cutest show of affection I'd seen outside of a movie, Hiroko and Garrett had kissed in front of everybody. Every student at the White Elm's Academy knew that they were an item. When they heard he was missing, every pair of eyes would be on Hiroko.

I couldn't change what had happened but I could change how she found out.

'Aristea, I mean it,' Lady Miranda added, as though she knew what I was thinking. I nodded instantly.

7

'Mm-hmm,' I agreed. 'I understand.'

'We'll need to draft a public statement regarding Aubrey,' Glen, a Telepath, said, looking around. 'We'll also need to advertise for applicants for our new vacancy.'

I hadn't thought of that until right then. With Aubrey gone, the White Elm council was down to twelve members. Incomplete. It seemed so soon to be replacing him, but I could see how it was necessary to do so as quickly as possible. How long would they wait for the right person? Only, I would be eligible in a bit over two years...

'Is there any point?' asked Anouk, Glen's cynical Russian telepathic counterpart. 'Last time we advertised, Lisandro threatened most of the potentials out of applying.'

'No advertisement,' Lord Gawain confirmed. 'I have someone in mind. We'll deal with that in the coming days. For now, just let the public know that Aubrey is no longer to be trusted.'

I supposed that two years was a bit too long to wait. They needed someone soon. The first position to come up after I turned twenty was meant to be mine, assuming, of course, that I lived that long. I'd not realised until tonight that it was not a given.

I'd been so stubborn and stupid earlier tonight, insisting I should be allowed to come along when Lord Gawain and Renatus confronted Lisandro. In reality, I'd had no place there. I'd nearly gotten killed, and had cost the council their Elm Stone – a storehouse of power Lisandro had been seeking for months – as well as their edge – my ability to scry Lisandro's movements. Tonight, he'd touched me, and now knew my essence. He'd block my every attempt to view him now. I was also, devastatingly, partly responsible for the disappearance of the four students, because my original instructions for tonight had been to stay here and keep watch on the house and its inhabitants. If I'd been here, like I was told, I could have warned Renatus as soon as Aubrey entered the estate. He could have been back in seconds.

Now how was I going to even face Hiroko, with this heavy realisation weighing on me?

'What about the ring?' Emmanuelle asked. An awkward silence answered her. Yes, what about the ring? The Elm Stone – the flat old gem, set into a plain platinum band, which held the source of the White Elm's power – had belonged to the council for hundreds of years, spending its time growing in energy, used only in times of great need against terrible threats. Last night it had fallen into Lisandro's hands, and no one knew what this meant for the magical community.

'Say nothing,' Lady Miranda said crisply. 'No one needs to know we've lost it. Again. There would be bedlam. Say nothing, and we will deal with this matter privately.'

The White Elm's usual plan of attack, I'd noticed. A conservative government, they tended towards quiet brushing aside of anything that could bring embarrassment or upset, and proactive rejections of anything with risk. Only days ago I watched them trial Renatus – think old-time medieval witch trials, it wasn't much better – with a paranoid fervour that had frightened me. They'd worried *he* was the spy in their ranks, and the threat to our fledgling partnership and our futures with the council had been very real. Things were good now, at least in that respect, but I felt that Lisandro really hadn't thought through his plan very well: he was trying to destabilise their political position as the unquestioned authority over about three quarters of the magical world, the mainstream of witch society, forcing the White Elm into survival mode, which made them scary.

At least their ferocity was aimed in the opposite direction from me, at the most despicable being I could imagine. That stopped them from realising how much anger I deserved from them for my stupidity and what that had cost them tonight.

They spoke and planned all around me but a lot went right over my fuzzy head. I wished they would go so it would just be me and Renatus. So I could tell him how sorry I was

9

for how tonight had gone down. So I could ask what was going to happen now. So I could sneak off, wake Hiroko and tell her everything, without worrying about getting in trouble.

Conversations carried on and ended. From his place behind the desk, Renatus had the door open for his colleagues with a flick of his hand. This whole house was attuned to his blood and his energy. Gates opened at his touch; doors opened at his thought. Some, like this office, wouldn't open *without* his thought.

'I need to write this down,' Glen said finally, overwhelmed with information, and looked around. Renatus wordlessly offered him a fountain pen and sheet of paper, and Glen took them hesitantly. In Renatus's old manor house, this was the height of technology. He leaned on the desk and began to scribe.

'Perhaps a keyboard would be faster,' Lord Gawain realised. 'Let's use my office.' Relieved, Glen finished his sentence and dropped the pen onto the desktop. Discreetly, Renatus moved it back to its place, in line with all his other fountain pens. 'We might be able to get it printed by the morning. Renatus, what's that you're working on?' he now asked while Glen folded his draft up and pocketed it. My master had gone back to staring at the list in front of him, but now glanced up. He handed it over when Lord Gawain reached for it. The older man looked it over, and when he spoke again, his voice was emotionless. 'I'd forgotten about this. I'm not sure it's worth your attention.'

Renatus was silent for a long moment, and I knew he disagreed. But eventually he nodded and took the list back.

'You're probably right,' he said. 'Good night, Master.'

It was polite but definitely a dismissal. The four councillors still present headed for the door, which was still open for them and closed upon the last of their number stepping through it.

Finally.

I turned to Renatus. I had a lot to say, and I wasn't sure where to begin. Well, there was one very obvious word that came to mind.

'Do not even go there,' Renatus said before I could speak. 'Do not apologise.'

'I definitely get to apologise this time,' I disagreed. 'This is all my fault.'

'No. Susannah said you coming led to the best outcome. That means things would be worse if you'd stayed.'

'How could they be any worse?'

'I'm not a Seer. I don't know what the other futures looked like. Maybe we wouldn't have found Teresa. It's unlikely that we would have realised Aubrey's death was faked without you, and he would have come here and taken the boys anyway without us knowing.'

'I would have been here. I could have told you.'

'He might have hurt you,' Renatus said abruptly. 'There's no point in discussing "would have", "might have". There's only what is. You came with me, we lost the ring, we got Teresa back, we all survived, and if I'm lucky, maybe I can finally make some sense of this.'

He waved the page he'd been poring over all night and unlocked a drawer, ready to put it away. I stepped over and reached across the desk with my left hand. The only evidence of my earlier trauma, my singed and tattered sleeve, hung awkwardly from my elbow. It had been burnt away by Lisandro's magic, as had my skin beneath it, but that injury was completely gone. My wrist was smooth and unmarked, except for the black tattoo on the underside.

Renatus whipped the aged, creased paper away from my fingers before I could touch it. I knew why. Sometimes when I touched things I tapped into impressions – a vision produced by residual energy. He didn't want me to get overwhelmed. So much had happened tonight, and I'd already had one meltdown (understandably, I thought). He wasn't sure how sensitive I was, what I might see and how I might react.

His movement was too quick for my hand but not too quick for my eye. The stained paper was home to a list of handwritten names, some crossed out, and while I didn't read them all before he folded it in half, a few caught my attention.

*Lisandro... ~~Cassán~~... Aristea...*

'It's the *other* list with your name on it,' Renatus confirmed as he buried it in a desk drawer and locked it away, 'and tonight is not the night for you to worry about it.'

My stomach tightened a little, suddenly remembering finding a list on his desk weeks ago and him freaking out about it. The list I'd found was harmless, a class list – *this*, whatever it was, is what he'd thought I had stumbled across.

'Why is my name on that list?' I demanded. I paused, thinking on the way he'd kept it from my fingertips. 'Lisandro wrote it. Didn't he?'

*Yes.*

I inhaled slowly, directing my attention to the back of my mind, where I was connected to my master. It was his voice I heard in my thoughts, not my own. From him I learned more. He was always a wealth of information. I sifted through his knowledge of the subject. He didn't block me from it, though he could.

All he knew for sure about this list was that it had been written by Lisandro, most likely sometime in the past four years but possibly earlier, and that Peter, a former White Elm councillor who had followed Lisandro upon the revelation of his betrayal, had hidden it, along with the ring, and left both for Emmanuelle to find after his death. Renatus didn't know why Lisandro had written it. He didn't know why Peter had taken it and hidden it in Emmanuelle's yard.

'The running theory is that he knew Lisandro was planning to kill him and so he hid the ring and the list, hoping to hinder Magnus Moira and help us,' Renatus said, referring to Lisandro's followers by their official name, 'but it doesn't explain how he thought this list would help the White Elm.' He paused. 'My name's on it, too.'

'Who else?' I asked, pushing again into his thoughts to see his memory of it, but he now blocked me. 'Is it a hit list?'

'Don't worry about it tonight,' he said again. 'I don't know what it's for, but it's not a hit list. Half the people on it are already dead, and were dead years before the list was written.' In his thoughts, mostly blocked, I saw a name. *Anastasia.* His sister. She was on there, too. 'Besides, Lisandro put his own name on it.'

'And us,' I agreed, trying to be reasonable.

'Are you saying that you doubt he intends to kill us?' Renatus sounded extremely sceptical.

'He *told* me that he let us live *on purpose*,' I reminded him. 'He said that it wasn't a mistake that we survived.' I ran a hand through my hair; my fingers met resistance in the form of knots. My hair had experienced a pretty bad night, too, getting rained on and blown around in a crazy storm. 'There's also the inescapable fact that he didn't kill me tonight.'

Renatus turned away to stare out the huge arched window behind his desk, one of his usual thinking strategies.

'I thought he was trying to,' he admitted after a minute, 'but Lisandro needed me to believe that, or I would have gone after him and killed him. You were in danger; I could hear your thoughts, your terror, and I could see how close each blast came to hitting you. But he wasn't going to kill you unless I followed him. It was a test. He just wanted...'

'Wanted what?' I pressed, when he didn't finish.

'To see what I would choose. He really didn't know which way I would go.'

I looked down at the oak desktop.

'I thought I knew what you'd choose,' I said. 'I was surprised.'

At the height of the battle, Renatus had been faced with a moment's choice between chasing down and confronting Lisandro or rescuing me. He'd chosen me. Lisandro had gotten away.

'You shouldn't have been surprised.'

'I know,' I said quickly. 'But I-'

I stopped myself. I'd been about to say something like, "I wish you'd killed him". That probably wasn't an appropriate thing to say, traumatised or otherwise. Did I really wish that? Did I really wish a man dead, and wish my master to commit such a soul-tearing act? I wasn't sure, which scared me, because the answer might be yes.

'But I wasn't thinking,' I said instead. I knew Renatus wasn't fooled; he had to know it wasn't what I was going to say, so I added, 'I'm still not thinking properly.'

'You need some sleep,' Renatus insisted. He put the list back in the drawer he kept it in. 'Emmanuelle's right, you're tired and your body needs rest to recover the energy she borrowed to heal you.'

So that was how she got around the exhaustion. Actually, someone might have told me that before, now that I thought about it. She used *my* energy to mend my injuries. It was a good idea, I thought, as it hadn't affected me at the time, but I was feeling it now.

'Lady Miranda doesn't want me to go back to my dorm, though,' I reminded Renatus. 'That would be re-joining the student body. Can I just sleep in here?'

I could easily curl up in my armchair again, or lay down on one of the two-seaters.

'No, come with me.'

I followed Renatus to the door, which silently opened for him, and we walked out into the empty hallway. Without speaking he led me off to the left, down a hall I'd never before used. This level of the massive house was not used for lodging of students or for classes, so unless a student was sent to Renatus, the headmaster, (as I had once been) there was no reason for them to be up here. My friends and I had explored much of the rest of the estate, but this seemingly empty floor was somewhat foreboding. It seemed obvious that this was the part of the house that Renatus lived in, and although it wasn't specifically said, it seemed equally obvious that students weren't supposed to be wandering through it.

Renatus opened a door, silent like all the others, and clicked with his finger and thumb. A warm, dull light flickered to life inside the room, casting our shadows against the wall behind us. I moved forward to be able to see into the room.

It was a huge, extravagant bedroom, with a tall four-poster bed draped in beautiful curtains dominating my attention. I looked around to admire the other tall, oak pieces of furniture, like the free-standing mirror, the beautiful duchess, the elegant wardrobe and the perfectly-stacked bookcase of hardcover classics. The light was born of the lit oil lamps and candles around the room.

'You can stay here tonight,' Renatus said, 'and this can be your room from now on, if you would like.'

There was a tone to his voice and a slight feeling I got from him that told me what a huge release it was for him to give this to me. This room had to be Ana's – his dead sister's. The sister he'd adored, who Lisandro had murdered and who Lisandro claimed I was replacing in Renatus's lonely life. The sister whose name was with ours on Lisandro's list. I wondered if hers was crossed out.

'Thank you,' I said, stepping hesitantly into the room. It was perfect, dustless, nothing to say it had been empty for seven years. No doubt, Renatus's caring staff had kept this room in its immaculate state. He stayed in the doorway, looking around expressionlessly. I left his thoughts alone.

'There's a bathroom through that door,' he said, pointing. 'It won't be like the one in your dorm. And there are clothes in all the drawers and the wardrobe. Anything you want is yours. Good night.'

He left abruptly, closing the door behind him, leaving me alone in Ana's bedroom.

# chapter two

On Tuesday morning I awoke to something I'd not woken to in weeks – a ray of pale sunlight dancing across my face. I opened my eyes and looked around, totally lost. This was not my room. It was not my bedroom at home, and it was not the dormitory I stayed in at Morrissey House. I was lying in a lush four-post bed in a huge, beautiful room furnished with tall, elegant oak wardrobes and dressers.

I sat up as last night's events came back to me. I'd nearly died. I'd cost Renatus the White Elm's ring. I'd been given this room, Ana Morrissey's old bedroom, and everything in it. I'd contemplated poking around and looking at everything but then pretty much passed out on the bed, exhausted.

I swung my legs out from under the covers. I'd slept very soundly, which surprised me. Although the bed was extremely comfortable, I happened to know that the last person to sleep in it had died over seven years ago, which creeped me out at least a little bit. She hadn't died in the bed or even in the room (thankfully) but she'd died violently and much too young, and her passing had derailed Renatus's life. It was not a nice story.

I got out of bed and walked slowly to the window. The dormitory I shared with Hiroko, Sterling and Xanthe didn't have any windows because it was in the centre of the house, without any exterior walls. I realised now that I'd become used to it, and that waking to sunlight today was something of a novelty. I gently shifted the draped curtain aside to look through the glass.

Morrissey Estate was beautiful, with green, rolling grounds sprinkled with the occasional shade-giving tree and edged with a solid stone wall. At the back of the property was a dense, overgrown apple orchard. It was off-limits to students staying at the house, but it might as well have been haunted, because nobody wanted to go in there anyway. The feeling of death and darkness was quite pronounced. It did look pretty, though, especially from up here with the early sunlight brightening its shadows.

I pushed the curtain with more force, letting more light into the room than I imagined it had seen in almost a decade. The lace hanging behind the curtain filtered the sunlight prettily, casting dainty patterns across the bedspread I'd messed up and the soft carpets. It was such a lovely room, like a princess's bedroom. I hadn't known Ana but knowing how Renatus lived now, I didn't think it was much of a stretch to imagine the late heiress as being treated like a little princess.

Reminded of my master by my train of thought, I subconsciously reached for him along the telepathic link we shared. I didn't want his attention; I just wanted a sense of what he was doing, what he was thinking. For the first time since I'd learnt how to do this, I found his mind vague and quiet – fast asleep. Imagine that; I'd woken earlier than he had.

*Anything you want is yours,* he'd said. I started to wander around the room, admiring all the pretty things that would be mine if only I asked. Atop the stately drawers were several glass jewel boxes. I wanted to get them down and go through them, but I forcibly kept my hands to myself. I'd touched something personal of Ana's once before and had been quite confronted by the impressions I'd picked up on. I'd had a rough night; I didn't need any further emotional shaking. Maybe another time.

The dresser, complete with three-piece mirror and stool, was tidy, with make-up brushes and nail files standing neatly in a glass vase and lipstick cylinders lined up against the mirror. Everything had a place. Had I not known her brother, I would have said that Ana's things were too neatly organised to have honestly been left as they were when she died. However, I did know Renatus, and I knew he wouldn't have let anything of Ana's be changed or rearranged. I also knew his obsession with neatness. Everything in his office had its own place, right down to the perfect row of fountain pens that lived in the upper left of his desk. Apparently it was a hereditary trait.

Or a learned coping mechanism against the same childhood environment. I didn't know much about it, except that Renatus had walked away from the family name and all their associates after the death of his parents, so I gathered it wasn't the same warm, supportive upbringing I'd shared with my siblings.

I cringed when I saw my reflection. I'd fallen asleep (passed out was definitely the more appropriate term) in yesterday's clothes, including my torn and singed jacket, but the crumpled look was the least of my problems. The hair. Oh, the hair. Rain plus wind plus violence plus sleep did not make for a good hair day, let's leave it at that. I impulsively reached for the paddle-like hairbrush lying parallel to the comb and-

*Night time, the room is lit with candles… A beautiful girl slowly runs the brush through long black hair… Staring at her reflection in the mirror… Brown eyes distant…*

I dropped the brush, but the impression had already passed. I felt silly. I'd known, or at least strongly suspected, that this would happen. Intense moments in time left energetic impressions on physical objects, like hairbrushes and lists, which could last years. What I'd just seen hadn't appeared particularly intense, but I wasn't to know what Ana was thinking at the time she'd last touched this hairbrush. She might have had an epiphany, or come to a difficult decision. That might have been a significant moment in her final days.

I carefully picked the brush up from the floor. I'd already tapped into its memories – it was unlikely to yield anything further, but I was still cautious. I spent a few minutes brushing the knots out of my hair, and felt a mild twinge of disappointment when my slightly wavy brown hair didn't look as perfect, soft or sleek as Ana's.

I put the brush back where I'd found it and went into the bathroom Renatus had pointed out. As he'd said, it was nothing like the one in my dorm, but nor was it much like the room I'd just left. Unlike the bedroom, it was brightly lit and totally pristine, obviously cleaned and prepared only in the past few days. Fresh towels were laid out, with new soaps and shampoos and hair clips should I want to keep my long hair dry. Not that there was much risk of my hair getting wet in the shower, considering there wasn't one. An elegant pedestal basin, an old-fashioned toilet, a wicker laundry basket and an ornate silver mirror surrounded a huge free-standing, claw-footed bathtub. That sounds like plenty, except when you need a shower. I lived for showers. I wasn't sure this new-bedroom arrangement was going to work, between the haunted hairbrushes and the stark lack of shower.

As it turns out, baths are not so bad. I actually don't know how much time I spent just lying there soaking, dirt from last night's confrontations with the ground coming away – I was so filthy, I was surprised Renatus had let me sit down in his office – and getting my hair clean. When I let the water out, it was satisfying to watch the grimy events of the night swirl down the drain. I got dry and wrapped myself in the towel, and then hesitated. What was I meant to wear today? Yesterday's clothes were wrecked and/or dirty, but all my other stuff was in my dormitory… two floors down. I couldn't very well wander through the house naked except for this towel to get clothes from my closet. Wait, what time was it? Maybe…

19

No. It was hardly decent. Morrissey House was currently the boarding house of thirty-something teenage witches, here to learn the fine magical arts from the councillors of the White Elm. Half of those students were boys. Thanks to some nasty (and totally untrue) rumours, at least half of those boys thought I was "easy". Regardless of the hour, I would not be caught walking around the halls in a towel.

Just no.

So what was the other alternative? Wear Ana's things. It was stupid, but I felt really uncomfortable with the idea of wearing someone else's clothes without asking her, even if she wasn't alive to ask. None of the clothes she'd died in would be here. They would have been ruined. All the clothes left behind were just abandoned possessions, like the furniture, like the lipsticks... Not creepy at all, I told myself forcibly. My wand, rarely used though it was, had belonged to my dead grandmother. *That* wasn't weird. Neither were Ana's t-shirts.

Almost convinced, I strode back into the bedroom, just as someone quietly opened the bedroom door. I froze, tightening my arm across the towel to hold it to my chest, and automatically built a series of energetic wards around my body, protecting me from most forms of attack.

But there was no need, of course. My visitor was Fionnuala, Renatus's head of staff and childhood nanny. She was oldish, in her fifties or sixties I supposed, with steely grey hair that spent all its time pinned up in an old-fashioned, lady-like bun. I didn't know her very well yet but she'd been totally lovely to me and clearly adored Renatus.

'Good morning, Miss Aristea,' she said pleasantly, pretending not to notice my defensive act, although I was certain she knew I was completely coated in magical shields. I dropped them, feeling dumb. Like I could possibly be attacked here.

'Morning,' I responded, eyeing the small bundle of fabrics in her hands. I recognised a girly hearts-and-kisses pattern as belonging to a pair of my underwear, and was certain that that black denim was a pair of my jeans. How had she known?

'I'm glad that Master Renatus has given you this room,' the housekeeper said. She left my fresh clothes on the end of the bed and went into the bathroom to collect my dirty clothes. 'It's a big step towards accepting what happened to Miss Ana. It doesn't necessarily mean *you're* ready.'

I felt strong affection for the old woman then. She understood, better even than me, what my problem was. Ana was gone and I reminded her brother of her. There was a connection there that I still needed time to explore. Stepping into her life wasn't something I was ready for.

'Thanks,' I said, and she smiled knowingly.

'I might be able to mend this jacket,' she said, critically examining the wreckage of my clothes. 'I'll see what I can do. Pancakes for breakfast this morning,' she added over her shoulder as she left the room.

As soon as the door clicked lightly shut, I dropped my towel and set about getting dressed. Breakfast. The White Elm always made serious announcements at breakfast. The kidnapping of four peers was pretty serious, and I still didn't want Hiroko to hear about it from anyone but me.

I strapped my watch on (to my right wrist, where I'd recently taken to wearing it), clipped my key back on around my neck, slung my dripping dark hair over my shoulder and hurried out of the room, taking care to close the door behind me. It still felt quite early in the dim, silent halls of the mansion, so I began to think of ways to quietly wake Hiroko up without disturbing our roommates. My plans were quickly shattered by the sudden ringing of a loud bell. I glanced at my watch as I hastened my pace. Why hadn't I looked when I'd put it on? Seven o'clock, the wake-up bell that went off every weekday to counter the lack of alarm clocks and assist students in getting to scheduled classes on time.

I jogged down two flights of stairs and followed the hall to my left. Two doors down was the dormitory to which my key would gain me entry. I pulled the chain over my head and slid the key into its hole, but paused before turning it. When I extended my senses, I could feel the energies of my three roommates moving around inside the room. Presently I felt Sterling and Xanthe moving further away from me, presumably into their bathroom, while Hiroko remained in the bedroom. I turned my key and gently pushed the door open. The two beds to my left were empty and unmade, sheets strewn about. The first bed to my right was as neat and tidy as I'd left it yesterday morning, and the bed to the far right was in the process of being made up by its owner and my closest friend, Hiroko.

'Hey,' I said softly, entering and pressing the door shut carefully to avoid a noise. Hiroko looked up at me, and her dainty-featured face broke into a relieved smile.

'You're okay,' she commented, and I knew she'd worried that I wouldn't be. She alone of all the students here knew what I was doing last night. 'I thought something-'

'Something terrible *has* happened,' I cut her off, still speaking quietly. The door in the left corner of the room was slightly open, which meant Sterling and Xanthe could easily overhear anything I said too loudly. I didn't want them to hear me or even know I was here. I could be in a bit of trouble if anyone on the White Elm (bar Renatus) knew I'd come here this morning. 'It's about Garrett.'

Hiroko's smile quickly turned into a confused frown, and I felt horrible. Maybe I should have left this to the White Elm, as I'd been told. Maybe Lady Miranda, in all her wisdom, really did know better. But I was here now, and the best-friend thing to do was spill.

'What do you mean?' Hiroko asked. Her words were clear and well-articulated but her speech rhythm was always slightly stilted, the tell-tale sign that English was not her first language. 'Garrett... He did not go. He is not an apprentice.'

'Aubrey was the traitor,' I whispered, hearing the sound of water running as one of the other girls turned her shower on. I sat down on the edge of my bed and Hiroko sat on hers.

22

'All along. He betrayed everyone; let us think he was in danger when he wasn't. While we were looking for him, he came back here and... he came back here and kidnapped... some boys,' I finished lamely. It sounded so melodramatic but it was so much worse than what I'd said. Aubrey had not only let his council believe he was in danger for weeks, he'd let them believe he was dead. And he'd not only kidnapped some boys, he'd kidnapped *Hiroko's* boy.

'Garrett,' she murmured after a moment. I nodded. I didn't know what else to say. 'Who else?'

'His whole dorm,' I said, watching her porcelain-pale face for pain and difficulty. 'Tyson, Enrico... and Joshua.'

Josh was another friend of hers. Like Joshua and Garrett, Hiroko was a Displacer, gifted in the ability to teleport. They were all in Elijah's top class for it and all got along particularly well – much better than I got along with other students in the top scrying class, anyway.

'The White Elm has not yet found them?' Hiroko asked. I shook my head, and she asked, 'Do they know why he has taken them?'

'Not really, but we assume he's taken them to Lisandro.' I paused, and she said nothing. 'I'm really sorry. I wasn't supposed to tell you; I just didn't want you to find out with everyone else.'

'Thank you,' she said immediately, although I wasn't sure whether she was in shock or actually capable of gratitude at the moment.

'I have to go. I'm not meant to be here. Will you be okay?'

'I am fine,' Hiroko assured me when I touched her arm concernedly. 'Just... I will be fine. And I am glad you are okay.'

'Oh, Emmanuelle fixed me up,' I said quietly, extending my arm and looking for marks. There was nothing to see or show, except my tattoo, so I let it fall. 'I'll see you at breakfast.'

'Yes,' Hiroko agreed, smiling as though I'd not just told her that her sweetheart was missing and possibly in danger.

Her show of apparent strength just broke my heart, and I g ve her a quick, firm hug. Her dark, asymmetrically cut hair fell over my shoulder, enviably smooth and straight even when it wasn't brushed.

'See you soon,' I reiterated, because I didn't want her to be alone for long, and I quickly left before Sterling or Xanthe could come back and see me. I shut the door behind me and leaned back on it, closing my eyes briefly, allowing myself this one moment of stillness. That exchange had been many times more awkward than I could have expected. Bearing bad news was painful and I didn't feel any better no matter how many times I told myself I'd done the right thing.

An unexpected voice projected from everywhere interrupted my hurried withdrawal from the dorm. I opened my eyes.

'Students, please ready yourselves and gather as quickly as possible in the dining hall for an urgent announcement,' Lord Gawain said from somewhere I couldn't see. Magically, his voice was cast all around the mansion, loud and clear like a dozen speakers were planted through the halls.

I hooked the chain bearing my room key back around my neck and shoved off from the door, starting toward the staircase. I wondered over Lord Gawain's odd behaviour. I often privately questioned whether he had any idea what he was doing. Why panic the students by hinting at an emergency, especially when the emergency actually occurred seven or eight hours ago? It was a big deal, but not one the students could assist with or were directly threatened by, otherwise they should have been woken as soon as the council and I had returned last night.

A door further up the hall opened and some boys stepped out, still yanking sweatshirts over their heads, and I hurried down the stairs before they could see me and ask what was going on. I was a pathetic liar.

*Why now?* I asked Renatus silently, utilising the telepathic link between our minds once again when I reached out and found him awake. I kept my doubts in Lord Gawain's choices to myself; Renatus would not share them.

*I suppose he wants everyone present so there's no miscommunication*, he said, although that didn't really answer my question. I decided against pressing the matter. Renatus was Lord Gawain's biggest fan. *He brought the boys' parents in throughout the night. Susannah and Qasim are with them now. Alerting the rest of the school community is next on his list.*

When I reached the first floor of the mansion, I found Emmanuelle and Jadon deep in conversation, standing together in the huge reception hall. The two looked much too fresh for a pair who had fought so hard and so viciously against Lisandro's men last night. Outsiders could never have guessed what strength and courage the White Elm's youngest members possessed, and even my admiration for these two had been intensely reinforced by the night's events. I'd always thought that Renatus was the council's warrior, but now I knew they had several.

Emmanuelle spotted me and cut Jadon off with a sharp look with her brilliant blue eyes. Last night she'd pretended to switch sides, fooling even some White Elm and almost fooling Lisandro into trusting her, in an attempt to rescue me. She'd not succeeded exactly, but her interference with Lisandro's spells was what had eventually enabled me to escape.

Jadon was years younger than her at not quite twenty-one and at first glance seemed completely different. He was the kind of attractive you didn't notice unless you were looking for it, able to go unseen and overlooked with his mousy brown hair shaved short and rounded features that could change from an easy, open grin to an intense, dark scowl in moments. However, he shared with Emmanuelle the same impulsive nature and reckless loyalty, and I had seen the physical embodiment of those characteristics in battle last night. Both were incredible and terrifying warriors and I was grateful to have them on our side.

'Did you sleep?' Emmanuelle asked me, both her eyes and Jadon's shifting in focus as they flittered over my face and around me, perhaps reading my aura.

'Not enough,' Jadon commented uneasily. 'Your energy is a mess. Are you alright?'

'She's fine,' the sorceress cut me off when I opened my mouth to respond. 'She is still sleeping off her injuries, that's all.'

Jadon was unconvinced and shook his head. He gestured at me and told his colleague, 'That's not recovery, that's a paradigm shift.'

'*Sans surprise*,' Emmanuelle muttered in French, as she tended to do when she was thinking out loud or getting annoyed. 'She will be fine. Try to take it easy today,' she advised me. 'Go inside. Lord Gawain is ready to start.'

She and Jadon offered me tight smiles but didn't move. I gathered that was my cue to keep going, and I left them where they were to finish their conversation, rubbing my arms self-consciously. My energy was a mess? I'd felt worried about my aura before, worried it was broken or freakish when I was told it had unusual markers or that it was very hard to find. Since I couldn't see it, I could only go off what others told me, and I was yet to be told how nice, normal, full or healthy-looking it was.

The dining hall was home to one huge, long table that had clearly been constructed for, if not inside, this room. That was where the students sat to eat each mealtime, nourished by a large buffet table that stood at the door. The White Elm councillors, who taught at the Academy, ate at a smaller table that had obviously been added later for this very purpose. It was a different stain from the rest of the wood in Morrissey House and much too new. It didn't look right in the room, off to the side, but it did give the councillors a distance from their students where they could also supervise. Several of them were already gathered there, minus Renatus, who I sensed was not far away.

I half-approached the throng of councillors, briefly surprised by how familiar they now felt, and paused not far from the door, unsure whether today I was one of them or one of the students. Elijah smiled at me from where he stood at the table with Lord Gawain; Anouk spared me a brisk 'good morning' on her way in. I decided to stay where I was. Individually, they were all good people, even those who didn't particularly like me or agree with my somewhat controversial involvement with the council's business. Individually, I had so much respect for each of them.

Collectively, I had the utmost respect for them, too, but you can respect something completely and still be slightly afraid of it.

I intuitively glanced over my shoulder as my master entered the hall behind another small group of students, flanked by Jadon and Emmanuelle. Together, I was struck once again how the White Elm's youth, perceived at times by older councillors as liabilities, were really the most impressive people in my world.

Though Renatus was clearly listening to his colleagues as he walked with them, his head tilted towards the speaker, his eyes scanned the room intently until they fell on me standing unexpectedly in the foreground. We'd had our differences in the months since we'd first met, most of them in the past week, but our connection was stronger now than it had ever been before, and somehow I knew there was still space for growth, providing we lived long enough to see it. He was not only my master – he was my protector, my leader, my teacher and my brother. I knew I was more than an apprentice, too; the master-apprentice relationship was complex and deeper than I could have imagined before I entered into it.

One thing I was still getting used to but that I thought I liked was the telepathic conversations I had with Renatus when were in the same room and perfectly able to speak out loud.

*I should have learnt by now that secrets never serve anyone,* he said as he nodded an acknowledgement to Jadon and stopped beside me. Jadon and Emmanuelle stood together a few feet away, sticking with the observatory spot I'd apparently selected and looking to their leader from the other side of the room. *Lord Gawain ordered Emmanuelle to withhold what Lisandro told us.*

My stomach twisted a little. Not talking about it last night had allowed me to numbly ignore the harsh reality of what I'd learned about myself. I wasn't just an orphan: I was *orphaned*.

I didn't *want* to talk about it. I didn't want anyone to ask me about it or offer me a devastated look.

*For how long?* I asked as I tried to avoid making eye contact with any of the students as they passed me on their way to their table. Did I really think they would guess what I was thinking if they saw my tight lips and furrowed brow?

*He said he wants to give us time to come to terms,* Renatus answered, *but that means keeping a secret that could hinder the search for Lisandro, so probably not for long. Jadon knows something's up. He's been trying to glean it from Em but can't get in. He's probably not the only one.*

Jadon was a talented Telepath, able to speak to other minds even through dense wards. I wondered how long Emmanuelle could keep him, and the other Telepaths, out. I hoped indefinitely. It was selfish of me, because as Renatus had pointed out, it was imperative that the news that had rocked me so badly be shared with the council.

I just didn't want to deal with it right now.

*I don't care if secrets cause bigger problems further down the road; I just don't want to deal with it right now,* Renatus admitted, surprising me, and we left the discussion there, but I felt minutely less lost and alone.

Within sixty seconds the whole school population had filed into the dining room and every remaining student was sitting silently at the long old table, watching the council leader nervously. Four absences were enough to be evident in a cohort as small as this one. Though I tried not to look at anyone, I couldn't help spotting Hiroko's face amongst the other familiar ones. She was sitting with Iseult Taylor, the only other student I could reasonably call my friend. Hiroko's face was impassive and her body was still; Iseult's pretty little elfin face wore a small frown and she kept craning her neck to see further up the table. Like nearly everybody else, she was clearly restless and on edge. I knew she was looking for Joshua, and I felt a dull pang of regret for her. I wished I'd thought of her earlier. I wished I'd had time to drop into her room after I'd visited Hiroko.

Elijah, Anouk and Lord Gawain ended their conversation and turned to face the student body.

'Good morning to all,' Lord Gawain began. 'An unthinkable issue has arisen at our Academy. Last night, the White Elm acted to rescue our missing councillors, and in so doing, we were able to retrieve Teresa...'

Damage control. Politics. I could live without this. I tuned out when I felt the intensity of gazes on my face. I looked up. Among the students, girls and boys were glancing at me for confirmation as the news unfolded. Not long ago, I was one of them, just another hopeful kid in the crowd, so the implication of my involvement in the rescue mission was intriguing and fascinating to my peers.

'Enrico Sanchez, Tyson Marks, Joshua Reyes and Garrett Fischer were last night convinced to leave the estate at the suggestion of Aubrey, presumably to into the presence of Lisandro...'

There wasn't a person who didn't return their attention to Lord Gawain in astonishment right then. Except maybe Hiroko, but I hadn't been watching her face. She was looking down at her feet. Iseult, for once, looked speechless, just like everyone else. I tried to listen to the remainder of Lord Gawain's short speech.

'We are in the process of notifying all of your families,' he was saying. 'So far none have requested their children withdrawn, but of course should that be the wish of anyone present, as always, that can be arranged. It should be noted, however, that while this act was unpredictable and shocking, the White Elm has taken every reasonable measure against a repeat of the situation. Despite the events of last night, this estate is still the safest place in the world for you to be.'

I knew it was true but also knew that it would be difficult for Lord Gawain to expect anyone to believe that immediately after being told that four of their friends had been snatched from within these so-called "safe" walls. I noted the significant looks my peers shared with one another.

Whatever Lord Gawain was in the process of saying next was cut off by the loud scrape of a chair being shoved back. Attention flew to the student who now abruptly stood and walked away from the table.

Hiroko.

I broke away from where I stood with Renatus, squeezed between Emmanuelle and Jadon to reach the door at the same time as my friend.

'Wait,' I urged quietly, reaching for her, feeling awful as waves of discomfort and unhappiness emanated from her in erratic bursts. The fact of Garrett's disappearance had just hit home for her. This was the scene I'd wanted to help her avoid, and now it was unravelling anyway, right in front of everybody, with every pair of eyes on her. On both of us.

My hand didn't close on hers. She spun away from me before I could catch her, and kept backing away, out the door.

'*Īe,*' she said forcefully, shaking her head. 'No! I... *Gomen'nasai.* Just...' Clearly conflicted, she couldn't meet my eyes; hers were brimming with tears of embarrassment. 'You must leave me alone, Aristea, please.'

She left the dining hall and I stood there feeling like the worst friend in the world, because if I'd been less arrogant only twelve hours before, I could have done something to stop this.

Believing I could have done a thing to prevent it was probably an even more arrogant thought to have, but knowing this didn't make me feel any less useless.

# chapter three

The staircase was central to the layout of the house. The largest rooms in the house, the library and ballroom, as well as the good-sized dining hall, came off the entrance hall on the bottom floor, from which the huge sweeping staircase dominated the eye and wound slowly one flight at a time up through the rest of the building to the bedrooms, parlours and dressing rooms. Now most of them were repurposed as dormitories and classrooms, spaces for hosting and educating the White Elm's society's most gifted youths in the finest magical arts in a multi-step effort to up-skill the general populace.

Until last night, Renatus hadn't appreciated how badly this initiative was needed. Lisandro was a danger to everyone in the community – he was a *killer*, a *traitor*, a *liar* – and he had followers willing to die for his ideals, whatever they were.

Renatus had known his godfather was a pitiful excuse for a man. He'd known Lisandro was without loyalty or morality. What he was still struggling with, however, was the *extent*.

'I don't know what you want me to do,' his seventeen-year-old apprentice, Aristea, commented, her hands wringing her wet hair onto the carpeted stairs as she followed several paces behind. How quickly things could return to normal when your life was everything but. Twelve hours ago, Renatus's deepest fear and worst memory had been revisited when he'd almost lost Aristea. Now they were ascending the central staircase, perfectly safe, talking as they always did, no hint at all in her demeanour or his of how close they'd come to losing everything, several times in the last few days.

They'd only met six or seven weeks ago. The bonding ceremony last fortnight had permanently fused their consciousnesses – skills and traits of hers had already started to slip across the connection to influence him, which was slightly unnerving, and he'd noticed incredible advancement in her abilities since gaining access to his life experiences as if they were her own. The rapid development in her unnaturally stimulated adolescent brain seemed to have only done her good.

The potential beginnings of *his* arrogance in her behaviour was another matter, and judging from her aura, swollen with new power but misshapen and turbulent with recent trauma, Lisandro's harsh truth wasn't doing anything to better her, either.

'I mean, if Aubrey or the boys left traces, you would have already picked up on them, right?' Aristea asked when Renatus reached the second floor, quickly dropping her sopping wet hair to jump aside when her elbow accidentally brushed along the staircase's smooth handrail. Unbidden, irrelevant images of her peers placing their hand on that rail on their way upstairs to their lodgings flashed through her mind. Mind melded forever to hers, Renatus saw the same montage and quickly dismissed it. Tapping into impressions was old hat to him; for her it was still only new, and still not entirely welcome.

'Right,' Renatus agreed, 'and I have, but you know I don't see what you do.'

She went silent and followed him along the hall. She was special, but not in a way that she generally enjoyed. Like him, she was a sorcerer, and like him, she was a scrier, and like him she was exceptionally powerful, but unlike him and unlike anyone else he'd ever met, she was also an Empath. She felt on a level that most others couldn't, and experienced the emotions of those around her with only a developing ability to prevent or control it. It was for this reason that she was down and sulky at the moment – the misery of Hiroko Sasaki, her closest and sometimes only friend here, was still affecting her, and likely would for some time yet.

Renatus hadn't known her long enough to find it annoying but imagined the gift had the capacity to make her typical teenage traits stand out even more. On the other hand, it also made her invaluable, because unlike any other sorcerer, when Aristea had a vision, she didn't just *see* it. She also felt the emotional states and motives of all persons present in that situation.

He'd looked through the Archives. The White Elm had made it their business to collect into their ranks the most gifted and talented sorcerers at any given time in history, and yet they hadn't had an Empath in two hundred years. She was quite the find.

Tian, a master swordsman and Seer, stepped out of the dorm room that had become a crime scene, looking calm and encouraged. Aristea and Renatus, both scriers, shared a gift and used it in the same way. Seers were much more varied in their approaches and methods. Some saw direct paths for individuals into the future; others saw choice points that would determine those paths; still others saw possibilities for the many or the few, and another group saw only concrete images of those events that could not be avoided on any path. All were fed their knowledge via a mysterious commune with Fate itself, which Renatus believed in but found difficult to properly comprehend, so tried not to think on it too much, because it only led to wonderings like *why did Fate let this happen to me* or *what good can possibly come from this.*

'Did you find something?' Aristea asked hopefully, hastening to catch up to him when she saw Tian's positive demeanour. The other councillor glanced at them, startled, and seemed to wake up.

'I went through the whole room again,' Tian reported to Renatus, crossing his arms and looking back into the room with a very slight frown. 'There is nothing helpful in determining the fates of the boys or of Aubrey. One item that will stand out to Aristea, though not to the council.'

Aristea looked at him inquiringly, not understanding, but Renatus did. Tian's foresight was drawn through objects. Fate spoke to him by showing him how weapons and other features of the physical world were likely to be used in upcoming moments of significance. With the boys' families upstairs in serious discussion with Susannah and Qasim, his task in investigating the bedroom of the four stolen students was to identify whether the residents would be back in the future to use any of their possessions, but unfortunately, it seemed, even if they *did* return, they would not be using anything in this room for anything memorable or worthy of note to Fate.

But Aristea might.

Her face had fallen when Tian admitted to having found nothing of use, but once she stepped curiously through the dormitory door something changed. Her thoughts, zippy and disjointed since last night, seemed to slow right down, and her expression smoothed out. Even the violent swirls in her aura evened out considerably.

'What happened?' Renatus asked her, put off by the change in her. She looked back over her shoulder – she was three paces away but might have been three kilometres.

'What do you mean?'

'Your energy transitioned very suddenly,' Tian said, apparently equal parts concerned and intrigued. 'Did you do something?'

'No.' Unworried, Aristea turned away and began running her fingertips over the surfaces in the boys' bedroom. She'd been hesitant on her way up the stairs. Now she was happy to do it? At her will, dozens of disjointed images took a mad dash through her mind; from his close perspective, he saw the same. She paused with her fingers on the cover of a hardback book lying open and upside down on the bed, and started reporting what she saw for Tian's benefit. 'Josh is reading. Someone else says, "Seriously, man, how old is that book?" and he says... "Haven't you seen the film version? Grace Kelly was a babe"... Then...' She looked back at Renatus and Tian. Shrugged. 'I guess that's when Aubrey got there.'

Four of her peers, two of them friends of hers, had been taken in the night and he knew she felt guilty about that, even though there was nothing she could reasonably done to prevent it, so her suddenly unflappable manner was not fitting. Not feeling right about it, Renatus walked in after her to see what... What? To see what? His worries fled. Which was a worry in itself.

Aristea was still moving around the room, engrossed in her task, fingers trailing after her. She reported some aloud and let the rest just process through her mind, and Renatus filtered the information the same way. He'd seen all of this already, when he'd come through last night after Aristea fell asleep. Enrico sitting on the desktop, demanding of Aubrey, 'What happened to you, man?' Joshua yanking the half-packed bag from Tyson and insisting they could not leave.

All of them eventually agreeing.

'But *why* did they agree?' Tian asked Aristea urgently from the doorway. 'Qasim is one floor above, telling four families that their sons left without coercion or threats. It is difficult for them to accept.'

'They didn't want to,' Aristea said, finally starting to sound uneasy, which grated directly against Renatus's frictionless mood. 'They didn't want to go. Enrico was worried about his cousin. Garrett didn't want to leave Hiroko. Joshua wanted to tell his parents where he was going. But... they all agreed to go when Aubrey told them to.'

How could they not, in a room *so damn agreeable*?

The spell broke.

So obvious.

'Ugh,' Aristea said suddenly, withdrawing her hand from the tidiest of the four desks. She looked up at her mentor. 'It wasn't them. It's *the room*.'

'The room's been atmospherically altered,' Renatus told Tian darkly, and felt the spell start to wear away instantly. The false good feelings faded. 'Aubrey's a Crafter. He must be able to do it.'

Without someone to believe in it, all things lose substance, and Aubrey's effect on the dorm's energy faded away all around them. The ability to affect the emotional atmosphere of a space was rare but not unheard of in Renatus's experience. Lisandro used to do the same thing to parlours or the dining room or the study on the top floor if arguments threatened to break out around him, especially between Aindréas and Ana Morrissey, and Renatus had never noticed until the familial breakdown that resulted in Lisandro's banishment from the estate. Ceasing to believe in his godfather had broken the spell of his influence.

'He made it all *obliging*,' Aristea noted, looking around uncomfortably. The unsettled swirls resumed their patternless movements in her aura; the speed of her thoughts accelerated. Turning her attention back to the desktop, she said, 'They didn't feel threatened at all, just shepherded. They didn't feel like they had a choice.'

*Emotional manipulation*, Renatus told Qasim through the thirteen-way connection he shared with the rest of the council. *Extremely persuasive. They wouldn't have stood a chance.*

He felt the older scrier's vague acknowledgement and saw Lord Gawain appear at the doorway, watching the proceedings with interest.

Aristea picked something small up off the tabletop.

'Is this what you meant?' she asked Tian, showing him the folded paper box. The councillor nodded.

'Significant to you?' he guessed, and she nodded, looking down at it.

'Kind of,' she said. She traced fingers along its neat and crisp folded edges and smiled wistfully at the images of Garrett Fischer writing on the base of the paper construction while his friends urged him to leave it, to hurry, to get out and go.

'Have we learned anything new?' Lord Gawain asked. Renatus shook his head and stepped out of the room, his apprentice trailing behind, still examining the origami box.

'Nothing much, except Aubrey has more in common with Lisandro than we suspected,' he said.

'You can fill me in on the way,' the council's leader stated, already turning away to start back for the stairs. 'I want you to come with me to check the beach.'

Aristea's head shot up and her energy spiked with unease as she came to an abrupt halt. Renatus didn't need to ask what that was about.

'Go and find your friend,' he suggested. *There's no reason to put yourself through it all over again.*

A little pause – Aristea liked to be involved in whatever action was happening, but rarely liked the reality of it – and then she nodded.

'Okay. Thanks.'

'I'm sure your friend will be alright,' Lord Gawain offered kindly as he and Renatus walked ahead. Knowing she was off the hook for returning to that dreaded beach (where she'd not only lost her family three and a half years ago but where she'd last night found out they were *murdered*) she started walking again, following at a distance.

'I hope so,' she agreed dubiously, but Renatus had access to her thoughts, which betrayed her doubt in Lord Gawain. He didn't think on it; she was young, and so new to the White Elm's world. She couldn't share his deep faith in the council's high priest – it was Renatus, not Aristea, whose life Lord Gawain had changed, and it was orphaned, blood-soaked, teenage Renatus that Lord Gawain had gathered into his arms following the deaths of the Morrisseys. There had been no one to pull the adolescent Aristea free of the wreckage of her home when Lisandro had dealt the Byrne family the same fate.

Yet still, she was the one who had turned out for the better.

At the stairs they waited as Susannah and Qasim brought the procession of traumatised families down to show them the dormitory. The parents of powerful young sorcerers were likely to have a plethora of enviable skills, and may learn something from the room that the White Elm in their objectivity had overlooked. It was also a PR exercise, in truth: the opportunity to show the aggrieved families what the council was doing to help their sons. Aristea drew back against the wall as the large group paused to talk with Lord Gawain, invisible wards of energy going up around her. No doubt they brought with them an immense weight of grief, worry, anger, uncertainty and guilt, and Aristea was painfully susceptible to it.

*Go*, Renatus urged, and she nodded quickly and slipped behind the group to the staircase, where Qasim brought up the rear of the crowd.

Aristea and Qasim exchanged no words as they passed one another, but the younger scrier did glance up at Qasim in acknowledgement. Doubtless, they had nothing to say to one another. They'd never gotten along on a personal level, although Aristea really admired the councillor and Qasim had been furious when Renatus had chosen her as his apprentice, mostly annoyed because it meant he'd missed out on her himself.

It had become politically incorrect to overgeneralise and associate the six magical classes with specific traits, but Renatus was convinced that the old parable had its merits. Scriers, like himself, Aristea and Qasim had historically been considered quiet observers of few words, generally deep of mind and intense of nature. Loyal; proud; stubborn. It was definitely true of both Renatus and Qasim and neither would deny it. Aristea would probably claim to be different, but she certainly was not. She was the most stubborn of them all.

Healers were gentle and compassionate, although with a hot temper when provoked; Displacers were patient and calm, still; Telepaths were usually outspoken; Seers were thoughtful and seemed erratic. And Crafters, like Lisandro, like Jackson, like Aubrey – the three traitors of the White Elm – tended to be discerning, motivated and manipulative. Way more trouble than they were worth.

For his part, Renatus had never particularly liked Qasim, either, mostly because Qasim had never liked *him*, but there were few people in the world he could trust the way he trusted Qasim. Not that he had a choice, really. Days ago, Renatus had made the precarious decision to open his mind – a mind the White Elm had long feared, for various valid and not-so-valid reasons – to Qasim in a bid to win back the council's trust. It had been a massive risk, because in his mind were many concerning details, including the details of the way he'd once killed a man. To his immense relief, Qasim had judged his past actions as irrelevant to his present character, and welcomed Renatus back into the council.

'Renatus and I are returning now to the beach where we encountered Lisandro last night,' Lord Gawain told the Reyes, Fischer, Marks and Sanchez families. 'Renatus is the White Elm leading the search for Lisandro.'

All of the eyes in the crowd turned to him then, some hopeful, some doubtful. He knew he didn't look senior enough to be heading a task like this one, and saw a few of the parents squinting to get an idea of his aura and power level. That seemed to satisfy them. He wondered whether Lord Gawain would ever have publicly alluded to Renatus's purpose on the council if not for this situation.

'Finding Lisandro is a duty I take very personally,' he assured them, bowing his head respectfully to avoid having to make eye contact with any of them. Loss was something he knew well, and theirs made him feel uncomfortable. 'I promise to do everything possible to locate him and your sons as quickly as I can.'

He nodded his goodbye and stepped away to take the stairs down.

'Thank you.'

He stopped and looked back. The woman who had to be Joshua Reyes' mother was looking straight at him with sad, hopeful, grateful eyes that looked exactly like her boy's. Lord Gawain had made it sound like his job was to find her son and his friends, when in fact that was the job of the rest of the White Elm.

Renatus's job was much less noble, much more primal.

It was too much. He wished he'd snuck away when Aristea did. He departed quickly. Lord Gawain finished up the conversation and followed.

'You were doing well,' he chastised when he caught up in the entrance hall. 'What happened?'

'Public relations wasn't in the job description when you initiated me.'

The council's High Priest left it alone. By now he knew his young friend well enough to appreciate that communication wasn't his strong point.

Outside, it was a clear, bright, early May morning. Rain from the recent days meant that the grass was still wet and squishy underfoot as they made their way down the sloping hill to the gate at the bottom. Protective spells had guarded this house always, since the first Morrissey to live here, and every son to inherit the house since had contributed his share (helpful or otherwise) of wards to the strong stone walls. Renatus's untimely inheritance of the estate had undone some of these, most notably his father's banishment of Lisandro, and countless days had been spent tediously rebuilding these spells and creating others on every metre of fence line.

Renatus pressed a hand to the wrought iron gate, and it opened for him immediately. The young scrier and the old Seer stepped out of the safety of the estate. They walked several paces away from the fence line until the enchantments woven over the estate were no longer affecting them. Renatus grasped Lord Gawain's forearm. With a power that only the most gifted sorcerers ever managed, he reached for the Fabric of space, opened a hole and stepped through, bringing Lord Gawain with him.

They stepped out of space at a cold, barren beach on the north coast of Ireland. Nobody was around to see them appear out of nowhere. That meant nobody had found the bodies yet, or the "shipwreck" they'd staged to explain the bodies to any investigating mortals.

'What are we doing here?' Renatus asked as they began walking east to where the battle had taken place last night. He pulled his cloak tighter as the winds picked up; Lord Gawain did the same.

'I told the others we would check it in the daylight, to ensure we made no mistakes in the darkness,' the older man answered, implying there was some other reason why they were here, and this was just the excuse Lord Gawain had used to get Renatus alone.

Alone was fine with him. The cold winds whipped about and brought only the noises of small waves rolling up and down the beach. The sounds of nature kept the sounds of unwelcome thoughts at bay, at least for a short time.

A minute of silent walking brought them into view of the fishing boat wrecked on the rocks, and in another minute they were close enough to see the stiff dead bodies of last night's enemies. Nameless adversaries, perishing when they fell unconscious into the turbulent sea.

'Such a pitiful waste of life,' the Welsh sorcerer murmured regretfully. 'They were too far away to rescue. And their people didn't make any attempt to pull them out of the water when they fell.'

It was a disgusting scene, but Renatus had seen worse, and it was hard to feel sorry for the dead when these men had wasted their final moments trying to stand against the council. They'd pledged themselves to Lisandro, and died fighting for him, trying to protect their leader and trying to keep Renatus from saving Aristea. It was hard not to think they'd gotten exactly what they deserved.

'Anouk is brilliant,' Lord Gawain commented when Renatus did not reply, keeping his distance from the scene as he checked for inconsistencies. 'It was her idea to turn the beach house into the boat and the nets, and it certainly looks convincing, doesn't it? I wasn't sure how it would appear in the light of day but it seems we did our work well.'

Renatus kept walking east, knowing he wouldn't find what he was looking for. The house was gone; Lord Gawain had just said so, so there was nothing for Lisandro to come back to even if he wanted to. The hidden beach house, which had housed Lisandro and his followers for months, had become the site of a brief but intense battle last night, originally fought for Aubrey's sake, although Renatus's priorities had immediately changed when Aristea was taken hostage. He'd suddenly no longer cared whether he was able to rescue his fellow councillor. He'd hardly cared how dangerous these people were, how dangerous his godfather really was – the murderer of whole families, including his own. He'd only wanted Aristea back, with a protective intensity he hadn't felt since losing his beloved sister seven years ago, and to wring Lisandro's neck. Or blow him up. Or rip his head off. Whatever gruesome opportunity Fate had awarded him.

As was his true ignoble purpose.

He'd had a chance, he recalled bitterly, slowing to a stop when he sensed Lord Gawain trying to keep up with his quick pace. Renatus had been awarded that chance, not by Fate but by Lisandro himself, and then – because Lisandro didn't really *take chances* – things had changed, as the lightning storm Lisandro was commanding had struck the supports of the beach house, sending the whole structure collapsing into the wild waves and taking Aristea down with it.

He'd known then, what Lisandro was actually communicating with that lightning strike, and any hesitation was only momentary. He'd had a chance, but it was never really a choice. Drowning had not been the foremost danger to Aristea; Lisandro was the only real threat. If Renatus had taken the chance to follow Lisandro and kill him, Aristea *would* have died. He had no doubt that Lisandro would have killed her before letting Renatus get too close, whatever garbage he'd fed her about keeping her alive with purpose. So there'd been no choice, and if there had actually been one, he hoped he was the kind of person who would still have made the same, righteous one.

Renatus glanced back as Lord Gawain rested a hand on his shoulder.

'There's too much on your mind, son,' the old Seer said gently. 'Share the burden.'

Lord Gawain was a talker; Renatus never had been. But he loved this man who had always believed in him, and knew his mentor wanted only to help, and so tried his best at these times to find the words to communicate the dark, horrible things that stewed away in his private mind in appropriate ways. It rarely made him feel better, but often helped him to piece things together. It was just so difficult to start. How do men usually just start discussing their fears and feelings, anyway?

'Lisandro confuses me,' Renatus admitted finally. 'I wish I could understand his motives. They seem... contradictory.'

'He is a complex enemy,' Lord Gawain agreed. 'He was my friend for eleven years, and I still cannot hope to understand his intentions. I can appreciate how much worse this is for you, of course.'

Renatus was not the only one Lisandro had hurt and betrayed. He was just the only one he'd hurt who also happened to be his godson.

'He insists that he loved my family, yet he killed them,' Renatus said, his words coming too quickly to maintain his calm, cool tone. 'He's said he never really liked me, yet he let me live. For seven, nearly eight years now. He told Aristea he'd kept her alive for a reason, then proceeded to try to strike her dead. I just don't understand, and I need to.'

'Renatus,' Lord Gawain said warmly, squeezing his shoulder gently before dropping his hand and moving away to better admire the grey view of the North Sea. 'You've been this way since I first met you. You convince yourself that you are powerless without all the puzzle pieces. You think you need to hold the power to win. Probably your father's influence, and Lisandro's. All that we need to know *does* come in time. I know you know this; you just need to believe it, and be patient.'

Renatus knew Lord Gawain was right, but he was not naturally all that patient. He followed the other's gaze to the still horizon. The night's storm had left the sea murky and grey.

'What do you think it all means?' Renatus asked after a minute of silence. 'Why do you think Lisandro killed my family, and then the Hawkes and the Byrnes? Where's the method to this madness?'

'If there is one.' Lord Gawain smiled grimly. 'I think we can assume, for now, that there is. Despite the years between them, the storms and the killings do not seem random. Your family, well, that one is evident – there was already a link with Lisandro. And the Hawkes, too. If Kenneth Hawke was your sister's godfather, then we can imagine he was probably a mutual friend of Lisandro's and your father's. The one I cannot figure out is the Byrnes. Aristea's present connection to you and to Lisandro is obvious, but the family's connection to him at the time of the storm is not clear. We are missing too many puzzle pieces, son. We can't see the full picture yet.'

'And why do you think Lisandro left me alive when he killed my parents?' Renatus pressed. 'He killed *Ana*, of all people. Why would he kill her and not me? Why kill the eldest Byrne child and not Aristea?'

'Not just Aristea,' Lord Gawain corrected. 'The sister lived too.'

That only confused the situation more. If Angela Byrne had died in the storm with her parents and brother, at least Renatus could have deduced that Lisandro was leaving alive the youngest member of each family he destroyed, for whatever sick, deluded reason. How inconvenient of her.

'I'm not sure why he chose the way he did,' Lord Gawain said now, in a way that told Renatus otherwise. 'I think you'll discover the reason yourself soon.'

Renatus folded his arms and glared at the sea, feeling sulky. Lord Gawain knew something, or theorised something, but he wouldn't give it up. It was a Seer thing. They were blessed by the universe with special knowledge of the futures, and few took this responsibility lightly. If he wasn't telling Renatus, it wasn't because he felt like keeping his protégé in the dark. It was because he believed there was a right time for him to gain this information, and now wasn't it.

'I was proud of you last night, so proud,' Lord Gawain said softly. 'You were right. You did not give in to him; I did. I admit you shook my faith in you over these last weeks, but last night you proved yourself.'

'I told you I would never willingly give Lisandro that ring,' Renatus said.

'I wanted to believe you. Did you?'

'Mostly,' Renatus admitted, then amended himself. 'I *did* believe what I told you, but I was not sure of anything else. I mean...' He paused, not certain he should say more. Qasim knew he'd taken life before; Aristea knew. Lisandro probably knew. But nobody else. Lord Gawain, he'd once promised himself, would never *ever* know what he'd done in the minutes before they'd first met. The unconditional love would end as quickly as it had begun. Renatus had few enough friends. He would choose his words very carefully.

'I mean, I am not sure who I am to become,' he managed finally. 'Am I really *good* because you tell me I am? If I tell myself, and others, that I am? Am I good because you make me good, or because Aristea makes me good? Am I good because I chose to save her instead of chasing my revenge?'

'Actions speak louder than words,' Lord Gawain counselled. A breeze tousled Renatus's shoulder-length black hair, and he tossed his head irritably when it fluttered around his eyes.

'Maybe so,' he said, 'but I can't know what actions I might choose in the end, when the day comes that I have Lisandro's life in my hands and I don't have Aristea's safety to consider. *If* that day comes,' Renatus reminded himself, because it was no certainty, just a determined dream. Or nightmare. He didn't know yet which it was.

'You are scared that one day you'll have your revenge and you won't know whether to take it,' Lord Gawain elaborated. He took Renatus's shoulder in his hand again and steered him back the way they'd come. 'I'm not going to tell you that killing Lisandro is the wrong thing to do. It's neither right nor wrong. He's dangerous. He won't stop so long as he's alive. As much as I don't like it, it's the job the council tasked you with when we initiated you into your current role. But I'm afraid that no amount of worrying or thinking on that one can possibly prepare you. Be patient. If the day comes, and the choice comes to you... you will know then, and only then, what to do.' He smiled as they began to walk together along the cold beach. 'I have faith you'll know which choice to make.'

# chapter four

I was glad Renatus had sent me on my way, and from the heavy thoughts I got from him in the following hour, I figured I wouldn't have been welcome anyway. He and Lord Gawain were talking about some dark and unhappy topics.

Escaping Qasim and Susannah's miserable crowd, I had a half-formed idea about finding Hiroko and checking on her. Was she okay? Would she even want to see me? *You must leave me alone, Aristea, please.* If I'd only been here, as I'd been told, maybe I could have prevented Aubrey from ever reaching the boys' room. Maybe I could have sounded the alarm. But it was futile to consider the possibilities, and totally lame of me to think there was anything I could have done that Teresa, a White Elm sorceress, didn't manage to do. Aubrey had overpowered her, and he could easily have overpowered me if he'd wanted to. I was only lucky that when I *had* encountered him, he'd not been of the mind to do so because he was too busy playing the part of a wounded, frightened hostage.

It was easy to feel stupid, I reminded myself, but really, I shouldn't. Aubrey had fooled everyone. I'd trusted him as everyone had – he'd once been my teacher, though for only a short time, and Renatus had involved me in the investigation into his disappearance. But I was hardly the most hurt by his betrayal. The council had risked their lives for him; Jadon and Teresa had loved him as their best friend; the boys from dormitory five had trusted Aubrey as their caretaker and protector. He'd played the whole council, the whole Academy, the whole *world*, really, and I was the least of his victims.

I needed to find Hiroko. If I was feeling guilty and depressed, I couldn't even imagine how *she* was feeling. She and Garrett had been dancing around one another for weeks, flirting, Hiroko more openly than desperately shy Garrett, until last night, they'd *finally* made progress and kissed… and now he was gone. I didn't want to wonder how long it would be until he came back, if he ever did or even wanted to. He could escape and just go into hiding. I probably would, in his situation.

I strode into the house, ignoring all the people I passed in the doorway. The other students probably thought I was a snob, walking around like I owned the place, but I knew they also thought other, worse things about me, and I wasn't interested in their sidelong glances and snide comments. I had a friend in need – the one friend I really had right now.

I stopped dead in the middle of the wide entrance hall when I noticed four girls standing around outside the library door.

'How could four guys just *disappear*?' the strawberry blonde with a cute ski-jump nose and fabulous curves speculated quietly. 'And how could the White Elm not know it was happening?'

'And how can we be expected to think we're safe, if they weren't?' the tall, comparatively lean Greek girl with narrowed eyes pressed, while the pretty, brunette identical twins with sparkling green eyes shrugged uncomfortably.

Most students here, I could care less about. Most people who were nasty to me could easily be ignored, but there were four girls whose comments could hurt me, and they now fell silent and stared back at me, equally disturbed my presence as I was by theirs.

Sterling, the somewhat ditzy strawberry blonde, and Xanthe, her total bitch of a counterpart, were my and

Hiroko's roommates. We hadn't spoken in weeks, after an epic misunderstanding with Sterling totally blown out of proportion by Xanthe. The incident had not only cost me their respect and friendship, but also the respect of the whole student body and the friendship of the Canadian twins standing opposite them. Kendra and Sophia had been good friends of mine, and Hiroko's, until they'd sided with Sterling and Xanthe in the massive argument we'd engaged in one fine breakfast time, and so I hadn't spoken to them since, either. My life had become very lonely since Xanthe had viciously (and *wrongly*) accused me of sleeping with Renatus, sparking lovesick Sterling's misplaced jealousy and destroying my relationships.

Except with Hiroko. Hiroko had stood by me, knowing how beyond incapable and disinterested I was in doing what they thought. And it was with this thought that I made myself keep going, stepping past Sterling to let myself into the library. I couldn't stop myself from glancing back once as the door closed behind me. Sophia Prescott was looking straight into my eyes. The door shut, and her sad eyes disappeared from my view. What did she have to be sad about, anyway? She still had her friends, she was still well-liked – her sister was dating the funniest, coolest guy at the Academy. She hadn't almost died last night, met her family's murderer and come back to school to realise that despite those life-changing events, nothing here had changed.

Hiroko and Iseult were sitting right at the back of the library, exactly where I'd expected to find them, in the comfy armchairs against the furthest wall. Iseult, so tiny, was kneeling on her chair, keeping her voice down as she pressed Hiroko for information. No doubt she'd worked out that Hiroko already knew about the incident and figured she'd heard it all from me. She was of the persistent sort, and looked like she did when she was concentrating and trying to solve a problem. Hiroko, in contrast to Iseult's determined body language, was slumped in her chair. She knew what I knew. The problem was not so easily solved. Garrett, Joshua and the others might not be coming back.

Her pain, her depression, hit me like a bucket of ice as I moved closer.

'Aristea!' Iseult's voice was a stage whisper when she spotted me. 'What's going on?'

I shrugged, feeling awkward.

'Exactly what Lord Gawain said,' I answered, sitting down on the floor in front of them. 'From what we understand, Aubrey just waltzed into the dorm, convinced the boys to leave... and then did. There are no signs of conflict.'

'So you think they *wanted* to leave?' Iseult asked, a bit cold. Hiroko stared at me.

'No, of course not,' I said quickly. 'I was just in their room. It's all... weird. Agreeable. They trusted Aubrey and his spell made them feel like they had to agree with him.' I swallowed. 'The whole council did. They're having as hard a time believing this as you or me.'

Hiroko sat back in her chair and looked away.

Iseult asked, 'Why was no one here to stop him?' and my stomach flipped over.

'It was a rescue,' I told her. I didn't go into details. I shared details of my life as Renatus's apprentice with Hiroko all the time, but my friendship with Iseult was less developed, not as deep. I also didn't believe she would really care for all the particulars. 'They didn't realise there was anything to protect the house from, least of all Aubrey. We thought he'd died. We *saw* him die,' I added, remembering how well-considered Aubrey's plan truly had been, until Lisandro had practically dropped me on top of the real Aubrey. Bringing me into the beach house, knowing Renatus, at least, would come for me and discover the real Aubrey, had been a hugely silly move on Lisandro's part. Was this a sign that he was capable of making stupid mistakes? Or was I missing something – was this all part of Lisandro's bigger picture? Just because it didn't seem to have benefited Aubrey didn't mean Lisandro hadn't, somehow, profited.

Iseult's eternal cold front softened slightly.

'I didn't realise you were there,' she said apologetically. 'It must have been a horrible night for you. Are you okay?'

I forced a smile.

'I broke my shoulder and got burnt,' I said with a tiny shrug. 'I'm fine now.'

'Well, you look good, considering,' Iseult said. She shot an appreciative glance at my shoulder. 'Did you fix it yourself?'

'No, I'm not that good yet. Emmanuelle did it.' I caught Hiroko's silent dark eyes on the paper box in my lap, and I held it up to her. 'I took this from Garrett's desk.'

I leaned forward onto my knees and she leaned out of her armchair to take it from me.

I knew I'd found Garrett's desk as soon as I saw it. Unlike the other three, it was an actual working space, without the spattering of paper balls and underwear that had graced the others. In the centre was a medium-sized folded paper box.

While Garrett's early attempts at origami had been quite laughable, he'd clearly come a long way in the hobby he'd taken up to impress his Japanese sweetheart. The box was very neat and the folds were very sharp and precise, unlike those initial, many-times-folded cranes.

When I touched it: *Garrett, holding the box in one hand and carefully scribing something onto it with the other... Aubrey's voice, 'Garrett, come on.'... All wrong, but who is Garrett to question Aubrey?... Garrett keeps writing... Aubrey's stress rises... 'Garrett, what are you writing?'... Enrico, '...you can't leave notes, they'll be able to find us.'*

Tian had foreseen me taking this from the room, so I hadn't hesitated in doing so. Watching Hiroko's porcelain-doll face and feeling the slow change in her mood, I knew I'd done the right thing. Hiroko gently turned the box over in her hands, the hint of a smile on her lips. I knew that she'd read Garrett's message.

*Hiroko, I've now made you so many little cranes and flowers. Here is a place for you to keep them. Wish I could give it to you in person. Maybe even talk to you.*

'They didn't want to leave,' I said. 'I don't know how, but something was done to the room. Renatus wanted me to look for trace energy and I didn't want to. As soon as I walked in, I just wanted to do exactly what I was told.'

In retrospect it was a very disconcerting thought. Aubrey's spell had made me eager to do things that scared me. What kind of world was I in that there were people with abilities like that? Wasn't that dangerous?

'That's a form of energy manipulation,' Iseult spoke up. 'It's a high-level Crafter ability and it's illegal. We're specifically taught *not* to do it.'

'*You* can do that?' Hiroko asked, speaking for the first time. Iseult looked uncomfortable.

'All Crafters can. But it was banned in 1958, along with pretty much everything else. So whenever I tried it to get out of trouble as a little girl I ended up with a hiding.' She smiled wryly. 'My da was right to do it. Spells like that take people's choices away.'

'How does it work?' I asked. 'How can you identify it quickly and break it before you end up doing something you regret?'

'It's an emotional atmosphere alteration, and I'm actually very surprised you realised you were caught in one. Generally, if a Crafter like Aubrey, or even me, was manipulating energy around you to make you more willing, more accepting, you *wouldn't* notice. That's the whole point. He would be able to make you happy just being around him, or make you dislike someone just because he seemed to.'

I thought on the other Crafter I knew of. Lisandro had never liked Renatus, and in turn, the council had innately disliked him, even after Lisandro had been revealed as a traitor. Was this an example of his deepest manipulations at work?

'The spell is cast on a space, not a person,' Iseult added before anyone else could speak. 'Once they leave the space, it would begin to wear off. The effects would be gone within minutes, but words or ideas imparted during those minutes would stick more stubbornly than usual. Once they got outside the gates, Joshua and the others probably began trying to justify their actions to themselves, using the ideas Aubrey gave them. Nobody wants to believe they've done something they didn't personally want to do.'

'Enrico said, "don't leave notes or they'll find us', like he thought *we* were the threat to worry about,' I said. 'Do you think Aubrey "manipulated" the room, and then told them that the White Elm was bad or whatever, and they just convinced themselves it must be true and followed him out?'

'Pretty much.'

Hiroko abruptly stood, still clutching the little paper box.

'I am going to write to my father,' she said automatically, as if she'd come up with the excuse some time ago and had saved it up for the moment when she could stand this conversation no longer. She started walking away, but slowed and paused just before she moved out of sight behind the library stacks. She glanced back at me, and for the first time since breakfast I felt graciousness and warmth entwined in her emotional profile. 'Thank you for finding this for me. I am sorry if I am rude earlier.'

'You don't owe me any apology,' I assured her, and her impassive face broke into a quick, uncontrollably relieved smile. She left to deal with things on her own, as she wanted, but I felt *so* much better knowing she wasn't mad with me, that she was going to be okay and that *we* were okay. Iseult was nice enough, but Hiroko was my best friend. I felt even more relieved than she did to learn that our friendship was unaffected.

In her wake, the library became awkwardly quiet. When we heard the door close behind her upon exit, I stood as well.

'I think I need to go for a walk,' I told Iseult, not because I didn't appreciate her company but because the quiet of the library was making me feel restless. Hiroko was the person I usually debriefed with, and since she was unavailable, the numb insanity of my recent experiences screamed around inside my head, unable to escape. I stood and made to leave, but then considered something. 'Will you be alright?'

'Without Josh, you mean?' Iseult asked. 'After Hiroko marched out of breakfast this morning everyone was talking about her and Garrett. You're the first person to remember that the other lads have people who care about them too.'

I shook my head. 'Their parents are upstairs. All four. There are a lot of sad people here today.'

She stared at me, deep in thought, then she said, 'Thank you for asking. Yes, I'll be alright. Hopefully they all come to their senses quickly and get the opportunity to escape before anything happens to them.'

I thought on her words as I struck out across the lawn a few minutes later, stepping over a rabbit hole. Iseult sounded positive that the students from dormitory five were alive, as was the White Elm. I couldn't shake the overwhelming cloud of grief and loss surrounding their families along the second storey hallway. I'd once lost my parents and elder brother, but imagine leaving your child with someone you trusted and then being called to say that trusted person had *lost* them? I was grateful to Renatus for sending me away, because I was in no state to manage their emotions as well as my own right now.

On that note, I was making a poor emotional choice right now, but didn't have any better coping mechanism yet. I was getting very close to the orchard, a dense and untidy part of the estate off-limits to students because of the deep sense of hurt and darkness that lingered in the place where three Morrisseys and one stranger had lost their lives. Most people couldn't stand the cold, repellent energy they felt when they drew close. My dorm was pretty much the last place I wanted to be during the day because of the likelihood of running into my other two roommates, so this was the place I went, where I really shouldn't go, when I needed time alone to think. It was the only place I knew where absolutely *nobody* would follow me.

I walked along the fringe of the overgrown orchard, kicking twigs and rotten apples that lay scattered across the grass, until, after many minutes of walking, I came across a gap in the trees that revealed a path stretching into the dimness of the orchard. Visually, the most unusual aspect of this path was the failure of every tree to drop fruit or leaves onto the ground here. It looked as though it had just been swept clean of all plant matter, but I knew I was the only person to walk this path in many years, and I wasn't sweeping.

The darkness was most intense here, and the first time I'd tried to follow the path, unnaturally drawn as I was, Hiroko had pulled me away, too disturbed to stay. Normal people hated the darkness. For reasons no one had yet been able to properly explain, I was not only attracted to it, I was empowered by it.

Like Renatus.

Like Lisandro.

I walked the path, deliberately skirting around the energetic epicentre that remained in the place Renatus had acted his worst. There was way too much power there, way too much for me right now. I continued to the end of the path, knowing it ended at that little black cast-iron gate just ahead. I'd never gone any further than that.

At the gate I stopped and looked at the graveyard beyond. Fully enclosed by a sturdy but aged and wonky cast-iron fence, the Morrissey family's graveyard was actually bigger and fuller than I'd previously realised. As many as twenty-five stone headstones faced me, marking the final resting places of Renatus's ancestors. Each headstone was unique, tall and grand and ghostly in the filtered light of the orchard. A few trees had been planted between graves, increasing the shade. I supposed that the purpose, aside from providing a deeper sense of austerity to an already depressing space, was to discourage the growth of creeping weeds by limiting their sunlight. The creepers had found the ideal way around this problem by simply climbing the stately tombstones to reach the light.

It was the gloomiest, stillest, quietest place I knew, and I had no intention of going through that gate. Since bonding with Renatus and accelerating my magical development, it seemed I was a magnet for distressing impressions of the past. I didn't even want to consider the number of depressing thoughts that had crossed the minds of people who had stood near or touched those gravestones. Every square centimetre of stone was likely saturated with intense emotive energy and memories I didn't want to access. I wasn't interested.

Well, it wasn't that I wasn't *interested*, I reconsidered, my hand hovering above the gate. I was extremely interested in this place, maybe too interested for my own good. I kept being drawn here, for the dark energy of Renatus's biggest mistake but also for my fascination with this final resting place of his mysterious family. My interest was only shadowed by my logic (which never lasted long when battling with my curious and imaginative nature, so it was only a matter of time), reminding me that a walk through Renatus's past could be almost as painful for me as it was for him. I withdrew my hand and shoved them both deep into my pockets to avoid temptation. I would have to be patient – patient and reluctant all at once.

Impressions could be confronting but they were not purposeless. They came to the people who needed to see them, and waited years sometimes to be accessed. There were many, many answers waiting in that graveyard – some to questions I hadn't even thought to ask yet – but I wasn't ready for them, and so they would wait.

With a frustrated groan I turned away. I was too chicken-shit to scare myself with answers, but driving myself insane with questions.

Lisandro had ruined everything. It was difficult to adjust to my own altered perception of myself, and more difficult still to decide how I felt about it.

I sat down against an old apple tree. The leaves fell mysteriously to one side only, apparently loath to mar the otherwise clear pathway with leaf litter.

What good reason did Lisandro have to attack my family? What good reason did he have to kill anyone? I let my eyes slide over to the graveyard. Even here, in this orchard where he'd killed them, three people lay still and silent because of Lisandro's madness. His *madness*. But though it comforted me to consider Lisandro mad, I knew it wasn't true. He was methodical and careful. He didn't do things without a reason. He'd befriended and collected Peter, a former White Elm, in an attempt to win the Elm Stone from him, and when, after untold months of loyalty, Peter had refused to share the power, Lisandro had killed him. He'd selected Aubrey to infiltrate the White Elm. He thought everything through and put his plans into action early, knowing they would be fruitful in good time.

He'd admitted to me yesterday that he'd *pre-set* the storm that had killed the Morrisseys. That someone could do that blew my mind; that someone would want to do that was even more incomprehensible. I stared upwards, through the leaves overhead and at the bright blue patches of sky beyond the canopy. I'd seen Renatus's memory of that day and then last night I'd tapped into Lisandro's. It had hurt him to do what he did to this family, but not what he did to mine. He'd not even cared that he was destroying good people and leaving two teenage girls alone.

'What do I have in common with you?' I asked the graveyard. Not even a breath of wind answered me. There was really no obvious answer. The Byrnes were not like the Morrisseys. We were not an old family, not a particularly powerful, traditional or well-known family like this one. We didn't share associates. The youngest of both families (me, and Renatus) were both scriers, both connected to the White Elm... Both dark-haired? Both pretty tall? The relevant similarities seemed to end quickly, except for the commonalities Lisandro had given us by murdering our families.

My connection to Lisandro seemed even less substantial. He wasn't a scrier. He was no longer affiliated with the White Elm, although had once held the secretive chair Renatus now possessed. He *was* tall with dark hair, admittedly, but so were a lot of people, and it really didn't seem a reasonable connection to explore.

I reached behind the tree for the nearest fallen leaf and began ripping it into little pieces. The only thing Lisandro and I had in common was a relationship with the Morrissey family. But I didn't have that relationship even as little as a month ago, while Lisandro had loved them so much and for so long... that he'd killed them?

None of it made any sense at all. I was missing too much information. My gaze drifted back to the graveyard, but I made myself think of Ana's room, how easy it was to pick up on glimpses of her life in the place she'd lived. I wasn't prepared for what I'd tap into in the place she'd been laid to rest, so close to the place she'd died. Just... over... there.

There were no answers, despite that I sat in the orchard for hours, thinking in circles.

# chapter five

*Who is Garrett Fischer's closest friend?*

I opened my eyes and stared at the bright snatches of blue sky that fought through the canopy when I received Renatus's very random question. Garrett's closest friend? Hiroko. She didn't count. She and Garrett weren't really *just friends*.

*Josh Reyes,* I replied, sitting up from the tree I was leaning back on, deep in thought. I'd calmed down a great deal just by sitting here and thinking through my situation, even though I was no closer to really understanding it. *And Addison James.*

There was a pause.

*Please bring him to my office,* Renatus requested. I got up and brushed dirt from my jeans. I hadn't even noticed Renatus's return to the property, so lost in my own thoughts I'd ended up. I couldn't understand what Renatus would want with Addison, and wasn't going to ask, but he added, *Garrett's parents want to meet him.*

Then Renatus's presence was quickly gone, closed off, because he didn't want any connection with where I was.

Tall, funny and outgoing, Addison was Garrett's polar opposite and had spent most of his time annoying Garrett or pushing him into awkward situations in an effort to "man him up". I'd never seen him in a bad mood. He had the enviable ability to seem comfortable in all scenarios, and to make those around him feel comfortable as well.

I didn't know, however, where I stood with him now, and how he'd react to me summoning him away from his friends like I was someone he was meant to listen to. I started back to the house, stretching my witch senses – built for identifying and locating sources of energy, though never so far-reaching – beyond myself experimentally to see if I could find him. Still inside the orchard, only paces away from the epicentre of black energy that Renatus's spell had left behind, I was surprised by how *full* my own energy felt, and how easily my senses flung themselves from my immediate vicinity. Across the lawn, through the house... Further than ever before, and hardly thin, either, because all of the feedback I received – *four warm bodies at the front steps, sixteen warm bodies in the dining hall, two in the library, six in the kitchens below the ground floor, two on the staircase, one in dormitory four, three in dormitory seven* – as I moved my attention upwards through the house seemed shockingly precise.

I wondered whether this was how Renatus and the other White Elm saw the world all the time.

Knowing where everyone was, it was easy to avoid people on my way through the house. The infusion of power the orchard gave me wore off the further from it I moved, but my confidence in the skill had been lifted, and I extended my senses through the door of dormitory four as I passed, noting Hiroko's energy signature within, and dormitory seven when I reached it, feeling for movement and energy. The three eighteen-year-olds within were quite still. Sleeping? Surely not, between breakfast and lunch? I forced myself to knock anyway. A few seconds later the door opened inwards, and an expressionless Jin stared at me through it.

'No one in here ordered an escort, thanks,' he said, leaning casually against the doorframe. His words stung – it had been a while since anyone had spoken to me like that and I'd started to convince myself that it didn't matter what so many people thought of me, but the malice still hurt. For a moment I didn't know what to say. I remembered why I was here, and looked past Jin into the room beyond. I saw Addison sit up on his bed.

'I need to see Addison,' I said, pretending I hadn't heard the first comment. Jin smirked.

'I'll bet you do.'

'Jin,' Addison said, warningly, as he got to his feet. I could see that he was just wearing his jeans and a singlet, but when he came closer I could also see the concern and curiosity in his expression as he looked at me. 'What is it?'

'Garrett's parents are here,' I told him. 'They want to meet you.'

He nodded immediately and turned away, eyes on the floor. When I followed his gaze, I saw that there was very little floor to be seen at all. Much like the interior of dormitory five, the carpet of their room was covered in a layer of clothes and *stuff*. Addison kicked a pencil case and a pair of boxers aside and then, apparently having found what he was looking for, grabbed a shirt from the floor and pulled it on. He slid his foot into a sneaker, and looked around for its pair. The third roommate, Constantine, silently tossed the second shoe at him from the other side of the room. Addison jammed his foot into it and deliberately shouldered Jin as he passed. He gestured for me to lead.

'Behave yourself, Add,' Jin called after us. I chanced a sideways look at Addison and caught him giving Jin the finger over his shoulder.

Neither of us spoke the entire walk to Renatus's office. I couldn't think of anything to say, and presumably, neither could he. We'd been friends, sort of, before I'd had *no* friends. Maybe we still were? We'd not spoken all month, but then last night, randomly, he'd stopped me on the way out to face Lisandro and passed on advice that had probably saved my life. Shouldn't I thank him for that? I couldn't work out how to begin, because it hadn't been *his* advice – it had come from his girlfriend, Kendra, who hated me. Normally I probably would have just said thanks, but after Jin's comments I was feeling self-conscious. What if Addison said he didn't care? What if he told me to shut up? I didn't want to open myself up for any further humiliation today.

As we approached Renatus's office, the door opened for me, and I led Addison through it, pulling emotional barriers around myself, guessing what we were walking into.

Not a moment too soon. The families I'd seen touring the mansion earlier were sitting in or standing behind the plush armchairs of Renatus's office with my master and his, Lord Gawain. I recognised the crowd of anguish that Qasim and Susannah had walked through the second storey hallway this morning, but then, I'd only seen the shock and confusion and anger and sadness on their faces. Now, protected from them and their unconscious shedding of pain, I *looked* at their faces. Josh's eyes. Enrico's chin. Tyson's forehead and hairline. At the forefront of the group was a tight-lipped couple. The man was clearly Garrett's father, milky pale with some freckles, the same shaped eyes and mouth. The woman didn't look much like her son, but Garrett had inherited her thick dark red hair.

Had anyone told them that the man who took their kids had left his traumatised best friend for dead in the library, and had anyone told them that the man he'd taken them to was a serial killer with a pattern of destroying whole families? No? Maybe that was a wise move.

'Mr James, thank you for joining us,' Lord Gawain said as Addison stepped out from behind me and the door shut. 'This is Louise and Linus Fischer. They are Garrett's parents.'

'Hi,' Addison said immediately, extending a hand to Garrett's father and shaking firmly when it was accepted. He turned to Louise and did the same. Normally witches don't do much hand-shaking out of our suspicious natures, but Addison was always so warm and open that people *wanted*, genuinely, to be around him. He was a very good-looking guy, with spiked black hair and flawless, tanned skin. His Australian accent added to the friendly appeal, and lifted the mood of the conversation. 'I'm Addison. I'm so sorry for what you're going through.'

'Don't be sorry for anything you didn't do,' Linus Fischer said gruffly, reminding me forcibly of Renatus, who often said something similar. 'Garrett's... predicament... is not your fault, so don't be sorry.'

'I'm sorry all the same. Garrett is a good friend of mine.' Addison looked up over their heads at the woman with Joshua Reyes' eyes. 'So is Josh. We practise Displacement together.'

Josh's mother looked momentarily surprised, then smiled, warming instantly to Addison. I kept silent behind him while Lord Gawain introduced the remaining people. I glanced at Renatus for guidance but he didn't say anything or even look my way.

Addison didn't need any guidance. He always knew what to say.

'I don't know Ty or Enrico that well,' he admitted to the other families gathered, 'but we have a few classes together. They always sit together, and they always seem to be having a laugh.'

The atmosphere we'd walked into had been one of awkwardness and private pain, but now the Marks and Sanchez camps, standing in isolation at opposite ends of the group with their arms crossed, looked over at each other with gentler expressions. Their sons weren't just kidnapped by the same person at the same time. They were friends.

Louise Fischer leaned forward and looked intently up at Addison. She had not yet released his hand from the handshake. In his casual way, he made that seem perfectly normal. Maybe she'd forgotten to let go, shell-shocked as she was.

'Pleased to meet you,' she said softly. Her gaze slipped to me, expectant.

'Aristea is Renatus's apprentice, and a classmate of your sons',' Lord Gawain added.

'Oh, of course,' Mrs Reyes said, a flash of recognition brightening her eyes. 'Josh mentioned you in a letter.'

I attempted a smile, feeling even less comfortable here than in my lonely dorm. What was I meant to say? Why was I even here?

'Mrs Fischer and Mr Marks are Seers,' Renatus told me, answering my wonderings out loud as he often did. 'They have shared a vision about the fate of their sons.'

'They could be wrong,' one of the men in the Sanchez group, either an uncle or Enrico's father, commented tightly, and several others in the room nodded just as tensely. I felt grateful for the walls around my sensitive soul. What had Renatus invited me into? This was much more than the misplaced shock and confusion of parents whose children were taken away. This tension was thicker, imbued with resentment and denial that came from a direct confrontation with someone's core beliefs.

From the way Renatus still refused to meet my eyes, I gathered that he was one of the people who was feeling challenged by whatever was going on here.

'We're not wrong,' Tyson Marks' father insisted. 'Do you think I would say I have foreseen my own son's death if I wasn't certain?'

I felt my eyes widen and I felt the confusion in Addison's aura, adjacent to mine and harder to block. Did that mean…?

'The timing is what makes it uncertain,' the woman beside him, perhaps his mother and therefore Tyson's grandmother, said in frustration. People from different families nodded again; whatever this disagreement was, it was not between families but rather within them. 'We all agree Tyson and the other children are alive and that retrieving them is our greatest priority-'

'Retrieving them alive,' Mr Marks interrupted his mother. 'I don't want Ty back in pieces, thanks.'

'Obviously. But there's no proof your vision will come to pass.'

'That's what Mr James is here for,' Lord Gawain reminded the group, gesturing at my classmate, and the room fell silent. Even through the barriers I felt Addison's discomfort spike underneath his calm exterior. Garrett's mother was still holding onto his hand. 'If he is to encounter your sons again in his future, Mrs Fischer and Mr Marks will see it.'

And Addison, who shared a short past with Garrett, was quite likely to have a future in which Garrett featured, *if* he were to return to the Academy.

'Fate knows already that my son will cross paths with you again,' Mrs Fischer said to Addison confidently, eyes glassy. Her accent was mostly British but with an exotic twist I couldn't identify. 'I'm too close to my situation to see him in mine, but I see him standing with you. I see... Joshua. With you and with Garrett. I see them practising together. I see them resuming school.' Josh's mother visibly brightened at the mention of her son. Louise kept staring into nothing, eyes looking straight through Addison. 'Tyson. He's thin. Older. Not here, not at this house. You must meet him again later in life.'

'What does that mean?' Addison asked, unsure. Louise didn't answer; Lord Gawain filled in the blank.

'When he escapes from wherever Aubrey has taken them, he won't come back here. He may return directly to his family.'

'You will see Enrico much sooner, though not as soon as Garrett or Joshua,' Louise stated, full of certainty. I watched her resolute stillness with amazement. I'd never watched a Seer channelling before. I knew different Seers did it differently, and this was only one example, but it was hypnotic. The Sanchez family was watching on with the same interest. 'Enrico and another boy. A cousin? It's a surprise reunion. Handshakes and laughter.' She dropped Addison's hand and abruptly stood. She reached past him for me but I stepped back in startled surprise, leaving her to float her hand across my chest without touching, dipping her hand into my auric field. Her dreamy tone changed; it was like someone had bumped the TV remote. 'You let Garrett in through the gate. It's late, he's dirty. Dragging someone. Joshua. Hungry, bleeding, both of them.' Everyone listened attentively as she seemed to fall deeper into her trance. I stayed out of her reach but it didn't seem to bother her. 'He has information for the White Elm. He has to speak with someone. He needs to tell them *right now*, before things get worse. He's bleeding but he escaped and he needs to share with the council what they saw.'

'What he tells us will take us to war with Lisandro's movement,' Lord Gawain finished sombrely, quietly. 'Officially; publically.'

Addison turned his head to look back at me with wide, disbelieving eyes. Like, *These are the kinds of conversations you people regularly have?* I was sure my return look was very similar.

'The only way to ensure this happens is if the White Elm *swears* not to act on any intelligence indicating the whereabouts of our children,' Louise Fischer said firmly, dropping her hand finally and snapping out of her trance. 'If any of your agents attempt a rescue of any of the boys, or to encroach onto Lisandro's encampment while our sons may still be on the premises, this future will be destroyed.'

Umm...

'Excuse me,' I spoke up, raising a hand slightly to gain attention and taking a step forward to the right to put Addison's looming figure between me and Louise, certain I was missing something very obvious, 'but *why* would we prefer a course of action that led to *war* with Lisandro over trying to rescue four people?'

*Thank you*, Renatus said, exasperated, still not looking at me. Perhaps what I was missing was not that obvious, since Renatus didn't seem to understand it either.

'Mr Marks' and Mrs Fischer's vision came to them while we were discussing possible rescue plans,' Josh's mother said uncomfortably. 'Lord Gawain's came straight afterwards.

They say...' She swallowed and glanced between them, taking in their grimly assured expressions, and reworded: 'They *realised* that all attempts by the White Elm to get our sons back, whether by storming a compound or by stealth, would result in deaths. Our children don't mean enough to Lisandro or Aubrey to protect them in a fire fight.'

'But if we do nothing,' Tyson's father said, speaking mostly to his own mother, who still looked unconvinced, 'Ty will come to his senses and make his own escape. So will the others.'

'Say that's true,' his mother snapped. 'How long are you willing to wait? Days, weeks? A year? He's been gone eighteen hours, and that's already too long.'

Mr Marks shrugged helplessly and looked at Mrs Fischer, the only other person who seemed as resolute as he was.

'I don't care how long it takes if it means we *all* get our sons back.'

Everyone went restlessly quiet.

'Does this mean no one's going to look for them?' Addison asked, dumbfounded.

'And that we'll go to war with Lisandro?' I repeated, stuck on this concept. The man was a psycho. Most of the people in the room didn't even know the extent of it. Declaring him public enemy number one and dedicating resources to finding him and bringing him to justice, whatever that needed to look like, was how the council had handled it up until now. War, though? Didn't that necessitate armies and soldiers? I thought of the men who had stood between Lisandro and the council last night. *He* had an army. He had more where those came from, I was sure of it.

Nervously, self-consciously, I moved my right hand to clasp my left wrist, the tattoo safely hidden under my palm. Renatus wouldn't hesitate to go head-to-head with soldiers of his godfather's, but I hadn't imagined when I'd accepted this tattoo and all it meant that it would involve *war*. I hadn't imagined I'd learn that my family, years dead, were murdered, and that their killer would scare me, chill me so thoroughly that I simply refused to feel anything about it at all.

We couldn't go to war with him. I might have to look at him again. I might have to feel something.

'That was inevitable,' Lord Gawain told me gently. 'Whatever Garrett will learn in his time with Magnus Moira, whatever secret he brings back to us when he makes his own escape, it will prompt us to take the battle to Lisandro ourselves. Evidently, it is significant; worth the cost of war.'

I thought that was terrible reasoning.

'We are talking about *abandoning* our children to their kidnappers,' Enrico's mother spoke out, heartbroken. 'How can we do such a thing? How can we leave our sons to such a fate?' Of Mr Marks she demanded, 'How will you explain to your son, when he returns to you in six months from now with broken bones and scars from which he will never recover, that you did not even *try* to save him?'

Her words hit home, I could tell from Tyson's dad's face, but he still said, 'I will tell him that I foresaw a day in May where the White Elm had a chance to rescue him, but in doing so he would have died, and his friend Garrett would have missed his chance to witness an event so significant it prompts the White Elm into a righteous war; I will tell him that an opportunity in June looked promising but that his friend Enrico would have been killed.' He swallowed. 'I will tell him I wanted him back as much as you want back your boy but I trusted his resourcefulness and believed he would have the strength and bravery to escape without help.'

Enrico's mother's eyes had filled with tears while he spoke, and now they spilled down her cheeks.

'We will need to agree, each of us,' Lord Gawain told the group. 'We have spoken all morning about courses of action. Instead we may be forced to agree to *in*action until further notice.'

Renatus finally looked up at me and I detected the resentment in him.

'I don't like it,' Garrett's dad said unhappily.

68

'Neither do I,' Renatus admitted. I saw now that it was taking all of his efforts to maintain the united front of full agreement with his leader. 'It doesn't feel right. If we agree to this and word gets out we've left four minors, nationals, in hostile territory, we could be in for even bigger problems. Vigilantes, riots – the results of which we cannot control.' *It's political suicide,* he added to me incredulously, but couldn't voice with the parents present. *How does a government recover from a proven example of negligence on this scale?*

'We are sometimes faced with almost equally unattractive options,' the Welsh sorcerer reminded the Irish one, and Renatus curled his hands into fists and flexed them open again in an attempt to restrain his feelings on the matter. Lord Gawain looked around at the families. 'We would need to agree to some sort of non-disclosure, for the boys' protection from such threats as Renatus just mentioned.'

My master looked away out his window.

'We came here prepared to do anything necessary to help retrieve our son,' Linus Fischer said to Lord Gawain. He didn't sound like his wife. He spoke in a Germanic sort of accent (Swiss?) with that same strange twist that Louise and Garrett shared. 'I did not expect we would leave having agreed to cease the search for them so early.'

'We didn't either,' Mrs Sanchez said softly.

'I did not expect,' Garrett's dad said, turning to stare at Louise, 'that my wife would be the one to suggest it. But,' he sighed, 'she is never wrong.' He looked to the other fathers. 'We knew this could happen when we sent Garrett here. We understood there were risks. But Lisandro... His movements do not yet affect our part of the world, but without the White Elm, his... influence... would spread. It would be selfish for us to keep our son's talents to ourselves. He wanted to do his part. That is why we sent him here. Now our inaction can enable him to help us all.'

I couldn't help but wholly admire the Fischers right then, even if I still struggled to understand their position. Their display of loyalty and solidarity was unlike anything I could imagine of anyone else in their horrible situation. Despite the White Elm's failure to protect their child, they recognised the true enemy as Lisandro and his followers and were willing to work together with the council to find Garrett and the others.

I doubted my own family would be so understanding if this were to happen to me. What would *my* guardian, my big sister Angela, think of the White Elm if she knew all I'd been through these past months? I suspected I would be strapped into the front seat of her car within two hours, on my way home.

'Are you *absolutely certain* that inaction is the only way to ensure all four of them survive?' Mrs Reyes asked Mrs Fischer desperately. 'Is there really no doubt in your mind?'

'None.'

The silence that followed went for so long.

'Do we... vote?' Mrs Reyes asked finally.

They did. Unanimously.

No energetic barrier between my emotions and theirs would have been thick enough to keep their heartbreak from seeping into my bones. I squeezed my eyes shut against the onslaught.

*This is awful.*

*This is democracy*, Renatus replied without any semblance of satisfaction. *This is the illusion of choice.*

Nobody in the room wanted to agree to the course they were all voting for, but they felt they had no choice, the way their sons had felt when Aubrey had shepherded them off the property.

I didn't like it. I couldn't believe it was the outcome. But there was no better choice.

Sometimes, I realised with an icky feeling that had to be a reality check, doing the right thing meant doing something that felt wholly and totally wrong. Maybe there was no right and no wrong, only right*er* and wrong*er*.

Renatus was fuming. Inaction was not in his nature. But I could feel that he had no argument. If action meant deaths, there was no choice in the matter.

'It's settled,' Lord Gawain said, voice gentle, as the hands of the very sobering vote went down. 'I'll brief the rest of the council on our decision. No action will be taken. We will keep you all updated on what intelligence we come into contact with but will not act on it, nor will we actively seek it.'

'None of you,' Louise Fischer repeated, looking at Renatus now. He stared back at her. 'I realise that you are tasked with seeking and prosecuting Lisandro, and I would never presume to issue you with orders, Sir, but in carrying out your assignment you *must not* redirect to seeking out our sons.'

'Really, he should avoid looking for Lisandro at all, if it's as serious as you say,' Tyson's grandmother insisted, and a few others nodded. Renatus's mouth tightened. Grounded.

'We appreciate everything the council was willing to do to save our children,' Mrs Sanchez agreed, 'but it is in Enrico and his friends' interests that they are left alone. They are good boys. They will return to us.'

'I and my colleagues regret that there is not more we can do,' Lord Gawain said diplomatically when Renatus said nothing. 'We will respect this arrangement and will keep everyone informed. I ask that you all do the same, with us and with each other.'

'What's your phone number?' Mr Marks immediately asked Mrs Sanchez, and they all got out their phones, only to realise they'd all fizzled out thanks to the immense electromagnetic energy of the spells tied all over the estate. It didn't matter – they grabbed pens from Renatus's tidy collection at the top of his desk and wrote on their own hands and wrists. Grief had transformed into solidarity and calm efficiency. Mrs Fischer turned back to Addison and me, laying affectionate hands on our arms, smiling warmly at us in turn.

'Thank you both for what you showed me,' she said, and her words got the attention of the other parents. 'Seeing our sons in your futures is such an assurance.'

'Yes, thank you for coming to see us,' Mrs Reyes agreed, making herself smile. 'I'm sure there are places you would rather be on a lovely day like that,' she pointed out the window at the glorious blue sky, 'instead of here watching us blubber.'

'We're just happy we could be of some help,' Addison insisted, speaking for us both. I was grateful. I didn't know what to say anyway. 'We wish you all the luck in the world.'

'This conversation is not to leave this room,' Lord Gawain said to the two of us, and we nodded and were dismissed, and I was grateful all over again. I gathered Addison was, too, because he casually took my shoulders and steered me toward the door ahead of him. Renatus waved a hand at the door and it opened without a word. I glanced back and caught his eye.

*Did we just watch the vote that will lead us into a war?* I asked, still reeling.

*History in the making.*

Addison let me go and I walked out with him right behind me. He stopped and closed the door; he'd never been in the study before so he didn't know that the door would actually close of its own accord if left for a moment. As soon as it clicked shut he leaned back against it with a loud exhalation of disbelief, and the confident posture he'd maintained through that whole exchange fell away.

'Holy shit,' he muttered, staring at the ceiling. 'They're not even going to *look* for Garrett and Josh.'

I stood there looking at him. I was glad it wasn't just me, or even just me and Renatus. It was tragic. Four families had just chosen the path to war, a path that demanded the best people capable of rescuing their children to stand down and make no effort to do so, because *Seers* had told them it would guarantee their safety. How accurate were Seers? Could you really risk your kid's future on their word?

Addison pushed off the door and stalked off towards the staircase and I followed him in silence, retracing our steps down the hall, down the stairs, and back to the dormitories. *I had risked my own life on the word of a Seer only last night. It had paid off. Who was I to judge?*

We paused awkwardly at the point where we should go our separate ways.

We each took one step away, ready to take the easy path and not speak.

Then we both spoke at once.

'Did you notice that-'

'I wanted to say-'

The awkward silence returned as we both stopped abruptly. Addison pointed at me and mouthed "you go first".

'Um, well,' I said, feeling put-on-the-spot. I should just say what needed to be said. 'I wanted to tell you, um, yesterday, I think you might have saved my life, maybe. So, uh, thank you.'

'Oh.' Addison looked like he really hadn't expected that. 'Well, I'm not going to say what I was thinking of saying now. It'll just sound dumb after that.'

'Why, what was it?' I asked, a deep sense of relief settling over me after my tense, frustrating day. Addison, at least, didn't hate me and didn't think I was some kind of school joke.

'It's really dumb,' he warned me. 'I was going to ask if you thought Garrett's mum and dad sounded funny.'

I choked on a laugh.

'Even funnier than Garrett,' he reiterated, unable to resist building on his own jokes. Then he sobered slightly, a sadder tone entering his voice. 'I guess I should have asked Garrett about it at some point, instead of just picking on him. Or maybe I've done him a favour, toughening him up for what he's experiencing now.' He paused, frowning. 'Too soon for that, isn't it? My bad. I'll stop now.'

He gave a quick wave and went to his room. I went to mine, sensing Hiroko still inside and in a more receptive mood, glad that the day, for all its downsides, hadn't been a total waste.

'Aristea?'

I looked back over my shoulder as I opened my door. Addison had paused again.

'Yes?'

'Are they serious about a war?'

I shrugged uncomfortably. 'I think so.'

He looked down at his door handle, deep in thought. I thought he was finished talking to me.

'Aristea?'

'Aye?'

'I forgot to say, "you're welcome".'

That night at dinner we were reminded that the estate's protective enchantments had been reinforced and that we were all perfectly safe, but that no genuine White Elm councillor would ever encourage a student to leave the estate without telling anyone. We were taken through the emergency protocols for alerting the rest of the council should we ever find ourselves confronted with an intruder or imposter. I kept to myself my thoughts about how these protocols wouldn't have protected the boys, who had now been missing for twenty-two hours.

After dinner, I went to my dormitory instead of Ana's bedroom. Following my experiences today with her things and my time spent at her grave, I didn't want to go anywhere near the room. I laid on my bed reading. Hiroko was soon under her covers with her back to the rest of us. We'd sat up talking for a while about mundane things like movies and music because, after departing from Addison, I'd given her the summary of the vote from that morning and she'd taken it well, but we couldn't discuss it in front of the other two girls. Quickly the fake conversation died and she went to bed. Sterling and Xanthe were cutting little words from a magazine to glue onto their nails, but I ignored them. It was like this every night – an invisible, intangible wall separating

74

their half of the room from ours – and was quickly moving from uncomfortable to familiar. It was preferable to fighting.

Everything was preferable to fighting. Wasn't it?

# chapter six

Jadon was smiling at a wall.

He wasn't going mad, or at least he hoped not. He barely even realised he was doing it, but he was practising his smiles and trying to choose the best one for the occasion. You have so many smiles, see, and they all mean different things. He smiled a wide, bright grin. An expression like that was best for delight or humour. He closed his lips to hide his teeth, but it felt tight – forced, unwilling. He relaxed one side of his face, making a playfully lop-sided smile. No way. Definitely not appropriate.

Nothing seemed right, but he needed to pick one and get it sorted, and soon. If he didn't, who knew what expression would leap to his features when Teresa opened that door?

Jadon was waiting in the hallway on the fourth floor of Morrissey House opposite the bedroom Teresa was using. She'd been inside for almost forty-eight hours, ever since he'd found her lying pale and still in the library. He'd thought of nothing but her ever since, but Emmanuelle and Lady Miranda had demanded the whole council give Teresa complete privacy until she was ready to re-establish contact with them. Only those two Healers had visited her, presumably taking the traumatised young councillor through some kind of rigorous magical therapy. They'd not told Jadon anything except to mind his business.

Until tonight, when, after dinner, Lady Miranda had mildly wondered whether Teresa would be ready to go home by now and if Jadon could take her. These were the exact musings Jadon had been waiting for, and he'd jumped at the chance.

'I'll do it,' he'd told Lady Miranda enthusiastically, jogging to catch her as she left the dining hall, because *waiting* to hear whether she was okay these last two days had honestly been the biggest drag of his whole life. It didn't help that his foremost choice of distractions from worry was to hunt for and rescue the missing students, and he'd been banned from it. By *their parents*.

Feeling useless, he'd taken to seeking clues as to Teresa's state of health from Emmanuelle's mind, which was usually quite open to him, but she'd kicked him out and was now actively avoiding him. She had a secret, something huge that she shared with Renatus, Lord Gawain and Aristea, and she wasn't giving it up. Glen and Anouk, the other Telepaths, had noticed too, but hadn't gleaned anything further.

The White Elm had lost four innocents and was opting to stand down the search.

The White Elm was keeping secrets from its own members.

The White Elm had an opening and was not advertising the position. Instead they were putting another councillor on leave and reducing their number even further.

Apparently, in some alternative universe he hadn't realised they'd all fallen into, it all made perfect sense, or so Lord Gawain made it sound.

Anyway, that was how he'd come to be standing here, smiling at walls. Frustration with the political gridlock he faced at every turn would have driven him to this point sooner or later.

Jadon detected movement inside the room. He wasn't sure she even knew he was there, but he couldn't bring himself to knock or disturb her in case he interrupted some sort of prescribed meditation or something. He didn't know what her mental state was like – he could only infer from Emmanuelle's protectiveness that Teresa was very vulnerable, and he could only imagine what she'd been through to get like that. Teresa had been a hostage of Jackson's for weeks, and she'd been a physical mess when they'd freed her. If she'd been that dirty and scratched up on the outside... what was going on in her head now? A natural Telepath, Jadon had been so very careful these past few days to studiously avoid Teresa's thoughts. Had they tortured her? Did they make her cry? Who had burnt the skin from her palms? Had anyone... done anything else? If Jadon ever got the answers to these questions he would have to kill someone. Or several someones. Jackson and Aubrey could be first...

The door handle moved slightly, and Jadon stood up straight, swallowing nervously and pasting a small, kind smile across his mouth. It would have to do. The tall, thin door swung slowly open and Teresa stepped through.

Her curly brown hair was gathered to the side.

Her skin was fresh and unmarked.

Her stance was relaxed, no sign of any limp or discomfort.

Her unburned hands clutched overnight bags and the fingernails which, two days ago, had been broken and bleeding were today pearly and healthy.

And she wore the same rehearsed little smile Jadon did.

'Hey,' was all Jadon could think to say, wanting so badly to grab her and hug her tight but guessing that wasn't a good idea. She looked perfectly normal but that didn't mean she *was* back to normal, and he didn't want to break her.

'Hey,' she whispered back. Her hands tightened on the bags she held and her cheeks flushed lightly. Damn, she was remembering that the last time they'd seen each other, Jadon had been dumb enough to kiss her. Dumb, dumb, dumb...

'Here, I'll take those,' Jadon said hurriedly, taking the bags from her.

'Oh, you don't have to,' Teresa protested weakly, but she let him and cast her eyes away as she gestured for him to lead. They walked together in awkward silence down three flights of stairs and across the reception hall. Teresa kept her eyes cast down and her shoulders were tense.

Most students had already eaten dinner but a few noisy teenagers could be heard laughing loudly in the dining hall. A particularly voluminous roar of laughter as they passed the doors seemed to startle Teresa, and she hastened her pace to reach the front doors. Jadon watched as she nervously patted down her pockets, fumbled with her key and dropped it as she tried with shaking hands to unlock the doors.

'Let me do it,' Jadon offered as she bent to collect the key. He noted the way her fingertips skittered across the floor. She shook her head and forced a tight smile.

'I can do it,' she said, and missed the keyhole completely when she tried to insert it.

'Teresa,' he said, putting the bags down and reaching to take it from her. She blocked him with her body.

'No, I'm fine,' she insisted. She dropped the key a second time. She went to reach for it but Jadon grabbed her hands. They were shaking.

'Stop,' he said. He looked her in the eyes. 'You're not fine. Let me.'

He stooped for the key, unlocked the door and shoved it open for her. She slipped through and he followed with the bags. He locked it behind them while she stood on a lower step. He waited in stillness and silence for her to speak. She stared at the starry sky.

'I really am fine,' Teresa insisted after half a minute. 'Lady Miranda and Emmanuelle fixed me up.'

She did look all better, but she was also a master illusionist, so for all Jadon knew, he could be looking at the Teresa she wanted him to see. Beneath, she could be scarred and scabbed and ruined. And beneath that... well, she wasn't back to normal. His Teresa was quiet, sensitive and cautious. This Teresa was shaky and honestly terrified.

'Come here,' Jadon ordered. She shot him a nervous look, and he sighed and took the stairs two at a time to reach her. 'I'm not going to kiss you.'

She blushed bright red but allowed him to drop the bags at her feet and gather her into a tight hug.

'And I am sorry about that, by the way,' Jadon added, resting his cheek on her hair. She slowly relaxed against him. 'I'm just so grateful that you're alive.'

He stood with her for ages, maybe longer than forty minutes. It didn't matter. She was alive and she was back, and Lisandro, Jackson and *Aubrey* were never getting near her ever again.

After a long time, Jadon shifted his elbow to itch a spot against his shirt. Teresa flinched and pulled away.

'Let's go,' she muttered. Jadon nodded and collected the bags, giving in to the temptation to browse her surface thoughts.

He dropped the bags straightaway.

Her mind was a minefield. She was thinking non-stop about the fortnight's experiences as a political prisoner of a war that hadn't officially started. Typical of a victim of trauma, the faces of her captors were blurred, the way all improperly processed memories appear. Constantly on edge, flooded with adrenaline and living on dangerously minimal sleep, the mind commits less to memory than usual, focussing sharply on minute details at the expense of the greater picture.

But that didn't prevent her from reliving those disjointed and disordered memories on loop.

She seemed to remember the hands with more detail than she did the faces. There were rough hands, wet hands, hairy hands, pale hands, hands with freckles, hands with dirty fingernails and a hand with a birthmark the shape of Africa on the back. That hand was the one she kept seeing in her waking nightmares, even now that she was safe and free.

Mostly, for two weeks, she'd been left alone, except when Jackson needed an illusion cast. That was what they'd wanted

80

her for. Her illusions looked as good as the real thing, and could last for hours or even days, and they'd used her to pay some of Magnus Moira's debts. But the hand with the birthmark had taken his big fake emerald and then come back for something else that wasn't his.

Lord Gawain said that Lisandro didn't seem to have known about her treatment. *And you believe him?* Jadon had wanted to shout. *Does that make him exempt from blame or something?*

There was no forgiveness for this kind of violation. Stolen. Injured. Isolated. Manipulated. Terrorised. Assaulted. Worst of all, locking her power from her with an enchanted chain around her ankle. A natural Healer, she'd been unable to fix her own wounds for the first time in her life. She had been cut off telepathically from the ring of minds that made up the White Elm. She'd never had the chance to call for help. She'd been unable to defend herself with magic, or cast one of her incredible illusions. The anklet had only come off when Jackson needed another gemstone.

She'd done what they asked. She hadn't antagonised her captors. Like all of the White Elm, she'd believed Aubrey was another victim, just like her, and when Lisandro had requested a lifelike illusion of Aubrey with which to deceive the council, she'd done it, worried her disobedience would result in harm to him or his pregnant girlfriend. *Teresa* had tried to protect *them*. She'd been captured in the first place because she'd stayed to defend Aubrey when she should have run away. She'd loved him like she loved Jadon, and he'd betrayed her to Jackson's filthy crew to be used, humiliated and hurt.

Aubrey was an utter bastard.

Jadon turned back to Teresa, hugged her again and kissed her hair. If only Telepaths could steal away the thoughts they read from minds, like ripping pages from a book, without risking massive damage to the person and without breaking a dozen laws.

Best to just turn the page and pretend not to have read that chapter.

'Emmanuelle got in contact with Samuel today,' Jadon said, trying to sound normal as he grabbed the bags and started towards the gates. 'He knows to expect you and he's cooking some pasta thing for you. She told me what it was, I just can't pronounce it.'

Teresa spared him a small smile. How could she bring herself to smile when she'd been treated as she was?

'I saw you, holding Samuel back,' she said, apparently talking about the Thursday night on which she'd been taken. 'You saved his life. Thank you.'

'*You* saved our lives,' Jadon disagreed. 'Your illusion protected us. We just wished there was something we could have done to help you.'

She looked uncomfortable, and Jadon berated himself for allowing the conversation to sway towards her imprisonment. She finally shrugged.

'It's done now.'

They said nothing else until they were through the gate. Jadon locked it behind them and walked in silence with his most favourite person for almost a further minute along the dirt road that would allow a well-directed car to make its way to Morrissey House. Certainly far enough now from the house's energy, they would be able to Displace without interference.

Jadon reached for Teresa's hand and gently pulled her with him as he opened space and moved between Ireland and Italy.

It was a pretty good Displacement for a non-Displacer, Jadon thought with pride as they walked up Teresa's quiet, sloped street. They were within a hundred metres of the house and no one seemed to have witnessed their sudden appearance beside a bird bath.

The lights were on at Teresa and Samuel's place, and Jadon started to feel sad when he saw the front door open and Teresa's Italian boyfriend step outside. He was only here to hand her back – Samuel was the one who would take care of her, cook for her, hold her tightly when she woke later tonight from a nightmare...

'Samuel,' Teresa murmured with a smile, a real smile, and ran the last thirty metres into her boyfriend's arms. Jadon maintained his pace to give them a moment before he came within earshot with the bags.

Samuel was not extraordinary, but he was honest and loving and stable. He was perfect for Teresa, and exactly what she needed now. Jadon had liked Samuel from the first time they'd met, and it had never mattered that Jadon had quickly fallen in love with the boring man's girlfriend. He'd never wanted to take her from him. Samuel was better for Teresa than he could ever possibly be.

Teresa huddled closely against her boyfriend's chest and Samuel raised a grateful, acknowledging hand to Jadon as he neared.

'Thank you, Jadon,' the Italian said. His English was not as good as Teresa's, but the couple had given themselves the challenge of speaking only in English at home when she'd been brought onto the White Elm. Both had improved markedly since Jadon first met them last year.

'You're welcome,' Jadon said, shaking hands with the one who brought real smiles to Teresa's face. 'Has Emmanuelle spoken to you about treatment and stuff?'

'She called me today. She filled me in. She was... insistent.'

The "let it be" message had gotten through loud and clear, then.

'Lady Miranda has ordered I take at least two months' leave from the White Elm,' Teresa told Samuel. 'She said I'm not needed unless I'm better, but I feel fine.'

Samuel smiled at her and cuddled her close. When her face was obscured by her hair, he glanced up at Jadon for confirmation. He knew Jadon could hear his thoughts and knew he was wondering how fine "fine" really was. Jadon shook his head slightly. No, she was not fine. She might not be fine again for a very long time. But if wanting to believe she was fine was part of her recovery plan, he could play along with that.

'You'll be back working with us in no time,' he agreed with her cheerfully. 'Take the break and work on your garden or cross-stitch or something.'

Teresa shot him an amused look. He put down the bags and stepped back from the door. He could feel that the house's wards were back, only stronger and better than before because they were Emmanuelle's work. Nobody was getting in here without a lot of work and without the French sorceress knowing about it. There was nothing else for him to do here.

'I'd better get going,' he excused himself. Teresa pulled herself away from Samuel and stared at Jadon.

'Do you have to?' she asked, and her boyfriend added, 'You could stay for dinner.'

'My mom is expecting me home. She's been complaining I'm never there,' Jadon said in a joking tone. It was true, and the couple accepted his excuse reluctantly. Teresa secretly feared that Samuel would start asking questions about her time imprisoned, while Samuel was wondering what he'd say to her once Jadon left, terrified that any conversation could inadvertently remind her of some unknown terror. They were both afraid of being alone together after this short but intense time apart.

Jadon adored them but he couldn't help, least of all by staying longer and prolonging the inevitable. Eventually they would have to be alone together and find a new rhythm for their relationship.

'Take care,' Jadon farewelled them, backing away with a wave. The couple called reluctant goodbyes and cautiously withdrew into their home. Jadon turned and walked down the street. He didn't stop until he was almost out of view, then he turned back and took a moment to watch their front light go out.

Teresa would be safe now. Not that Samuel, or her huge Romanian family, really had the skills to protect her if she were attacked again – only her White Elm family could do that – but they were the people she needed around her while she recovered. Time away from the council would be good for her. She didn't need their constant hunt for Lisandro, Jackson and Aubrey reminding her of her horror. She didn't need their over-protectiveness at this time. This was the right place for her.

Space shifted, and Jadon turned.

'Hello, Jadon.'

Aubrey stood a mere metre away. His coppery hair hung into his eyes in bangs, like a late nineties pop star. He wore a casual sort of suit with the buttons of his shirt open. He would be judged with raised eyebrows by Jadon's hometown friends, but Aubrey wasn't the sort who would care. He was always comfortable with himself, with the kind of easy confidence inspired within a person who knows he looks rather good. Even today, after a fortnight of confinement, he looked rather good.

It took Jadon a few seconds to remember that Aubrey was no longer his best friend, but was in fact an utter bastard. He stepped away and drew his wand.

'Aubrey,' he answered, trying to sound angry rather than hurt. He'd trusted this man implicitly until only nights ago. He'd gone to war for him. He'd watched him die, and mourned him, and then learned that Aubrey had faked his own death to fool him. There was more than a little bitterness. 'You stay away from her, or I'll murder you where you stand.'

'Jadon, wait,' Aubrey placated, opening his hands, or one of them at least. The other held a sort of sack. '*Frère*, brother, I just came to talk.'

'We have nothing to discuss, *brother*,' Jadon spat. This had to be some kind of surprise attack. Or some other kind of manipulation. Lisandro must have sent him.

'You're angry. I understand. I didn't mean this to happen.' Aubrey's French accent, though not as strong as his distant cousin Emmanuelle's, did little to incite trust in his one-man audience, but when Jadon did not strike, he continued. 'I didn't intend to break your trust. I never intended to *have* your trust, Jadon. Your friendship was an unexpected gift.'

'I thought you were dead. I hurt people and let them drown to avenge you. But you were nothing but a shit.'

Aubrey looked the same, but when Jadon's focus moved from his former brother's face to the space around him, he saw that this was not the same person at all. This man had done darker deeds than the Aubrey he'd known a month ago. This Aubrey was practising dark magic, or had at least done something very uncool very recently. Everything about his aura was out of whack, stronger in some ways and weaker in others. If Jadon were to strike him now, Aubrey would not be able to heal himself. Such gifts were reserved only for the good.

'I've been selfish. I always have been. I can't help that. I've used a lot of people. I used Emmanuelle to get onto the council. I used Renatus to keep suspicion off me. I used you to make life easier for myself.'

'And Teresa?' Jadon couldn't help but glance in the direction of her house. Were Aubrey's new minions even now attacking the home while their traitorous leader kept him distracted? Nothing moved or seemed out of the ordinary at the house. 'You used her and then threw her to a pack of bullies and rapists.'

Aubrey sighed and looked down. He said nothing for so long that Jadon began to feel uncertain. Was there a chance that this situation was not as he expected?

'I can't say I'm sorry enough for what happened to her,' Aubrey murmured. 'I didn't know, Jadon. I didn't know they would take her. It was never part of the plan. It was only to be me, and the Elm Stone. They took too long to arrive – Jackson should have been there before Teresa cast her illusion… The mix-up wasn't meant to be.' He shook his head bitterly. 'I didn't know. Jackson was supposed to take me and the ring, Lisandro was to "kill" me and I was meant to disappear. That was the role I was chosen to play. That's why I was with you that day when we both applied for places on the White Elm. That's all I knew, I swear to you, *je te promets.*'

Jadon stared at him. It seemed so wrong to be having this conversation with Aubrey, as enemies rather than as brothers, but it wasn't until later that he reflected on how furthermore strange it was for this traitor to be spilling on his master's plan. Maybe it didn't matter now.

'They locked her up,' Jadon said finally. 'They-'

'I know what Jackson's scum did,' Aubrey interrupted flatly. He dropped the sack at his feet. 'His team – they're filth, the worst of the worst. Murderers, child molesters, animal torturers… I didn't know this until today when Lisandro took me to them. Only one touched her, *morceau de merde,*' he hissed, and Jadon now remembered him pronouncing his curse like that a dozen times but not making the connection a week ago when a French speaker was overheard trespassing onto White Elm allied lands. 'But they all knew. They did nothing. And so.' He kicked the bag and a number of stiff, organic, five-pronged shapes fell out. Jadon stared, uncomprehending; when he realised, he sprung back, disgusted. Aubrey was still talking. 'Lisandro sends sincere apologies. He didn't know either. The team's been disbanded, needless to say.'

'So Lisandro approves of kidnapping, murder and the burning of little girls, but draws the line at sexual violence? What a champ.' Jadon's tone was scathing. He deliberately kept his gaze up and away from the sack of dismembered hands, knowing that there would be rough hands, freckled hands, hands with dirty fingernails and a hand with a birthmark in the shape of Africa. 'And he clearly doesn't flinch when dismembering his employees.'

'He didn't do this. He left them to me.' Aubrey was expressionless. 'It was my sister they touched – they were mine to pull apart.'

'Who *are* you?' Jadon asked in disbelief. 'You, *brother*, are an excellent actor. All this time, I was sharing my meals with a psychopath. It's not a stretch to call you a killer, is it?'

'No, but I wasn't either of these things when you knew me. I've changed a lot these few weeks.'

'Apparently. I got that impression when I found Teresa unconscious in the library.'

Aubrey sighed again.

'How many times do I need to tell you I'm sorry? Of course I regret that, but it was necessary. It was the kindest way to silence her. I risked my life every day of this year as Lisandro's spy on the council. I couldn't let everything unravel in one moment of mercy.' He ran a hand through his hair. 'I don't expect you to understand my motives, but suffice it to say that this year, *everything* I've done, betraying you and hurting Teresa, it was all for Shell. This was the only way for me to be with her. She belongs to Lisandro; to have her, I needed to make a deal. So I did.' He shrugged unhappily. 'I regret that I made and lost friends like you and Teresa. I'm sorry a thousand times over, and I know you'll hate me forever. But this is for Shell's freedom, and for the life of my son.'

'Shell's freedom? What are you talking about?' Jadon asked in frustration, but space was shifting. Aubrey could feel it too, and began backing away.

'I'm sorry, Jadon,' he said. 'I-'

A blast of blackish lightning struck a hasty ward just centimetres from Aubrey's face as Renatus appeared beside Jadon. The French Crafter was quick to build another, and it only occurred to Jadon then that *he* hadn't thought to build a single ward against Aubrey. Talk about trusting.

'Renatus, I'm here to talk,' Aubrey shouted as he ducked beneath a second blast. 'I just want-'

'Why would I care what you want?' Renatus demanded, stepping over the scattered hands to shove Aubrey's chest, wand still raised threateningly. 'You turned the council on me, and then nearly cost me my apprentice. I have no interest in what you want.'

'Then go,' Aubrey snapped. 'I didn't come to talk to you, anyway. I'm just here to promise Jadon that the pain is over for Teresa. She's safe. Lisandro has declared her, her kin and her property off-limits to all in his command.'

'For how long?' Jadon asked, grabbing Renatus's arm and yanking him back when he tried again to have a go at Aubrey. The three of them were about the same age but Renatus was the oldest, the tallest, the strongest, the highest ranked, the most powerful... the most everything. Jadon had never tried to be physically assertive with him before; he had long suspected he would probably come off second-best. But Renatus allowed himself to be restrained. The thoughts he didn't try to block from Jadon indicated a sense of relief that he'd been stopped before he could lose himself.

He was struggling as much as Jadon with the forced inaction within the council and had as much, or more, pent-up rage to let out on his next confrontation.

'Until Lisandro changes his mind,' Aubrey said, 'and then they'll answer to me. She won't be touched as long as I live.'

'How convenient,' Renatus noted darkly. 'Are you suggesting it would be unwise to kill you?'

'It could be.'

'Where are the boys?'

Jadon wished he'd thought to ask that.

'Safe. Safer than Teresa was.' Space was shifting. Aubrey was preparing to escape. 'I know it doesn't make up for what I've done, Jadon, but I *am* sorry and I *would* undo Teresa's hurt if I could. You have my word she's safe now. I can't promise the same for you... I'm sorry. It's all for Asheleigh.' He opened a wormhole and glanced warily at Renatus, but the Dark Keeper made no move to stop him. 'I wish it wasn't this way – I wish you hadn't been such a good person, Jadon, and such a good friend. I hope this is the last time we meet.'

He slipped away into some other place. Jadon and Renatus were alone. The young Dark Keeper stalked away a few paces, clearly fuming. They stood in silence for a while. Nobody came out of their homes. The locals hadn't heard or noticed a thing.

'You didn't call for me,' Renatus said eventually. 'You didn't alert anyone.'

Jadon realised that he was right. He had eleven minds connected intimately with his, a mere thought away if he wanted their attention. The appearance of an enemy as powerful as Aubrey should have been immediately reported so that backup could arrive quickly to support him. Renatus must have scried their exchange. Aubrey was a Crafter and a strong sorcerer. Jadon had never sparred with him before so he didn't know if he had the firepower to take his old friend on, but knew that if Aubrey had wanted him dead, he would have had the element of surprise on his side at almost any point. Jadon still thought of Aubrey as his friend. It was a weakness.

'I didn't think to,' Jadon admitted. 'I didn't feel threatened.' He paused, then stated the obvious. 'You didn't kill him.'

Renatus seemed to consider his answer carefully.

'It wasn't worth it,' he said. He looked down at the ghastly and bloodied hands. 'Perhaps I was wrong. Who is Asheleigh?'

'Shell,' Jadon clarified. 'Ash-shell-leigh. He said all this was for Shell, and their baby.'

And then Jadon remembered the photo he kept in his front pocket. He withdrew the low definition scan Shell had given him of her baby when Aubrey had first gone missing. It had inspired him even more deeply to find his friend, soon to be a father to this beautiful unborn life. He'd planned to give it to Aubrey when he found him. He'd forgotten all about it, even though he still put it into his pocket every morning. But now Aubrey was an enemy. And, apparently, so was Shell.

'Ash-shell-leigh,' Renatus repeated, accentuating the syllables the same way Jadon had. It was an unusual pronunciation of an otherwise common name. 'Asheleigh Hawke?'

Jadon nodded. Renatus thought for a few moments and then disappeared.

Life had become so complicated all of a sudden. Both of Jadon's closest friends had changed forever; one was a broken victim and the other was a traitor and an enemy, though a sympathetic one at least. It was mind-blowing; Aubrey an enemy, Renatus a friend? Jadon wouldn't have ever imagined it. The council had a hole in it, only twelve members when they should have thirteen – they all lacked their potential strength when their council wasn't whole. If they had to face Lisandro and his followers now, they might not be as successful as they were on the weekend when Aubrey's power still fuelled their circle.

He stared at the gross spectacle of hands, cut from their natural owners at the wrist. Aubrey, his friend, his former brother, loving boyfriend to Shell, future father, soft and talk-first-act-later Aubrey, had done this to countless men. Well, not countless, not if Jadon could bring himself to tip the bag out onto the road, and not really men, either. Scum. Dirt. The filth that took advantage of Teresa when she couldn't fight back or knew but did nothing.

He looked up at her house. Should he call her out and show her Aubrey's gift? Might that calm her nightmares, knowing these monsters had been taken care of? Or would the ghastliness just worsen them?

Jadon raised his hand and channelled energy through his body. He couldn't create magic – it wasn't something that could be just made – but like all living things it could flow through him; being a sorcerer, he had the added bonus of having an awareness of that energy flow and the ability to manipulate and direct it. He sent a small amount along his arm and directed it to transform. A fire ignited in his palm. He watched it as it grew, cool and safe to his skin but deadly to anything else it touched.

Life was not so complicated at all, he realised with a sense of comfort. Life was about doing good and protecting good people. Life was very simple really.

He tipped his hand and dropped the ball of fire onto the sack at his feet. It immediately caught alight and the flames spread all over, burning feverishly as it moved unnaturally fast. Jadon walked away, and even before he Displaced home, his fire had reduced Teresa's nightmare hands to nothing more than hot ash to be blown away in the night breeze.

# chapter seven

For the first time since arriving at Morrissey House on the first of March, exactly two months ago today, I was missing my computer. It was Friday, after lunch, and I was sitting in Renatus's office poring over yet another stack of old letters. I had no idea where he kept producing them from, but ever since he'd faced Aubrey two nights ago he'd been analysing old documents – everything his mother and father had ever written, as far as I could tell – looking for mentions of the Hawke family or Lisandro. There had been journals, account books and letters from distant family and friends. So far we'd found little of interest or relevance. Occasionally I'd tap into some old energy and access an impression, but not many people recorded their monthly expenditures while in a foul or passionate mood, so not much energy had lingered on any of these documents.

If I had a computer, and the internet, I'd just be able to type "Asheleigh Hawke family tree" into any given search engine and let the computer do the browsing for me. Wouldn't that be easier?

'I think the name is proof enough that she's who we think,' Renatus said, and I remembered that thinking in questions was a quick way to have my thoughts overheard. It was like broadcasting, Anouk had said once, an invitation for good Telepaths to listen in. 'Aubrey told Jadon that Shell *belongs* to Lisandro. What chance is there that an orphan

Hawke in his service is from a different line of Hawkes than the one he once considered family?'

I'd learned already that coincidences did not exist in the world of cunning dark sorcerers, magical rings and powerful councils.

'Then what are we looking for?' I asked tiredly, shifting a letter from one Desmond O'Malley. 'Was this a relative of Declan's?'

Renatus glanced up and noted the name.

'Yes, his father. And I don't know what we're looking for. I'll know when we find it.'

'How will *I* know if I've found it?' I countered.

'You just will.'

Snappy. He'd been like this since Tuesday. One word answers, long cold silences, annoying me with restless habits like tapping pens against the edge of the desk – typical signs that Renatus was intensely frustrated with his own uselessness while outside the house that felt like a prison, the world kept turning, bad kept happening and opportunities to do something about it all kept passing him by. He wasn't saying it but I knew that he was angry about the meeting between my classmates' parents and Lord Gawain, and the vote that had left him feeling powerless. Going after Lisandro was *his job*, and right now Lisandro and Aubrey had four hostages. There was nothing he wanted more than to get out there and track them down.

Instead, he was unofficially grounded.

I knew that despite the assertions of the Seers involved, and later Susannah and Tian as well, Renatus felt sure that there was more that could be done for the missing students than simply *nothing*. He believed there was more *he* could do.

I guess I knew where my newfound arrogance was stemming from, but in his case, I tended to agree he was probably capable of it. Renatus was a resource the White Elm heavily underutilised, kind of like having a dragon and keeping it chained up in the backyard.

Let him fly free, I found myself thinking privately, and let him set Lisandro's camp on fire. He wouldn't hold back, and the world would be a safer place. One less family-killer on the loose.

Four kids dead. I could see why nobody was putting me in charge.

Renatus was silent for a long time, then sighed, perhaps realising he'd fobbed me off, and added, 'We're looking for something to explain why Lisandro murdered his former friend and his wife, and then later seems to have conscripted their surviving daughter to his ranks.'

'You think he would have put that in writing?'

'No, but someone may have mentioned something special about her *somewhere*,' he gestured at the piles of paper in frustration. 'He collected her. He didn't do the same to you or me.'

But Renatus was wrong about that. Lisandro had long played two sides. Onto one side, his secret underground army, he'd conscripted Asheleigh Hawke. Whatever was or wasn't special about her, it had already paid off, because through her he'd been able to control Aubrey. On the other side, the White Elm council, Renatus had conveniently been sworn in. Renatus had once told me he felt Lisandro hadn't wanted him on the White Elm but who knew? And who knew what he'd maybe planned for me if Renatus hadn't found me first? I was younger than Renatus and Shell. Maybe he'd been collecting us onto his two teams, unsure which he would choose in the end? If that were the case, he probably now regretted putting Renatus where he had.

I silently read through the rest of the letters in my stack. The Morrisseys received very different mail than my household. When Angela or I checked the mailbox, it was typically a combination of bills, bank statements and junk mail advertising specials at the local shops. Renatus's parents did get their bank statements as letters, but seemed not to have gotten any official bills – not being connected to the power grid or having a telephone must have an upside at times. I tried not to read the amounts on the bank letters, but couldn't help noticing that there were about twice as many digits as I'd ever seen on a bank statement before. The Morrisseys were more loaded than I'd thought. Short letters from any number of acquaintances were polite and formal and usually hinted at some kind of unnamed business transaction to be undertaken. Those were probably the sort of business transactions one did not record on paper for fear of being arrested. I was of the understanding that the Morrisseys had made a good deal of their fortunes through illegal trade of dark artefacts and information, and by selling their services as practitioners of darker arts to the desperate and well-paying.

I made it my business to not know anything more specific than that.

'The trouble is that we have only one side of the correspondence,' Renatus complained eventually. 'We can only surmise as to what my father put to paper to get these responses.'

'Which is why email would have made this so much easier,' I muttered. 'We could have just scrolled down and read the conversation history...'

He shot me a look, but probably had no idea what I was talking about. I knew for a fact that he'd never sent an email, just like he'd never driven a car or watched a soap opera. He'd lived such a different life from mine.

I finished my very boring pile without a single mention of Kenneth Hawke and reached for more. The very first letter caught my attention as previous ones had not.

> Dearest Aindréas and Luella,
>
> I do hope that this note finds you and your family fit and well. I write to thank you for your generous gifts to my Teagan on her recent fifth birthday. She and I are very grateful and were honoured by your family's presence at the party.

*For my part, local business is still suffering, and expansion is challenging without international reach. I still marvel at your genius, Luella, in suggesting an alliance with Reilly Murphy. As discussed at the party, with my Caitlin soon to be of age, the time to cement this alliance is nearing.*

*I greatly appreciate your offer, Aindréas, to broker this alliance, and enclose the documentation you requested proving Caitlin's lineage, as well as your payment.*

*As promised, I have made contact with Cian Ó Maoilriain and expect to host him and his wife next weekend for tea, over which I will discuss the prospect of both Anastasia and Keely spending the summer studying the arts under his tutelage. I understand that he is increasingly in demand.*

*Please write shortly with your response.*

*Kind regards,*
*Thomas Shanahan*

I lightly touched the aged paper and tapped into a very vague impression of a slightly overweight blonde man as he wrote this very letter, focus and hopefulness etched all over his face, a blot of ink from his pen making the date illegible.

'Am I reading this properly?' I asked of Renatus, waving the letter at him to get his attention. He followed it with his eyes and frowned.

'Hold it still and I'll tell you,' he said, irritated when I kept waving it, unable to resist because his bad mood was boring. He snatched it out of the air and scanned the words. I continued speaking as he read.

'Was your dad helping arrange a marriage?'

'Yes, I remember the wedding,' Renatus agreed finally. 'It was at the end of May, a week or so before Ana turned eighteen. It was... memorable.' He squinted at the date at the top but couldn't make it out either. 'They arranged it well in advance, then. Teagan's fifth birthday... She must have been nine or ten at the wedding.'

'And how old was the bride?'

'The same age as Ana.'

I did the math in my head.

'They organised this when she was only thirteen?' I demanded. 'She was only a kid and your dad was trying to marry her off?'

'Shanahan got his alliance. As far as I know, he and the Murphies are still tight. Caitlin was happy,' Renatus assured me, rereading the letter. 'I'd forgotten about old Cian. *Studying the arts.*'

'Which arts?' I asked.

'Art forgery,' Renatus replied. 'Outspoken, independent heiresses like those two needed a trade in case nobody would marry them.' His brow furrowed and he tilted his head in thought as I struggled to articulate a response in my self-righteous outrage. '*You're* nearly eighteen. Have you considered art forgery? Sewing?'

Deeply offended, I opened my mouth to retort, then caught the glint of amusement in his eyes and felt my anger dissolve. I clamped my mouth shut and tried not to smile.

'Marrying off your daughter to secure a business alliance is prehistoric,' I said. 'Caitlin was only my age.'

'And I'm not marrying you off to anyone, so relax.' Renatus handed the letter back to me. 'This was a tradition. Still is. That whole community would have killed each other off generations ago if they weren't all emotionally invested in one another's families. Kenneth Hawke,' he said now, tapping his fingers thoughtfully on the tabletop, more alert and present in the moment than I'd seen him in days, 'must have had alliances and connections beyond my family and Lisandro. If he was their friend, chances are he was *like* them – from the same tradition. His mother would have been promised to his father when she was a girl-'

'In exchange for chickens and goats,' I filled in peevishly.

'In exchange for land or money or leniency in some ongoing transaction, more like,' Renatus corrected. 'You underestimate the value of a good, obedient young woman with nothing controversial to say.'

I threw a pen at him. He ducked and it fell over his shoulder.

'Okay, does that mean there would be people still alive today who could tell you about the Hawkes?' I redirected. Renatus pushed his chair back and got up to go and fetch his pen.

'I expect so.'

'So you could ask them and we could pack all these letters and ledgers away?'

'No.' He shook his head and came back to the desk with the pen. 'I'm not in contact with those people anymore.'

'Could that change?' I prompted sweetly, glancing again at the piles of useless paperwork conspicuously to remind him of what we could avoid. He leaned forward over the desk. The playfulness I'd seen in him a moment ago was far gone by now and he was back to cold, stony, one-word answer Renatus.

He placed the pen back in its usual arrangement, not breaking eye contact with me.

'No.'

Somebody knocked. He flicked his hand to let Lord Gawain and Susannah through the door, and I gathered that it was not their arrival that had caused the shift in his emotions, but I didn't push it.

'Have you learned anything new?' Lord Gawain asked us. I shook my head.

'Nothing,' Renatus confirmed. 'These documents are too recent. There's nothing in here about the Hawkes. My father quit contact with them before I was born. I think I'll be searching for a long time.'

'And we can't just *ask* people,' I made sure to mention, earning me a sharp look from my master.

'What exactly are you hoping to find?' Susannah asked. I looked down. The fact that Lisandro had murdered my family, along with the Morrisseys and the Hawkes, was still not common knowledge yet on the council. It had been a few days since I'd gleaned the facts from Lisandro's memories, but only Renatus, Lord Gawain and Emmanuelle had been there to hear me spill the truth. None of them had passed this on to anyone else on the council. Admittedly, there was nothing immediate to be done about Lisandro's mysterious pattern of killing witch families, leaving it as my and Renatus's personal little project, but I knew this bubble of numb silence couldn't last.

'Who Shell Hawke really is,' Renatus said smoothly. 'I know her family was connected to mine at some point. Lisandro seems to have used her to manipulate Aubrey against us. She was probably the one passing on the information and the instructions the whole year.'

'Renatus, we have a task for you,' Lord Gawain artfully changed the topic. 'We have been waiting for the time to be right and Susannah and I have seen the path that leads to the future we want.'

'To the future where Aristea's classmates come back on their own and help to spark a war?' Renatus asked coolly, and I turned in my seat to await the Seers' answer. They glanced at each other.

'The time is tomorrow afternoon,' Susannah said instead, 'which will be late morning where you're going.'

'Her name is Oneida, and we want her to replace Aubrey on the council.' Lord Gawain sat down beside me and looked across at Renatus earnestly. 'We contacted her last year for the same position but we think Lisandro got to her first and scared her off. She wasn't interested. We're hoping she might have changed her mind.'

'The only future in which she might be convinced is if you two approach her and ask,' Susannah said, glancing at me. 'She's a powerful Seer, and a lot changed when you two were bonded. With new futures to pursue she might be persuaded.'

'Oneida is linked with a number of groups that currently do not answer to the White Elm,' Lord Gawain continued, 'which complicates matters. We must tread carefully. An alliance with some of these groups, particularly with Oneida's family clan, would be of immeasurable value. To offend her is to offend them, so you must be tactful.'

'I don't think it's a good idea we go,' Renatus said, voicing my own thoughts. If they needed somebody tactful, they really should be sending two different people.

'I don't know what you're going to say or do, but you're the only one with a chance of convincing her,' Lord Gawain said with a helpless shrug. 'It needs to be you. I'd like you to go.'

Renatus, still standing, looked down at the pen he'd just replaced and fidgeted with it, shifting it so it was perfectly in line with the others. He was my master but Lord Gawain was his. The council leader had the right and the job of directing his councillors. He could get Renatus to do whatever he wanted just by issuing the instruction, yet I'd noticed many times that he was unwilling to order Renatus around the way he did others. He preferred to ask, which in my opinion was going way too soft on the Dark Keeper.

Renatus didn't want to go, and he was being allowed to say no.

'Fine. Where will we find her?'

Because how could he turn down the opportunity to *do* something?

Lord Gawain smiled, slightly relieved, while Susannah and Renatus consulted a world map and pointed at some Native American reserve on the western edge of the United States. His affection for my master had always been evident, but he seemed even more comfortable about displaying it since our confrontation with Lisandro. Until Monday night, despite adoring Renatus, Lord Gawain had feared for him, never sure whether his deepest loyalties lay with him and his council or with his estranged godfather. Now it appeared that his years of support and guidance had paid off. I had to be grateful for Lord Gawain's input. Renatus wouldn't be the mentor he was to me now without it.

Hiroko was withdrawn when I found her that evening, and didn't really want to talk. This had become her usual state of being this week, and I tried to be supportive and sensitive. I tried to gauge when she wanted companionable silence and when she wanted me to just talk and drown out the chatter of people around us.

'I wonder what she knows?'

'They were so together.'

'But wouldn't he have stayed for her if they were really that close?'

'... got to know something...'

'You'd think they have better things to talk about,' Iseult commented loudly, silencing a group of older guys as she passed them. One coughed awkwardly, and another shoved a whole slice of garlic bread into his mouth. Iseult was always good for putting people in their place.

'I'm surprised they are speaking all about us anyway,' Hiroko noted, stirring her soup and nodding in the direction of the dining room door. I sneaked a glance at the young male student entering alone. 'That is Miguel. Enrico is his cousin.'

Other than the twins – Kendra and Sophia Prescott – and another brother and sister pair – Suki and Isao Tanaka – I hadn't realised that there were families attending the Academy. It made sense, since magical blood tended to flow through families, but it hadn't occurred to me how obvious this should be.

'His uncle came to get him two times. He does not want to go home.'

I thought of Enrico's father, mother and uncles. With reluctance they'd agreed to leave Enrico to his own devices; I couldn't blame them for wanting to bring their younger boy home with them before they lost him, too.

'I didn't know they were cousins,' Iseult said, surprised. 'Aubrey's spell must have been pretty potent to make Enrico leave his cousin here and Garrett leave you. But we're not talking about it,' she decided firmly, going back to her soup, 'because gossiping about Miguel would make us no better than the rest of them.'

I nodded, glad she'd stopped where she did. Hiroko's dark eyes had slid down and away at the name.

Hiroko's mention of Enrico's cousin played on my mind, but I didn't want to continue along a line of conversation that upset my friend. Later, as we got ready to go to bed, I nervously asked her, 'Why doesn't Miguel want to go home?'

She spat her toothpaste into the sink and looked at me.

'He say to me, when the White Elm fights Lisandro, he wants to be here to help,' she said. 'I think that is fair.'

She went to bed without another word. I inhaled slowly and turned the faucet to wash her toothpaste away. I knew it was selfish but I just wanted to catch her in a decent mood. Normally I told her everything, and having her to debrief with was an excellent means to straightening out how I felt about the overwhelming things that happened to me as a result of my involvement with the White Elm. I understood, completely, why she was so distant and unavailable right now. I did. The problem was that until I could blurt my own problems out to her, my best friend, I felt like I was walking around inside a cloud. Numb. Unfeeling.

Until I could tell her that my previously tame sob story about dead parents now featured premeditated supernatural murder mirroring the premeditated supernatural murder of Renatus's family, I wasn't sure how I was going to feel about it, so I went to bed as well, still in limbo. Still numb, still unfeeling.

The next afternoon I followed Renatus through the front gate and several paces away from the fence line. Too close, and a Displacement would be warped, inaccurate.

'If you don't want to come, you don't have to,' Renatus said, stopping and turning to me. He'd told Lord Gawain that *we* would go, but was offering me a way out if I wanted.

'Am I likely to come off any worse than I did on Monday?' I asked, a bit dryly. If there was ever a time when I should have taken an opportunity to stay behind when Renatus went out, that was it. Any other expedition he suggested really only paled in comparison.

He seemed to accept my point and took my upper arm in his hand. I'd recently learned how to teleport myself, but I'd only ever managed a few times and only over short distances of a few hundred metres with no specific destination. In trying to get from rural Northern Ireland to a Native American Rancheria in California, there was zero chance that I'd get us even close to where we were headed and a worryingly high chance that I'd get us in an ocean, so Renatus would be managing the Displacement. He opened a gap in the Fabric and we stepped through.

The first thing I noticed, before I'd even finished my step onto the sand, was the intense and sudden wall of heat. I took a sharp breath and closed my eyes against the glare of the hot sun. The air was dry and unfamiliar in my throat and lungs. I'd never experienced 37°C desert heat before – this was at least ten degrees hotter than my idea of too hot.

'But... it's only May...' I argued against the temperature. 'It's not summer for another month.'

'I couldn't agree more,' Renatus told me grimly, turning and leading me in the other direction. 'Welcome to the Mojave Desert.'

I followed him over a grassy sand dune, marvelling at the expansive landscape. Much like the world beyond Morrissey Estate, the earth here rolled away in easy hills and dips, but they were dry and scorched and brown. The sky was a washed-out, whitish blue, and the sun was merciless. There was little life to be seen or felt, but beyond this dune I sensed what Renatus was heading for – people.

Why they would choose to be here was outside my comprehension.

We reached the top of the dune and looked down upon a small cluster of maybe fifteen simple boxy buildings. I withheld the term "town" because there didn't seem to be any shops, roads or other infrastructure that would elevate the cluster to such a classification. Perhaps I was wrong, but through the haze I wouldn't have known any better. Each building was quite house-like, with short wooden poles to keep them off the ground, four walls and a pitched roof. I noticed a few dogs but couldn't see any people.

'Probably inside, if they have any sense,' Renatus muttered, peeling his jacket off. I wished I could do the same, but I'd dressed for the beautiful, deliciously warm 18°C day I'd woken to at Morrissey House, so I was in a black t-shirt, purple tartan skirt and lace-up boots, and I couldn't take any of it off without being completely inappropriate or burning my feet. It really wouldn't do to greet a potential council applicant in my underwear and knee-high boots.

Renatus started down the slope and I reluctantly followed, shading my eyes with my hand. There was little shade here, with nothing much to create it, although beyond the homes was a high rocky outcrop, which possibly cast shadow across the little neighbourhood late in the day.

I wasn't sure what I expected, but I was surprised when people with long dark hair and reasonably normal clothing appeared in the front doorways of each house and stared at us while we approached. They waited patiently for the several minutes it took for us to reach them. Nervous, I extended my senses over these strangers. I detected that they were all witches of varying ability, with two standouts somewhere amongst the small population. I felt curiosity from some, wariness from others. There was no animosity.

Renatus's eyes slanted towards me and I remembered that he couldn't feel what I felt. He could feel their energy but didn't feel people's emotions, intentions and desires. Through me he now had an awareness, but only by reading the information in my mind.

We got within raised-voice speaking range of the first house, and Renatus stopped. I waited beside him, hoping he knew what he was doing. He bowed his head respectfully to the woman standing at the door. I copied.

'You're here for Oneida,' the woman guessed, sounding unimpressed.

'We seek an audience with her,' Renatus confirmed. 'That is all.'

The woman folded her arms and frowned. She was in her mid-sixties and her dark, wavy locks were streaked with silver. She was tall and thin and had unusual tattoos on her arms and chin.

'Oneida doesn't want to see you,' she told us. 'You should leave.'

'My name is-'

'We know who you are.' The woman's voice was flat. 'You are the White Elm. You are at war with a darkness that you brought *here*.'

I assumed she was referring to Lisandro and whatever unpleasant visit he'd made last year.

'Oneida told you then and she will tell you the same today. Nothing has changed.'

'Everything has changed,' Renatus argued, turning his right wrist over. The spiky black marking appeared stark and dramatic against his pale skin. A few of the locals craned their necks to better see. One, a woman of about thirty, stepped down from her house and moved closer. The older woman hesitated, but then shook her head.

'Nothing has changed,' she repeated. 'Once again you bring danger to us.'

'Aunt.' The one who was even still approaching stopped in front of the first woman's house and addressed her. 'He's right. The futures... they have shifted. Perhaps Oneida would prefer to meet him.'

'I doubt it,' the older woman said moodily, 'but if you wish, take them to her. And tell her it was your idea, and I am in disagreement. *Strong* disagreement.'

She gave her niece a meaningful look and turned back into her house. Many of the others did the same. The second woman gestured for Renatus and I to follow her, and she led us between the houses to the one she'd come from. I hoped it was cooler inside. We followed the thin Native American sorceress up the steps and through the door.

It was noticeably less hot inside, but not cool enough to be "cooler". I fanned myself with my hand, breathing deeply. The building was basic, a kitchen and a bedroom and a bathroom and somewhere to sit, but nothing more. It was sparsely furnished with mismatched items. Our guide walked to the end of the shack and turned back to us. She was not a pretty lady, and way older than I'd first assumed – maybe into her fifties. Her skin was rough and creased, something I'd not noticed before, and her eyes were small and dull. She was bony and her listless hair was shorter than that of the other locals. Her appearance kept my attention, though it was not unusual or attractive enough that it should. I felt her power – not comparable to Renatus's, but not unlike anyone else on the council – and felt the magic wrapped all around her. I wondered if she was Oneida's mother.

'Firstly, who are you?' she asked. 'We have never seen you here before.'

'Renatus, and Aristea,' my master said, gesturing to me when he said my name. 'Where is Oneida?'

'Listening,' the guide said cryptically. 'She does not meet strangers. She will listen to your words and decide whether she will reveal herself to you.'

'We are not here to make threats, present danger or cause upset,' Renatus said, staring intently at the woman with a peculiar expression. 'We are here to offer Oneida a position on the White Elm.'

'Why does Lord Gawain not come?' the woman quipped.

'He…' Renatus thought through his answer. 'He foresaw that I would have the best chance of persuading her.'

'I wonder why?' The ugly lady smirked. 'Because you're so pretty, or because you're so intimidating?'

'I imagine he thought this might interest her,' Renatus said, taking my left wrist and turning it over to expose the tattoo that matched his. The witch moved closer, eyes on my arm.

'I imagine he's right,' she agreed. She looked up and met my eyes. I couldn't help but look at her, unwaveringly. Why did her face demand my attention? 'Oneida will be quite interested in *you*. Your future is quite a tale, and our Oneida likes a good story.'

I recalled that the one we were here to find was a Seer, and I supposed that this lady, who I still assumed was her mum, was probably one, too. She squinted into my eyes.

'The war has become a certainty,' she stated, not a question. Renatus nodded once.

'It seems that way.'

'New paths have been set in motion. You took an apprentice. Lisandro's foster daughter is having the French Crafter's son. And Lisandro has your council's weapon,' she added, letting her eye turn slyly to Renatus. She wasn't meant to know that, but Renatus acted unsurprised. 'Some paths lead where we all want to go. Others lead us to dead ends. One thing is still certain, though.'

'What's that?' Renatus asked. The fascinating witch shifted her whole gaze back to him.

'Your war has been an uphill battle of uselessness since before it started. Lisandro fights for reasons you don't understand, and without those motives you cannot hope to defeat him. He wants what he wants more than you want to stop him. Why should Oneida risk everything to join a doomed crusade?'

'She will know that it isn't doomed. Not anymore.' Renatus looked around the room, hoping that the great Seer was still listening, however she was doing so. 'She must know that the stakes have changed.'

'You mean, she must know that your godfather's treachery has been revealed to you, and that you both thirst for revenge,' the woman stated, stirring something akin to emotion under all the numbness I'd wrapped around that topic. 'Yes, she does. She knows this and more.'

'She knows, then, that I will beat him,' Renatus said firmly. The conviction in his voice made me shiver. Unlike me, he had given this issue serious thought. He had made up his mind. He was going to kill Lisandro at the end of it all.

I blinked, reality giving me a kick.

Renatus was going to *kill* him.

Conflicted reactions rose in my chest against the denial I was living in. I wasn't sure how to feel. Premeditation was a bit frightening. So was Lisandro. A world without Lisandro sounded like a much less frightening place.

But I didn't want Renatus to kill Lisandro, because *I* wanted the chance to try first.

I hurriedly buried that thought, horrified with myself.

The woman smirked again and extended a hand to me. Hesitantly, I took it. Had she heard that heartless, careless thought?

'She knows you will need to if you intend to protect *this*.'

She withdrew a knife from behind her back. I kept my gaze locked with hers. She couldn't stab me quicker than I could throw up a ward and blast her backwards, and Renatus wouldn't let her get that far. She lowered the blade to my hand and I didn't move, even when I felt my master's radiating tension with the situation. She ran it along the edge of my hand. It was super sharp and cut deep enough to draw blood without much pressure or pain. I refused to flinch or pull away. Renatus glared at her but did not interfere. The ugly woman held the knife up between her face and mine and we all watched as a trickle of my blood ran down its length.

'Everything is at stake, Renatus,' she said meaningfully. 'You have no idea.'

'But you do,' said Renatus. He reached over and took the knife. 'Oneida.'

Our guide did not act surprised. She smiled, and her face shimmered. The illusion she'd worn since she'd led us here fell away. Beneath it was the sorceress we'd come to find.

She was very pretty, with huge dark eyes and long wavy hair that hung in locks and braids, except for a neat, straight fringe that reminded me of Sterling's. She was about thirty, like I'd thought when I'd seen her from a distance, which was still older than I'd expected our new councillor to be.

'I do have a good idea,' she agreed. 'Your unorthodox relationship; the connection Lisandro forged between you both when he did what he did; your new power; your passion for revenge... The past lunar month has tipped the scales in your favour, and the future we all want is now within grasp.'

'Then step forward and grasp it,' Renatus urged her. Oneida smiled again. She still held my hand, and he held out his for the other.

'You know, I think I will,' she said, and accepted his offered hand.

This was the easy part. The hard part was getting Oneida out of the village. As soon as the agreement was made, the door was opened, and several members of her tribe, including the unhappy aunt, demanded that she reconsider. They'd sensed the changes to the future when she made a decision, and didn't like it. It turned into an argument very quickly. Oneida insisted it was for the benefit of their people; her people asked her if she remembered what Lisandro had done the last time she entertained the idea of leaving them for the council.

In the end she did come with us, but it was with everything she wanted to keep packed into a bag. Her aunt told her if she left she wouldn't be welcome back. Renatus was clearly as uncomfortable as I was through the whole commotion, and tried to convince Oneida to delay her departure, to spend some time talking it through with her family. She declined.

'The last time I bowed to Lisandro's manipulations, he burned down my village anyway,' she answered boldly, and a few of her tribespeople looked away. 'I'm not making the same mistake twice.'

# chapter eight

Whenever Hiroko and I got together to practise magic, we would find an unused room, hoping not to be disturbed.

'It will be some time before Teresa returns to classes,' she said as we shut ourselves inside our old Illusions classroom. 'Do you know if she's better?'

'No one mentions her now that she's on leave,' I answered, gathering up our usual pile of pillows. 'I suppose she's recovering.'

'Will she come back for this initiation?'

I shrugged. I was pretty unclear on the whole process, from who needed to be involved through to how long it would take. Apparently there were lots of boring routine sorts of things to get through before a new councillor could be initiated to the White Elm, so Renatus sent me away when we brought Oneida back to Morrissey House. To begin with I insisted that I would prefer to stay and take part – she would undertake a formal interview with the council, perform various feats and have her mind read and entire history scried by Qasim, among other things – but Renatus reiterated that he knew I would be bored beyond belief, so I took his word for it and left.

And stayed away. All day, all night, and now all day today.

Kind of relieved, actually, because though I would have hated to admit it to anyone, Oneida made me a bit uncomfortable. It wasn't *her*, per se, but whenever my thoughts touched on her, they moved stealthily to the dark, quiet moment in her house where, for the shortest breath of time, I'd almost *felt*.

And I'd felt... bad things.

Better to stay distracted.

We had a routine. We always started with wards. I was already quite adept, so I would instruct Hiroko on what I knew. She was an excellent student and could now quite reliably protect herself from my onslaught of thrown pillows. It was a benign threat, admittedly, but her progress over just a few months was impressive, especially compared with my results in Displacement – the dreaded second half of our tutoring sessions. I always tried to put this half off for as long as I could manage.

'Lift your hand a little,' I directed, holding my latest pillow over my shoulder, ready to heft. Hiroko did as I said. 'Aye, that's better. It'll be strongest in the space you direct it to, so if your hand is too low the armour will be thickest in front of your hips or legs.'

I threw the pillow as hard as I could, and it bounded off the shimmery wall she built before herself.

'Many people seem interested in Oneida,' Hiroko commented as I went after the redirected pillows. Details of the soon-to-be-councillor's unique homeland and her memorable hiding technique had fascinated Hiroko when I'd told her all about my short adventure yesterday, although the minor bloodletting had understandably freaked her out. I wasn't yet very good at healing, despite my appreciation of the art, and between Hiroko and I we'd both had a good go at sealing the cut on the edge of my hand, but all we'd really done for all our meddling with the natural clotting process was keep it open and oozing dark blood well into the evening.

Much to the interest of Sophia Prescott, former friend and Healer, who'd cast me glances all through dinner. Gloating internally, no doubt.

'She's very interesting-looking,' I offered, thinking of the woman's exotic appearance this morning at breakfast when Lord Gawain introduced her to the student population, explaining how she would be taking the position left open by the departure of Aubrey. She'd elected to wear a long natural cotton dress with ties at the back, and her hair was the most intricate, fabulous combination of braids, knots, beadwork and feathers I'd ever seen on one head. As powerful sorcerers so often were, Oneida was very beautiful. The illusion I'd met yesterday was long gone.

Iseult Taylor had leaned back and around Hiroko's chair to tap my shoulder and whispered, 'Isn't she a bit old? You know, not *old* old, but I thought they pulled new initiates from a pool of young talent?'

'Apparently they've wanted her for a long time,' I'd whispered back. Oneida's doe-like eyes had drifted over me right then, and I'd sat back in my seat. I still didn't know if she'd overheard my horrible thought in her house. My stomach tightened even now at the prospect, not that she'd heard it but that I'd had it at all. I reminded myself that she was a Seer, not a Telepath, so there was nothing to suggest she'd heard.

'Did you notice she smiled at what Lord Gawain says?' Hiroko asked, opening and closing her hand several times in quick succession, experimenting with creating and closing down wards. The result was a sort of flicker of magic in front of her. 'He says, "Oneida is a master academic of many magical arts and methods not known or used by more conventional styles of magic".'

No, I didn't miss Oneida's sidewards glance and her flash of amusement, but I hadn't realised anyone else had detected it.

'I don't even know what that *means*, so I can't begin to suggest why she found it funny,' I admitted. Hiroko was thoughtful as she readied for the next onslaught of pillows.

'I think it means she does not practise white magic,' she said. 'This should not be a surprise because she is not from the White Elm's nation, but it *is* a surprise that the White Elm wants her if she uses uncontrolled magics.'

'Uncontrolled magics? It's all white magic, isn't it, unless it's bad?'

Hiroko lowered her ward and stared at me, thinking how best to answer, and I took the opportunity to lob pillows at her.

'White magic is the magic Jadon teaches us here,' she explained carefully. 'This is the type of magic the White Elm con.... Condone? Condones and monitors. They say it is *clean*. It is energy. The rest is...' She struggled to articulate. 'It is clean like when you scrub the dirt *and* the skin away. Bare. But there are other ways to channel and shape magic. These ways are older and difficult to predict. Wild magic. These are not legal in communities controlled by the White Elm.'

I'd never considered that magic could be *wild*, or that there were other methods beyond what I was being taught here. The White Elm's methodology was identical to what my parents and aunt and uncle had used, and that pretty much encompassed my entire exposure to the magical world.

Actually, I realised, that wasn't true. I knew that there were other types of magic. There was dark magic – Renatus's job was to study it, learn it and know it, for when other sorcerers skilled in these arts challenged the council.

Hiroko smiled slyly, privy to an inside joke I wasn't in on. She said, 'Lord Gawain is careful. He calls her *an academic.*'

Like Renatus. Just an academic. I thought of some of the spells I'd seen Renatus use. I thought of the fireball I'd used on Lisandro to keep him at bay on Monday night, the magic that had come from the part of my brain I now shared with Renatus's memory bank of magical skills – that had not felt like the magic I was used to casting with. Wild magic. Dark magic.

*He's been teaching you bad things, sweetie.*

I'd gathered, of course, that this particular spell wasn't legal, and as such I'd neglected to mention it to anyone else on the council. But it had come from the same place as the incredible feat of Renatus using my own power and filling my cupped hands with water out of thin air. *That* was beautiful, and I remembered the delight I'd felt at knowing I'd one day be able to do that and other magic like it unassisted.

Wild magic.

If those two examples were one and the same, or at least from the same source, was all wild magic necessarily also *dark* magic?

'Time to swap,' Hiroko decided, interrupting my wonderings and rebounding two pillows in succession. Determined to put the changeover off as long as I could, I tossed the last two pillows, one at her head and one at her feet. There was no ward; there was no Hiroko. The pillows landed softly on the floor behind where Hiroko had just been. A pair of hands covered my eyes from behind. 'You will not get better at Displacement by throwing cushions at me.'

I groaned and pried her hands from my eyes.

'I might,' I tried. She had moved away to push furniture back against the walls. 'Who knows?'

'*I* know,' she answered. 'We will practise for twenty minutes only. Alright?'

I nodded reluctantly. I felt Renatus checking in with me and recognised his approval of my activities.

*Hiroko's instruction has hardly hurt.*

Yeah, yeah.

'You must improve with...' Hiroko struggled to remember the right word for a moment, clicking her fingers until it came to her. 'Judge. Judgement. You must improve with your judgement of distance. You seem to understand direction and dimension but distance is Elijah's third "D" of Displacement. He says it is the finest point of the art. It is very difficult to pinpoint in the Fabric.'

I nodded again and asked, 'Where do we start?'

'Elijah says non-Displacers cannot judge distances in the Fabric with their own eyes, so with Iseult he teaches her to feel for it. She says she Displaced one metre many times, became accustomed to what one metre distance felt like, and then learned what two metres felt like, and so on.' Hiroko backed up about five metres. 'You will never need to Displace one metre unless you are playing. We will start with five.'

She was a very practical teacher. I'd seen her and Addison Displace over tiny distances to show off, and it was very impressive, but she was right, it was a party trick. It wouldn't help me escape Lisandro, Jackson or Aubrey in a dire situation, and these days that dire situation was not improbable. She must have been thinking the same thing.

'I will catch you,' she said, extending her open hands to me. 'Close your eyes and look for me.'

We'd done this before, the very first time I ever Displaced myself. I had to find and open the Fabric of space by myself, but Hiroko's hands would be waiting for me at an opening she'd prepared, ready to pull me back through into the real world. I didn't know what was between; I didn't know what happened if you didn't manage to find or create an opening. I had never asked.

A sentient being, I was accustomed to feeling the physical world around me, floor beneath my feet, air against my arms. As a sorceress, I was accustomed to feeling the energy that lay across all of that, the magic of the world. As an Empathic scrier, I knew that this energy held within it memory and knowledge, some ancient and unimaginable. But the Fabric is beneath, between, within and *is* all of that. I had to reach deep to feel it, just out of sight and mind but very much there, holding everything together. Delicate yet unbreakable. Pliable. Again, I felt its familiarity and this time didn't need Renatus to tell me how the Fabric is so entwined with Fate. My own initiation in my recent memory and Oneida's upcoming one on my mind, I immediately recognised the golden light of Fate in the Fabric of the universe. What's there is there, and what is written is written. Both can be manipulated but neither can be restructured or broken.

The Fabric isn't the same shape as the world you see around you. It's endless, dimensionless, or maybe dimensionful, I couldn't say, but when it's warped you can tell. It sinks away, like I felt now right in front of me. I reached into that space and felt Hiroko's hand close on my fingers. I followed her through, trying not to panic as my step forward was met with resistance, like water, and in a mere moment I was right in front of her. Five metres away from where I'd started.

'Did you notice the distance?' Hiroko asked, going to the corner, ready to try again. 'Did you feel how it was different from other times, when you have Displaced further?'

'No, I wasn't paying attention,' I apologised. 'Let's try again.'

Teleportation is kind of amazing, even when you're not that great at it. Hiroko dragged me through space dozens of times, for way longer than twenty minutes, but when she decided to graduate me from being caught and left me to my own devices, it was clear that I had not gotten Elijah's third "D" down pat yet. I turned up in a linen closet on another floor.

'You were better at this the first time you learned,' Hiroko commented when we found each other on the stairs and went back to our practise room. 'You found me in the dining hall very well.'

'That was different,' I said, laying a cushion on the floor and taking five huge steps away from it. 'I felt for you and went *to you* – I didn't know how far that was. It's easier to go to someone or something.'

Like on Monday, when in my desperation to escape plunging into stormy grey seas I'd grasped at the only nearby location I had any emotional connection with and I'd teleported myself right to the site of my own childhood home, long knocked down except for the foundations and basement level... I closed my eyes again and felt for that pillow. There it was, squishy and covered in my energy and traces of Hiroko's wards. Deeper, it was inconsequential, just a stitch in the indifferent and infinitesimal Fabric. I maintained in my mind where it was and folded the Fabric the way Hiroko had taught me, made a split between my space and the cushion's space and stepped through...

'Careful!'

I lost my footing on uneven ground and Hiroko caught my arm to steady me. I looked down as I stepped back. I'd landed right on top of the cushion.

'Success!' I exclaimed, pleased. Hiroko grinned.

'I think I should be glad you have not landed on my head yet,' she said. 'This is not the same as selecting a distance but perhaps you will get a feel for the same distance. Try again. This time go *beside* the target. And try to feel for how far you are moving.'

I did as she told me and landed exactly where I had before, both feet squarely on the cushion. I stumbled backwards to regain my balance.

'Are you really surprised that I always put this half of our tutor sessions off?' I asked, backing up to try again.

'You are trying hard but you are not convinced,' Hiroko stated. 'Each time you are just hoping for the best. You *can* Displace. You *can* learn this. Stop being surprised.'

'I know I *can*, I did it on Monday night, but even that really surprised me.'

Hiroko swiped the pillow up off the floor before I could make my next attempt.

'You nearly died on Monday, didn't you?' she asked me flatly. 'Terrible things happened.'

'Aye, Aubrey took the boys from-'

'Terrible things happened to *you*. You said you broke your shoulder and Emmanuelle had to heal it.' She waited and I shrugged. She looked down and bit her lip. 'I know, I should ask already. I know. I... was too afraid.'

'Why were *you* afraid?' I asked. She blinked her dark, dark eyes.

'It was self... self? *Selfish*. I am so worried for Garrett and Joshua. I am worried, if I know what happened to you-'

'You'd know what might be happening to them,' I guessed, and she nodded, still not looking at me.

I said nothing for a long time, regarding her. She was my best friend. We'd met in the library only a short while ago, but we'd gelled so amazingly and I trusted her implicitly. Usually I told her everything that I took part in with the White Elm – against the rules, I know, but whatever. In this case I had told her nothing more than I had on Tuesday morning. She hadn't asked, and my initial desire to discuss it had waned in light of understanding. Discussion meant acknowledgement. I wasn't sure I was ready for that.

More to the point, I didn't *want* to be ready. Just the prospect of opening up about Monday night and all that came with it – the truth about what Lisandro had done, most significantly, but also the little things, like the heart-stopping terror of being taken by Lisandro, of thinking Emmanuelle was an enemy, of seeing Renatus powerless, of watching nameless men drop, dead and dying, into the waves, of the storm itself and the immense guilt of costing the council their ring – rose my heartrate instantly.

But.

Almost four years ago, a tragic not-accident killed my parents and brother Aidan. For months, my sister and I had avoided the topic, and our aunt and uncle, who took us in for a time before Ange could get government assistance as my new carer, had indulged the choice in the name of being sensitive. When I arrived here at Morrissey House, Qasim had found a latent gift for scrying trapped in me behind a wall of undealt-with trauma. *Not* talking about it had helped me get through the tragedy, but at a cost.

Skating through life pretending everything was okay had only set me back in the long run.

Obviously, I needed to talk about it, so I said, 'I don't want to talk about it.' Because I was mature like that. And I added, 'You were right to avoid the topic. I don't blame you at all,' because I didn't want her to feel bad for her delayed inquiry into my emotional wellbeing. Right now, I needed friends like her. Enablers.

Hiroko opened her mouth but the door opened before she spoke.

'I'm sorry to interrupt,' Lord Gawain said, smiling at us both, then looking around at our scattered pillows. 'What are you doing?'

'Studying,' Hiroko answered promptly. I nodded once in confirmation and said nothing. Was it not evident, what we were doing? Was it not evident that the door was *shut*, and we were in the middle of a serious conversation that I probably needed to have? Lord Gawain seemed content with our answer, whether he believed us or not.

'Aristea, could I ask you to join me in Renatus's study? I want to speak with him about something and I think you should be part of the discussion.'

I should have known that this wouldn't be something I wanted to be part of, but I jumped at the chance to escape Hiroko's oncoming interrogation. I promised her I'd see her straight after. She nodded silently and went to collect up our cushions, aura slightly hard with worry for me, guilt at her own distance and hurt from my rejection.

I hurried after the White Elm leader, assuring my own guilty conscience that I would fix things with my friend soon.

'What's going on?' I asked, touching base with Renatus as I spoke. His thoughts were regular, nothing out of the ordinary to indicate distress. He didn't know what I meant when I asked him the same question; he didn't even know we were coming.

'There's no emergency, Aristea,' Lord Gawain said, leading me to the staircase. 'I want to speak with Renatus about something and think you should be there for the discussion.'

I hadn't had many one-to-one conversations with the Lord but the few I'd engaged in told me that I would get nothing more from him until we reached our destination, so I stopped trying. He took me to the top floor and led me to

Renatus's door, which opened for us. My own master was waiting for us, leaning against his desk with his arms folded.

'What's wrong?' he asked as soon as the door closed behind us.

'Nothing, Renatus,' Lord Gawain placated, hands raised soothingly. 'You two are so suspicious.'

'You got my apprentice for me,' Renatus noted.

Lord Gawain sighed and crossed the room to sit in one of the stiff-looking armchairs.

'I was coming to see you, noticed her presence on the third floor and stopped to pick her up,' the old man said wearily. 'It seemed the efficient thing to do, rather than climb all the way up here only for you to call her here anyway.'

Renatus seemed to take that as a reasonable answer and relaxed his arms to his sides. I came over to sit opposite Lord Gawain. I wasn't feeling as interrogatory as Renatus seemed to be, but it didn't escape my notice that Lord Gawain had come to me first (something he'd *never* done before) without telling Renatus he was coming to see him.

'Alright,' he conceded in the silence that followed, apparently giving in to pressure only he could feel. 'I knew you wouldn't want her here for this conversation but also knew that she needed to be.'

Renatus folded his arms again, tighter this time, and fixed his intense gaze on me. Like this was somehow my fault.

'Which conversation is that?'

'Renatus, it's as much her business as yours,' Lord Gawain said sternly. He adjusted his position to include me in his gaze. 'I want to talk to you both about Lisandro, and what he has done to both of your families.'

Deep inside me, I felt something close. A door, maybe. I didn't want to talk to Lord Gawain about it. It was a big enough deal to wonder about opening up to Hiroko, and I liked her a good deal better.

'Aristea, you can go if you want to,' Renatus said shortly, but Lord Gawain shook his head and raised a hand to signal me to stop.

'Don't,' he said in a firm voice that made me freeze in my chair. To Renatus he said, 'There is only so long I can excuse keeping this knowledge from the council's collective mind. Eventually we will need to share what was learned – it will be recorded for the ages and Anouk will lock it into the Archives for future councils to study. Holding back to give you both time to come to terms with your grief in privacy has been a personal favour, but it is also preventing new information from coming to light.'

'What new information?' I asked.

'I don't know; no one will until we take the step,' Lord Gawain told me. 'I just know that sharing this revelation with the council will trigger someone's memory and provide us with new possibilities, which is what we will do at Oneida's initiation.'

'Aristea had to meet Lisandro and let him scald her for us to learn what he'd done,' Renatus said coldly. 'We lost a significant advantage for this information. Now we have to recount the experience in circle to learn something else. Forgive me for questioning these exercises of faith in Fate's plan.'

I nodded tightly, glad he'd said it the way he did. I had no reason to discount the validity of Fate but neither did I have any inclination to jump off cliffs or walk through fire at its behest, and this felt comparable.

'You are the one who wants the puzzle pieces,' Lord Gawain reminded my master, a knowing look in his blue eyes that made Renatus immediately back down. My chest tightened to see him react like that – no, no, he was meant to fight this off for me! I stood, awkwardly because I'd only just sat down.

'I don't want...' I started to say, but my voice trailed away as my throat went tight like my chest. Damn feelings! 'I'm not...' I swallowed a few times and sat back down when tears stung the back of my eyes. *So* embarrassed. I was the first White Elm apprentice in thirty years, and the first female apprentice to a Dark Keeper (council resident badass) *ever*, and I couldn't even produce a full sentence. Lame.

'You don't have to say anything,' Renatus told me, voice low and uncharacteristically gentle. I didn't turn to look at him. I worried I might actually cry; I might actually *feel*, and have to manage these overwhelming feelings. 'You can leave whenever you want.'

We sat in silence for almost a minute. I fought against the tirade of horror that threatened from behind my eyes, from within my chest and woven around my trachea. Got it in my grasp. Locked it in a metaphorical basement and breathed through it.

Nope. Not dealing with you today, emotional trauma.

'I don't want to leave,' I said finally, and it was just a stupid whisper, and I couldn't raise my eyes to make contact with either of the men, but the words came out even and whole. 'I want to be here.'

Lord Gawain spoke up again. Gentle. 'You only need to recount it once, to me; I can repeat it to the council. I understand that it will be painful, but sadly your personal traumas fit into the larger picture of the White Elm's hunt for Lisandro, making this disclosure a legal and ethical matter.'

I finally looked up at Renatus, opting to let him take the lead. We couldn't share everything we knew. We couldn't let anyone else in on Renatus's memory of his family's deaths. Qasim was quite enough.

'What do you need to know?' Renatus asked finally. Lord Gawain sat back in his seat, a resigned expression passing briefly over his features. Perhaps he knew his protégé well enough to know this story would be the lean version.

'Just the parts I don't understand,' he suggested. 'Aristea, when Lisandro had you, just as we offered him the ring, you said it was him, that he was the one controlling the storms and that he was the killer of both of your families. How did you know this?'

I ran my hands along the armrests of my seat until my arms were outstretched and my fingers were curled around the edges. This was okay, I told myself. I could handle this line of questioning. Keep it objective and I could handle it.

'I scried it,' I stated. Easy.

'But you would have scried the events of that day a thousand times,' Lord Gawain countered. 'What made this time different?'

'I've never scried the storm, not once,' I insisted, shaking my head, determined not to feel anything about that claim. He frowned.

'That's strange,' he said, glancing at Renatus for confirmation. 'Your families were murdered and the events went unsolved and unquestioned. That's the exact sort of information that comes to scriers. It's strange that *neither* of you came across this on your own.'

I shrugged and scratched my knee. I didn't have an answer for that. So I'd never scried it – that was probably for the best, right? Like that was something I wanted to see.

'Well, anyway, I knew it was Lisandro because it was *his* memory of events that he wasn't meant to have been present for,' I said, getting back on track to get this over with. 'He remembered the storm that came through here, felt regret, wished it hadn't had to happen, but just sat at a desk with his head in his hands as he felt them dying... He stood on the side of the road and conducted another storm. He regretted that too. But then when he killed my family...' I swallowed, hoping I wouldn't cry. Trying to remain objective wasn't keeping the emotion at bay, and as an Empath, emotional vulnerability was high on my list of prominent qualities. 'He did that from the beach house. He...' I swallowed again. 'He didn't even care. He said that, too, when he took me to the house. He said it was easy.'

Lord Gawain regarded me with a serious expression. Renatus glared at the floor.

'What else did he tell you?' the High Priest prompted.

*He's been teaching you bad things, sweetie. You think he loves you? You are a substitute. You're a project, just like he was to Gawain.*

'I asked him if he'd made a mistake when he left some of us alive,' I blurted, angry. *Feeling.* 'He said no, he left us on purpose. He let Renatus and I live.'

I still couldn't comprehend what this meant, but Lord Gawain turned now to Renatus.

'He can't kill you,' he said. 'He's sworn oaths to protect you.'

'He's found some neat ways around that.'

'He's wronged you but never touched you. To kill you would irreparably damage him. But as for Aristea, and her sister... I can only speculate as to why he chose not to kill you two. I can't work out the link.'

Lord Gawain scrutinised me for a second. Renatus moved his gaze from the floor to me.

'Lisandro told me what the link was, without meaning to, I'm sure,' he said. 'He knows who her grandfather was. Cassán Ó Grádaigh. He said her grandfather, mine and Lisandro's mother were on close terms.'

'Were they?' Lord Gawain asked, frowning again. Renatus shrugged lightly.

'Obviously my grandfather knew Lisandro's mother; their sons were friends from infancy,' he said. 'I knew that they knew Ó Grádaigh but didn't think it was a close association.'

'So,' Lord Gawain said slowly. 'This, whatever this is, goes back as many as three generations.' He paused a moment. 'Come to think of it, the last time I saw Ó Grádaigh, Mánus Morrissey was there, too. Perhaps they were meeting.'

'You knew my grandfather?' I asked, startled. Lord Gawain smiled.

'I met him, twice. Once at a party and once before that at a bookshop, where he was selling copies of his work. He was such an engaging presence, very knowledgeable and interesting to listen to. That first time I met him, I stood outside that shop for more than an hour, just listening to his spiel as he signed books for other people.'

'What did he talk about?'

'His work,' the old Welsh sorcerer said, remembering. 'Fate, Magic and the way both are entwined with human relationships. It was influential and groundbreaking. No one was doing any research into magic in those days – the White Elm of the time had just laid down laws that made it very difficult. Ó Grádaigh wrote anyway. He didn't publish widely; he was careful to stay underground. He was something of a celebrity rebel in our world, for a short time. He had quite a following, but I don't think fame suited him. He was very private. He'd already started withdrawing from society by that last time I saw him, and then a few years later he disappeared completely.'

I sat back deeper in my seat, considering this, glad for something else to think about. I'd never known my maternal grandfather. Even my mother, his only child, had no memory of him. He'd married his Greek holiday love, Anthea, brought her to his homeland, had their daughter... and then just not come home one day. Apparently his family weren't the only people who had wondered where he'd gotten to.

I thought of that strange dream I'd woken from the night I'd met Lisandro. The memory was faded and wispy now, yet when I first woke from it the details had been fresh and crisp, right down to the year. Now those details were gone. Was Renatus right? Had I scried that? Too bad I couldn't remember anything but a few faceless men standing about and a dripping pipe.

'The third storm you saw would be the Hawkes, of course.'

I nodded vaguely, unwilling to be pulled back into this conversation. I wished Lord Gawain hadn't thought to include me. The fight to remain distant and unbiased on the matter started up inside me again. I hadn't even realised it had died down; the grandfatherly stories had distracted me sufficiently, and I'd grasped that distraction oh so willingly.

127

'I suppose,' I agreed sulkily.

'Can we talk more about that? Determining Lisandro's crime pattern will be a large focus for the White Elm when I share this with them.'

'I want to tell them,' Renatus spoke up suddenly. 'The council. It should come from me.'

Lord Gawain nodded slowly in the silence that followed; I felt his surprise that Renatus's apparent indifference should lead to this proclamation.

'Whatever you prefer,' the old man said finally. 'I am sorry, for what it's worth.'

I looked down. Sympathy is not always easy to accept. Renatus, for one, had long since abandoned it completely.

'You've done nothing wrong,' he said immediately. 'There's nothing to be sorry for.'

But I'd done something wrong. I used the armrests of my chair to pull myself up again.

'I changed my mind,' I announced. 'I don't want to be here after all.'

Renatus raised a hand; the door opened for me, and I left without another word.

I just didn't want to talk about this.

Hiroko was back in our dorm, in our bathroom, washing her hands. She looked up at me as I walked in.

'I thought a few times I was going to die,' I said outright, no introduction, standing vulnerable and terrified in the doorway. 'Lisandro can control weather. I didn't know anyone could do that but I saw him do it. He can cause and control storms. He stole me away from Renatus and hurt me and he almost killed me with lightning and that sounds *so freaking ridiculous* but it's so ridiculous that I would never try to make you believe it unless it was true, and I was so afraid because I really believed I was safe with Renatus and Gawain and then I wasn't. I wasn't safe.'

I sucked in a breath, disappointed by how painfully it went down, because painful breaths were the breaths of feeling too hard. Hiroko was still staring at me, faucet still running. I made myself keep going, even though every instinct said *no, piss off, I'm not dealing with this, not now, not ever.*

'You tried so hard to teach me to displace and I know I've been such a hopeless student,' I confessed, all the words tumbling out of my mouth. I was surprised they fell out in the right order, they came so fast. 'On Monday I had the choice of displacing or drowning, and I was able to do it. I wasn't sure I would but I *had* to so I did. And I was *so* scared it wouldn't work, and then there was still the storm and the thunder, and then *Aubrey* and everything else that came with that... And all this isn't even the worst thing, Hiroko,' I told her desperately, striding over and turning off the flow of water when she still didn't. 'This is just me rambling about all the little things, trying to avoid telling you that Lisandro made the storm that killed my mum and dad and my brother. He killed them. On purpose.' I exhaled, hard. 'And I have *no idea* how I'm supposed to deal with that, and that's why I don't want to talk about it.'

Hiroko stood there, hands dripping into the sink, and I stood there, tears running down my face, though I hadn't noticed them before now and they hadn't yet choked up my voice. My feelings had not yet broken through the wall I'd built but they were lapping at the very rim of that wall, so close to spilling.

My friend slowly reached for a handtowel and dried her hands. I hurriedly wiped my eyes, embarrassed. I'd held off the tears all through that meeting with Lord Gawain and Renatus.

'I don't think there is a correct way to deal with this,' Hiroko said finally, clearly stunned. 'I am... grateful... you have told me.' She thought for another long moment, and then suggested, 'Do you want to play snap? I have some cards.'

An unexpected laugh escaped me, and it felt good to feel that. Not all feeling was bad. I nodded and went with her to her bed, and we sat together and played cards for hours, mindless and tranquil.

I still didn't want to deal with the truth and its implications, but this little step today was me listening to my head instead of my self-protective instincts for once. Naturally I wanted to avoid dealing with trauma. Everyone does. But trauma had held me back from progress before. Avoidance of the topic of my parents' and brother's deaths had walled off a talent that was fast becoming a core component of my identity. How much damage might I have done to my future self if I'd never broken through that wall?

I didn't know the answer to that, but I did know that I didn't break through that wall until I opened up and shared my heartbreak with Hiroko.

# chapter nine

As much as you might love your family, there is only so much of them that you can take. Tian forced himself to continue smiling and to avoid looking up at the clock on the sitting room wall. His well-meaning wife had invited his sister Mei-Xing and her husband Gan for dinner and tea, which was fine, because he loved them, but this was the third day in a row they had been over for dinner and tea. The day before that was lunch. They'd been over almost every day since they'd heard about Aubrey's betrayal.

'We received a letter from Lien Hua yesterday,' Mei-Xing said in their native Cantonese, referring to her nineteen-year-old daughter, a student at the Academy. 'It takes some time for mail to arrive, sent traditionally. It was sent last week, on the day of the upset, before she knew. It sounds like she is enjoying herself, when she is not endangered.'

'Hmm,' Tian agreed, unenthused by this conversation topic. They'd already spoken about the letter, yesterday, when it had first arrived. His wife, Cai, shot him a look, and he corrected himself, downplaying their fears like they wanted him too. 'I've told you, Lien Hua was never in any danger on Monday. Aubrey didn't hurt any of the students, and was only there to collect the ones he had a pre-existing relationship with. Lien Hua's dormitory is under Qasim's supervision.'

'Did you speak with Lien Hua and ask her to write to us again?'

'I thought you already told her that.' Tian had brought his niece home to her parents for a day since classes were postponed following the "upset". They hadn't wanted her to return, but their daughter was stubborn.

'I did, but she listens to you,' Mei-Xing pressed, and Tian repressed a sigh. His older sister was insufferable. It was not difficult to see how Lien Hua had gotten the way she had.

'Yes, I told her,' he promised. 'I told her that if she writes you another letter, I would bring it to you immediately. She must be being lazy, because she has not yet given me anything. Busy,' he corrected himself hastily when Mei-Xing glanced worriedly at her husband. The idea of their daughter behaving lazily in any way while representing their family at a prestigious school horrified Mei-Xing. 'She must be too busy.'

Gan leaned past his wife to address Tian more directly.

'In her last letter, Lien Hua spoke of another student receiving an apprenticeship already,' he said, and Tian continued to smile, nodding, knowing already where this was going. 'I thought it would take much longer for those White Elm who are seeking apprentices to find appropriate students. Lien Hua has not yet been offered any placements?'

'Not at this time,' Tian said. He understood their disappointment but wished they wouldn't pin such high hopes on their daughter. She was extremely talented, but so were her competitors, and there were many more students than there were White Elm. Worse still for Lien Hua, she was a Displacer, a rare breed of sorcerer, and the council had only one possible match. If she didn't succeed at becoming Elijah's apprentice, she would excel at something else. No matter what, her parents would be proud of her, because she wouldn't stop until they were. 'Elijah is not in any hurry.'

'Lien Hua will be twenty years old in August,' Gan reminded Tian.

'Fate will guide,' Tian said. His brother-in-law nodded, slightly glumly. 'What is meant to be will be.'

Mei-Xing opened her mouth to say something, but seemed to think better of it. Tian was glad. He didn't want to hear her suggestions of how he could help put Lien Hua at the top of Elijah's list. He had no intention of playing any part in Elijah's selection of an apprentice, even if staying back and staying quiet meant that his niece missed this opportunity. It was not his place, despite what his sister believed, to influence Elijah's choices. He had deliberately avoided using his gift of Seeing to divine Lien Hua's future, because just knowing what *could* happen would inevitably affect the outcome.

The phone rang, and Cai went to answer it. Gan finished his tea.

'We should go,' he said, looking to his wife. She looked unwilling to do so. 'We have guests coming tomorrow; we should go home and prepare.'

'Of course!' she said, suddenly remembering her plans. She stood, eyes lit with that frantic brightness they took on whenever she had something important to do. 'Did we tell you, Tian? Mr and Mrs Chen – I never remember their given names – have a son at the university-'

'Say no more,' Tian interrupted, raising his hands. Closer in age to his niece than to his much older sister, Tian's relationship with Lien Hua was a brotherly one. She told him things she didn't tell her parents, and her parents told him things he felt compelled to warn her of. Undoubtedly, Mr and Mrs Chen's son was a prospective partner for Lien Hua that Mei-Xing and Gan had scoped out, and if tomorrow's meeting went well, Tian expected that Lien Hua would be introduced to this young man at the first opportunity. She was probably grateful to be safely locked up at the Academy right now.

'You are keeping an eye on her, aren't you, *Sai lou*?' Mei-Xing asked anxiously, referring to him affectionately by his title as younger brother, and he nodded dutifully. His sister had made it clear to both Lien Hua and Tian that Lien Hua was not to be dating fellow students while at the Academy, "wasting her time". Mei-Xing and Gan wanted her to find an upstanding husband and make a respectable marriage into a well-to-do family. They left it unsaid that this ideal family would be Chinese. So far his niece had showed little interest in pursuing any other students (though her friendships with fellow Displacers, Addison James, Garrett Fischer and Joshua Reyes, were probably closer than her parents would like to know) but if she did, Tian had an equally low interest in telling his sister. This was Lien Hua's first chance to be truly free to be whoever she was going to be, and whatever or whoever she needed on that journey was not going to be impeded by Tian.

'I have a circle with the White Elm tonight,' he said before his sister could say more. 'I need to go.'

'Yes, of course, work,' she agreed, gathering her coat and going to the door. Cai returned from the phone call to see them off. Mei-Xing stopped in the doorway and turned back to her brother worriedly. 'She really is safe there, isn't she, *Sai lou?*'

'Mei-Xing, *Jeh je,*' Tian answered with a sigh, taking her shoulders in his hands. 'Do you believe I would risk her if I thought otherwise?'

Tian was not a tall man, but he'd outgrown his tiny adult sister in his teens, and so she had to look up to see into his eyes. He was sure she knew already what she'd find there.

'I trust you, *Sai lou,*' she murmured finally. It took some effort, but eventually Mei-Xing was convinced to leave and Tian locked the door behind her.

'I have to call my mother back,' Cai told him, kissing his forehead before going back to the phone. 'I'll see you when you get back.'

Family was such a huge part of her life, so it was nothing to her to have her in-laws over every day. Tian loved his family, but leading a life so different to his sister's had given him different values and priorities. It was more important to him to work towards keeping his family safe than it was to see them daily. On the White Elm, he had the unique privilege of being able to do this in the most firsthand way imaginable, and he completely respected Lien Hua's desire to do the same.

Tian went to his closet and got changed into his white robe. For the first six years of his service to the council, and for decades prior, circles had been a monthly gathering, a regular cycle that fit easily into all lifestyles, modern or traditional. Since Lisandro's departure last autumn that regularity had become shaky, and the establishment of the Academy had eliminated it completely. Circles were as constant now as they were inconsistent – tonight's would be the sixth in a month. Councillors saw each other all of the time. Those who lodged at Morrissey House saw each other every day. The forced proximity had sparked tensions, to say the least, between the many strong personalities of the White Elm, culminating in a near-total breakdown in the weeks leading to Aubrey's departure and Teresa's recovery. The clarity that came with Aubrey's deception had calmed things, but Tian knew, even without checking on the futures, this was only temporary. Circles were once beautiful, peace-bringing gatherings. Now, every circle brought new complications to already complex issues, and tonight could be no different.

Although, in at least one respect, it *was* different. This was Oneida's initiation.

Tian paused in the hallway and touched the sharp blade of his favourite sword, hanging in its place on the wall. Perhaps to others it would seem irrational, but Tian had long found that objects spoke to him. Fate knew what was coming, who would be necessary for an event to transpire and which aspects of the Fabric, which mundane objects, would aid the event. A man's weapon can cause, alter or interrupt a Fateful event in both positive and negative ways, and Tian had always *known* when he would need his weapon. Susannah and Lord Gawain, both Seers also, did not experience this odd gift. Their Sight was greater, clearer, obviously – they

135

were greater sorcerers than Tian – but he was grateful that Fate had given him this insight instead.

Tonight would bring tumult and fear, Tian felt, but no need for defence. Something was coming to light.

With that thought, he left quickly, ensuring that he locked the door and checked and tightened the wards around the home.

By the time Tian arrived at the ballroom of Morrissey Estate most of the council was gathered inside. They were a large family of thirteen but there were bonds within that family that were tighter than the greater circle of minds. Glen stood apart from Anouk, several spaces between them but probably deep in mental conversation as the pair usually was. Lord Gawain always seemed most comfortable with his co-leader, Lady Miranda. They balanced one another beautifully – one idealistic, the other grounded – and their partnership had so much more to offer the magical world, if only that world would settle down and return to peace.

The most recently established alliance on the council was the unlikely trio of Emmanuelle, Jadon and Renatus, the latter of whom was not yet present. They were young, volatile and had drawn together suddenly out of a mutual hatred for the enemy. Both Emmanuelle and Jadon had lost their closest friends to Lisandro's army, so their bond made sense; the inclusion of loner Renatus was the oddity to Tian. The cold possibility occurred to him that perhaps the last Morrissey represented to the pair the best chance of getting revenge upon the object of their hatred.

Oneida stood alone, trying not to look small and nervous in her new white robe. Her large dark eyes skimmed the group and when she caught Tian's gaze he offered her a smile before she could look away. She uncertainly made her way across the expansive room.

No one else said a word to her.

'May I stand with you while we wait?' she asked. Tian gestured welcomingly at the empty space beside him. The last time the council had sidelined a new member, they had missed countless opportunities to realise that he was a traitor. Seers were not typically retrospective but in this instance the past was too fresh to ignore, and Tian was not willing to make the same mistake so soon.

And beside all this, it never hurt to have allies on the council.

'You didn't invite any family for your initiation ceremony?' he inquired, noting the lack of extras in the ballroom. The actual ritual was a private affair, but for his own initiation, his wife, sister, brother-in-law and niece had been present for the celebrations before and after, sparking Lien Hua's determination to follow in her uncle's footsteps. Oneida shook her head with a wan smile.

'My family isn't particularly excited for me,' she admitted. 'Our people have stood apart from the Elm for centuries, practised our own magic and lived by the laws of our ancestors. I have betrayed that tradition. My aunt isn't talking to me. After tonight I will no longer be welcome in her circles.' She pursed her lips, playing at casual. 'She's our high priestess.'

Tian allowed a moment for the implications to sink in.

'You're being excluded from your community for your choice to join us?' he realised, shocked. He'd never heard of such a thing. Well, there was Renatus, who claimed that his decision to join the council had burnt any bridges he had within the traditionalist society his family had come from, though that claim had never been tested and Renatus had done a good job of burning most of those bridges himself through icy distance and failed communication. Anouk was the closest similar case, a recruit from an independent colony, and though there were those who grumbled about her split loyalties, she was still welcome in her home city. She even held a chair on the city's leadership council. He tried to imagine his own family cutting him out over *anything* and could not.

'It's more my sanitised magic that she wants to keep out. After tonight,' she reminded Tian wryly, trying to keep humour, 'I'll fall under White Elm law, which condemns the magic of my people. It'll be a crime for me to weave with my family. Unless I use the white magic. Look, I've been practising.' She pressed her hands together and separated them slowly, channelling energy down her arms and into the growing space between her palms. A white translucent ball of power sparked to life and swelled for a few moments, shuddering with the inconsistency of her control, then blinked out when she clapped her hands back together over it. 'I haven't found any practical application for this magic yet but the rest of you seem to get on well enough with it. What was your tradition before joining the Elm?'

Tian worked at stamping out the welling of pity he'd felt watching Oneida produce her pathetic spell. She was powerful, his level or a little higher, and definitely capable of wielding incredible magic, but her spellcasting had always been done in another way. She may as well have been told to communicate henceforth only in a foreign language, despite being a poet and wordsmith in her native tongue. And now her native tongue was banned, and her homeland refused to have her back speaking only her new language. Such a huge pity. He forced a smile to cover the momentary lapse in conversation.

'I was raised in the modern way, essentially; the way of pure channelling, so there was no transition for me,' he said. 'There are forms within the form, I'm sure you realise, but my family's magical form-'

'Still *con*forms,' Oneida finished, nodding. She looked away and around the ballroom.

'If I may ask,' Tian prompted gently, trying not to prod at fresh hurts but intensely curious, 'why are you taking this vow if the sacrifice is so great? Your magic, your family?' Your very identity? So much of a person's sense of self is tied to their home, their language, their culture, their customs and practices. Who was Oneida without all of that, and hadn't Lord Gawain considered this obvious impending mental health crisis before inviting her onto the council?

Oneida waved a dismissive hand. 'It's not a sacrifice, not really. My aunt will get past this. My learning in your arts will be swift. My service to the White Elm doesn't have to be lifelong. And Lord Gawain has already agreed to enter talks with my aunt and I, when she comes around, to draft a set of exemptions for Native American ancestral magic,' she added with a quick smile, 'or else I would not be here.'

Like the Valero Agreement, and like Valero's "loan" of Anouk to the council. It was a sensible enough motivation to join, Tian thought, for an independent – to benefit one's colony and their political position, and he said so. Oneida seemed to hesitate.

'Last year, Lisandro came to my village,' she said, and nearby, Emmanuelle and Jadon stopped talking to listen. 'I didn't see him. He spoke only to my aunt. He said I wasn't to apply. He burned down our houses. All of them.' She looked around and met the watching gazes of the council's two junior members. 'I listened. We rebuilt.'

'But here you are,' Jadon commented. He was one applicant Lisandro hadn't counted on and so hadn't tried to dissuade.

'Nothing could have stopped him,' Oneida said. 'Nothing could stop him if he comes back tomorrow. And he might,' she admitted, as Renatus and Aristea arrived. The apprentice was wearing the same white robe as the full councillors – it had been decided that she would replace Teresa in order to stabilise the circle, since her initiation, with only eleven councillors, had been so volatile. Oneida was watching the apprentice. When she continued, her voice was too low for the newcomers to hear: 'When I cut the girl, I saw what Lisandro will put her through. She is only one. What will he do to others? I can rebuild houses. I can reclaim my aunt's favour. I can learn new magic. That child,' she murmured, jabbing a finger in Aristea's direction, 'cannot rebuild her soul if he's allowed to live long enough to tear it apart. He must be stopped.'

As Susannah, the last, came through the doors, Emmanuelle crossed the floor to demand what Oneida meant in a hushed voice. Tian cleared his throat and shifted away a little from the sorceresses to give himself space to contemplate what was just said.

When Aristea was first assessed by the council for her suitability to become Renatus's apprentice, Tian had declined to lend his support. He'd liked the girl, of course, but Fate had offered him glimpses of a wayward future Renatus, and had sent him a rush of acknowledgement when Susannah had spoken of Fate's slideshow of possible terrible paths for the prospective apprentice. Renatus was not old enough nor experienced enough to have an apprentice. She should have been Qasim's student. Renatus cared for Aristea, that was evident, but bonding with him had slashed the girl's chances of survival. Aristea *could* become a strong and powerful sorceress, first a successor to Qasim's role as Scrier and then the first female Dark Keeper, but most possible futures saw a burnt-out Aristea, exposed too early to magic more powerful than she could handle. The weeks since the initiation had allowed Tian to put that out of his mind, but Oneida's words brought this fact uncomfortably back to the surface.

The circle was called, and the councillors moved into their positions, Oneida in the centre. Tian tried to keep his attention away from Renatus's apprentice, squeezed in at her master's side where she could lend her energy to the ritual. Soon Fate would be invoked, and bring with it the calm and positivity and assurance its golden light always left in its wake, and Tian's discomfort with what he'd not spoken more strongly against would be carried away.

The windows of the ballroom were closed and the door was locked yet the clothing and hair of the council leader now lifted gently in a sudden magical breeze. The breeze drifted slowly to Lady Miranda, and her dark hair flecked with silver lifted lightly as well; Renatus's hair, curling at his shoulders, was caught next and the ends floated in Aristea's direction. She leaned away instinctively – despite the insistence all humans seem to harbour that they want to know, they rarely actually do – but her shoulder bumped into Qasim, and her long hair picked up briefly in that soft wind before it passed to the Scrier, and all around, eventually to Tian, who, unlike Aristea, practically leaned into it. Drowned in it, for just a second.

*Her face. Grey house. Broken letterbox. That voice. Another tattoo. A birthday.*

The wind brushed on to Em and he was standing where he was before, breathing deeply, invigorated and soothed. He'd seen... heard... felt... *known*... And now he didn't know. The breeze had brought with it visions and knowledge he didn't have, and just as quickly as it had revealed all, it had taken that knowledge with it. And moreover... it felt like *someone*, rather than *something*.

Fate, to a Seer, felt like a friend.

And that friend assured Tian that it had a plan, and he need not worry right now.

The breeze moved from councillor to councillor, moving faster with every round, coming from nowhere and going nowhere except around and around this circle of sorcerers, invisible at first but obvious in its soft breathiness against their left sides and then brightening to a glorious gold after a few circuits.

The main attraction was Oneida herself, since it was her initiation. She stood in the middle of the circle and repeated the necessary pledges Lord Gawain and Lady Miranda recited to her. The growing light of the ever-hastening wind that whipped through the rest lit her features and her determined dark eyes. Tian was glad to have taken the time to speak to her; it gave context and gravity to that determination.

The golden light left the circle to envelop her. Tian felt it rip away and spiral inward, but the tearing didn't hurt. It left a warm sensation of calm behind it. It soaked into Oneida until it was all gone, the room going dim, and then in the dimness *she* started to glow, or rather her aura, bright white and silver-edged, the marker that irrefutably proved her new status. Lady Miranda, the high priestess, stepped out of the circle to drape a royal purple sash over Oneida's robe, and to hand her a well-preserved but very old wooden staff etched all over with runes. All heads dipped in a respectful bow. The entire ceremony was beautiful and sombre, typical of all White Elm rites or the rites of any religion, steeped in ancient tradition and ritual. Most witches never got to see this, didn't even know this went on.

Tian felt blessed, and, drunk on the gold of Fate, overwhelmingly gracious.

'Fate has granted you a place among our ranks as a sister, Oneida,' Lord Gawain said now as the rest kept their eyes on the polished floors of the ballroom. 'I invite Fate to show you to your chair.'

Fate was still present, and unlike at the recent bonding ceremony, it did nothing drastic. The room slowly brightened with a dull, golden light. Tian looked up as the others did, too. The light was soft, ethereal, and emanated from an unusual source — a human-sized pillar of light between Elijah and Anouk. It lasted a few seconds, and then ebbed away to nothing, and its universal presence left the room. The circle was over.

Even contented by Fate's assurances, Tian felt as surprised as his brothers and sisters looked in that moment. Elijah and Anouk glanced from each other to Oneida in the centre of the circle. Oneida was new and the White Elm valued experience, loyalty and commitment. By this logic she should be at the bottom, below Jadon. But the council also ranked its members by age, with the one exception of the Dark Keeper's role, and apparently up until now, this had also happened to align with years of council experience.

It wasn't envy but it was something akin to it that rose in Tian right then. He had been on this council for seven years. Oneida had been on it for seven seconds, and she was now his senior.

'Take your place, please, Oneida,' Lord Gawain said eventually, trying hard not to sound as surprised as everybody else looked. 'Fate has spoken, and it is only through Fate and its Ultimate Powers that we have our power at all.'

Tian tried to swallow his feelings and hear Lord Gawain's words all the way through his being. Fate knew what it was doing, and this council served Fate. Looking embarrassed, Oneida moved to the place Fate had set glowing for her. She knew she was cutting the queue and it was as unexpected for her as anyone else. Elijah and Anouk shuffled over slightly to fit her in.

'Fate sometimes surprises us like this,' Lord Gawain admitted now. 'It chose not to show us this – any of us,' he added, looking to Susannah and Tian for confirmation, and they both nodded, because they'd had no clue this would happen, 'but it always has its reasons. Your rank doesn't matter in this moment. Oneida, we welcome you as our sister to the White Elm, grant you the position awarded by Fate, and bestow upon you the chair of council Scribe. Blessed be.'

The closing sentiment echoed softly around the circle. Efforts were made to settle any emotional reactions to her placement and to simply revel in the saturation of residual power from the initiation.

'Please, nobody leave,' Lord Gawain requested, unexpectedly. 'While we are gathered together, I have news to share. This particular circle is overdue.'

No one said a word but the restlessness in the ballroom was not silent. Tian didn't need to be a Telepath to know that others in the circle were thinking the same as he was. These days, any circle overdue? Far from it.

'On the night of the twenty-seventh we encountered Lisandro and lost our Elm Stone to him,' Lord Gawain went on, aura full and strong. 'A lot happened that night. We have not yet fully debriefed following those events and I expect that we have a lot to talk about.' He paused, as though giving the rest of the White Elm a chance to interject or share their thoughts or feelings. They were all still high from the initiation. Tian felt only reluctance to revisit that miserable night while he was feeling so good and so empowered. When no one spoke, the leader added, 'Also, those of us who spoke with Lisandro at length came into certain information that has been withheld from the wider council until now.'

Tian glanced around the circle, unsure what to think of this. Others seemed to react similarly. Anouk shared a significant look with Glen; Jadon frowned, unsurprised; Elijah looked to Lord Gawain with patient interest. Emmanuelle, beside Tian, studied the leader briefly and then averted her gaze to the floor. She already knew. She was there.

And if she knew, then so did Renatus, and Aristea, too. The poor girl had been getting around with an aura that looked like it had been attacked with scissors. Even now, she looked frayed. This "certain information" was serious. Tian felt himself tensing against the assurances of the gold light, even though he knew there would be no violence or danger tonight.

'Withholding information regarding our opposition could have been quite debilitating to our efforts,' Susannah commented coolly, frowning. 'Your reasons must have been extraordinary.'

'I elected to wait because of the nature of the information,' Lord Gawain said. 'As far as I could see, wide knowledge of it did not serve to benefit our immediate chase of Lisandro, and when that was suspended by the will of Fate, it became even less urgent. My choice was also a compassionate one, to give those who it most affected a chance to come to terms with what was learned.'

'Who did it affect?' Elijah asked when the Lord left his words hanging again.

'Me,' Renatus said, 'and my apprentice.' The teenager at his side looked away, fidgeting with her fingers. 'Aristea tapped into memories of Lisandro's that implicate him in crimes more numerous and sadistic than we ever expected.'

'What has he done?' Qasim asked sharply.

'He can control the weather,' Renatus answered. His voice was carefully calm and distant. 'Atmospheric pressures, perhaps. The violent storm we were caught in that night was his creation and followed his direction. He used it to threaten Aristea in order to draw me away from his trail.'

'That's not possible,' Jadon claimed. No one backed him up. He looked around. 'It isn't. That's movie magic.'

'It is real,' Oneida corrected. 'I've seen it done. Extremely complex spell work.'

'Lisandro can do it,' Renatus said, voice still flattened. 'He can form storm cells and control them.'

'And?' The Scrier's tone was hard in comparison to the Dark Keeper's.

'And he has used them in at least three other instances to commit and hide multiple murders.'

Aristea exhaled shakily, staring hard out the window. Tian hadn't yet put the pieces together but could see the futures shifting in response to this new information.

'Here?' Qasim demanded, disbelieving. Renatus nodded once, stiffly. 'Then who...?'

'I know,' the Dark Keeper interrupted, sounding angry. He calmed himself. 'I mean, I don't know. But I know what it means.'

'We can discuss that later,' Qasim emphasised, clearly referring to a shared understanding, 'but in the meantime... Lisandro initiated and controlled the storm that came through here seven years ago?'

'Nearly eight now,' Lord Gawain agreed grimly. 'And two other families: the Hawkes and-'

'Mine,' Aristea broke in. Many councillors had been wondering for weeks now why Fate had allowed Renatus the honour of Aristea's life and trust, but this new knowledge brought light to Fate's choice. Both young scriers had been tied together by Lisandro's actions before they'd even met. Her interruption brought a stillness upon the circle, and Tian felt a hint of Fate's golden light return to the evening. At the

145

same time, Aristea suddenly jerked back, grabbing her own hand. 'Ouch.'

'What?' Renatus looked down at her; she only clasped her hand inside the other, glancing up at Oneida with disbelieving eyes. For her part, Oneida said nothing, and as far as Tian could tell, had done nothing, and after a moment Aristea said, slowly, 'I'm okay.'

'What does this bring his death toll to?' Lady Miranda asked eventually.

'At least eight with the use of storms,' Renatus reported, casting one last worried look at his apprentice. 'Peter is the ninth that we know of.'

Tian took a slow breath as others asked worried questions of the council leaders. When he'd been initiated, seven years earlier, Lisandro was the council's Dark Keeper. He'd been likeable, charismatic, interesting. The sort of man one looked up to and admired. 'He's recently suffered a loss,' Lady Miranda had told Tian in an aside, 'so if he seems off, he doesn't mean it.' It was the Morrissey storm she'd referred to, but he'd rarely seemed off, apparently handling it very well, until Lord Gawain had reported at a monthly circle that he'd reversed the decision to place the Morrissey orphan with the Avalonians and had reinstalled the boy as the head of his family's estate. Lisandro had been completely furious, the only time Tian had ever seen him upset, shouting that Renatus was *his* charge and that Lord Gawain had no right to interfere.

'You're welcome to try to put him back,' the old Welshman had said, 'but I don't expect he'll go quietly and I'm not sure they'll take him.'

Lisandro had gotten past this upset very quickly and had even seemed proud when his godson had been honoured with a place on the White Elm with him. There had been no other signs of displeasure with Lord Gawain, Renatus or anyone else on the Elm, so his aggressive defection had come as a terrible shock to Tian. Lisandro had tortured Peter before them all, threatened to destroy the council, attacked

146

Emmanuelle and left with two other Elm members and the Elm Stone. An event so huge should have been obvious, Tian thought, but he'd not seen it coming and neither had the other Seers. Fate had chosen to blindside them. Sometimes even Seers needed to be surprised for the right future to be written.

He could speculate as to why this had to be but couldn't be certain, probably not for years yet. Probably the council had needed the surprise betrayal to give them the motivation to move against this new enemy; if they'd seen it coming, might they have tried to stop it and led the council down a less honourable or less favourable path? Fate had chosen to surprise them and leave them bitter and hurt for a reason.

'Why has it taken so long for us to realise this?' Elijah spoke up. 'You say that the weather control is a cover for murder but murder can't be hidden. Isn't that right?' he checked with Qasim. The Scrier nodded and turned back to Renatus.

'You should have known this already,' he said sternly to the younger man at his side. 'You should have seen this. You've been hiding from it. You too, Aristea.'

'Lord Gawain said the same thing, but I never scried any such thing,' the girl snapped while Renatus folded his arms in annoyance. The three scriers often seemed to rub one another the wrong way but they were each integral to one another's futures. 'Never, so it's rubbish.'

'You never *dreamed* about the storm that killed your parents?'

Aristea frowned, hurt.

'Of course I did.'

'Every night?'

She didn't answer. Tian guessed the affirmative and saw the Scrier's point. She'd *known* all along and not known it.

'Does that seem normal to you, Aristea?'

'I was traumatised. It's not meant to be normal.'

'Your sister experienced the same trauma but doesn't dream it over and over like you do. What's the difference?'

'She's older-'

'She's not a scrier,' Qasim interrupted. 'The universe has been sending messages of your parents' murder to *you* because you're equipped to read them.'

'Clearly she isn't,' Renatus said coldly, and the other rounded on him once again.

'You are even worse,' he said. He continued speaking to the apprentice. 'Did the dreams stop when you came here, Aristea?' The girl nodded mutely. 'That's because-'

'We're not talking about this anymore,' Renatus cut him off. Tian thought it was well-timed, because his apprentice was looking paler and more upset with each cutting word the Scrier spoke. 'Focus on the issue at hand, Qasim. Lisandro is a serial killer.'

The phrase set nervous murmurs through the circle like waves. There had been many magical murderers in history but very few serial killers. The difficulty involved in hiding even one such act was extraordinary – to carry out a number of them over time was an impressive if despicable feat.

Susannah closed her eyes. Tian touched Fate to see whether it would share whatever she was channelling, but nothing was forthcoming. Susannah was an incredible Seer – she saw most things, much of which Tian did not. He did not concern himself.

'Hawke, like Shell?' Jadon asked suddenly. Renatus nodded. 'Aubrey told me she was an orphan and when I saw him last week he made it sound like Lisandro had some stake in her life. That was why he did what he did, he claims.'

'It's unclear but it seems that he has taken her in, in some way or another, sometime after killing her parents,' the Dark Keeper confirmed. 'I don't know why. I don't know why he didn't kill all of us.'

'Does Shell have any particular talents that might appeal to Lisandro?' Lady Miranda asked. Jadon shook his head.

'She's a Seer, but she's half-mortal and Aubrey said she was the usual type, low-power.'

'Aubrey said many things,' Emmanuelle spoke up, having been unusually quiet for the most part of this circle. 'Sometimes that type still have visions.'

Magic is complicated, and magical genetics is a complicated science. Powerful sorcerers tended to have powerful children, usually with very similar capacities and often with inherited gifts. The Morrisseys, for example, had always been scriers and had long married strong sorceresses into the family, and true to form, every child for generations had been magically powerful and gifted in scrying. But this family represented the common pattern, not the rule. Like theirs, Tian's family had been without mortal influence for many generations and had maintained a reasonably high power level in its descendants, but they all had different gifts. Lien Hua, his niece, was stronger than either of her parents or her uncle, and was the first Displacer known to be born into the line.

Mortal blood and low-power lineage mixed with higher capacities confused matters even further. Usually, when there was a non-magical parent, the offspring would be born very low power, like Shell Hawke was suggested to be. They were typically Seers or Telepaths of little ability and with limited control of that ability. But then sometimes a half-mortal could be born to be outstanding, exponentially stronger than their witch parent, and other times magical children could be born to perfectly ordinary parents of no witch blood at all.

To even call it a science was sometimes laughable, because in so far as Tian could tell, blood only *suggested* what or who someone should grow to be. In the make-up of any human being there are so many variables beyond the scope of modern understanding.

'Excluding Peter,' Anouk said now, glancing apologetically at Emmanuelle, 'what's the pattern? There's a storm, there's a family... Someone always survives to tell the tale. What links them all?'

'It appears that an ancestor of Aristea's may have known, at least superficially, an ancestor of each of these families,'

Renatus said. 'But that isn't a very substantial clue. My father and Kenneth Hawke were childhood friends of Lisandro's, with whom he had a falling out. Probably he held my mother as accountable as my father, but there is no current explanation for his attacks on Hawke's wife, my sister or Aristea's family.'

'I am so sorry.' Susannah's voice wasn't loud or forceful but the crack in it brought everyone's attention to her. Her expression shook Tian – he had never seen her looking so *broken*. She raised a shaky hand to her mouth, staring at Aristea. 'I'm so, *so* sorry.'

She turned away suddenly and strode from the ballroom, breaking circle for the very first time. The sacred atmosphere of the ritual dissipated immediately, leaving the councillors blinking and staring after her in confusion.

'There we have it,' Lord Gawain said to Renatus.

Fate reached for Tian this time, casting its light on him. This moment was significant, but not for him. For Renatus and Aristea.

Oneida leaned forward to meet Tian's gaze, and he knew she'd felt the same thing.

# chapter ten

Renatus left my side to follow Susannah. I hesitated a long moment, frozen in place, holding one hand inside the other. I was already feeling shaken. I couldn't think about what Qasim had forced me to realise. It was too much, especially alongside the rest of the circle's discussions and the blood that was pooling in my palm. Hearing my story repeated to the White Elm, even briefly and objectively, was even worse than sharing it with Lord Gawain the other day. It was *my* story, my very own personal heartbreak that I'd kept all to myself until coming to Morrissey House, where I'd eventually told Hiroko and, later, Renatus. Both of those conversations were difficult, but sort of relieving.

This, tonight, had not left me feeling relieved. My story was out, only now it wasn't *my* story. It had been wrested from my unwilling grasp and now it was Lisandro's story. And it had changed from being a story, a moving tragedy, to only a chapter of some huge cheap thriller. When I'd entered the conversation and tried to take ownership of my tragedy, the scabbed-over, mostly healed cut on the edge of my hand had *opened back up*, and was bleeding steadily once again. I'd immediately assumed Oneida had done something to me, but she hadn't owned up or taken responsibility.

All in all I was left feeling degraded and small by this night, the wall holding back my massive emotions barely holding together. The biggest event of my life was just a plot point in some greater tale.

And Susannah, it seemed, knew why.

It was that thought that drove me after my master as the door shut behind him. I ran across the ballroom and shoved through the swinging door with my shoulder to keep my bloody hands off of it. I didn't bother feeling for their energies so I nearly ran into them, standing together in the entrance hall. Susannah had her head in her hand but she must have felt me approach because she looked straight up at me.

'Aristea,' she said, her voice tight, like she might cry. I didn't know if I could handle it if she cried, not after everything else. She was one of the eldest women on the council, strong and borderline heartless, and didn't seem like the tearful sort, so the prospect was quite terrifying. 'I didn't know. I never Saw this, I promise. If I had, I would never have said anything.'

'What are you talking about?' I asked. I was surprised by how steady my voice came out.

'This is why Seers shouldn't share what they See,' Susannah implored. 'Even we don't know how far the ripples of a tiny action will move through the future.'

'What did you do?' Renatus demanded. His tone implied a threat, and I knew he was worried.

'It was before we knew,' she insisted. 'He was my brother on the council; we were friends. I didn't know what he'd do with the information. Fate didn't show me *this* outcome. I thought I was helping a friend.'

'Lisandro?'

'Yes.' Susannah nodded in response to Renatus but still looked at me, as though suddenly seeing me in a different light. 'I didn't know the harm. I won't make this mistake again, I promise.'

'What mistake?' Renatus pushed. 'What did you do?'

'It's the worst mistake a Seer can make,' Susannah admitted now, wiping the edge of her eyes with shaky hands. 'I had visions that I shared with him. I just didn't want to see... I didn't want...' She shook her head, long brown hair escaping her low ponytail. 'What I saw frightened me, and he was my friend. I wanted to save him.'

'From what he was becoming?'

'No,' Susannah corrected, and continued quickly, 'but do not ask me to explain. I've learned my lesson. That vision is confidential.'

'So what can you tell us?' I asked, a little more bluntly than intended.

'A lot changed when you two were bonded,' she reminded me. 'A lot of futures opened up that had looked hopeless before. Some of those futures are not futures Lisandro wants as options. He didn't know about you, precisely, Aristea, not then, but he knew... because of me, he knew...' She looked unable to continue, but after a while turned to Renatus and redirected. 'You weren't on the council yet so you won't recall the long process of finding replacements for Lady Jennifer and Frank. We had so many names to sift through. Miranda was ascending to High Priestess so we needed a new Healer, but the other position could go to anybody. Lord Gawain handed around a list of names. There was a brother and sister pair being considered. He was of age and she was only just too young, by a fortnight or so, but for the right person, we can wait a couple of weeks before initiating. They both had a considerably limited knowledge of magic but they ranked high enough on the Trefzer Scale to make the list. I got the list; I Saw it all straightaway. I took Lisandro aside later and I said...' She breathed deeply as her voice cracked, and a tear escaped the corner of her eye. 'I said...'

'I don't care what you said!' I exploded, startling both of the councillors. 'Whose were the names?'

I knew, I knew, but I didn't want it to be them...

'Aidan and Angela Byrne,' Susannah answered, barely whispering. I felt like she'd struck me, though I'd known what was coming. 'We were leaning towards the brother but the future would have played out the same with either one. I see now what it was I was trying to avoid. Any Byrne on the council would have brought *you two* together sooner.'

I took an unconscious step backwards. Too much, too much...

'My brother was going to be invited to apply for the White Elm?' I managed eventually, trying to imagine our old house, my big brother sitting at the kitchen table opening his mail while sharing toast with me, and reading *that* in a letter. 'But... He was going to be a carpenter, like Dad.' I looked at my master. 'Aidan and Angela... are their names on Lisandro's list?'

His mind flashed on the list in his desk drawer, the one he'd told me not to worry about. He didn't have to answer. I knew.

'He would have been initiated, you would have met Renatus...' Susannah shook her head, her gaze imploring me to understand. I couldn't. Neither could Renatus.

'Why was this so important to delay?' he asked, annoyance evident in his tone. 'Obviously it was going to happen anyway.' He must have seen me open my hand to check my small wound, because he demanded of me, 'What did you do?' and produced a tissue from mid-air. I took it and shook my head to convey how little understanding I had of the cause of my bleed, to match my understanding of everything else that was happening.

'Why did you try to prevent us from meeting?' I prompted Susannah, staying focussed. My voice sounded like stone, rock-hard and cold. I wiped my palm cleanish and pressed the bunched tissue against the cut to stem any further bleeding. Susannah stared, seemingly transfixed by the sight of my blood.

'Fate did that,' she murmured, nodding at my hand. With effort, I did not throw the bloody tissue at her.

'*Why*?!' I shouted, and Susannah squeezed her eyes shut, visibly shaken by my volume.

'I didn't... I didn't know I was only postponing the inevitable. I thought...' Again, Susannah trailed off, struggling. She jumped onto another track. 'Renatus, think back five years. Lisandro was our brother and protector; you were a liability, a probable danger to us all. You were a boy,' she added, seeing his expression. 'Seeing is not like scrying. What *you* see is fact; what I see is truth, and the truth is different for everybody. Naturally I wanted a future that protected the interests of the council as I knew it and the people I believed to be good and righteous. Even you might have done the same with the information available.'

Her logic sounded valid enough but I balked at her words.

'Neither of us would have told Lisandro, or anyone else, to kill a stranger to make sure he never got the chance to introduce his little sister to a teenager we didn't like,' I snarled, furious with everything. Before tonight I'd not minded Susannah but now, the implication that she and I, or even she and Renatus, were anything alike, was mortifying. My story had been taken from me, which was upsetting, and now, worse, Susannah had stepped forward and admitted to being its ghost writer. 'We aren't like you at all.'

Susannah's mouth fell open; beside us, the ballroom door inched open, and Lord Gawain peered through. He had a talent for that, poorly timed entrances. I resisted the urge to shut the door on him and chose to ignore him instead.

'I did not tell him to kill the Byrnes!' Susannah insisted, taken aback that I would assume this, though I couldn't figure out what I was *meant* to assume she'd said, since she wasn't sharing. She was talking all around the point. A skill of a great Seer. 'I told him what the Byrnes meeting the White Elm represented – a catalyst for a great many things – and I kept an eye on their futures as we on the council deliberated... One morning their futures with the White Elm dissolved, the path just went away-'

'Because he'd killed my brother?' I interrupted. I felt numb and my voice was stony.

'No, the Byrne storm was a week after we agreed on Peter Chisholm,' Lord Gawain told me, through the door. I wanted to scream at him to go away. 'It happened a few hours after the initiation. When we learned of it, we understood that this was why their futures with us had suddenly ceased to be possible. One was to die and the other was to refuse the offer in light of the tragedy.'

*One was to die.* That *one* was my big brother. *The other was to refuse.* That *other* was never asked, so how would they know? I bit my lip, hard, to keep myself from answering. I had nothing nice to say.

'Lord Gawain, I broke the rules,' Susannah confessed, looking to him as though for forgiveness – as if *he* were the one she needed forgiveness from. Was it *his* mother, father and brother's blood on your hands? Was it *his* life ruined by your stupid choices? No, didn't think so. 'I never Saw this outcome. Fate kept it from me. I was trying to keep the White Elm together.' She glanced at Renatus quickly. 'I couldn't see then what you saw in him.'

Lord Gawain's expression softened while Renatus's hardened. I didn't like the contrast.

'For someone who claims to be acting for the White Elm's benefit,' I said coldly to Susannah, 'you've spent a long time working very hard against the best person on it.'

Lord Gawain opened his mouth, perhaps to defend his Seer, perhaps to scold me, and Susannah did the same, though I couldn't guess what she'd meant to say. I didn't find out either councillor's choice of words, because I turned on my heel and left. Nobody tried to stop me.

I fumed all the way to my room, where Hiroko was already in bed, pretending to be asleep, and Sterling and Xanthe were sitting between their beds, cutting up magazines, rolling the little rectangles into tubes and sticky-taping them to maintain their shape. I rarely bothered to guess what they were up to these days. Their goings-on seemed so trivial now, especially with mine and Hiroko's spiralling in and out of control.

I went to the bathroom to wash my hands and cover my cut. I had no spare energy for wondering what magic had reopened it. When I returned to the dorm I grabbed the photo of my family I kept beside my bed and laid down. I'd taken it as a little girl with my own camera, and it wasn't a great picture. Angela's eyes, so unique and amazing with that sea-blue-green colour, were closed against the glare of the sunny day, and nobody was posed quite right. I ran my fingertips across the glass, removing a fine layer of dust. Angela was such a pretty girl – I'd grown up wanting to be exactly like her, so lovely, so likeable, so polite and tactful and smart and well-mannered. In this picture she was seventeen, the same age I was now. Her hair was like gold, tied in a high ponytail as it absolutely *always* was, and she had a wispy sort of fringe she'd soon grown out, but if I looked long enough, maybe I'd see myself in her features. Were we alike? People said we were. This Angela wasn't even out of school – she had no idea what future Fate was going to throw at her. This Angela was going to study in Dublin, but didn't know she'd only get one year of that life before coming home for the summer, watching her parents and brother die and deferring indefinitely to raise me.

I usually avoided looking too long at the other three loved ones in the photo, but this time I found my eyes drifting to and sticking with my brother Aidan. He looked a lot like our dad, I reflected, with the same tall build and strong shoulders, the same golden hair, those workers' hands. His eyes, though, were like mine, like Mum's. Most people complained about their brothers but I'd never had much reason to complain about mine. He'd taken good care of me, made room for me in every game he played with his friends and never allowed anyone to slight me. Angela and I were his personal responsibilities and everyone in town knew it.

I remembered quite clearly the first time I'd taken the school bus alone, and I'd accidentally taken the seat at the back, which apparently was known by everyone else to be reserved for Rory Dermot, a bully three grades above me. He'd boarded two stops after I did and made a spectacle of me for the viewing pleasure of the busload of kids, emptying my schoolbag onto the floor and ridiculing the pink cardigan he found amongst my possessions, and stopping only when he read the name written on the tag – *Angela Byrne,* a hand-me-down from my sister. He'd thrown it all back at me, muttering, 'Sit where you want, then, stupid,' and plonked himself down somewhere else. My brother and sister were in high school by this point so I couldn't tell them until after school, by which time I'd decided it would be childish and lame of me to snitch on Rory, but the story must have made its way to the high schoolers somehow anyway, because two mornings later, Rory Dermot boarded the bus with a black eye amid hushed whispers. Months later, when one his friends tried to start me, Rory had actually stepped in, reminding the friend whose sister I was.

I hugged the photo to my chest as I felt it constrict, missing my brother and sister intensely. They'd both loved me, still did, in Ange's case, but for both, I'd always been the *other* sibling. They'd been closer with one another than they ever had been with me, the years-younger baby, and though I knew my sister adored me, I'd spent the last three years studiously avoiding wondering whether she wished the tree had fallen differently, taken me instead of the kindred spirit that was her brother and best friend.

It hardly mattered now, I decided. What Angela wished had never been a factor. Fate had been bent in our case, by the spite of Lisandro and the ignorance of Susannah, all to disadvantage Renatus.

As I my thoughts touched on Renatus, the only brother I had now, I felt the tightness recede. I'd once asked him what I'd never asked Angela, whether he'd prefer to have Ana, his blood sister, the hero of his childhood, instead of me. He'd said no. He was glad I was here. For whatever anyone else thought of him, whatever he'd done, he was still –

I sat up suddenly, still clutching the photo frame. Across the room, my roommates' curiosity spiked at my odd behaviour, but they deliberately did not look my way. I ignored them, my thoughts spinning again. Something painfully obvious had just struck me – something I should have thought of last week, when I'd first found out about Lisandro's betrayal of both my family and Renatus's. I clambered off my bed, unlocked the door and ran from the room.

I'd been so selfish, so self-absorbed all week, thinking only of how all this bad news made *me* feel. I'd hardly spared a thought for my master and what he must be going through. He'd gotten the worst news of all, and it hadn't even occurred to me.

It was odd, I thought vaguely as I strode for the staircase, how quickly priorities and feelings could change. Two weeks ago I'd tapped into a memory of Renatus's and seen him at his worst. I'd scried the day he'd lost his parents and sister and found a total stranger carrying Ana's dead body, beaten almost beyond recognition... and killed him. Viewing the memory, I'd felt no sympathy for the stranger; I'd never seen anything more gruesome than the condition Ana Morrissey had died in. It had never occurred to me to judge Renatus poorly for his act that day. I couldn't imagine that anybody would have acted any differently, certainly not myself, but most still wouldn't condone it. Renatus had long hated himself for it, loathed the evil he felt he'd done in vain, because he'd been unable to revive Ana, and lived in perpetual fear of being found out, knowing that not everyone would see it the way I had.

But now we knew something we didn't know before – the stranger was *not* Ana's killer. Lisandro was the one who had designed and initiated the storm that had caught the Morrisseys up and thrown them about like dolls into the trees, battering them to death.

So, this left the awful question: if the stranger was not there to kill Ana, what was he doing on Morrissey Estate in that terrible storm, and who was he?

Whose life had Renatus cut short?

Now that I asked myself this question, I heard it all through my mind and Renatus's, racing in useless circles and eating him alive. To avenge your family is an ancient, nearly honourable motivation to kill another person; there is no honour in mistakenly killing somebody else.

I stopped very suddenly in the middle of the second flight of stairs. Susannah was waiting on the next landing with her hands hanging loosely by her sides.

'I'm not looking for you,' I told her immediately. I knew I was being rude but I wasn't in any state to accept further emotional battering from her, and I didn't want her to get any ideas.

'I know you're looking for Renatus,' she said, nodding. 'You don't find him tonight. He's outside, sulking, but you won't go to him.'

Says you. I frowned and started forward.

'I'm going there now,' I retorted, moving past her.

'You are *now*, because you've made the decision to do so,' Susannah agreed, turning as I passed, 'which paves the future for this series of events, but I have also made a decision, and mine will counteract yours and spin a new future in which you *don't* speak with Renatus tonight.'

I stopped and looked back from the edge of the landing.

'When I saw *what I saw*, and told Lisandro, *what I saw* was certain because Lord Gawain had made the decision to add Aidan and Angela Byrne to the list of candidates,' she went on. 'Decisions and choices take us on unique paths into our futures. It was certain because the list would shorten all the way down to Aidan Byrne, Emmanuelle Saint Clair and Peter Chisholm, and Byrne's bloodline would become apparent and would secure his position.'

I folded my arms over the photograph. My connection to my once-famous, long-dead grandfather had been a total mystery to Renatus, Lord Gawain and Qasim, yet Susannah seemed to have known all along.

'Futures are complicated because they change whenever new decisions are made that can redirect or completely counteract those of other people – just like your present circumstances are affected by the immediate decisions of others. The morning I woke to find the future of Aidan Byrne on the White Elm eliminated, a decision must have been made. These decisions can be small. Wrong place, wrong time, that sort of thing. It doesn't have to be malicious. In this case, unfortunately, it was.'

Susannah eyed me for a long moment. I adjusted my grip on the picture frame I still held, intensely aware of how odd it was to be wandering the manor with it.

'It was not *my* decision to end your brother's life, nor those of your parents,' Susannah said, eyes on the picture, 'but it was *my* poor decision-making that provided Lisandro with the information he needed to make that decision himself, and for that, I am endlessly sorry. I am so, so sorry, Aristea, and I only hope that I am beginning to make up for it with this.'

She offered me an envelope. I took it without hesitation or graciousness – did she think she could buy my forgiveness with a sympathy card or some cash? It was very light and thin, with one slip of paper in it. I slit it open and withdrew the note.

I don't know what I expected, but it was not a time and place.

'What's this?' I asked. Were we to fight it out?

'A choice.' Susannah's tone gave nothing away. 'It may seem clearer when the time comes, but the choice still falls to you. Arrival at this place, at exactly this time, will enable a very specific future. You don't have to take this path,' she reminded me when I looked dubiously at the handwritten date, the twenty-sixth of June, more than a month away, 'but just as I did for Lisandro without realising, I am now giving you the information you need to make a choice that can impact heavily on many futures.'

'I thought that was bad practice for Seers.'

She smiled wryly.

'So you do listen. It is bad practice to try to change the outcome, yes. After what I've already done, this is no longer relevant. The ending is the same to nearly all paths now, but how we all get there remains to be seen, and to be *chosen*. Whether or not you use what I've given you, the outcome will remain the same. You can, however, ease and quicken many of our journeys to that outcome.'

I fidgeted with the paper, feeling that it had become somewhat heavier in the last few seconds.

'Coordinates?' I asked. She nodded once.

'Scotland. A wood, national parkland.'

'What will I do when I get there?'

'That will be up to you.'

'But *why* am I going there?' I pressed. 'Scotland in the middle of the night – what can I possibly want there? What will I find? How am I meant to get there? Anyway,' I added, an afterthought as I shifted the picture frame under my arm, 'last time I was in Scotland I nearly died.'

'I don't know what you'll decide to do,' Susannah answered, somewhat airily, totally unhelpfully; and then, 'I recommend you wear shoes you can run in, though, if you *do* choose to go. And bring the rabbit's foot.'

'Bring the rabbit's foot,' I repeated, slowly, incredulously, because it was the most *ridiculous* piece of advice I had ever been given. She had stopped speaking and I waited for more, but it seemed she had said all she was going to say. I started down the stairs again.

'I'm still going to see Renatus,' I said, feeling childishly determined that she not be correct in her earlier claim. I refused to look back as I heard her soft footsteps. I shoved the note into my pocket and kept my eyes on the carpet. 'I'll think about what you've said.'

She spoke, so softly I barely heard, but my mind processed the whispered sounds and stopped my feet with a suddenness that nearly tripped me.

'What?' I asked, grabbing the banister to maintain my balance and looking over my shoulder. Susannah looked sorry again, solemn, as she too leant on the elegant handrail. 'What did you just say?'

'Renatus is going to kill Lisandro,' she said again, still quiet. 'That's the ending. That's what I told Lisandro and that's why he killed your family – to try to prevent it. But there's no stopping it. It's Fated.'

I stared at her, with her soft features crinkled with grimness and pity, and allowed myself to let these words sink in. I couldn't feel her grimness. I felt nothing she could pity.

I felt satisfaction. The notion of Renatus taking our revenge was appealing. I'd forgotten already my reason for being here, on this staircase, to discuss his feelings on murder with him.

'That sounds like great news,' I said eventually, wanting to smile but sensing it would not be appropriate. The Seer had cared deeply for Lisandro; I tried to appreciate the emotional difficulty she faced. It was tough. 'He'll be pleased to hear that.'

'You may never tell him,' Susannah ordered firmly.

'Why? It's good news.'

'Is it?' she countered, raising an eyebrow. 'Do you think he wants to hear that? If I told you that you're to commit murder, that you had no way of avoiding it, how would that make you feel?'

'Am I?' I heard myself ask, though immediately I wished I hadn't opened my mouth. She was right – it wasn't something you wanted to know.

'I didn't say that.' Again, her tone gave no clues. I was relieved. She absentmindedly pulled her long brown hair over one shoulder and fixed me with a piercing look. 'You can't tell him because he can't know. Renatus is stubborn, like you. If you tell him what he's to do, he'll try to change it, and attempts to divert this path would be disastrous.'

'Can it be changed?' I asked. 'I thought you said it was inevitable.'

'It is. Lisandro's death can only be by Renatus's hand, or...'

'By me?' I guessed, and my heart leapt in a slightly frightening manner. Why would I want that possibility? Why would I want her to say yes? I clutched the photo a little tighter.

'I didn't say that. Lisandro will die, but how, when, where, how many lives he takes or ruins first... All is determined by our choices. There are many choices between now and then.'

I took my family picture in both hands and looked at the four precious faces as I allowed my feelings to settle. Lisandro was going to die. I was going to live to see my family avenged. The White Elm would be victorious. I felt... peace.

'Thank you, Susannah,' I said, hating her so much less. 'Knowing that we're going to win... You just fixed everything.'

'Win?' she repeated. Her tone made my stomach flutter, like I was falling all of a sudden. 'Our enemy's death doesn't guarantee that we prevail. The council may not survive this war. There are many futures, Aristea, and none of them nice. I don't survive them all; you don't survive them all. Your master doesn't survive them all. Even the smoothest path is wrought with death, loss and heartache.' She paused, seeming to weigh her words carefully before using them. 'You were right, what you said before. Renatus is not a bad person. Yet. He made a righteous choice last week to save you instead of fulfilling his fate and killing his godfather, but you won't always need rescuing. I don't know what he's done in the past – I don't *want* to know – but what he is yet to do will change him. Renatus's soul is the price for our "win" over Lisandro. I'm not sure any of us can call that a win at all.'

I battled with that wall inside me and my voice was crumbly when I asked, 'What do you mean, the price?'

'What do you think I mean?' Susannah pushed lightly off the banister and came down to stand on the same step as me. She gently grasped my wrist for a second, a reminder of the black marking I bore there. 'As I Saw when you asked me for support for your apprenticeship, you may still live to regret this tattoo.'

164

She offered me a sad smile and carried on down the stairs. I stayed where I was, listening to her footsteps as they receded beyond my range of hearing, and for several minutes after they faded into the deep silence of the mansion.

I absolutely hated for her to be right, but when I started to move again, it was back up the stairs to return to my room. Surely even great Seers had to have a fail rate, and if Susannah did, I'd rather she be wrong about all the other stuff. She could be correct just about this one little thing, because I definitely couldn't face Renatus with what I now knew.

# chapter eleven

I didn't sleep at all after my encounter with Susannah and as I sat in the dining hall long after breakfast the next day I was silent and withdrawn, sitting with my head in my hands, waving away questions of what was wrong.

'Headache,' I claimed, not really lying. I felt crappy, plagued with my impossible cyclic thoughts. Hiroko and Iseult didn't believe me, I could tell, but they didn't push it. They were absorbed in Displacement talk, books spread around them, protractors and pencils in hand as they completed a theoretical assignment for Elijah's top class. I tried to listen in. I gathered that the angle of a Skip through space affected the angle in which you came out the other side, just like momentum, but that careful calculations prior to opening the wormhole could allow a Displacer to change her angle, so that you could disappear at a steep downward run and reappear somewhere else facing more upright to avoid a faceplant into unexpectedly flat ground. Good to know, but not likely something I was ever going to master or understand. Add it to the list. A few classes were running but some other people were sitting around, too, finishing off breakfast or studying or talking or playing board games. Worry about the missing boys had dulled following the White Elm's announcement that the families had foreseen their safe return, and asked the council not to interfere. Not far from Hiroko sat Kendra and Sterling, playing checkers, while Xanthe and Sophia watched on. I'd seen a lot of

Susannah's students playing it lately, actually. I wondered if they'd been set the game as a task, learning to predict the other's moves.

And thoughts of Susannah started the cycle again.

*Renatus is going to kill Lisandro. That's the ending.*

Renatus hadn't come to breakfast, which was not unusual, but what *was* unusual was the lack of mental contact from him. I supposed he was giving me space to process Susannah's revelation, the part of it he knew of, as running away and keeping to myself had been my pattern of dealing with upset in his experience. I tried not to uncomfortably realise how distant he'd been overall this past week. Normally – funny that we had a *normally* after so short a time – he was in my head all the time, checking in, but this week he'd been conspicuously absent, only the very occasional conversation. He had a lot to deal with; I'd been a lame excuse for a friend, selfishly absorbed in my own problems while he struggled with the same issues. I'd fully intended to talk to him last night. Even now, I could so easily nudge his thoughts and get his attention, try to open a dialogue.

Now, though… I didn't know what to say to him, and so I left his thoughts untouched.

*Renatus's soul is the price for our "win".*

Susannah hadn't come, either, for which I was immensely glad. I'd been carrying around so much latent anger since learning that Lisandro had killed my family – last night I'd felt it rising up against the Seer. Call it shooting the messenger, but how was I not meant to feel angry with the woman for her part in my parents' and brother's deaths? She'd *told* Lisandro that Aidan would help Renatus kill him, and Lisandro had done what any psychopathic sorcerer was inclined to do. *He* had acted within reason. *She* had not, not in telling him about Aidan and Angela, not in telling *me* about Renatus. It was completely unreasonable to saddle a person of my age with that kind of knowledge about someone they care about less than twenty minutes after hitting them with *Oh, I'm responsible for your orphan status. Sorry about that.*

Oneida *was* there, the only councillor still eating, and I studiously avoided looking at her, with her big full aura, still swollen from the circle last night like the rest of the council. My initiation had wiped me out. How come hers was so nice and empowering? Even I felt stronger after that ritual, though not as much as the councillors.

Despite the power boost my mood was awful, made worse when I peeled one end of my plaster off and saw the stupid cut from Oneida was *still open*. Like a whole night had done nothing at all to help it heal.

'Damn Seers,' I muttered harshly, an opinion I knew was more Renatus's than mine but I said it before realising this, dropping the plaster and grabbing a napkin. Hiroko and Iseult looked at each other discreetly and continued their conversation. I dabbed at the blood and took a slow breath. Calm down. Get a grip. I was a *sorceress*. I closed my eyes, gathered energy and prepared to channel it. I could deal with this.

Turned out, I couldn't.

I found the skill of Healing fascinating, but had practically no talent in the area. If I did, I was yet to tap it and begin the turbocharged learning curve that I had come to consider normal now that I was bonded with Renatus. I glared at my hand. Concentrated. Hard. Nothing happened, unless you counted a tingly feeling and another ooze of dark blood. I sat back in frustration, hand left lying on the tabletop as if I could drop it there and walk away. I could just as soon get away from my hand as I could escape the echo of Susannah's voice last night.

*Renatus isn't a bad person. Yet.*

What was I even meant to make of that?

Further down the table, through my distracted exhaustion, I felt someone's uncertainty and curiosity, and I made the mistake of glancing over. Sophia Prescott quickly turned her head away to look straight down at her empty plate. I turned back to glaring at my cut hand. She'd been watching me, I realised, as I failed persistently at the skill she was most gifted at. Did that make her feel better about herself? Did she like watching me fail?

I decided I didn't want the answer to that. I had enough to avoid feeling without worrying about my aborted friendship with the Prescotts.

I sighed and pressed a napkin against the open cut, and lowered my forehead into my waiting palm. Life was so screwed up. *You must never tell him.* How had it dissolved like this? Renatus was my master and I trusted him – I'd never had secrets from him before now. We shared a connection I could hardly explain. *You must never tell him.* How? How could I possibly *not*? Didn't he deserve to know? Wouldn't he *expect* me to tell him? Wouldn't he be furious with me for withholding something like this?

Last night, among other horrible things, I'd been made to realise that I had not dreamed about the storm for three and half years straight, but *scried* it, every night. Some part of me had *known*, or had been open to knowing, and ignorant me had missed the message every time. Renatus had done the same. We'd both failed to notice and use the information made available to us, for *years*.

But that was on us, down to immaturity and wilful ignorance. *This* was different. *I* was informed. Renatus was not. That wasn't fair on either of us. How could Susannah ask me not to tell him? How could Fate?

Fate was a jerk.

Questions warred away inside me. Why hadn't I ignored Susannah and been strong enough to go ahead and tell him anyway? Why did I want to if there was a risk of making things worse? The impossibility created feelings, heavy and painful feelings, which smashed themselves against the wall I'd erected inside me. I pressed my hands against my ears and hummed like I could block them out like noises. If anyone saw me they no doubt thought I was insane, but how far wrong would they be? Everything, inside me and out, was falling apart, and I was ill-equipped to deal with it. I was *seventeen.* I wasn't old enough for all of this. I wasn't strong enough.

*Wear shoes you can run in. Bring the rabbit's foot.* What did that even *mean*? A metaphor for luck?

Hiroko tugged my hand away from my ear, worried about me.

'Are you sure you are alright?' Iseult asked.

'It must be this headache,' I mumbled, adjusting my hold on the napkin that was doing a terrible job of stemming my bleed. Hiroko twisted my hand to get a better look.

'This is strange,' Hiroko pointed out to Iseult, who leaned across the table to look closer. 'This is where Oneida cut you? It still bleeds?'

'It opened back up after her initiation,' I said, glancing toward the staff table as Oneida herself got up and departed the room, but didn't want to discuss the circle, so left my hand lying bleeding on a new napkin and used my clean hand to turn Hiroko's homework toward me. Vectors, distances, formulas for force, speed and acceleration all swam before my eyes. My uncle, who had home-schooled me through my mandatory secondary education, had taught me these once, but having never found use for them beyond my exams, I'd soon forgotten. Printed across the page in Hiroko's neat, round script, it looked as alien to me as her native language of Japanese did. I was glad not to be in her class for this subject. Elijah would never throw equations like these at my class. All we did every lesson was fall over, trying desperately to teleport across the lawn. 'How much of this could be useful to me?'

'In deflecting questions? Most of it,' Iseult quipped, meeting my annoyed glance with cool eyes.

'None.' Hiroko shot her a warning look and me a quick smile, then took her homework back. She measured out an angle with her protractor and recorded its degrees beside it, and began mathing. 'I doubt even Elijah uses this. And he is best.'

'I'm exempt from that page,' Iseult said triumphantly, reaching for one of the sheets in front of Hiroko. I don't know how she could tell it apart from the rest. 'Displacers only. I'll never be able to affect my momentum like you can, so I don't need to study the theory behind it.' She read over it anyway, clearly interested, and glanced at me over the top of the page. 'Just so you know, your aura looks like someone gave it a bad haircut, so while you're busy trying to avoid everybody's attention and mull over whatever you're dealing with – and I won't ask – just be aware that others will probably overstep the mark and ask how you're doing, too.'

I sighed again. I was being a bad friend, *again*.

'I'm sorry for blocking you both out,' I said quietly, looking at my hand so I didn't have to look at either of them. I curled my clean hand around the napkin, holding it in place over the cut. 'I'm just…'

'Dealing,' Iseult finished for me. She didn't sound bothered by it. 'Continue. We'll be here.'

She went back to her work, content with her offer of constancy, which I really did appreciate. Hiroko smiled at me again, gentler this time, and squeezed my wrist affectionately.

'You can talk, if you want to,' she said, because in most things I told her everything, but this – *this*. All this. Where to even start, and before that, *should* I even start? Susannah – trying to protect her friend, trying to keep her council together but betraying her own ethics in trying to do the right thing. Her note – June was ages away, or felt it, and no further clues to explain it were forthcoming. Lisandro – murdered my parents and brother to keep me from meeting Renatus.

Renatus.

*Renatus isn't a bad person. Yet.*

Renatus had killed someone. It didn't matter to *me* whether the stranger had actually done the deed of murdering Ana: he was still holding her when she died, had done nothing to try to save her, and had been just about to hurt Renatus, too. Regardless of what he was actually doing

171

here in Lisandro's fatal storm, he was still guilty... in my opinion.

But Renatus and I had differed in opinion before, and no doubt would many times more in future. The fact that the stranger was not Ana's murderer had changed Renatus's opinion completely against himself, and I knew that this morbid mystery was eating him alive even now.

Renatus was not allowed to know it, but he was Fated to kill Lisandro. Good riddance, the angstiest part of my brain said, but the slightly more alert, worrisome sections did not agree. Susannah hadn't *said* it, exactly, but she'd made it sound as though either the act of or the path to killing the White Elm's enemy would turn Renatus into someone I wouldn't like. Maybe the council's long-held fear that Renatus would turn dark – as most of history's Dark Keepers did – would be realised when he took joy and satisfaction from hunting down and killing the person he hated the most.

Or when the guilt of a second murder consumed him.

If he went bad, how long before I followed suit? Less than a month bonded and I was exclaiming his biases about Seers instead of my own. Slowly but surely, I was becoming more like him. His magic and his knowledge of spells had already started to slide across the connection. I doubted it was possible for one of us to go wrong without pulling the other down with us.

Hence, the council's reluctance to let us pair up at all.

Somehow, though, I wasn't feeling the appropriate concern about my own fate in all of this. My destiny wasn't the one Susannah had spoken so miserably of. I was a kid, maybe I still had a chance, but Renatus, if she was right...

Renatus was screwed.

The wall shuddered inside me and tears stung the backs of my eyes like little needles. He had to know, he had a right, I owed it to him... He would know what to do with the information, better than I did. But if he couldn't do anything about it... As always, I sought to run away from my feelings.

'I can't,' I told Hiroko, my voice cracking, and shoved my chair back and got clumsily to my feet. I turned–

And bumped straight into Sophia, and froze, almost nose to nose.

She didn't look so surprised and didn't give me a chance to react. She grabbed my elbow with one hand to keep me still and wrapped her other hand over the two of mine, clutched protectively in front of my chest. I should have cast a ward but I didn't think to. She held on, forehead pressed to mine, looking me straight in the eyes. Hers were pretty, a sort of light crystal green. I'd never been this close to her to see the little flecks of grey in the irises, but that said, I couldn't remember being this close to anyone. There was an intensity between us, something my strung-out brain didn't recognise until a moment later as magic.

She was healing me.

She released me, and I released the breath I hadn't realised I was holding. She stepped away, pulling my hands apart. I saw her handiwork. The blood was still on my skin and seeped through the napkin but the cut underneath was sealed. No evidence remained of it, not even a scar.

'Yuck,' Xanthe said with rolled eyes from where she sat with Kendra and Sterling, who were both watching Sophia and I curiously. 'That explains why you're always staring at her.'

It was the closest she'd come to actually addressing me since our big fight.

'Go to hell, Xanthe,' Sophia answered over her shoulder without effort or bite. She looked back at me while her friends talked in tense, quiet voices I couldn't hear. 'Magic made that cut. It wasn't going to heal on its own.'

I stared at her, caught up in the warm intimacy of being healed. You don't heal someone you don't care about, right? And it's not done by accident. It wasn't just *whoops, you ran into me and I tripped and accidentally healed you*. She touched me, held me still, held eye contact, like Emmanuelle did when she performed her art. This was deliberate. A deliberate act of kindness.

She didn't hate me. The truth of the fact rolled around in my head, incredible and amazing against everything else I was struggling with. She emanated anxiousness and uncertainty but she stayed put. The tears behind my eyes quit their relentless push and did not fall.

Hiroko stood up beside me, cautious, and took my hand to turn it.

'It is gone,' she said. I nodded and continued staring at Sophia, not sure whether to believe my luck.

'Thank you,' I murmured, and I really meant it. This was the last thing I'd expected today, and such a welcome change in my life's otherwise bleak outlook. She smiled, a little nervously.

'It's the least I could do.'

'*Excuse me?*'

Sophia, Hiroko and I looked around upon hearing the indignant exclamation. Kendra had suddenly stood up from her checkers game and was glaring down at Xanthe. Nearby conversations slowed, the better to focus on this confrontation.

'I was only *saying*,' Xanthe said coldly back to her.

'Only saying what?' Kendra asked, angry. 'Only insinuating that my sister's sexuality is *any* of your business?'

Every teenager in the room was suddenly listening attentively, watching on with cautious interest, hoping that this argument didn't end badly. Sophia and I glanced at each other and my heart sank. This again.

'If Sophia's a lesbian,' Xanthe stated, 'then we all deserve to know. I mean, we share personal information with her; before now we wouldn't have thought twice about changing in the same room.'

'Oh, no, not *personal information*,' Kendra mocked. 'Imagine what a lesbian could do for her malicious gay agenda with your *personal information*.'

'Leave it alone, Xanthe,' I called, and I felt all the attention in the room double because *I* was involved. The troublemaker, the centre of all controversy on this estate. I waved my hand, still stained with drying blood, still clutching a scrunched bloody napkin, to show her. 'All she did was heal my hand.'

'Says *you*.' And that was directed straight at me, the first words she'd spoken to me in a month. They didn't hurt; I felt the arrow of spite she sent with her words but it landed atop the arsenal of other hurts that had been thrown my way of late and paled in comparison.

'Aye, says me,' I retorted. There were no councillors present. No one to make me behave. I was pumped full of my own emotions and looking for a good distractor. 'Shockingly, the people around you are hooking up a lot less than you seem to believe, you paranoid bitch.'

I got the narrowed eyes. Ooh. Like that was going to scare me.

'I don't care if she's gay,' Sterling offered from the other side of the table, an attempt to diffuse the situation.

'So she is gay, then.' Xanthe was cool and calm, and Kendra's eyes narrowed, too.

'That's not your concern. But if she is, don't stress about her checking you out while you're getting changed. She's way too good for you anyway,' Kendra snarled, but Sophia left my side now, moving over and taking her twin gently by the arm.

'Ken, it's okay,' she soothed, although it was clear that she was upset with Xanthe's attitude. 'Don't worry about it.' She looked back at Xanthe as she, too, stood. 'I'm not gay-'

'And she doesn't owe you an explanation,' Kendra inserted. Sophia paused for the interjection and continued calmly as if it hadn't happened.

'-and I'm not into you. Alright? What's the problem?'

'The problem?' Xanthe repeated. She pointed over at me. I folded my arms, ready for whatever she thought she was going to throw at me. Bring it on. 'I didn't realise you two were like that, girlfriends or whatever, but it's wrong and it shouldn't be on display like that. It's shameful.'

I dropped my folded arms. I was so ignorant of these sorts of things, which was how I'd triggered Xanthe's belief that I was involved with Renatus in the first place. I took things on face value, and forgot to consider how other people might perceive what I thought of as perfectly innocent. The same way Xanthe and Sterling had misinterpreted me returning late at night from an attractive man's office, breathless and with runs in my stockings, skirt twisted and unwilling to discuss what had happened, Xanthe had now constructed her own idea of what it meant when Sophia held me close and looked me in the eyes.

Ugh, why did people need to make things so complicated? What twisted societal problems had caused this obsession with sex and romantic relationships? Did every positive interaction between two people need to be deconstructed for some deeper or less honourable motivation?

'Shameful?' Kendra scoffed, while Sophia tried to calm her and pull her away. 'Holding hands is shameful?'

'They were kissing.'

'No they *weren't*. They were holding hands. Like this,' she added aggressively, leaning across the table to grab a surprised Sterling's hand off the game board. She held it for a second in the air to make sure her example sunk in before letting go. 'Harmless. And if they *were* making out, what the hell difference does that make to you? You're hardly pure, shoving your tongue down that poor guy's throat yesterday in the ballroom.'

Xanthe coloured, folding her arms uncomfortably while a few people audibly covered their amusement with light coughs.

'Well,' she said after a moment, 'he's only one guy, Kendra, not eight. At least I'm not whoring my way around the school like you have been-'

Out of nowhere, Sophia's fist appeared, striking Xanthe solidly in the face. A huge crack alerted the rest of us to the moment when Xanthe's nose broke. With a muffled shriek, Xanthe backed away, and Sophia advanced, screaming, 'Don't you speak to my sister like that!'

Cue brawl. The emotional energy of the room surged and so did I. Hiroko and I, along with nearly everyone else, stood on our toes to see better as Xanthe clawed and scratched at the furious Canadian, which only served to incite further anger in her twin. Sterling got well out of the way. Addison, sitting nearby, vaulted over the table to reach their side and bolted over.

It was over within five seconds. Addison intervened, catching Sophia around the waist and lifting her clear of the scuffle. Dylan arrived next and separated Kendra and Xanthe, who stood opposite one another, tensely glaring and panting slightly. Kendra sported a long red scratch across one cheek.

White Elm Displaced in from all over the estate, Qasim and Jadon and Oneida, but the students had taken care of it. A self-managing populace. I felt a familiar presence nearby and looked to the door.

I hadn't seen him since last night, just after the circle, so when I saw Renatus striding over with a grim expression, I met his eyes and sort of froze up in spite of all the excitement coursing through me.

Here was the person who had chosen me over all the others at the Academy, sparking tensions with Qasim and even risking his standing with Lord Gawain in his fight to have me as his apprentice.

Here was the person who shared my awful past, with both parents and an older sibling stolen from life by Lisandro, and whose future was *my* future.

Here was the person who had saved my life instead of chasing down his demons.

Here was the person who would one day kill Lisandro, but may lose all that made him decent in the process.

I had to tell him what I now knew. I couldn't tell him.

'Disgusting,' Qasim was saying to Xanthe and the Prescotts. Renatus stopped at my side and listened. 'Headmaster's office, *now*. I've already summoned your council supervisors.' He gestured and, shooting one another a final hateful glare, Kendra and Xanthe left with him. As he passed me, Qasim didn't miss the opportunity to add, *No surprise that you are involved.*

Addison waited until Xanthe was out of sight before letting Sophia's feet touch the ground and releasing her. She breathed deeply, already composing herself.

While everybody else stared at Sophia, shocked by her sudden show of aggression, Renatus looked to me.

*What was that about?*

*Sophia healed the cut on my hand. Xanthe mistook that as us holding hands,* I explained, feeling uncomfortable mentioning what she'd *really* thought, and my words flinched with untruth. Not fair – I didn't want to talk about kissing with Renatus, and magic should be on my side in that regard. I felt his thoughts beginning to intrude on mine and kept talking, aloud this time, not wanting him in my head until I knew whether I wanted him there. 'That's not all,' I said in an undertone when Sophia meekly came over. I avoided her eyes as I told him, 'Xanthe deserved that. She called her sister a whore.'

Renatus accepted it and left my thoughts alone, to my immense relief, which I was glad he could not feel the way I did. He beckoned to Sophia as she stared at me. *I suppose you think that means I should let this one out of punishment?*

I shrugged. Our viewpoints on justice likely deviated greatly but in this instance I felt that Renatus personally agreed. In his role as headmaster, he could not always be subjective.

'Come,' he said to Sophia, and she nodded obediently, following him from the hall. The other councillors stayed for a moment but seemed content that the trouble was gone, and left as well.

As soon as they were gone, the conversation resumed, twice as loud and excited as before the fight. I turned back to Hiroko and Iseult, who was the only person still seated, opposite us, while everyone began to gossip and speculate. I forced the feelings of others away from mine, closing myself off.

'Do you think he'll expel them?' Iseult asked.

'No,' I responded immediately, thinking of the time Qasim had dragged me to Renatus's office for a much worse crime, unknowingly setting me on the path that would lead to Renatus's selection of me as his student. He hadn't expelled me; to expel Kendra and Sophia would be unfair.

Khalida Jasti, a resident mean-girl from my scrying class who had been one of the driving forces behind the rumours and lies that had turned the student population at the Academy against me, pushed through the crowd.

'Aristea,' she called, her voice one of wonder. Her gorgeous cronies, Bella and Suki, were not far behind, hopeful expressions lighting their model-pretty faces. 'Why didn't you tell us you were gay?'

I stared at her while everyone stared at me.

'You can't have it both ways, Khalida,' I responded coldly. 'I can't be gay *and* screwing Renatus, or else I'm not only violating the natural laws of magic, I'm also damn confused.'

She stopped suddenly. She and her girlfriends had been so jealous of the time I spent with my master before my initiation was announced that they'd happily helped Xanthe's rumour-spreading. I had no love for them, and no patience left to manage them today. I was so sick of this, and felt grateful to Sophia then for breaking Xanthe's nose, because it was by Xanthe's design that the student body was so insensitive to my privacy.

'But if you *are*, you could have just said so, ages ago,' Khalida said, apparently not privy to how tactless and insensitive she sounded. Why were we having this conversation? Did she think we were friends, after all she'd done to me? 'You-'

'Get out of it, Khalida,' Addison snapped as he approached us. 'Wouldn't be your business either way. Renatus doesn't want to invite you to bed, and neither does Aristea. Is that what you want to hear?' Khalida had no response except to look very hurt and sour. I turned away from her, feeling very satisfied and wishing I could have thought of that comeback. Addison looked me over quickly. 'You alright?'

I could have laughed. Was *I* alright? I wasn't the main victim of Xanthe's nastiness this time, nor was I the one sporting a broken nose. Was I alright?

No. Not even close.

'I'll be fine,' I said, and it rang true, no flicker of deceit, because eventually I *would* be. He nodded, running a hand through his spiky black hair, and went back to his seat, passing Sterling on his way.

'Your friend's a mega bitch,' he commented mildly, perhaps unfairly because Sterling hadn't done anything to encourage or inflame the attack. 'Get her to check her calendar tonight. It's the twenty-*first* century.'

Poor Sterling just sat back down where she'd started and stared at her lonely game of checkers. Not alright, either.

Join the club, sweetie.

'I have to go,' I said to Hiroko and Iseult, already jogging out of the dining room. They had to be used to my erratic behaviour by now, because neither one tried to call me back. I reached for Renatus and felt his familiar energy signature on the staircase with Sophia, so I hurried in his direction. I found them most of the way up.

'Renatus,' I called as soon as I could see them. They both stopped and looked down the well of the stairs. I kept going, trying to catch up. 'Wait. We need to talk.'

'Not now, Aristea,' he said, turning and continuing up the stairs. Sophia followed him slowly, still looking down at me. Worried. 'I'll see you after I've spoken to-'

'This can't wait,' I insisted, opposite them now, two flights down, looking up. 'It's important. Please.'

'Aristea,' he sighed, still ascending even as I ran along the next landing. *Not now.*

'Renatus,' I repeated, jumping over two steps at a time to catch up and grab his arm. He stopped. I opened my mouth – I had a million things to say, but most weren't allowed – and closed it again. I *wanted* to share Susannah's words to Lisandro with him. I *wanted* to promise that I didn't believe her, that I *knew* he'd never turn, not now that I knew him properly, whatever all the previous Dark Keepers had done. I *wanted* to talk about my brother and sister, and the parts they'd never been able to play in the grand tapestry of our relationship. I *wanted* to discuss the whole situation in depth and at length. But it was all off-limits, not even to be thought about in case he overheard, in case he tried to change his own fate.

'Can you go on ahead, Sophia?' he asked the other girl when I didn't speak, starting down the stairs now with me in tow. 'I'll be there in only a minute.'

She nodded and, with a last cryptic look at me, hurried up the stairs to leave us well alone. We both listened to her receding footsteps. Renatus kept going down, trying to put more distance between us and her. I swallowed, uncertainty strangling me. Maybe if I told him, and told him not to try to change anything, maybe then it would be alright. If he understood the importance of letting Fate take its course, surely he wouldn't do anything to jeopardise it. It was better to be informed, surely.

'I mean it,' he said as we crossed the landing. 'One minute.'

'One minute,' I agreed, pulling him to a stop. He turned to stare at me, casting a silencing ward that kept our voices between us. 'That's all I need.'

'What for?'

What for? His question rebounded through my head. What for? To tell him everything, and to make him swear not

181

to change anything? When even my telling him was the beginning of changes? Susannah, damn her, she was right – if he knew what was coming, things would be different, whether he or I intended it or not. He'd think about it, make choices based on it that he might have made differently before. He'd spend the coming months or years before the actual deed expecting it. How severely could that warp a good soul? I couldn't risk anything that would allow Susannah to be right. I couldn't tell him anything, no matter how much I wanted to, so waiting in the stairwell while I stewed on it was hugely useless.

I'd made the mistake of thinking in questions, and Renatus frowned when he noticed my internal conflict. I felt him reach for my thoughts; I tucked them away quickly, trying to think of nothing at all.

'Never mind,' I mumbled, letting him go and starting forward. There was no safe territory, nothing I could say that totally skirted all the topics I wasn't allowed to broach. If I kept going I was going to pierce that wall inside me and let all those emotions out. I was going to cry. Best to shut up. 'The girls are waiting-'

'Aristea, what's wrong?' Renatus asked, concern darkening his tone. 'What are you hiding from me?'

'It's just everything,' I claimed, trying a small smile over my shoulder to reassure him. He didn't buy it. I tried harder. 'You know, Lisandro, everything.'

He shook his head. I kept walking, wishing I'd not been so rash, wishing I'd stayed away until I'd thought this through properly...

I couldn't tell him. It could ruin him. *I* couldn't be responsible for that. He thought of me as family.

'That's not it,' he said. He followed after me. His mind probed at mine; his was stronger. 'That's not why you *ran* after me, wanting to talk, after avoiding me all day.'

He knew, he knew I was keeping a secret – how was I meant to keep it from him now? I couldn't lie, I couldn't tell the truth... He closed the gap on me and grabbed my wrist.

'The whole school thinks Sophia and I are together,' came tumbling from my mouth, and I felt Renatus drop his hand and withdraw suddenly and completely from my mind. Completely. 'When she healed my hand it looked like we were kissing, but we weren't. That's what Xanthe thinks happened.'

He stared at me, looking both stunned with my outburst and also a bit disturbed.

'You... You don't need to tell me that,' Renatus said after a very long moment of silence, sounding more awkward than I'd ever known him to be. He paused a little longer, then shook his head once and continued on his way *up* the stairs. I could feel the effects of his discomfort following him. I myself felt like melting into the floor. Talking about kissing with my master was kind of like discussing it with my dad or my brother. I hadn't meant to bring that up, but at least it had diverted Renatus from learning of Fate's plan for him.

Renatus was a whole flight away now, stoically ignoring my gaze and wondering why I'd wanted so badly to tell him something so irrelevant. I sighed; I knew he had something important to do but there were also important things to say.

'Are you coming or not?' he called back without looking.

'I wasn't involved,' I said, following, making no real attempt to catch up. 'But there's something else I'm going to say that you don't want to talk about.' I gave him a moment to respond; he ignored me except to maybe walk a little faster. 'I've been thinking about the stranger.'

'Sophia and a stranger now? Maybe next time you should ask for a name.'

I stopped, stung.

'I'm talking about *your* stranger, smartarse.'

Renatus stopped too; I'd never spoken to him like that. I never spoke to *anyone* like that. His surprise radiated from him, but more unsettling was the fact that his surprise registered on his face. I'd dislodged the mask. Instinct told me to fill the silence before he could react.

'The stranger in the storm,' I said quietly. His expression darkened and he looked around for eavesdroppers, but his ward was still in place. Our words were private. 'If he didn't do it, what was he doing here? I know you've been thinking about it.'

For a moment, though his face kept its look, I could see emotions chasing one another behind Renatus's eyes. Then I felt him let it all go; the mask came back.

'What's done is done.'

'You don't need to feel guilty.'

'You don't need to worry about me,' he countered. 'It wasn't your problem to be thinking about in the first place.'

'It *is* my problem,' I insisted. 'He's the only difference between our stories. If he didn't do anything, how does he fit into the puzzle?' I paused, and then couldn't help adding, coming closer, 'Who was he?'

'I wouldn't know the first place to start in finding out who he was.' Renatus looked away. 'I don't want to know. Especially now.'

*Now that I know he was innocent, and I killed him anyway.*

'No,' I said forcefully, moving up the steps to meet him, to regain eye contact, 'he wasn't innocent, and you aren't guilty-'

'I killed a man,' Renatus hissed, leaning close to me to keep the words between us, as if anyone else could overhear. 'I'm as guilty as they come, whatever Qasim told the council.'

'He knows,' I reminded him softly, thinking back to words exchanged at the circle, annoyed that the Scrier had worked it out before I had. 'He hasn't acted on it. He hasn't declared you dangerous or terrible.' *He doesn't think you're guilty.*

'Well, he can hardly do that now,' Renatus responded. 'Backtracking never looks good, and admitting he knew makes him an accessory. He'd be charged, too.' *You have no clue what he thinks.*

'You were a kid – it doesn't count, no matter whether he was good or bad,' I retorted, very quietly. 'You weren't far off the age I am now.'

'Do you know right from wrong, Aristea?'

'Of course I do.'

'Then it counts.' He left the silence hanging, my argument shot down, and turned away, frustrated. His guilt and self-loathing bubbled away. For a moment it threatened to engulf me, even as I barricaded myself emotionally, until he pulled his reaction into check. I was grateful. My resilience was running low. He said, softly, 'It won't change anything to know who it was, you know.'

*It won't change anything.* How could he know that? He had no idea what his future held – he probably suspected he'd be Lisandro's killer, because it was what he'd been hired for, but he didn't know what Susannah had Seen. He didn't know what she said he was to become. I was his apprentice. I was part of him. I was his responsibility but so was he mine. I'd promised Lord Gawain I'd look after him. How could I possibly keep that promise if I couldn't share with him what I'd learned of his Fate and help him avoid it? Lord Gawain had done so much to prevent this very thing...

'No, it won't make a difference to me,' I agreed, then amended, 'It *doesn't* make a difference to me. But it might make a difference to the investigation. Anyway, I didn't want to argue with you. I just wanted to tell you that...' All the things I wasn't allowed to mention raced through my mind, from one lockbox to another. '... that I don't care what you've done, or what you'll do, or what awful things were done by other people to bring us here. It doesn't change anything.'

'That's good,' Renatus said, nodding at my arm, my mark to match his, 'because it's a little late to change your mind now.'

There was no changing my mind. Worries and ideas that had been floating, disjointed, around my head all week suddenly clicked together, problem with solution. Instantly, everything was clear.

'And backtracking never looks good,' I reminded him. I couldn't tell him what was coming; I couldn't let him change it. Nothing he did would divert the path anyway. But *I* knew what was coming, and no one had said *I* couldn't make a difference. I didn't know what decisions I was currently fated to make that would help lead Renatus astray but I only had to make one to make all the difference.

I would be the one to kill Lisandro.

I wasn't good enough yet, but I was Renatus's apprentice. I could only get better. I would only get stronger. And while Susannah had said *Renatus* must be the killer, she'd alluded to some sort of escape clause with her "or... ". I felt with certainty that I was that "or... ".

Renatus couldn't hear my thoughts. His eyes darted to the space around me, my aura, which was surely smoothing over for the first time since I'd met his godfather – who I'd just decided I would murder. Making one's mind up after a period of upset and uncertainty has a calming, settling effect on one's energy field. I experienced a grim peace with my resolve, too tired to really appreciate the reality of what I planned to do. For now, it made me feel better.

It was extreme but it might save Renatus. He would do the same for me, given the same information.

'Do you want to find out who the stranger was?' he asked finally, reaching for my hand and taking the scrunched napkin, stained with smears of blood. He twisted it between his fingers; it was gone. His abilities with magic were amazing. Slowly, day by day, I was accumulating those same abilities. One day, years from now, I would be almost as good at it as he was.

'I think we should.' Because then he'd see that the stranger deserved what he got, and he'd maybe let that demon go. Maybe we could free them all... *Maybe this will save you*, I thought, but didn't share with him.

'Alright. We'll look into it. Later.'

'Alright, good.'

Renatus never smiled, or at least, I'd never seen him smile, but when he was meant to be smiling, his eyes would do it for him, softening slightly. He did that now, pleased to see me settled, thinking it was because we were on the same page and we'd talked through our different opinions to come out the other side stronger. Part of it was, but not solely.

He couldn't know any more than that until after the deed was done.

# chapter twelve

Anouk kept her eyes on Renatus's the whole time he spoke, though he didn't glance at her even once. He was extremely skilled at keeping his mind quiet and blocked off, which was very annoying as Anouk sought to pry into his thoughts to see what he was hiding.

The revelations of the previous night's circle were still filtering through her disbelief system, not yet ready to be added to the data banks that made up her "established fact" cortex. Lisandro, a murderer of whole families? Susannah, partly responsible? She'd found it difficult to sleep after the hyper-stimulating effects of the initiation and the impossible knowledge that had come with it.

After the dramatic exit of Susannah and the White Elm's most controversial duo, Lord Gawain had gone to check in on their conversation. But Telepaths like Anouk, Glen and Jadon hadn't needed his report when he came back alone. Renatus and Aristea's shocked reactions had rolled off them in reckless questions, subconsciously bypassing any wards they might have been wearing, giving Anouk access to the trail of their thoughts.

Aristea's were the typical self-centred thoughts of a traumatised child getting more bad news. Anger, denial, blame, etc. Renatus's thoughts were only open for a moment, just that moment of surprise that *Susannah*, saint of the council, had screwed up so royally, and in that moment,

Anouk had latched on to his wandering thoughts, read the anger, read the resentment, read the *guilt-*

Then had been shut out.

The young Dark Keeper had always been a driven, tortured soul – this had not changed, but seemed more evident since their confrontation with Lisandro earlier in the week. Now it seemed it could be explained by this news, but Anouk was dogged by a feeling that there was more. Aristea's aura was a terrible mess. Everyone on the council must have noticed how scattered and cracked her energy suddenly appeared as she struggled internally to come to terms with something new and disturbing. *His* energy was subdued, still, and pulled in close to him, dense like a layer of armour. No cracks. His thoughts were, mostly, deathly quiet. Something had focused him, aged him. The guilt. What did he have to feel guilty about in regard to what Lisandro had done to his family?

In this one instance, even Anouk, who was by no means a fan of his, had to admit he was truly the innocent victim Lord Gawain made him out to be.

'I think the three of you have some deep thinking to do,' Renatus said, clearly coming to the end of his lecture. Sitting silently in front of his desk were the three girls involved in this morning's tussle, including the Prescott sisters, who were Anouk's only remaining students at the Academy. The twins' chairs were close together and their hands were clasped between them for comfort. Xanthe's chin and cheeks were streaked with blood and tears but Emmanuelle had healed her broken nose and stemmed the bleeding. 'And to facilitate this thinking process, I am issuing you each with detention. Xanthe, you need to learn to think more before you speak. Each night for the next two weeks, you will spend one hour assisting my staff in the cleaning and maintenance of the house. Do you see this as fitting, Emmanuelle?'

'*Oui, absolument,*' the younger sorceress standing beside Anouk agreed firmly when her student glanced back at her nervously. 'This is not the first time your words 'ave gotten you into trouble with your friends. If it 'appens again the punishment will be much more severe.'

'You'll report to this office at eight tonight,' Renatus told Xanthe, and she nodded vehemently.

'Yes, sir,' she promised.

'Good. You may go.'

The seventeen-year-old stood and pushed her chair in. She deliberately avoided looking at the twins' faces but her gaze drifted naturally over their laps as she turned away. Kendra gave her a cold look and lifted her arm, clearly displaying her hand and her sister's joined together.

'What? Does this make you uncomfortable?' she asked in an acidic, challenging tone.

'Kendra,' Qasim warned from Anouk's other side, and the students said nothing else. But both sisters kept their attention locked onto their friend of only half an hour ago until Xanthe turned on her heel and silently strode to the door, which opened for her. The door clicked shut and Kendra dropped her arm, apparently satisfied. Anouk tried not to feel a sense of pride in her girls. Attitudes like Xanthe's were not appropriate in their world. Or in any world, really, but they were even more outdated in the magical community than they were regarded to be within the mortal one. Renatus considered them across the desk.

'Feel better now?' he asked of Kendra, earning him a sharp look from the Scrier. The student's smug expression was replaced by a brief look of surprise, and then a small smile.

'A lot better,' she admitted.

'Now that it's out of your system, I'm sure I can trust you both to stay clear of Xanthe in future,' Renatus said, reaching for one of the neatly arranged fountain pens in the left corner of his desk and etching a quick note. 'My gardener, Emily, comes on Saturdays. You'll spend five hours next Saturday and five the week after as her assistant, Kendra, to channel some of that physical energy into something useful. The equivalent of two weeks' detentions. Anouk?'

'Sounds fair,' she said, although she overheard Qasim closing off his thoughts in response and recalled that Aristea, the first student to receive a detention at the Academy, had been issued three weeks just for speaking disrespectfully to Qasim. These girls had hit and scratched and verbally abused one another and were only getting two weeks?

*They've got actual duties, though,* Glen said reasonably, commenting on her thoughts as he often did from far away. *Aristea's time was longer but she spent her detentions sitting in his office doing nothing.*

*Nothing other than, apparently, bonding with the headmaster,* Anouk noted cynically, as was her role in their telepathic friendship.

'And Sophia, I can't ignore that you broke another student's nose, so you will be spending up to four weeks as Fionnuala's assistant in the kitchens,' Renatus finished. 'She may want help with dishes after meals, or she may like for you to take part in preparing meals. She'll oversee your detentions and she'll decide when you've learnt your lesson. Report to her now; your duties start today. You can both go.'

'Cocky,' Qasim commented when they were gone, levelling a cool look at Renatus. 'Aristea's friends. Are we surprised?'

Renatus shrugged as though he had no idea, when in fact he enjoyed complete access to his apprentice's every thought, memory and emotion if he bothered to look.

Anouk and Emmanuelle shared a discreet glance. They didn't need to share thoughts to know they were thinking the same thing. Aristea and the Prescotts hadn't been near each other in weeks, since the last fight to break out over breakfast here. Also, Anouk recalled, involving and possibly instigated by Xanthe Giannopoulos. Why the twins would side against Aristea in that original argument and now apparently change their minds was beyond Anouk's comprehension. She only had to teach and supervise teenagers – understanding one was Renatus's problem.

'Thank you both for being here so quickly,' the Dark Keeper said, putting his pen back carefully and sparing a brief glance for both Anouk and Emmanuelle. 'I'll write it up for the council records if you like?'

His question was for Anouk, who managed the White Elm's vault of records. Technically, she shared the job with the council's Scribe, but that job was almost as ill-fated these days as Dark Keeper. For years she'd worked with Jackson, though not particularly well after his mysterious injury. When he was replaced by Aubrey, she'd struggled to share the load with him, even though he was much more eager and helpful than Jackson ever was. No wonder, though – he was trying to gain access to the vault for his own amoral reasons. Now she was meant to work side by side with Oneida. It was going to take some getting used to, and a good deal of trust, but Glen, a constant voice in her head, insisted it would be a smooth transition.

*She's just like you. Another independent. You'll have so much in common and you'll get along so well, I'll probably feel left out.*

Doubtful, but he was always the more optimistic of the pair.

'Yes, please,' Anouk answered him. She had a box dedicated to the Academy with enrolment forms, contact details, ongoing anecdotal reports of student progress for the future. Their students were the best and brightest of the whole White Elm nation. Some would go on to be councillors; some would be heroes in other ways, miracle workers. Some might go wrong. Like Lisandro. Like Jackson. Like Aubrey. And if they did, it was better to have a record of where it started, even if that was in a catty girl fight in the Morrissey family's dining room. 'Seems early to be asking that of Oneida.'

'I agree,' Renatus said, and started arranging a legal pad ready to start the incident report. Anouk noted the way he happily leapt onto the excuse to distract himself from his thoughts and she tried again to get into them.

'How is Aristea this morning?' Emmanuelle asked, concerned for the girl. Qasim, too, looked to the younger scrier for the response.

'Much better,' Renatus replied. 'We just spoke.'

Emmanuelle gave him a condescending look that he ignored, keeping his attention on his notes.

'She is far from alright,' the Healer warned, 'and a word with you makes everything *much better*?'

Renatus paused his writing and looked up at her, annoyed. 'Why is that so hard to believe?'

'Susannah got 'er family killed,' the French witch said boldly. 'She only learned less than a week ago that 'er family was murdered. Yours, too. She 'as not dealt with any of this properly. This is not 'ealthy.'

'Thank you for your assessment, Dr Saint Clair,' Renatus said, more heatedly than Anouk thought was necessary. 'If you already knew that, why did you have to ask?'

'Susannah didn't do anything the rest of us probably wouldn't have done in her stead,' Qasim corrected diplomatically, but that only irritated Renatus and Emmanuelle more, albeit managed to dissolve their tension.

'Don't cover for 'er,' Em argued, while Renatus pointed his pen at the Scrier and said, 'None of us in this room would have done what she did, *you* least of all. Betray your own code? I doubt I'll see the day.'

'Maybe you already have.' Qasim went to the door, thoughts all closed down, inaccessible to Anouk and her curiosity. What did *that* mean? 'Let me out of this office.'

Renatus acquiesced. The door swung open. The Scrier left. The Healer stood her ground, and Anouk, the Historian, hesitated.

'Aristea,' Emmanuelle prompted, waiting for a more detailed response from the girl's master. Renatus made a visible effort to be patient.

'Will be fine,' he promised. 'I don't think she slept. Her energy was even more wired this morning. But we've talked.

We've got a plan to concentrate her attention on something productive.'

'And yours,' Emmanuelle noted. 'You 'ave a lot on your mind, too.'

'What's the plan?' Anouk asked, when Renatus shrugged, dismissing Emmanuelle's concerns for him. He went back to his notes.

'It involves you, actually.' He finished the page with a signature and she saw he wasn't writing up the incident report at all. He tore off the front page and held it up for Anouk. She stepped closer and took it. 'An official request for Archived materials.'

'Missing persons reports,' Emmanuelle read over her shoulder. 'What for?'

'Lisandro's conscripts,' Renatus answered, *now* starting on the incident report. 'They're very loyal, willing to die for him. He's been collecting for a long time.'

'Interesting choice of time period,' Anouk commented slyly, and felt a tiny touch of satisfaction to see Renatus's pen slow on the page. Just a second, then he carried on, smooth and unruffled.

*Don't be spiteful*, Glen warned. She ignored him.

'It's a starting point,' Renatus said, giving nothing away. He looked up at her, eye contact made, a distinct challenge, mind utterly blocked. Anouk checked her own defences. She was a Telepath and knew a lot of Telepaths, but had never known anyone like Renatus – a non-Telepath with a gift for it so strong he surpassed a lot of natural Telepaths in ability. He could hear through some types of wards, listen through touch, tap into the mind with eye contact: all abilities usually restricted to the naturals only. He was an anomaly of the highest degree, and it was one of the many reasons Anouk didn't trust him.

'What exactly do you expect to find in files this old? We don't have any names to work with, no identifying information,' she brought up. He still regarded her, and it was a moment in which Anouk was reminded that he probably didn't like her any more than she liked him.

'*We* don't,' he agreed, implying the council. Anouk narrowed her eyes, disliking the situation even more.

'But *you* do.'

'If we find anything from it we'll report it to the circle,' he said finally, a cold shoulder. He went back to his notes. 'One of the beauties of my job is not needing to divulge my sources to anyone below me—'

'*Taisez-vous*,' Emmanuelle cut in. 'Aristea isn't the only one not sleeping. You're being childish.'

Renatus looked like he wanted to bite back but chose not to. Their friendship was something very strange, and something else Anouk chose not to try to understand. He inhaled slowly.

'I apologise,' he said after a moment, not meaning a word of it but at least making the effort to say the words, which was more than usual. 'Stress.' He struggled for a change of topic and tone. 'How are the proceedings in Valero?'

Anouk had been summoned here from her native Russia to be present for Kendra and Sophia, but wasn't interested in playing punching bag for Renatus's mood swings and Emmanuelle's attempts to retrain him in appropriate human interaction. She took one of his fountain pens from the tidy arrangement, careful to knock a few with her fingers, and signed the note he'd given her.

'You'll hear all about it in the next circle,' she said coolly, dropping his pen and his note on top of what he was working on before turning and walking away. 'Your application is approved.'

Renatus surprised her with her name, but she kept walking, knowing the difference between spoken and mental dialogue, listening with her mind instead.

*Anouk,* he said again, sending her the mental message without opening his thoughts, giving her no access whatsoever. *Give it up. You really don't want to know what I'm acting on. Trust me.*

She pushed through the door as it opened for her and left, pondering his words. *Give it up.* He knew she was prying. So what? Of course she was prying. He was keeping a secret. *You really don't want to know what I'm acting on.* Did he mean that the information only served to complicate matters and that she would find her job easier to fulfil if she didn't know? *Trust me.* There it was. The hard part.

Renatus was not Anouk's favourite person. She'd long been convinced that he could only be bad, that he could only grow to embrace the same darkness that had always distinguished his family from other sorcerers. The rest of the council had once believed the same, but seemed to have changed their tune this week. It would take Anouk longer than a week to accept that Renatus could really be everything Lord Gawain had always insisted.

*Dear Anouk,* Glen said affectionately. *So consistent.*

Valero, her home town, was her favourite place in the world. When she arrived on the outskirts of her hidden city five minutes later, she took a moment to admire it. Before her, for kilometres, lay a stretch of barren, rocky and deserted land, cold and desolate. It was the most beautiful façade she knew of any city. She walked for several minutes until she felt the air pressure change, the air gripping to her arms and face like spider webs. The air shimmered and the illusion of uninhabited land dissolved into the true image of Valero. All around her, magic crackled as tiny little alerts were sent to the keepers of the city, letting them know that someone had entered the perimeter.

Valero was a fortress. The illusion and the alert system were only a first defence. Spell casters and archers posted atop the high stone walls had an enviable view of the surrounding wilderness and any approaching individuals, and had control of a massive iron gate that could be lowered at a moment's notice. Thousands of wards protected every square centimetre of the city's walls, but supposing that anyone managed to defy all of these, the city was also filled with angry homebody Russian sorcerers, all trained to protect themselves and all prepared to fight for their way of life.

It was a way of life that sometimes needed to be fought for, Anouk reflected. Valero was one of several all-magical colonies around the world, like Oneida's, though hers was totally disconnected from the modern world, both mortal and magical. Electricity, telecommunications and even plastic were shunned by the Valeroans. They lived exactly as they had for the past five or six centuries, rarely even leaving their home unless they were a special case, like Anouk.

Unlike some such colonies, Valero had very tight ties with the White Elm, tightened in the most recent decade by the council's acceptance of Anouk (both the town's favourite daughter and a traitor at the same time, depending on who was asked for an opinion of her). The city had for many years complied with "The Valero Agreement", serving as the White Elm's imprisonment facility in exchange for protection and exemptions from various constitutional amendments that disadvantaged their medieval way of life. She couldn't see it from here, over those towering walls, but she could imagine the city prison, rising from the centre of the city, several storeys above everything else. Surrounded by another wall of stone (topped with looped, barbed wire) and guarded by Valero's best men and every relevant spell known, the prison was originally built to contain captured soldiers of whichever nearby magical settlement they'd been warring with at the time. Time had passed, and those enemy settlements had either moved on, been destroyed or been amalgamated with Valero itself, and so now the prison held only the occasional delirious idealist who thought he might try to attack the city's outer defences, and the White Elm's convicted criminals. Nobody had ever broken out – but one *had* broken in, just the other week, and killed an inmate. The townspeople were only starting to get over the shock that their impenetrable city and impregnable prison had been breached.

The archers gave Anouk a salute and a wave as the gate was dragged up and open, and she entered her home city. By modern standards, she knew, it was not a pretty place. It was colourless and cold, the architecture bland and primitive. There were no windows. The hardened dirt roads had never been paved. The city smells were less than pleasant unless you were standing inside a bakery first thing in the morning.

But it was the sense of order, diligent activity and tight community that Anouk felt most keenly as she moved through the closed-in streets. The relaxed, pointless holiday atmosphere of some other major cities was not to be found. Every person bustling about had a purpose. The farms at the back section of the city would not take care of themselves. The sick didn't become well by themselves. And the city keepers didn't stop planning and conferring.

She went straight back to the city hall, where she'd been before Sophia Prescott had broken Xanthe Giannopoulos's nose and Qasim had called her to Ireland. She'd pretended to be annoyed to be called away, but really, it had been a relief to get away for half an hour and clear her head, even if only to go forth and be further irritated by Renatus.

This reaction was not to be mistaken with any dislike of the proceedings, her part in them or the other town keepers. She loved her city, its leaders and its policies, and she absolutely loved the honour of being included as she was. In her unique role as both a Valeroan citizen and a White Elm councillor, Anouk held the powerful position of playing the mouthpiece of each group, representing views and overseeing each group's interests. Despite the defences of the city, Valero's very continued existence actually depended quite heavily on the White Elm's ongoing discretion regarding their position and their boundary control. The White Elm were Valero's customs officers, helping to keep out potentially damaging modern influences. It was in the council's interests to keep the Valeroans happy, of course, because without Valero's state-of-the-art prison and their cooperation, the White Elm would have nowhere to put its bad guys.

This was the topic of today's discussion, and Anouk could hear that the town keepers were coming to the end of the meeting. She suppressed a sigh – they'd reached the last point on the agenda, the one she'd hoped to be away for. She took her seat at the table, seamlessly re-joining the conversation.

'Apologies for my short absence,' she said in Russian. 'Are we almost finished?'

'We must only discuss our plans for Lisandro and for Aubrey, when they are caught, and then we will be finished,' Grigoriy, one of the older keepers, told her. Anouk nodded, her stomach sinking. This would not be fun. 'Demyan suggested moving old Jaska into lower security and using his cell for Lisandro.'

'Jaska is hardly a threat anymore,' Demyan added. 'It isn't as though he's going anywhere, regardless of which cell he's in. He's had his day as our biggest problem; these days, I wonder if he even knows where he is.'

'It's the most secure by way of magic, for sure, but I'd prefer Lisandro imprisoned at the top of the building, so he'd have the hardest time getting out.' Lev laid his scarred hands on the table. 'The more of us he has to pass, the less likely an escape, and the better I'd feel.'

'Underground has always been best for his type,' another city keeper commented darkly. 'Lock them up tight; no light; no noise; no contact…'

Anouk made herself nod. The White Elm usually chose to overlook Valero's strong collective sense of justice and its various manifestations. In the modern world, magical and mortal, these measures were seen as grotesque, inhumane, medieval…

*Those measures* are *grotesque, inhumane, medieval,* Glen couldn't help mentioning passively.

Here, well… It was just how it worked.

'Those are all good suggestions,' Anouk said now, knowing she would need to tread very carefully for the remainder of this conversation. 'Jaska is most certainly less concerning today than he was a decade ago. If it weren't for the severity of his crimes, I would even go so far as to say he is no longer a threat to society. That said, of course,' she amended, before anyone could become offended, 'Jaska was ruled guilty of his crimes by both our courts and the White Elm,' (who'd had to intervene in order to save the paranoid would-be terrorist from being publicly stoned to death without a trial) 'and I agree that he is exactly where he deserves to be. I'm told he's settled down since moving into his current cell. I wouldn't want to create problems for the jailors by moving and upsetting him.'

'It's the strongest and most cursed cell in the prison,' Demyan argued. 'Lisandro is a bigger problem.'

'As I'm sure I've mentioned before, informally, the White Elm is uncertain whether it will be invoking the Valero Agreement in the case of Lisandro,' Anouk told the table of silent city keepers. 'He is highly dangerous and prone to explosive acts of aggression towards our councillors. It is likely that, in the event we are able to overpower him, he will be killed. Apprehension seems implausible.'

There was a low rumble of unhappy mutterings about the table as the men and one other woman sitting at it absorbed this news, some for the second or third time. They must have all known, really. Lisandro was the most powerful enemy anyone at the table could ever recall worrying about. How could they have expected he would end up here? Alive, at that?

Demyan glanced up at her and she quickly looked away, berating herself for being stupid enough to wonder. Thinking in questions, wondering, is like an invitation to Telepaths to read your thoughts. It essentially broadcasts your thought to anyone nearby listening, searching for someone to answer you.

*He sent his spies to infiltrate our city*, Demyan reminded her. *Doesn't that anger you?*

*Of course it does. But being angry doesn't change anything. The fact remains that Lisandro will never come in quietly and to even kill him could cost the White Elm several lives.*

*Perhaps.* Demyan folded his arms. *If we cannot have Lisandro, we'd best get the other one.*

The table quietened and Grigoriy sat forward in his seat.

'I suppose we can understand the White Elm's dilemma,' he gave in, begrudgingly. 'Lisandro is a great threat and to wish for a simple and bloodless ending to him would be unrealistic.' He paused. 'What of the other?'

Anouk said nothing.

'The infiltrator, who caught both Valero and the White Elm with their eyes closed,' Lev filled in. 'Aubrey.'

Aubrey. Indeed, what of him? A week ago he'd been Anouk's missing little brother, with whom she shared the sanctity of the White Elm's Archives. She'd been so prepared to move earth and stone to find him, whatever it took to save him and bring him back safely. Now… now she felt like a fool, just as the rest of the council did. He'd never deserved her loyalty. He was a liar, a traitor, a murderer. There was no forgiving his transgressions and no forgetting the embarrassment of letting him into her life and council.

'The council is undecided,' she said finally, which was true, because they hadn't yet formally discussed how they should proceed with dealings with Aubrey. He'd disconnected himself from the council, saving them the bother, and they'd barred him from re-entering Morrissey Estate, but nobody had been brave enough to ask what should be done if they came into contact with him. He'd actually approached Jadon, who had said later that it hadn't occurred to him to capture or strike Aubrey down. Even Renatus hadn't killed him when he'd had his chance.

Yet another reason to wonder whether to trust the last Morrissey.

'On what?' Lev asked sharply. Anouk resented him briefly for making her clarify an obviously sensitive issue, but dispelled the feeling quickly. She only knew a few Empaths

201

but even normal sorcerers could sense emotional changes if they could see auras.

'On how to approach Aubrey and what to do with him if an opportunity presents itself,' Anouk explained. 'He isn't the same as Lisandro.'

'He's worse,' Demyan muttered, stirring a soft chorus of agreement around the table. Anouk shook her head, feeling tired. It was too hard sometimes to sit on this precarious fence between her two deep loyalties. 'You disagree?'

'Let us leave it here,' Anouk suggested. 'It is too early in the White Elm's investigation to make definitive judgements about Aubrey's character and crimes, and therefore his sentencing. We will keep you updated, of course.'

'Of course,' Grigoriy agreed coolly, 'but our people will still ask questions and scream for justice, Anouk, even as you promise investigations and cite proper procedure and legal nonsense. We'll need assurances. If Aubrey is apprehended,' and his tone demanded that she ensure he *was*, 'and once the White Elm has tried him for his crimes, will you see to it that he is sentenced to Valero to face our own courts?' When she just blinked, he added, 'Remembering that Valero has maintained the White Elm's confidence this week in keeping the news of our mutual issues with Aubrey from the ears of the outside colonies.'

The entire table waited silently for Anouk's response. She swallowed. This was why her privileged position was also a tight, dangerous vice, pressuring her from each side. Valero wanted to punish Aubrey themselves. They were hurt and angry. Their idea of punishment would be something the White Elm wouldn't be able to allow or overlook. Aubrey was only being charged with one murder, one they couldn't conclusively pin on him, and despite committing treason and being a terrible person, he wasn't Lisandro, slaughterer of whole families. Valero would tear him to shreds anyway, and the whole magical world would be watching, high profile as the case would quickly become. A former White Elm brother slain by the justice system of an independent colony? The council couldn't allow Valero to set a precedent like that, but also couldn't afford to lose favour with Valero, and certainly couldn't risk them releasing information about the break-in and murder to other groups out of spite. Valero's information made the prison execution look more like Renatus's crime than Aubrey's. It was in these uncomfortable moments that difficult decisions were made, out of necessity rather than for any greater benefit.

*Do what you need to do,* Lord Gawain agreed tiredly when she asked him for permission. *There aren't a lot of options.*

'I can promise, on behalf of the council,' Anouk said finally, 'that *if* Aubrey is captured alive and whole, and *after* his trial and *if* he is found guilty of murder *and* deemed unfit for mortal imprisonment, he will of course be sentenced to serve in Valero's prison.'

The men and woman sitting with her at the table shared triumphant, satisfied or eager looks. Anouk caught their thoughts and saw their imagined punishments for the traitor they all so hated. Most had never met Aubrey but had come to hate him instantly when Anouk had reported days ago that it was he who had breached their defences. Now she saw as they imagined him screaming, begging, torn open, strung up... None saw what she saw in those images – Jadon's struggle to ignore his former friend's call for help, Emmanuelle's horror at watching her cousin tortured, Lord Gawain shaking with moral indecision, Lady Miranda itching to run forth and heal the traitor's wounds. His pregnant girlfriend crying. Aubrey was a betrayer and Anouk was eternally embarrassed not to have realised, but his pain would hurt a lot more than just him.

*They have no idea,* she thought, and felt Glen's agreement.

*Anger is a powerful motivator and a heavy blindfold,* he answered, and she couldn't help but think there was a message hidden in that for her.

The meeting was adjourned and Anouk left, conflicted. She knew that her conscience would never let her hand Aubrey to her people. They were happy with her promise but she had no intention of letting the situation get that far. Aubrey would never have a trial. He would never be found guilty or assessed for appropriate sentencing.

He would have to be killed in any attempt to take him in.

# chapter thirteen

I was going to kill Lisandro. It was such a huge pronouncement to make, even privately, but the reality of it, the immensity of it, hadn't really sunk in yet, and wouldn't for a while. It was still just words. I had no plan, no real sense of what it meant to do what I had decided. All I had was a made-up mind, and that solved the most pertinent of my many problems – the risk of losing Renatus to something horrid and possibly avoidable, which was a totally unacceptable loss and not something I could bear to think about. Thoughts of him dying or falling from grace were direct channels to thoughts of my own mortality and my own brittle, still-forming identity. He was older and stronger. If he could be killed or compromised, there was no hope for me.

My insubstantial plan was an adequate antidote against dealing with that worry.

I arrived at Anouk's classroom bright and early, enthused by the thought of her ever-entertaining History class. I took my seat at the front of the room and opened my book. I carefully wrote the day's date in the margin; got it wrong, crossed it out, tried again. I *was* tired. I looked up when Anouk stepped into the room, awkwardly balancing a pile of cardboard boxes in her arms while she tried to hold open the door. I got up and ran over to help.

'Thanks,' she said, purring Russian accent beautiful as always, as she slid the top two boxes to me. They had handholds built into the sides and were sturdy, lidded. They looked like the sort of non-descript file storage boxes used in police dramas. I didn't suppose the boxes themselves had seen a lot of drama, but the information within might hint at a lot.

'It's okay,' I said, following her to her own desk and placing them down. She glanced at me, apparently realising for the first time who had helped her, but I was eyeing the boxes still. They were dusty, as though they'd been sitting in storage for a long time, and had labels written in striking Russian alphabet. I had no hope of reading them but I looked at the dirtiest one.

Пропавшие без вести лица 1996

'You look much better,' Anouk commented smoothly, eyes gliding over the air around me. 'Renatus said the pair of you talked things over this morning.'

Something about her casual tone caught my attention and I met her eyes. They were a pretty hazel-green, similar to mine in colour, I noticed for the first time, but unlike mine, clear and well-rested. She still looked as we all felt after the initiation.

'That's right,' I agreed, a little guarded. Anouk was a Telepath, a listener of thoughts. I ran my attention along the inner wall of the wards around my mind, checking for gaps. None. I was solid. 'It's a lot to take in.'

'Mm. That circle took us all by surprise but I don't think any of us can fully appreciate how it affected you. Still, you seem to be managing extraordinarily well.' She regarded me a while, eyes boring into mine, mesmerising; then she gave me a reprieve, broke eye contact and tapped the pile of mystery boxes. 'These are for you. Take them to Renatus after your lesson, will you?'

She pushed the boxes towards me. Surprised, I picked up the ones I'd carried in.

'What are they?' I asked.

'Confidential,' she answered unhelpfully. She helped me stack them beside the desk in the front row I would work at so no one else would go through them.

'Is that what it says on the labels?'

'Don't you read Russian?'

I placed the last box on the top of the pile and turned to look up at her. Seriously? But she was hinting at a smile, and I saw behind it a hint of her sense of humour.

'Nobody else on the council does,' she relented. The door opened and a few students made their way inside, greeting Anouk as they went to their seats. To me, Anouk continued, 'All files submitted to the Archives must be in English, as was the original White Elm and hence it is the official language; but when labels peel off and I write new ones, I often forget. Whoever will inherit the Archives after me will need to extensively relabel, if they are not Russian.'

She went back to the front of the room to prepare for her lesson. I gazed down at the boxes beside my leg. I longed to open them and satisfy my curiosity – files from the White Elm's Archives! – but she hadn't wanted to discuss it, and I didn't think it would be proper to go through the contents in front of other students, who were casting interested looks at my collection. When everyone was seated Anouk introduced the day's topic as duelling laws and launched into an elaborately detailed story about life in the sixteenth century. Once she began talking, accent rich and riveting, I found it easy to ignore the temptation of the files, engaged as I always was by her passionate storytelling and insightful understanding of our people's history. I guess a decade in the White Elm's vault of histories would give you that understanding, as would a childhood spent outside of the majority nation, learning about it in an academic sense instead of passively living it like I had.

'Agnes Bristol seems to have been the first to describe disorientation and illusion used in duelling in her account from 1598,' Anouk said, turning to sketch this fact quickly onto the blackboard. 'I'm sure she had no idea what to think

207

when she saw her son use these spells against the unnamed neighbour. Before this time there are only accounts of expressly offensive and defensive magic used in duels, across documented magical forms, of course,' she stressed to add. 'To apply trickery in this way was unheard of but certainly a turning point in the development of duelling, possibly even a positive one – Robert Bristol the Second overcame the neighbour's offences almost immediately with only minimal injury to either of them.'

She turned to write more, still talking, now describing some of the spells detailed in later accounts. I copied her notes, trying to write legibly, but when I reread what I'd written, something was definitely not right. I scanned again and narrowed it down to one word. I clicked my pen thoughtfully, trying to work out why the word looked wrong. *Disorintate*. I'd missed out an "e". I tried to write it in, very small, between the "i" and the "n", but it wouldn't fit. Now it just looked messy. Frustrated, I scribbled it out and rewrote the whole word above the old attempt. I was tireder than I thought.

'You can improve a dangerous practice, however, and still not make it a good practice,' Anouk said now, turning back to us. 'The application of disorientation as a battle strategy was certainly an improvement but lives were still being lost and irreparably damaged by unchecked violence in duels that were wrongfully cited as disputes of honour. Agnes Bristol's account was brought to the White Elm's attention countless times in those centuries, every man's defence, and for a disappointing number of years this was permitted.'

Something small flicked my ear. Startled, I flinched, and looked down at the little white ball of paper as it landed on my desk before me. Had someone just thrown this at me? Nervously, I extended my little finger to brush against the paper. Tiredness made the mind lax, more vulnerable and more open to impressions, such as those left on a scrunched-up paper ball.

*Kendra, sitting a few rows back, tearing the paper from a notebook...*

Anouk was still talking and writing notes on the blackboard, and I struggled to pay attention. I hurriedly wrote her last two sentences, trying to keep up. I ignored the stony, anxious feeling in my stomach. Perhaps I was wrong – perhaps Kendra hadn't thrown anything at me. After all, her own twin had healed that cut on my hand, spoken to me and even gotten into a fight for it, only hours ago. And Kendra herself had had a vision that, when shared with me by her boyfriend, had probably saved my life.

A second ball of paper missed my shoulder and tumbled to the floor beside me. I refused to look. *It's not important*, I told myself. *She's not my friend. She's not important.*

I'd misinterpreted the very public argument between Kendra and Xanthe this morning, obviously. Kendra hadn't been sticking up for me. I'd just happened to fall on the same side of the dispute as her sister, and she'd gone to battle to defend Sophia. The paper ball flicking seemed a very juvenile way to let me know that I was not back in the good books.

'So, in 1947, when Lord James wrote the draft for the new laws, it was the next Lady, Anita, who recognised the need for the prevention of duelling,' Anouk was saying. 'It was not until 1952 that this draft was finally formalised and passed as law, a precursor for a number of changes that would be made in the following years, culminating in a mass of amendments known as The Oppression in 1958...'

1952. I concentrated hard, pressing my pen a little hard against the paper in my efforts to stay focussed on what I was writing. Laws passed in 1952...

Something hit the back of my head and I felt my restraint snap. Closing my book, I stood. Anouk glanced over her bony shoulder at me.

'I need to go,' I said, by way of explanation. I didn't expect her to ask why, and she didn't. She nodded once, turning back to her quick, striking chalk script.

'Don't forget your boxes,' she said, and I opened the top lid and threw my book inside without looking. I scooped them up, noting now that the Russian lettering on the sides reflected the same hand as Anouk's board writing, despite being in totally different alphabets, just like Hiroko's English print still looked round and neat like her Japanese script.

I balanced the boxes in my arms and secured them firmly with my chin, and quickly moved towards the door. Behind me, I heard someone else shut their notebook with a snap, and I heard Kendra's voice.

'Anouk? Could I please be excused to the bathroom?'

*Oh, no.* My stomach tightened as I turned side-on to shoulder through the door. Anouk stopped writing to turn and address her student.

'Is that a good idea, Kendra?' she asked, perhaps a little sarcastically. I didn't hear the rest because I shut the door behind me and hurried down the hall. Kendra wouldn't really come after me just to confront me, would she? After all this time not talking, it was only now that she wanted to have it out with me? She and I didn't even have a quarrel with each other – my problem was with Xanthe and Sterling. We should technically be on the same side, shouldn't we?

I heard the door open and close behind me and I heard quick footsteps. *No, don't.* I tightened my hands on the lowermost of the cardboard boxes and tossed my head to get my loose hair out of my eyes. Something that didn't belong there came loose and tumbled over my shoulder, onto the top of the boxes. The paper ball.

'Aristea!'

I froze, feeling ill. I didn't want this. I stared at the paper ball, my insides twisted with the terror of confrontation. I couldn't very well run away, as much as I would have liked to. Very reluctantly, I turned to face her.

Standing very still about ten metres back was Kendra. Her glossy chestnut hair was tucked neatly behind her ears. The scratch she'd received from her fight with Xanthe was gone. I supposed that was one of the perks of having a twin with the gift of healing.

'Kendra,' I acknowledged nervously. Was she angry that Sophia had gotten in so much trouble because of me? Would she yell at me? Was she going to hit me?

'It's a note,' she said. 'You're meant to read them.'

I stared at her, and her green eyes moved to the paper ball on top of my armful of files. I tentatively lowered the boxes to the floor and picked up the ball. A note? I unfolded it and recognised her handwriting.

*I'm sorry. Please talk to us again.*

I looked back up at her, my exhausted brain slowly clicking through the possible meanings and their implications like an old slide projector. *I'm sorry. Please talk to us again.*

'You... You're sorry?' I repeated, wondering what I was meant to say to this. *That's okay.* It wasn't. She hadn't spoken to me in weeks because Xanthe had accused me of something I'd soon been proven innocent of, and which wouldn't have affected her even if I had done it. *I'm sorry, too.* I wasn't – I'd done nothing wrong. *Forget it even happened.* Would it be that easy? *Go away.* But I didn't want her to.

'We both are,' Kendra said. 'We're so sorry that we listened to Xanthe and not to you. We should have heard you out. We shouldn't have taken her word. And we should never have sat back and let her talk to you and Hiroko the way she did. I've wished a hundred times I could do that morning over and say something, but...' She trailed off, clearly struggling. I thought she would shrug and come at the apology from an easier angle, but she surprised me by keeping at it. 'But we were both cowards. I was scared of getting involved, I was scared of the rumours about you being true and looking like I'd picked the wrong side... which I had anyway. And by the time I worked that out, it felt too late to say anything. Pride, I guess,' she finished lamely.

I stared at her. I couldn't believe this was happening. I'd honestly thought we were in for a confrontation. I was ready for one this morning; I would have managed one now. At least I would have known what to say and do in that situation. In this one I was totally useless.

'Sophia was really upset after that fight,' Kendra went on, watching me, waiting for a response. 'She wanted to fix things with you and Hiroko straight away, even before your initiation proved it was all bull. I think she worked it out before I did.'

'Worked what out?' I asked finally.

'That you were telling the truth. That you'd *never...*'

'Of course I wouldn't,' I said quickly, before she could finish reciting the embarrassing rumour. 'Not just because he's practically our teacher but because Sterling was into him, and she's... She was my friend.'

'I'm really sorry I didn't believe you straightaway. Xanthe's... Ugh.' Kendra shook her head, unable to come up with anything appropriate to say. 'Sterling can have her.'

'Sterling isn't bad,' I said, surprising myself. I had no good reason to want to defend Sterling, but I still knew that she was not at fault for any of this. It was Xanthe who had put stupid ideas into people's heads and started these fights.

'Yeah, you're right,' Kendra conceded. 'She's only as spineless with Xanthe as I was.' She paused. 'Sophia said you stuck up for her when Renatus asked what happened.'

'I just told him that Xanthe had gotten what she deserved,' I said. I hesitated, the temptation to be friendly again battling with the memory of hurt. I took a chance. 'Sophia did a real number on her nose.'

Kendra smirked.

'We all got detentions,' she said. 'I'm working in the gardens on Saturdays. Sophia is helping in the kitchens. And Xanthe has to report to Renatus's office at eight to start cleaning duties. I wonder how she sold that one to Sterling.'

I couldn't help a sly smile. My time spent alone with Renatus was what Xanthe had used against me when she'd destroyed my friendships. Now, the paranoia she'd inspired in Sterling may work against her. I was glad.

'I'm sorry that it came to this – another fight, and you both in trouble,' I said. 'It doesn't seem fair.'

'I'm not,' Kendra said. 'What Xanthe said about my sister and me, in front of everybody, made me realise how stupid I've been. It was *exactly* what she did to you. And I just let her, and I let everyone get carried away with it when really, I should have known it was lies. I'm sorry it took so long for me to come around. And sorry for throwing paper balls at you. I wish there was something else I could do to fix things.'

I regarded her, wanting so badly to go back to the way things were a month ago but also scared of being cast aside again. Trust, as I was quickly learning, is a precious commodity. But if you never invest a little trust, never take that risk, you never reap the rewards.

'The paper balls were a good start,' I said eventually, 'but you could tell me how you've been.'

Kendra's face broke into a bright, genuinely relieved smile, and I felt the same relief inside. It was over. The icy silence with the twins was over, and we could go back to the way we were.

'I've been good,' Kendra began, still smiling. 'It's our eighteenth birthday tomorrow, and we got presents from our mom and dad in the mail today. I wanted to open them but Soph's making me wait until tomorrow. She's such a spoilsport.'

'It must feel like Christmas, seeing the presents just sitting there but not allowed to open them until the right time,' I mused. Kendra was already nodding in agreement.

'Exactly, minus the tree! I said, Mom won't know we opened them early, but Soph won't have it. She wants to do everything like we would if we were at home.'

It occurred to me that my own birthday was now only two months away, two months to the day actually. What would I be doing on my eighteenth birthday? Last year I'd made vague suggestions to my sister about getting dressed up and spending the night out on the town with her, but now I was pretty sure that wouldn't be happening.

'Hey, I know this is totally lame,' Kendra said, shyly, which was totally uncharacteristic of her, 'but... if you're not doing anything tomorrow, you know, do you want to come and hang out in our room while we open our presents? Pretty sure Mom sent us a whole package just of candy and snacks from home, and there's no way we can get through it all ourselves. You know,' she relented, as the classroom door opened and our classmates filed out. Apparently the lesson had finished without us. 'Unless we, like, rationed it and ate it over about a week. So not going to happen. You could come and help us eat it? I bet when I tip it all out on the bed, there will be stuff there you've never tried.'

I didn't doubt it, just as I imagined there were chocolates and treats that I'd grown up eating that weren't available in Canada.

'Kind of like a party?' I asked apprehensively. Kendra sighed.

'Yes, but without cake. So... not really a party at all. But almost. It would just be great to catch up, you know?'

'Yeah, that would be nice,' I said, amazed by how relieved I felt the more I talked with Kendra. I'd left the classroom thinking she hated me; now she was inviting me to an impromptu birthday party. 'Can Hiroko come?'

'For sure. With Xanthe and Sterling on my shit list, it's going to be a quiet affair.'

'What about Addison?' I asked, teasingly. 'Doesn't he eat Canadian goodies?'

'We broke up the other week.'

Broke up?! I froze, quickly reassessing the climate of the conversation. I'd fallen so easily into our old pattern of friendliness that I'd traipsed carelessly over new issues. Had I just ruined everything? Was the ice and silence coming back?

'I'm so sorry,' I said, feeling my expression fall in both worry for the life of the conversation but also in disappointment for Kendra and Addison. 'I didn't realise.'

'It's fine,' she said, and her confident, nonchalant wave of dismissal told me this was true. 'No harm done. In fact, "broke up" is probably too strong a term for what happened. We weren't that serious and just decided to leave it be. We're still on good terms and he understands. It's for the best.'

What "the best" was became quickly apparent, as a lad walked out of the classroom long after the rest of the students and stopped beside us.

'You left these,' he said, handing a book and pen to Kendra, and the pen I'd forgotten to me. I took mine gratefully and said thank you, but Kendra's smile was extra bright, and it was her he addressed when he added, 'I won't get a chance to get a card so I've written it in here for you.'

'Thanks, Heath,' she said, flipping the pages open to read the message. She gestured to me, ever the social degreaser. 'You know Aristea, don't you?'

'Who doesn't?' Heath remarked in a motley English accent. I wasn't sure whether he meant this in a good or bad way, but he smiled, and he had brought me my things, so I decided to give him the benefit of the doubt.

'Heath, was it?' I checked, offering my hand. He shook it and nodded.

'Heath's in Susannah's Level Three class with me,' Kendra added helpfully, finishing reading. 'Aww, that's sweet!'

She winked playfully and he grinned as he turned down the hall. Kendra turned back to me with the same sparkle in her eyes I recognised from when she'd been reeling Addison in. Heath seemed to be coming along just as willingly, and he seemed just as nice, but considering Addison had saved my life a week ago, I found myself planted deeply on Team Addison. It would take me some time to get used to. I picked up my pile of boxes – 'Delivering something from Anouk to Renatus.' – and we slowly started in the same direction the other students had gone.

'Heath's really talented,' Kendra gushed, casually taking the top box from me to reduce my load. It wasn't terribly heavy, just high and awkward. 'His whole family are Seers and he knows heaps of old techniques I'd never come across.

We've been working together in class on mapping the futures.'

I nodded as if I knew what this was. We were silent until we reached the stairs.

'On the topic of futures,' I said, 'Addison passed on your message.'

She gave me a cautious, sidelong look.

'He told me he had.'

'It was helpful. Thank you. I was... I felt like I got to make an informed choice because of what he told me.'

Kendra tightened her hands on the box she carried.

'I should have told you myself,' she apologised. 'It should have come from me, but I was a chicken and I was scared you wouldn't want to talk to me. And besides that, Seers Ethics is quite clear that if in doubt, visions should definitely not be shared. Susannah is super firm on that. But if it helped, I'm glad Addy told you.'

I cleared my throat against the build-up of incredulity that lodged there. Susannah and her morals, those *super firm* morals. I let it go.

I had to go up but I had some time, so we started down the stairs, still talking avidly, still catching up. She asked about my tattoo, marvelled over how it looked kind of like a capital A entwined with an R. We made it one level down when a movement down the next flight of stairs caught my eye. I looked over and saw Hiroko standing there with Kendra's identical twin, Sophia. Both were looking up at us nervously. From their proximity and body language I could guess that they'd just experienced the same re-bonding session Kendra and I had.

We'd been double-teamed. The twins took every challenge on together – Xanthe, for example, and they'd even worked together to win Addison over for Kendra – and now they'd done the same to Hiroko and I. To regain our trust and friendship.

'Hi,' Sophia said to me in a tiny voice. Despite her display of aggression yesterday, she really was the softer of the sisters. 'Is everything good now?'

Both Kendra and Hiroko looked at me as well and I realised that *I* was the one they were worried about. They thought I'd be the difficult one, the one with the grudge, the one unwilling to move forward. They didn't understand. They didn't understand that I had enough problems in my White Elm life to want to carry any more grudges in this life than were necessary. Lisandro had murdered my family – that was a worthwhile grudge to carry. Kendra and Sophia hadn't spoken up when Xanthe called me a slut – well, lots of other people had stood by, too, and done worse, joining in the bullying. The twins had never called me names. There was no grudge to hold.

'Everything's good now,' I told Sophia, starting carefully down, looking around my pile of boxes. Kendra followed, confessing to her sister she'd felt too scared to initiate a conversation so she'd resorted to throwing notes disguised as paper balls, and we'd just met in the middle when two other people stepped into the stairwell from the second floor.

Tension filled the air around me. We all fell quiet. Xanthe, leading, slowed, locking hateful gazes with each of the twins, the traitors they were for standing with Hiroko and I, but behind her, Sterling had stopped dead, eyes wide and a hand at her throat. She seemed unable to breathe. I felt an alien mixture of panic and determination burst from her.

'Sterling?' I asked, despite being very *not* on speaking terms. It was enough to snap the tension that had risen between the rest of us, and everyone turned their attention to the choking American.

Then the moment passed and she grabbed the handrail, exhaling.

'Are you alright?' Xanthe asked her, in that bored tone she often used. I hated her for it, that lack of care that it both implied and meant. Sterling righted herself, expression calm, and continued down the stairs. Right past us.

'I'm fine,' she said smoothly. 'I missed that step.'

'What are the boxes for?' Hiroko asked me, ignoring Xanthe completely, and with that, things went right back to normal. She moved past us as if we didn't exist. I hefted the boxes higher against my chest to firm up my grip on them.

'Not sure,' I admitted. 'Anouk wants me to take them to Renatus.' I looked up the stairs, knowing that's where I needed to go, but reluctant, because this friendship was so freshly renewed and I wanted to enjoy it for longer. 'Can I see you all later?'

'There's still a few hours of daylight,' Sophia said, winding an arm through Hiroko's but talking to her sister. 'We need some time outside on the lawn with this one. When I was trying to think of a starting topic and brought up soccer, she asked, "Is that the one with the spotty ball?"'

'I was only making a joke,' Hiroko insisted, hastily. Kendra shook her head slowly, disgusted with Hiroko's lack of sporting knowledge.

'*Spotty ball*,' she repeated, horrified. She put the box back atop my burden as she demanded, 'Tell me you know they're checks, not *spots*.'

I had to assure the twins I knew how to play before they departed with Hiroko, who seemed calm and pleased to be going with them. I went upstairs alone, glad. The fight that had initially broken up our friendship group had centred around me and my actions. Hiroko had lost friends for standing by me, and deserved more than anyone to have her friends back.

# chapter fourteen

I dumped the boxes on one of the armchairs and turned to Renatus expectantly. He gave me an innocent look from his side of the desk but said nothing.

'Anouk said they were for me,' I prompted. 'What are they?'

'Don't you read Russian?'

I rolled my eyes and brought over the top box, *1996*. I set it in the middle of his desk, right atop the map he was etching all over, and removed the lid. I grabbed out my history book and looked underneath.

'She's quick,' he said, standing to lightly catch my wrist before I could touch any of the stapled documents or manila folders inside. 'I thought when she approved me straightaway she would make me wait for weeks for the delivery.'

'Who, Anouk?' I asked. I watched as he lifted the top document out. 'She said they were from the Archives.'

'Missing person reports from 1996 to the year 2000. I thought we should start looking for the stranger as soon as possible.'

I recognised the timeframe as being two years either side of the Morrissey storm and eyed the document with even deeper interest. He tilted the document so I could skim its front page. I was surprised he'd gotten on top of my request so quickly.

'What did you tell her?'

'I said we were looking for early accomplices or conscripts of Lisandro's,' he said, 'which could be true. It's too much of a coincidence that the stranger was on the property at the same time Lisandro had chosen for the storm, so we can assume they have a connection.' He showed me through the file he held. 'Name, date reported missing, date last seen, date of birth, country of origin, and there's usually a photo stapled...' He flipped to the back to show me a Polaroid of an old lady with a toddler on her lap. 'Here. We're looking for a male, Irish, probably born in the late sixties, last seen sometime before June nine, 1998. It could have been months or years before anyone actually reported to us that he was missing, but *last seen* before then. Brown hair, Caucasian... You know what he looks like.'

'What makes you think he was reported missing to the White Elm?' I asked, reaching for the next document in the box, this one thicker, the pages held together with an alligator clip. Again Renatus pushed my hand away and got it out so I didn't touch it.

*There's a lot of emotion attached to these pages,* he explained, heading off any uncomfortable visions I might experience before they could happen. Out loud he said, 'He was a sorcerer and *most* sorcerers fall into the White Elm's nation. Even if he wasn't one of ours, many other groups report disappearances to us, too. Our government has the greatest reach of any of them and when you've lost someone, you take any help on offer. Or when a Morrissey *kills* your someone-'

'You didn't kill him,' I said staunchly, taking a stack of unrelated envelopes from the desk and flicking through them. The outgoing pile. He'd already addressed, sealed and stamped them himself. Our friendship had been built on me doing this for him. I supposed he'd been feeling cramped and caged, unable to seek out Lisandro by order of Lord Gawain and the boys' families. 'You said you wiped him off this plane. He can't have died if he wasn't alive to be killed.'

I didn't really understand what Renatus had done, almost eight years ago, to remove the stranger from his orchard, but I remained adamant that he was at no real fault for it.

'Splitting hairs doesn't make it right,' was his response. He flicked through the pages he held. 'He might have run off years before I met him, or he mightn't have been noticed missing until a long while later. Depends on how big of a scumbag he was, I suppose, and who he had left to miss him.'

'He was prepared to let two kids die,' I said starkly. I tossed the envelopes back where I found them and grabbed the next, smaller pile. 'That's a pretty big scumbag. It'll be a wonder if we find any record in here. Whoever knew him was probably too glad to be rid of him to report it.'

'Full of assumptions,' Renatus commented, without bite, 'but probably not wrong. Still.' He dropped the documents he held on the tabletop and reached back into the box with both hands to pull the lot out. There were a worrisome number of reports, and all from just one year. I hoped this included resolved cases. 'It does,' he answered immediately, and elaborated when I glanced up, 'include resolved cases. But we have to start somewhere, and it's not as though I can go to one of my contacts and tell them I'm looking for the man I killed.'

'No, I guess not,' I acquiesced. I found, among the letters he'd received today, one that stood apart from the others. The textured paper envelope had already been slit open, the contents probably already read and put back, and the hand-inked print on the front addressed the contents to *Renatus Morrissey*.

A name I knew he no longer associated himself with.

On a very strong impulse I opened the envelope back up and pulled out the card inside, the most interesting letter I'd ever opened for him.

'I'm so glad we have such a mutually respectful relationship, with healthy boundaries and consideration of privacy and all,' Renatus said without looking up at me. His tone conveyed his irritation. I ignored him. Inside was a single rectangle of heavy paper, so beautifully decorated with flocking and written out in perfect calligraphy that I recognised it straightaway as an invitation even before I read it. I traced the elegant writing over the words *cordially do invite Renatus Morrissey to celebrate the engagement of their son, Gearoid Raymond, to...*

'Who is Gearoid Raymond?' I asked, waving the invitation at him when he didn't answer straightaway. He grabbed the card from my hand and slapped it back down on the desktop, facedown so he didn't have to look at it.

'Society climber,' he answered. *I should have torn it in half when I opened it.* He made to pick it back up but stopped at a noise of protest from me. It was too pretty to destroy. He slid it across the desk, away from himself. 'Someone from an old life. From before.'

He rarely spoke about that life, except to get irritable and insist he couldn't resume those relationships.

'He's engaged.'

'So I saw. I'm sure his father is delighted with the match, since he probably negotiated it years ago.'

'Are you going?'

'No. No one expects me,' he explained before I could ask why out loud, 'and because I don't want to.'

'Were you friends with him? Gearoid?' I asked, sitting down in my usual armchair. Renatus refused to look up at me, but I could tell he wasn't impressed with my choice of topic and my persistence with it.

'No,' he answered firmly, unsurprisingly, since he seemed to have precious few friends, and he dropped the file he'd just finished reading on top of the other ones he'd set aside, presumably the ones he'd already read and written off. His hand froze on the next one; I felt the jolt of familiarity that struck him. 'Huh. No coincidences.'

'What do you mean?' I asked, leaning forward. He ignored me and scanned the file before him. 'Renatus?'

'Nothing.' He tossed the file atop his "done" pile. I reached for it and again had my hand pushed away. I glanced at the cover sheet and caught the name and part of a date:

*Keely Shanahan. May.* Renatus started on another report. I frowned, a sense of familiarity itching at me, too.

'Why do I know that name?'

'I don't know. She was a… a friend of Ana's, before she ran away. They never found her. Hopefully she lived a good long life, far away from everything she detested about the old ways.' He flicked to the attached photograph and discarded the whole file. 'Are you helping or not? This was your idea.'

'Depends. Am I allowed to touch the files?' I asked, extending my empty hand expectantly. He had another one in his hands; he looked at me warily, as though verifying I was finished with my line of questioning.

'Check your wards first,' he said finally, and handed it over. I closed my fingers on it. Nothing. Not all disappearances were traumatic dramas, and not all forms were filled out amid tears and confusion. He grabbed another from the box and we sat down to settle into research mode.

There was more in the box than we anticipated. The year of 1996 was full of runaways, husbands that never came home, old people who checked themselves out of hospital and wandered off, the occasional kidnapping, but mostly, miscommunications that were soon resolved. Thankfully, the majority of the documents I read included a later-added page that explained the manner in which the person was found, usually perfectly safe and sound.

None of the people reported missing to the White Elm in 1996 had a photograph that matched Renatus's memory of the man he'd killed. The face was burned into his memory, and the image was sharp in mine, too.

Years 97 and 98 had less in them, but 99 had a lot.

'Millennium cults were a problem at the time,' Renatus told me, tossing a handful of checked files back into the box and scrubbing his eyes with the heel of his hand. It was dark by now, and we'd been sitting here for hours. 'People kept leaving their homes without warning to go follow these apocalyptic nutcases. It was a bit of a mess for the council, as I remember it. Mass suicides, big rituals that drew a lot of mortal attention. Anyone who stopped off to buy milk after work without warning their wife first was immediately assumed missing and running about with one of these cults.'

'Crazy,' I commented. I'd started off reading each file quite thoroughly, fascinated, but by now my eyes were tired and the lack of early success had me bored with this research method. I grabbed each file, flicked straight to the photo, discarded, and repeated. As usual, my conversation with Renatus was more interesting than what I was doing. 'You wouldn't have even been on the council yet when that was happening. Hey, here's one.' I happened to notice the words *millennium cult* on the cover sheet, and slowed down my relentless pace to read more closely. "Mother has noticed increasing millennium paranoia over the recent months. Suspects disappearance linked with millennium cults'.'

'People really thought the world was ending,' Renatus said. His eyes skimmed through documents so quickly, settled on photographs, and with a hardening look he would throw them aside even as he reached for another. As we became more similar, our combined stock of patience was running low. I went to the photograph at the back. It was taken in a bar of a laughing young man with sparkling dark eyes and white teeth and a paper umbrella tucked behind his ear. Bryce Guthrie. His case had no added page to explain its resolution. This man was never found. I thumbed back through the pages to read about him. He had a mother, who had given his description to the interviewing councillor and detailed the last time she'd seen him.

'For some people in these boxes, the world *did* end,' I noted, running fingers down the page of handwritten notes. Hair colour, eye colour, age, last seen, usual haunts. One person, all summed up here on a single page in his ongoing absence. Was his mother still alive? Did she still wonder what became of him? My fingers stopped suddenly at the bottom of the page, and my questions stopped, too. 'Renatus? This interview was conducted by Jackson.'

He looked up, unsurprised, and said, 'A lot of these were.' He showed me the bottom of the page he was reading and I saw the same name printed in block capitals. *JACKSON.* 'He was the council's Scribe at the time.'

I turned the nearest box around so I could see Anouk's striking Russian and compared it with Jackson's quick caps lock. I hadn't seen his writing before, and it was unreasonable that it should bring me any sort of fear, but it did. My one meeting with the man was as much exposure as I ever needed. Lisandro was frightening in his charisma, control and unpredictability. Jackson didn't seem to have that control. He was big, he was brutish, and the way he'd leered at Emmanuelle, the idea that he'd knowingly let his men assault Teresa while she was in his care… it scared me.

'I thought Anouk was in charge of the Archives,' I said, realising I actually knew very little about the council's record keeping system. Renatus dropped the pile of completed and discarded files, all of them useless to us, back into the box.

'She's its keeper, yes. She's Historian, but a better word would be librarian. She catalogues everything that we record – circle minutes, legal proceedings, letters, financials, laws we pass. It's one of the busiest original roles on the White Elm. The Scribe's job is to make those records.'

'Jackson's job was to go and interview bereaved families?' I asked, disbelieving. 'Doesn't that require a certain level of sensitivity?'

'The irony is not lost on me,' Renatus agreed, 'but Fate chose him for that role. I'm told he was different back then, though I only knew him as he is now. He had some sort of accident, some head injury. Probably he should have been taken off the council then before he had the chance to defect to Lisandro's cause.'

Lisandro's cause. I put Bryce Guthrie's file down, feeling a little unwell. The man who had written this out, acted concerned for Guthrie's mother – he followed Lisandro and helped him conceal the fact that he'd *murdered* half of my family. Renatus's *whole* family. Asheleigh Hawke's parents. Peter Chisholm. Maybe others.

We were sifting through these boxes for the identity of a man Renatus had killed to try to alleviate my master's guilt, but he had *nothing* to feel guilty about, not when he stood beside the monsters we should be looking for.

The monster I was going to kill, and his sidekick, who I'd probably leave to someone else to take care of because that was just pushing my luck. *They* deserved what the stranger had gotten. They deserved worse.

My hands were still on the Guthrie file and my wards were solid when I was hit by an overwhelming vision that blocked all other stimulus.

*The cold, bare room of a hostel... Bunk beds with snoring male forms under threadbare, mismatched old sheets... Window open, raining outside... A man sitting on the windowsill, bright ember of a hand-rolled cigarette quivering in a shaky, cold hand... Knotty, dark red hair and beard... Terror... A glance around the room... Everyone's dead asleep... Maroon hooded robe hanging from a hook in the wall... Leaning out the window to flick ashes, the other hand is busy, reaching... A small plastic bag taped under the window ledge... Inside, a pen, a rusty razor blade, some leaves, rock salt, some other things... Still pretending to smoke placidly, the free hand hurriedly scrawls a series of symbols on the forearm... Body shifts to ensure the motion can't be seen... The pen drops into the rain, replaced by the razor... Discomfort, terror, no time to risk hoping... Another symbol, cut into the arm with the razor... Can't make a noise, can't risk responding to the pain... Salts rubbed into the wound, leaves crushed and mixed with the blood... Still no gasp, only cringing... A break in the magic... breath held... no one wakes... a faint glimmer of hope... a near-soundless whisper... 'Paul; brother. Paul, please – please find me'... A struggle to hold back tears... Now or never... Cigarette crushed into window ledge... Shaking hands push off and he's falling into the rain... A loud crunch, he lands in a scrubby bush three storeys below... Dogs barking, men enquiring, the bearded man on his feet and running in the grey night...*

I must have held my breath for the duration of the vision, because I came back to awareness of the present with a deep gasp to find myself still sitting in my armchair, hands on the pages in front of me. I shoved away, breathing heavily.

'That shouldn't have happened,' I protested, shaken, jumping to my feet and backing away from the pages. 'My wards... I didn't drop them, it shouldn't have gotten through-'

'That didn't come from the files,' Renatus said, blinking away the same vision. He wasn't sitting anymore. He was up, rounding the desk to reach me, and he grabbed my shoulders and bent to look me in the eyes. 'That came from elsewhere, outside. Qasim saw the same. Now, focus,' he urged me. 'Tune back in. We're going to keep looking.'

I nodded even though I didn't want to see any more of that, closed my eyes quickly against the sensory stimuli of the study and tried to reach beyond my own shaky body after that vision I'd just been struck with. It was receding, drawing away from me and off into the past, but I caught up with it and-

*Running, breathing hard... Blue eyes blinking against rain... Dogs barking... Fear... Boxy communist architecture in contrast with quaint and classical little free-standing buildings... Oppression, not what he signed up for... A glossy onion-like spire of an old church, high enough to be seen from here... Signs over the doors of closed-up shops written in an unfamiliar language... Limping, pain, gasping... Leg injured from the fall... 'Please, Paul, help me...' A tear in the world... Graciousness, a cry of thanks... Reaching... Gone.*

The vision ended as abruptly as it had started and I was left breathing hard like the man in it. Renatus was no longer standing before me, but was at his smoky-glass cabinet, fishing around inside it for various magical artefacts.

'He Displaced,' he explained. 'That's the end of the events in that location so we won't be able to see any more.'

*A warm handshake in greeting... 'Knew it wouldn't take you long to see the way'... Familiarity... 'What other way is there? Free magic for all'...*

'Wrong,' I argued. My heart was still pounding from the longer two snippets but this vision was less shocking, more passive in the way it slithered past my awareness without overtaking it.

'That's not connected. Or not the same man. Those are leaks.'

'Leaks?'

'Other moments, past and present, from the same place, that the man we saw has let out of a contained zone.'

'Who is he?' I asked, breathless. Renatus shrugged and I knew he didn't know, but already he had deciphered my Empathic interpretation of the same visions and was acting on it. Leaks, contained zones, free magic for all... My mind was spinning but I latched onto his, and that helped centre me. In his head, I heard the incoherent chatter of his fellow councillors reacting to the vision he and Qasim shared with them. There was a wall between them and me, preventing me from taking part in their sacred discussions, though I doubted they were particularly sacred right now, and I could still hear Renatus's own thoughts. They seemed to mirror what all the other White Elms thought.

They'd just seen someone escape Lisandro's camp.

'Wait, how do you know?' I asked, feeling overwhelmed by the sudden change in circumstances. One second, sorting through ten-year-old files, safe, bored, chatting; the next, readying for departure for an unexpected mission into Lisandro's base of operations. Assuming that's what we'd seen. I detected no explicit evidence of that. 'And if it is, why would you rush into it? You said that all visions you get from Lisandro are because he *chooses* to let you see them.'

*Laughter, chatter, accents... A shared roast dinner... Camaraderie...*

'This is different,' Renatus told me, slapping the cabinet shut and starting for the door, beckoning to me as he went.

Enchanted chains and a necklace that bound magic inside the body hung from the pockets of his jacket. I didn't know the purpose of the string of runes he wound around his wrist, or the two vials of what looked a *lot* like blood that clinked inside his pocket, or the slim sharp knives he hid away. I didn't really want to know. I followed him, still listening. 'The spell he did *broke* the seal on a concealment ward. Little scraps of information are leaking out through that tiny rip. Elijah can identify the Displacement point as Orsha. Belarus,' he filled in, when I offered a blank look. 'It's in the region we suspect Lisandro to be staying in. We thought Lithuania, but there's nearly just as much activity in Belarus...'

'A man breaks a concealment spell and jumps out of a window,' I said, heart in my throat – we were leaving to confront Lisandro and I was so not ready – as I followed him out the door, 'and that's the only conclusion? Is Lisandro the only one in the world with a concealment spell?'

'Against the White Elm specifically? No, probably not,' Renatus admitted, still walking with purpose, 'but he should be the only one using it to hide a roomful of men with red cloaks on the wall.'

*Red cloaks, twelve, hanging in a barren closet...*

Right opposite the door was a hidden portal, and Renatus had already taken a step into it when he reached back for me. I wrenched my hand out of his grip – I couldn't go through without him, or so I suspected – and he had to pause. In that moment I caught his arm and pulled him a pace backwards, back into the hall.

'Stop,' I begged, realising what we were walking into and utterly terrified. Hours ago, only hours ago, I'd told myself I would kill Lisandro. *Kill* him. For Renatus, to save him, because he deserved it and because I owed it to him. Now, looking up at him and his impatient face, I didn't feel it was wrong, and I didn't feel like I ought to relent or back down, but I did feel it was too soon. I wasn't prepared. I had to do it. I would do it. But not today. 'What's the significance of the red cloaks? I don't understand how you can be so sure.'

Renatus clearly didn't feel he needed to justify himself, but he did, for me.

'That's what Lisandro's followers, Magnus Moira, wore when they watched him drown Peter,' he said. 'It's a rather distinctive clothing item. Can we go?'

'No.'

We both turned to Qasim as he approached us along the hall. He looked conflicted and deeply unhappy.

'No?' Renatus repeated. 'That man broke the seal. The closer we get the easier it'll be for us to scry inside the perimeter. We don't know how long it'll take for Lisandro to notice the tear in the cloak and put it back up.'

'It doesn't matter how long it takes,' Qasim said firmly, even though he looked like he'd rather not be saying it. 'We promised we wouldn't act.'

'We what?' Renatus spat. 'Free magic for all. That's the message Lisandro is spreading. It's *his* camp we saw.'

'The parents,' I realised, heart sliding back down from where it sat in my throat to the depth of my stomach, disappointed. The boys. This was where they were being kept. And we weren't allowed to go after them.

'We promised to stand down,' Qasim confirmed. '*You* promised to stand down.'

'We don't know it's where the hostages are,' my master insisted, irritated by us both now, me for slowing him down first of all and Qasim for telling him what he didn't want to hear. 'All we know is it's Magnus Moira. They could have a dozen camps.'

'They could,' Qasim agreed. 'But this is the one we know about, so this is the one we can't storm. The rest of the council has stood down.'

'We don't have to storm it. We could drop right into the middle-'

'Elijah tried before I could stop him. The Fabric's pulled taut. He bounced off, landed somewhere on the outskirts of the city, left immediately. We'd have to approach from the ground.'

'There's thirteen of us,' Renatus hissed. 'It's not even a fair fight. Any one of us is worth twenty of his men. We'd be out so fast-'

'Renatus, you aren't hearing me,' Qasim said heatedly. '*Any* action here will result in innocent death. We heard it firsthand from *two Seers*-'

'Forgive us for not being all too ready to take *Seers* on their word.'

I looked down, realising his opinion had come from my mouth once again. Qasim's perfect memory joined the conversation, merciless.

'*I will tell him that I foresaw a day in May where the White Elm had a chance to rescue him, but in doing so he would have died, and his friend Garrett would have missed his chance to witness an event so significant it prompts the White Elm into a righteous war,*' he repeated Tyson Marks' father's words from a week ago. 'Those Seers have no reason at all to misrepresent the truth. Their children will *die* if you act on this information. No,' the Scrier said, gentler, laying a heavy hand on Renatus's shoulder, just briefly, 'you are not the only one burning to do *something*, but the fact remains we cannot. The consequences are too great. The honour of our word would come into question. We promised. It's not worth it.'

Renatus stood there for what felt like very long, very loaded seconds, glaring at the wall where he'd almost disappeared through an invisible portal that would have taken him to the kitchens where he wouldn't have been stopped by Qasim, where he could have chosen to ignore the Scrier's voice in his head. I wrapped my arms around my middle, feeling oddly cold, definitely uncomfortable. His tempestuous emotions rocked about inside him and bumped into me, hard, several times. All the barriers he'd prompted me to check earlier protected me from him.

With extreme effort, he pulled it all – the disappointment, the anger, the thrill of the chase, the guilt that he would have risked those lives to satisfy his own desires and the disgust that he'd desired to chase and kill at all – back under control and nodded, once.

'I understand,' he said, and turned around. He went back inside his study and the door shut behind him. His mind shut along with it. I stood in the hall with Qasim, feeling immensely sorry for Renatus. Strangely, I sensed that Qasim felt the same.

He didn't come back out.

'What, that's it?' I demanded, my pity morphing into frustration, with him and with the situation. I stepped over and banged on the door. 'Aren't there maps to scribble on? Am I not qualified to help with that?'

I got no answer from Renatus. I gathered he was sulking. I completely sympathised and felt hurt that he wouldn't allow me in to sulk with him. The first chance at getting my classmates back, Hiroko's Garrett, Iseult's Josh – and we weren't allowed to act.

Which meant my date with Lisandro was delayed. Probably for the best. I stopped banging. I'd only hours ago made that decision, to kill this ringleader of terrible people, and it probably wasn't a good one, but regardless, I was definitely not ready to carry it out. Time was in everyone's interests.

'He found it,' Qasim commented unhappily, and I looked back at him. He shook his head. 'Lisandro found the tear. He's repairing it. We won't see anything else out of Belarus.'

I pressed my lips together and stared at the door, shut and silent. I waited for another passive vision but Qasim was right. Nothing else came.

'Give him some time,' Qasim urged me, waving me away from the closed door. 'He'll be okay.'

It was true, he was okay. The next morning Renatus was talking to me again, though he didn't want to talk about Belarus, understandably. We spent the morning going through the last box, but no photo matched Renatus's memory of the stranger, and only a few descriptions caught our attention. When we turned up nothing, we petitioned

Anouk for more boxes so we could expand our search to include disappearances as far back as 1990. Post-2000 seemed a waste of time. If nobody had noticed the stranger's non-presence after a couple of years, chances were no one was going to report it.

It took us well over three weeks of periodic, fruitless reading and sorting to reject fifteen years' worth of missing person reports to deem the search method a massive failure.

What wasn't a failure was my revived friendship with the Prescotts. On their birthday I sat with Hiroko and Sophia on Sophia's bed while she and Kendra opened presents and, yes, tipped a huge helping of chocolates, sweets and crisps from an overstuffed post pack. To my immense surprise, both Addison and Heath were in attendance, and any tension between the exes was totally unapparent. Addison lounged along Sophia's bed behind us, cracking jokes and throwing screwed-up wrappers at us, mocking Kendra's communication method. She rolled her eyes and threw the wrappers back at him. Iseult sat curled up beside Heath, and that's how we remained for hours, eating our way through the twins' birthday snacks.

It was clear that I wasn't the only one glad to have the gang back together, albeit in a new, updated form, and missing a few kidnapped figures.

May progressed into the dullest, most stable month of my time at Morrissey House. Whispers of Lisandro's movements were non-existent, as were those of Jackson and Aubrey, so there was no need for me to leave the estate's grounds, and we were banned from moving in on Belarus. I focused on my research with Renatus, tried to improve in my study areas and spent time with my friends. I kept my secrets and no one suspected I was plotting a horrific crime to save someone else from committing it and worse. Hiroko turned eighteen; Sophia had the idea of writing her a book, so in the week before her birthday we each took turns smuggling the hand-stapled sheaf of printer paper between us to continue scribing and illustrating the insanely wacky story of a little witch called Roki. On the day, Iseult, the twins and Addison came to our room to see her reaction to the gift. The six of us sat on the beds and laughed ourselves to tears as Hiroko read the finished copy out loud, interrupted frequently by her own uncontrollable giggles. Her father sent her a pair of diamond earrings, which delighted and surprised her, as she said birthday gifts weren't normally given in her family, and the Fischers sent her a stunning ruby-red sari, embroidered with gold thread. None of us could work out how they'd learnt of her birth date or how they knew of her connection to their missing son.

That May was so uneventful, unproblematic and *normal* that I went to bed each night without a care in the world and mostly fell straight to sleep without ever noticing that, on at least three of those nights, someone else in the room was sitting up in bed, watching me sleep.

# chapter fourteen

*1959 – Manchester*

The feeling of exuberance almost overwhelmed Cassán as he stepped into the club. The lights were bright, the music was loud and lively, the food smelt amazing, the drinks were flowing and the people were smiling, laughing, dancing. It was New Year's Eve, with less than an hour to go until the new decade. It was a good time to be alive, young and powerful. Cassán breathed it in.

Colourful skirts flared out as girls spun on the dance floor and through the movement and happiness Cassán spotted his associate leaning against the bar.

'There's a Stepping Stone here,' Andrew commented, tapping his foot to the beat of the song and winking at a girl in a purple dress who kept trying to catch his eye. 'I can feel it. I just can't work out which one it is.'

*Which one*, he said, not *who*. People weren't people to Andrew Hawke. They were pieces in a giant game of chess. Cassán turned to the bartender to order himself a drink. This Manchester club was a common hangout for sorcerers and most of the faces were becoming familiar. The young bartender recognised Cassán immediately.

'Usual.' Cassán had to raise his voice to be heard over the music. 'No umbrella this time.'

Everyone around him, even Andrew, had a colourful, frilly-looking cocktail in hand, courtesy of both the times and the fussy, well-dressed bartender. He, sadly, was many decades ahead of his time, living in an age where it was okay to love as many people as you liked, so long as none of those people were of your own gender. Andrew nudged Cassán to get his attention.

'I think it's him,' he said, pointing into the crowd of dancers at a fair-haired youth. 'With the lass in red.'

Both were blonde, good-looking, drunk on too much drink and high on the energy of the night, if nothing else. Both were familiar, and not only from this club. They danced and laughed like there was nothing else in the world. Cassán raked his memory for their names.

'They're going to leave together,' Andrew decided. 'I'll make sure of it.'

'Why can't you leave the future alone?' Cassán asked. 'It's New Years; let it be.'

'Did Mánus tell you he wasn't coming?' Andrew redirected. 'I thought he would be here. It's not far for him.'

'Do you really think Morrissey has nowhere better to be on New Year's Eve than a bar in Manchester?' Cassán rolled his eyes. 'He and Áine probably had a dozen invitations to choose from.'

The song changed and all the male attention in the room shifted to the pair that waltzed through the door. More precisely, the male attention went to Moira Dawes, whose dark hair was piled onto her head to expose her long, graceful neck – not that she needed to, with all the skin she was already showing off with her tight, mostly sheer, totally-inappropriate-for-the-season party dress. Eugene walked in with her, looking immensely pleased to be seen with this goddess.

'Andrew! Cassán!' Moira hurried towards her friends as though she hadn't seen them in some time, whereas in fact, they'd seen her the day before for a circle. She pressed kisses onto each of their cheeks; Cassán found it hard to choose a polite place to rest his hand when he hugged her obediently. Everywhere seemed to be bared. 'What a great party!'

'It's noisy,' Eugene commented, shaking Cassán's hand. 'I would ask if you agree... but you do.'

'Where's Mánus?' Moira asked, frowning. 'He said he'd try to come.'

'Cassán seems to think he had better offers,' Andrew said sulkily. Moira smiled and leaned against his side for another hug, earning her a jealous glare from the girl in the purple dress.

'I doubt he had any better offers than us,' she purred. She accepted a drink from Eugene and raised it high. 'To us!'

'To us,' the three chorused, and drank. Cassán eyed them over the rim of his glass. When he'd first met most of these people, only eighteen months ago, he'd really not known what to think of them, but it certainly hadn't occurred to him as a possibility that their mutual quest for knowledge would consume so much of his time as to rival his writing for attention, nor that they would grow to know him so well. Some days he regretted their closeness, but he always rebutted this feeling with pitiless reminders of what these connections had gained him. These four shady friends were more useful than a team of trained researchers for finding forbidden information. The things he'd learnt, seen, done, since meeting in Moira Dawes' basement fell outside the realm of belief he'd held beforehand.

It had started as Moira suggested, quiet meetings over books, but had escalated quickly into circles in graveyards, animal sacrifices and bloodletting. Each frightening step up had felt like the last, but afterwards there was always an obvious *next* step, and the exhilaration of doing something new, or so old there was no memory of it anywhere, pushed them all onwards.

They worked, made and manipulated magic at least twice a week together now. They sourced ancient texts from hidden libraries; they romanced archaeologists to get access to cave drawings of interest; they woke the spirit world to ask for the secrets of the dead. A long-time enthusiast of magic's mysteries, Cassán was constantly amazed by how their every

237

manipulation of magic only further proved his written works. Magic, Fate and human relationships *were* entwined, in ways he'd not even previously understood himself. Moira, Andrew, Eugene and Mánus were *meant* to be in his life, and always would be. Their influence on his path, he saw now – even when he was sick of them or wished them away – was inescapable, and was so significant that it would be felt for generations to come. The group's investigations, their hard work and their successes were part of Fate's plan. It was hard not to find that fact incredibly empowering.

At the same time, however, Cassán was also haunted by a tiny, niggling worry at the very back of his mind. All things end. No staircase continues upward forever. Eventually, one of them would hit a ceiling... or try to take one step more than was available, and tumble from a great height.

'Let's do this again, a hundred years from tonight,' Moira suggested jubilantly. 'Right here, even if the building is knocked down. Promise.'

'Yeah, alright,' Eugene agreed lightly, as usual voicing the opinions of those around him. 'I think I'm free. Let me just write that down on my 2059 calendar that I carry everywhere with me just in case. Wouldn't want to double-book myself.'

'No, silly,' Moira giggled, 'I'm being serious. Let's do it. Let's do the spell. Let's live forever.'

Her announcement was met with laughter and awkward silence. Cassán was the silent one. She'd suggested this before; he had entertained the notion, but not with any real seriousness. This seemed to him to be that ceiling he'd been dreading. Living forever sounded at first perfectly ideal but he strongly suspected unhappy consequences. Not to mention the initial price – to live with *this* cost for even a normal lifespan would be difficult, so to live with it for always might prove impossible.

He thought of Anthea, the stunning Greek angel he'd fallen so deeply for on his recent trip through the Greek Isles. He harboured a wild dream of returning to her tiny island community and finding her still as enamoured with him as he was with her. He hadn't mentioned her existence to his friends, but after doing what they were suggesting, would he be able to face Anthea? Would he have the gall to ask her to love him if he became the man Moira was asking him to become?

The topic changed, and Cassán turned his mind from that dilemma and back to the party. He danced with the girl in the purple dress, knowing fully that she was only trying to make Andrew jealous but not minding at all. He was even less interested in her than she was in him. He drank with his friends. He watched with mild interest as a troublesome drunkard was thrown unceremoniously from the bar.

With only one minute to go until midnight, the countdown started, and Moira gathered them all back together to watch the hands of the clock above the bar. The anticipation in the room built with every second the partygoers shouted, and Cassán let himself get swept up by it, all that wasted emotion, even though he knew it was foolish, just a sixty-to-zero countdown to midnight, whereupon all the anticipation would prove to be for nothing, because nothing would happen, nothing would feel different.

'Forty-two, forty-one, forty, thirty-nine,' everyone shouted, and Cassán glanced back over his shoulder as he felt a sudden familiar presence enter his vicinity. Mánus Morrissey, dressed in a tailored suit much too formal for this place, jogged through the doors of the club and hurried over.

'Just in time,' he noted, reaching for the glass of whisky Andrew offered. Hawke must have known, because he still held his own drink in his other hand.

'You came!' Moira squealed, disentangling her arms from Andrew and Eugene to seize Mánus around his middle. 'They said you weren't coming!'

'I wasn't,' Morrissey admitted, politely peeling Moira's arms off him. 'I have to head back straight after this drink.

Áine and I are at a party in Verona tonight, and midnight isn't for another hour there.'

'Twenty! Nineteen, eighteen,' the crowd chanted, getting noisier, more excited. Moira's bronze-brown eyes narrowed slightly at Mánus's mention of his wife. She never liked reminders of the stunning sorceress to whom he was completely devoted, and Cassán knew she simply hated it that tonight, like all nights, he would choose Áine over her and the others, and was only slipping them in between other engagements. Her jealousy was tangible but useless. Mánus was not the pitying sort, and even Moira must have known that openly admitting her desire for him would only lessen his opinion of her.

'You're here now, that's the main thing,' Eugene said over the swelling noise of the crowd. 'The now is all that matters.'

Moira slanted her eyes in his direction, and Cassán could feel that she disagreed. No doubt Eugene knew exactly what she was thinking, but he continued smiling at the clock as the countdown fell into the single digits.

'Nine! Eight! Seven! Six! Five!' The partygoers leaned forwards to see the clock and the five friends were pushed closer together. Cassán lifted his arms out of the crush, where they were pinned to his sides, and lowered them behind Andrew and Moira to give them all some space. 'Four! *Three! Two! ONE!'*

The hyped atmosphere of the room built to its crescendo. The calls of 'Happy new year!' and 'Zero!' were drowned out in an incoherent scream of collective joy and excitement, accompanied and followed by the clinking of dozens of glasses. Cassán's glass met the glasses of his four friends and he drank. And drank, until the drink was gone. His friends had lowered their glasses after one mouthful but Cassán's impulse-control was limited in high-strung situations like this one. He felt things that those around him were feeling, and these other feelings, when intense, drove his own emotions. He had spent his adult life blocking these alien feelings but in the last year he had found it less important to do so. Some days he worried about his changing priorities and where this would lead; other days, like this one, he revelled in the freedom from his own sensibilities. Life has so much to offer – why fail to experience all of it?

'Cassán Ó Grádaigh?'

Over the concurrent waves of golden good feeling and jubilant conversation came the querying voice, and Cassán turned to look. The fair-haired youth Andrew had pointed out earlier stood with the blonde in red. Both were drunk, but the boy's blue eyes were lit with recognition.

'Aye?' Cassán replied, trying to place the vaguely familiar young face. The youngster opened his mouth to introduce himself when Cassán was struck with a sudden memory of a dreary day in New York City and a less than memorable book signing at a dingy occult bookstore. 'Harrington. From Wales, on holiday in New York with your parents?'

'Yes, that's right.' The youth, who couldn't have hit twenty-one yet, smiled widely with pleasure at having been recognised. 'Gawain Harrington. I bought your book in New York when I was holidaying there with my mum and dad. Boy, that was a long time ago. I was still in school.'

'And what do you do now?' Cassán asked, trying not to feel old.

'I'm studying law at Cardiff University,' Gawain enthused. Behind him, unseen, Cassán felt Moira's condescension at the mortal career choice. 'It isn't what I expected but I enjoy learning and I'm hoping it will put me in a better position when I start applying for work in our world. Mr Ó Grádaigh is a writer,' Gawain filled in for his date, who was looking away, bored. The blonde spared Cassán a glance, and both she and Cassán started when recognition passed between them, too. She blushed bright red.

'Kathleen Franklin,' Cassán noted, disappointed. 'It's been much too long. Where is George tonight?'

Gawain looked expectantly, obliviously, at his date. The blonde, even drunk, was quick.

'My *brother* is at a function of my father's,' Kathleen covered, smiling sweetly at Gawain and shooting a nasty look at Cassán as soon as the younger man had looked away. If she thought a look would hold back Cassán's tongue, she clearly underestimated who she was speaking with.

'I'm sure he is,' Cassán replied calmly, 'but I'm not asking about Thomas, I'm asking about George, your-'

'Cass, aren't you going to introduce us?' Andrew interrupted deftly, smiling at the young pair with a cunning sparkle in his eyes. He offered his hand to them each in turn. 'Oh, wow. What amazing energy, from both of you. You know, I normally don't do this, but Fate is really pushing me to tell you something about your futures.'

'What is it?' asked Kathleen, eager to redirect the conversation, while Gawain hesitated. Cassán could see in the youth's aura that he was a Seer himself, and of a power level comparable with any of the five friends.

'There's probably no point; we're too drunk, we won't remember,' he said cheerfully, possibly the most sensible thing he would suggest all night. Andrew ignored him, speaking mostly to Kathleen.

'Tonight is special,' he intimated, and she leaned close to listen. '*You* are special. You two,' he gestured here to Gawain, tempting the younger Seer to lean in too, however reluctantly, 'are Stepping Stones.'

'They can find this out for themselves,' Cassán said, more firmly than he intended. He'd gotten used to Eugene's mental intrusions, Mánus's mysteriousness and eccentric millionaire lifestyle and Moira's reckless, flirtatious influence, but Andrew's insistence on sharing people's futures with them, permission or no, was something he'd never fully accepted. His research was pretty conclusive – sometimes, people really shouldn't know what was coming to them. In the case of young Gawain, a powerful Seer in his own right, Andrew had no business telling him anything. Surely, if Fate had wanted

Gawain Harrington to know this, it would have told him already.

'No, please tell us!' Kathleen begged, alcohol fuelling her silliness. 'We want to know.'

'Relax, Cassán,' Eugene soothed, patting his shoulder meaningfully. He knew what Andrew was thinking; did that mean it was something harmless? 'It's New Years. New beginnings.'

'You two meeting tonight was Fate's plan,' Andrew told the young pair. 'This is the start of something really special. Your love is going to change the world. This is huge.'

'*Our* love?' Kathleen asked, wide-eyed, indicating Gawain with a nod of her head while she unconsciously rubbed her empty ring finger. Cassán tried not to roll his eyes at her stupidity. Like this fling with the Harrington boy could last more than a few nights before her husband found out, so how their "love" was going to evolve into anything particularly epic was anyone's guess. She seized her date's hands and stared into his eyes. 'Yes. I knew it when I saw you. Didn't you? Didn't you feel that golden feeling?'

'I... I think so,' Gawain said, caught off-guard.

'You know, I can see gold all around you,' Moira said suddenly, wrapping her arms around Cassán's shoulders as she leaned into the conversation with a bright smile. She reached toward the couple as though trying to touch their auras, every bit as theatrically gifted as Andrew, if not more. She paused and let go of Cassán to approach Gawain. 'Especially around you. You're going to make such a difference, did you know?'

'I don't see the gold,' Gawain said uncertainly, glancing nervously at Cassán for direction. His nervousness soon faded, however, as the atmosphere of the room began to settle and envelop them all in complacency and calm.

'Of course you do,' Moira insisted smoothly, laying her hands on either side of the Welsh youth's face. She caught his gaze and held it. 'Right here.'

The party's noise was still going on but it might as well have been silent in their little circle. Gawain stared, hypnotised by the false energy she'd created, into Moira's eyes, while the others looked on. Kathleen seemed to suddenly realise what the older woman was suggesting.

'I saw him first,' she said, trying to keep a friendly tone but definitely not feeling friendly things. Moira did not break eye contact with Gawain.

'I saw him second,' she responded. 'I'll have him second, too. I don't mind waiting for your epic love story to play out, little girl.'

Mánus, who had waited out the conversation at the bar behind them, finally seemed to lose patience and pushed between Cassán and Eugene to grab Moira's arm.

'Give it a rest,' he said, pulling her back to the bar. 'He's too young for you. He's barely legal.'

'Let's go,' Kathleen said to Gawain, tugging on his hand. He nodded.

'Alright.' He turned to Cassán and shook his hand. 'I'm glad I ran into you again.'

'The same,' Cassán agreed, genuinely. 'Good luck with your studies. I'm sure you'll do well. I hope we meet again.'

The youth smiled as he was dragged out by Kathleen. Andrew sipped on his drink.

'You won't. Meet him again, I mean,' he said tactlessly. 'Probably for the best.'

'Hawke, I can't tell you how much I hate hearing your stupid voice,' Cassán snapped. 'I've told you I don't want to know. Knowing ruins lives. And that kid – he's a good kid, and you've just sent him off with George Franklin's wife thinking something good will come of it. What happens when he finds out she's married? Or worse, when George finds out about Harrington?'

'George won't find out. This will be the best thing for him. Harrington will have his little heart broken and Kathleen won't step out on George again. See? I'm looking out for old George.'

'Meanwhile the poor boy George's tart wife picks out of a crowd comes off second-best?'

'Absolutely,' Andrew replied emotionlessly. 'So what? He'll get over it. Harrington's going to be a pain in our sides on the White Elm someday. And he leads a remarkably pleasant life from here on. He deserves this one bad date.'

'He is not,' Mánus argued, irritably plonking a new drink in front of Moira, who was still sulking about his comment about her age. 'He said he's studying mortal law. He won't leave Wales with that sort of qualification.'

'At least I'll know where to find him when he's old enough,' Moira quipped.

'I promise you, Harrington will be on that forsaken council. He's exactly their type anyway, goody-two-shoes he is.' Andrew ordered a new drink and sighed contentedly. 'At least he'll die before any of us.'

'You always find the silver lining, Andrew,' Eugene commented dourly, while Mánus asked, 'Why?'

'I *don't* want to know how that boy will die,' Cassán interrupted angrily, 'or any of us, either.'

'We're not *going* to die,' Andrew said, rolling his eyes. 'I've looked a thousand times. Fate hasn't got a death in store for any of us.'

Mánus stood straighter.

'Are you certain?' he asked seriously. 'Is that really possible?'

'He means it,' Eugene noted, sounding awed as he stared at Andrew's forehead. 'He's Seeing it now.'

'But is it possible?'

Cassán folded his arms, trying not to think. Mánus was the other "sensible" one in their group, the sceptic who never really believed until he saw it. When Moira cooked up really crazy ideas, Cassán could count on Morrissey to think along the same rational lines as he did. Because of Moira's adoration of the millionaire and his social influence, whatever position Mánus took on a situation was usually the position that they went with. If Mánus could be convinced, that left

Cassán alone in his belief that asking for eternal human life might be asking a little too much.

'You're not alone in thinking that, Ó Grádaigh,' Eugene assured him. 'It sounds insane. But if Hawke can See that none of us will ever die... Fate must have planned this for us already.'

'Oh, Cassán,' Moira said suddenly, grabbing his hands. 'Promise you'll think about it. That's all. I know you need to read all the books and do all the experiments before you'll be sure, but please promise to give it fair thought. Eternity wouldn't be the same without you.'

'It's going to happen,' Andrew mentioned. He accepted his new drink from the bartender. 'You've already made the decision, really – the future is already written. All that needs to happen now is the ritual.' He raised his glass to Cassán. 'Just say the word. All this,' he gestured to the room around them, obviously including the bright lights, the music, the dancing, the fun, the jubilation, the hope and anticipation, 'is ours forever. Let's just not get too old before we take it.'

Cassán didn't know what to say. Moira hugged his middle excitedly; Eugene shook his head, blown away by this revelation. Andrew smiled, enjoying his newfound leadership of the group. At the bar, Mánus still sipped his drink quietly. Cassán pulled away from Moira to approach the other Irishman, leaning close to address him privately.

'This is a bad idea,' he murmured, beginning to feel frightened, oppressed, despite the good feelings in the club. He felt his control slipping – if Fate had already decided, as the others suggested, it meant he had no choice in the matter, yet with Andrew's unwelcome prediction he should have felt *more* empowered, armed with the ability to change what was coming. That feeling was not present.

Mánus Morrissey's violet eyes were always guarded and cold, but now they softened slightly in understanding and, possibly, some alien form of pity.

'Of course it is,' he agreed quietly. He averted his eyes briefly to the countertop, where, Cassán now saw, he had been meticulously straightening the line of coasters before him. 'It's a *god-awful* idea. That said, now that we know it's possible, do you really think we'll be able to stop ourselves from doing it? The idea has been planted and it's inevitable that it will grow.' The final coaster in place, Morrissey swallowed the last of his drink, placed it on the centre coaster and stepped away from the bar. 'Look around you. No one here knows how or when they'll die. For some it might be tomorrow. For others it's not until next century.'

'That's how it's meant to be,' Cassán pointed out.

'But not for us.' Mánus walked with Cassán away from the others on his way out. Out of earshot of the group, he said, 'Hawke cursed us tonight. Be realistic. Now that you know, you'll never forget it. We'll never live the same way again, fearing consequences, fearing a death that isn't coming. He made the decision for us when he told us.'

Cassán clenched his hands, trying to control his feelings. Mánus was perfectly correct, and if *he* believed it, what chance did Cassán have of convincing himself otherwise? The future was written. It was an unfinished novel with no foreseeable end. Cassán hadn't even been allowed to read the blurb or critics' reviews before being thrown in. What kind of developments would his character take in a story as long as time itself? Who would he become? A marginal, inconsequential rebel now, maybe a villain later? A plot device to how many other people's stories?

'But just because it's a terrible idea doesn't mean it will be terrible,' the millionaire added. 'Hawke's given us eternity but he can't choose what we do with it.'

'What are you talking about?' Cassán asked, still struggling to bring his panic under control. His friend clapped his shoulder and leaned in to be heard over the music.

'Marry the Greek girl,' Mánus said quietly. 'Don't look so shocked, of course I know. Go back and find her, settle down, have a family, write a bunch more books. Hawke, Dawes and Dubois are an inescapable fact of the now but forever is a very long time, and the world is a big place in which to lose people and forget all about them.'

Cassán stared at the scrier, feeling both shocked and stupid. He shouldn't feel shocked. *Of course* Morrissey would have seen him in Greece. Of course Morrissey would keep that fact to himself. He was the single one in the group with any scrap of real honour, the only one Cassán would have chosen as a friend outside the circumstances that had brought the five together. Funny, given the Morrissey family reputation. Cassán buried thoughts of Anthea and her seaside town as the others come over.

'Are you alright, Cassán?' Moira asked silkily, sliding her hands up his arm and pulling a curtain of calm over their group. He felt the panic slip slowly away. 'Tell me you're alright.'

Cassán would have liked to get annoyed with her for altering the mood, for taking away his choices regarding how he wanted to feel, but he was too busy feeling exactly the way she wanted him to.

'What are you thinking?' she asked. She glanced back at Eugene. 'What's he thinking?'

'I'm thinking forever is a very long time,' Cassán said before the Telepath could do so, 'which gives me quite a while to think about it.'

Moira smiled and hugged him again, saying something about knowing he'd come around eventually, while Mánus straightened his jacket and gave Cassán a meaningful nod.

'Happy New Year,' he said to them all, and left.

'Just think, Cassán,' Moira said shortly afterwards, beaming. 'We really can wish each other a happy new year in a hundred years' time. And a hundred years after that. Oh, you won't regret this, I just know it. None of us will.' She sighed and leaned against a table to watch people start to leave. 'At least, not for a really long time.'

# chapter sixteen

*You won't regret this. Not for a really long time.*

I opened my eyes to the near-total darkness of my dorm room, breathing very slowly as I grasped at the slippery edges of my dream. The more I reached, the harder it became to retrieve, but a few details were slow enough to be caught – a year, 1959; names, Cassán, Moira, Hawke; a feeling, of utter pleasure; a pair of violet eyes that I would recognise anywhere. I clung to these fragments jealously as I was struck with a sudden fear of forgetting the lot, and sat up abruptly. I'd never done it before but intuitively snapped my fingers and a sourceless, washed-out light bloomed within the room, light enough to see my way to my desk but not bright enough to startle awake any of the other girls.

I snatched at one of my school books and opened it to a random page and began scrawling. To my relief, the process of writing it all down brought a lot of details back to me, like the purple of a girl's dress and the retro clock on the wall that had captured the attention of all as it ticked closer to the New Year.

*You won't regret this. Not for a really long time.*

I couldn't recall the entirety of the conversation in any sort of detail but the woman Moira's parting comment kept ringing in my mind. It had the chilling feeling of words spoken much too soon.

Questions (like, how come after months of dreamless sleep here I'm suddenly dreaming? or, did this really happen to my grandfather? or, where did that new ability to create lights come from?) bubbled up in my head, bringing me to a level of alertness that in no way resembled the sleep I'd just been in and which would be difficult to wind down from. I continued to write, probably illegibly, because I couldn't see what I was doing in this pale werelight, when a miniscule movement to my right caught my attention and I looked up. My breath caught.

Sterling was sitting straight up in bed, eyes trained on me silently, looking super-creepy in this unnatural light. I waited for her to say something, but several seconds passed without dialogue, enough to be clear that she didn't intend to speak. This didn't exactly surprise me, as we'd gone two months by now without speaking at all, but the silence coupled with the deliberate eye contact and strangely upright posture was off-putting. I put my pen down.

'I'll turn it off,' I whispered, referring to the light, though I wasn't sure how I would do that as I didn't really know how I'd turned it *on* in the first place. I expected Sterling to roll over and go back to sleep and back to ignoring my existence, but instead she shoved her covers back.

'It'll wear off. Can we talk?' she whispered eagerly. I had been trying to click my fingers but her words startled me and the click lost its force. I stared at her. Talk? Us?

'Uh,' was all I said, dumbly, lost for words. She got out of bed and went to the door without my answer. The werelight reflected oddly in her eyes, I saw as she glanced back at me. A sheen of emerald green shone back at me and I shivered, wondering if I looked the same. I wanted this light gone.

After more difficulty than seemed usual for her, Sterling located her key, unlocked the door and pushed the door open gently to keep from waking the others. Extremely on edge now, I followed, coating myself in discreet wards. Sterling had never displayed any physical aggression towards me or anyone else as far as I'd seen – Xanthe was another story – but one should never be too careful, and as my sister would attest, paranoia was a survival skill.

The hall was better lit, which made me feel slightly less freaked out. Sterling walked ahead of me, strawberry blonde plaits swinging and woolly pink socks padding softly on the floor. She looked the picture of innocence but I was more than just curious as to what she wanted to discuss. I found it too hard to believe that she suddenly wanted to pull a Prescott move and apologise, three weeks after she missed her opportunity to side with them against Xanthe.

She stopped suddenly beside a boring tapestry I'd noticed a while back and stared at it. I slowed, keeping my distance.

'Where has it gone?' she asked, a tone of disbelief to her usually cheery voice. She touched the wall, running her fingers along the rectangular silhouette that marked the wallpaper. 'Where is it?'

'Where's what?' I asked warily. As long as we'd lived here, that ugly rug had hung right there, and probably had for many years before that, too.

'The portrait!' Sterling answered, shooting me a suspicious look, as though I were being deliberately dim. 'The big painting from the Treasaigh family used to hang here. It was here for so long. Look, you can still see the outline, where the wallpaper has faded around it.' She looked up and down the hall suddenly, as though seeing it for the first time, and made a sound of surprise. 'They're *all* different.'

'What's going on?' I called after her as she hurried to the next modern wall hanging and looked behind it for the fade lines. Sterling was a Seer, not a scrier, so it wasn't as though she could have tapped into impressions that showed her the old paintings. Maybe she read it about the old art here in a book from Renatus's library, but Sterling wasn't the bookish type, and if she was so interested in the house's art, how was it that she'd not noticed the art already hanging over the past three months? She lifted a frame away from the wall disdainfully to check the wall behind it, muttering, 'What's he done? Where's it all gone?'

'How do you even know what used to be here?' I demanded, feeling more and more uncomfortable with every passing second. Her emotions were so flat, so un-Sterling, that I knew it wasn't *her* that I was tapping into. Not normal Sterling. I had no real fear of Sterling, even though we were apparent enemies, but the vibe she was giving off tonight and her weirdo behaviour were making me anxious. My words seemed to startle her.

'I don't,' she assured me, making a visible effort to contain her attention to me only and to ignore the hall decor. She came back over. 'I really wanted to talk with you.'

'I don't think it's a good idea,' I said. I started backing away, feeling better with each step. 'I'm going back to bed.'

'No, wait, don't!' Sterling begged, suddenly desperate. 'I've been waiting so long! It never seems like the right time,' she added, when I gave her an odd look. 'Please, can't we talk?' She paused, as though something was only now occurring to her. 'Why, aren't we friends?'

'Uh, no, not really,' I said, stopping. Something was truly wrong here. Her eyes shone with that greeny light again, though we were away from the werelight of the dorm room. 'Sterling, are you alright?'

'You're Renatus's apprentice. Aristea,' she said eagerly, bounding over to me. With my mind I reached for my master's thoughts, worried. I found him awake, outside, but when I asked him to come, I knew he abandoned whatever he was doing and came straightaway.

'You know I am. That's why we aren't friends, remember?' I reminded her pointedly. Sterling ignored my words and grabbed for my hand. She took it in hers, but didn't actually touch me – my skin was coated in a fine layer of strong wards. Her eyes flickered, cocoa brown with a faint shine of emerald, upwards to meet mine, knowingly, and I felt something from her. Amusement? She turned my hand to admire the tattoo.

'What's he like?' she asked eagerly, breathlessly, much more Sterling-esque now. She stared into my eyes. 'He has this same mark on him now, doesn't he? Why did he choose you? What work do you do together?'

'I'm not talking about Renatus with you,' I said firmly. 'I'm-'

'What about you, then?' Her grip on my hand tightened; her expression turned feverish with excitement. 'We should fix this rift. Let's start over. Tell me all about yourself. Pretend we've never met.'

'I'm not sure we *have* met,' I stated, pulling my hand free of her jealous grip.

'Alright, I'll go first,' she said, straightening her shoulders. 'I'm Sterling, and-'

'Sterling who?' I interrupted on a hunch. She floundered for a second.

'Doesn't matter,' she covered, extending a hand. 'You're Aristea Byrne, pleased to meet you-'

'Sterling *who?*' I asked again, quite certain now that I was speaking with a total stranger. I wished I had brought my wand from the dorm, or something else weapon-like that I could draw on now. Generally I cast my magic without a tool but having something to show for how defensive I was feeling would have made me feel a little more secure. Sterling, or whoever she was, tilted her head to the side.

'Have you always been this suspicious?' she asked, clearly annoyed. I put my hands on my hips.

'No. I learnt to be because of jerks like you.'

Her eyes narrowed, but then she smiled tightly.

'You're becoming *him*.'

A noise on the staircase saw us both spin swiftly on our heels to look, and Sterling seemed to choke on her gasp of surprise. A shiver ran through her body and she grabbed at the wall – a total overreaction to what turned out to be nothing more than just normal night-time creaks of an old house. A flurry of genuine emotions rushed through her (confusion, fear, distress) and the anxiousness that had plagued me since I saw her sitting up in bed faded. She blinked a few times and then she was staring at me.

I stared back. The confident body language and discerning expression of seconds ago had been totally replaced by wariness and puzzlement. She didn't say anything, but this time it wasn't creepily deliberate and I wasn't so put-off by her silence. Her totally brown eyes were shadowed by a slight frown that told me she had no idea why I was staring so intently at her and made me wonder whether I'd imagined the whole exchange.

Ten or so awkward seconds passed before she pushed off the wall and edged past me to return wordlessly to the dorm, leaving me standing there in my pyjamas feeling like *I* was the crazy one.

'Is that such an impossible conclusion?' Renatus asked me the next day. He'd spent an hour that morning in his study with Sterling, Emmanuelle and Glen, trying to get to the bottom of what I'd experienced. Apparently Sterling had been utterly overwhelmed by the chance to be inside his office, even with other adults present, but had absolutely no memory of getting out of bed last night, let alone talking to me in the hallway about paintings and tattoos. Glen had found no signs of forced entry into her mind. Emmanuelle had examined her and found no hint that she'd been hexed or cursed (apparently, those were things, and apparently those were things that required carving or marking the body to enable it as a vessel for someone else... so I was grateful Emmanuelle hadn't found Sterling marked or carved) and had taken blood to run medical tests, for whatever good that would do.

It didn't leave many explanations, but Renatus's suggestion was particularly unwelcome.

I folded my arms and glared at his back. We were outside, standing in the rain, although an elegant umbrella forced upon me by Fionnuala was keeping the majority of me quite dry. Renatus was opting to just get wet as he used both hands to feel and weave invisible braids of magic in the air above us.

'I am *not* crazy,' I retorted. '*She's* the one who can't remember an entire conversation.'

'Could you have been sleepwalking? That could explain why you remember it as real.'

'No. I'd just *woken* from a dream-'

'Vision,' he corrected, as always adamant that I was unable to dream while asleep on this estate.

'-so I can't have woken up only to sleepwalk out of there after Sterling,' I finished reasonably.

'So she was the one sleepwalking,' he offered. 'Despite your insistence to the contrary, everything she said *could* have been hidden somewhere in her mind – wanting to make amends with you, noticing the evidence of previous paintings, might be things she thinks about subconsciously and might have surfaced while she was sleepwalking.'

'But she doesn't sleepwalk.'

'She did last night.'

Seriously? I was so annoyed with him for not believing me. It was bad enough that Sterling had fallen straight back to sleep upon return to our room last night, unable to be woken by my gentle prods and whispers, and had ignored me as usual over breakfast, giving no indication that anything weird had happened between us in the hallway and making me wonder whether I really had imagined it. I glared back at Renatus, thinking fleetingly that here was a man I'd decided to kill for, and the best gratitude he could show was to make fun of me.

He sighed. 'I'm not making fun of you,' he promised, and I quickly stashed away the rest of my thoughts, realising he'd caught the tail end of that thought and could have, if he'd felt like it, followed it back to its source and seen the forbidden beginning of it. He was distracted, however, and didn't really notice. He continued his weaving, squinting against rain falling in his eyes as he stared upward and reached into the air, fingers twisting like they were braiding something unseen. 'I just don't know what else to tell you.'

'Well, I think you're being short-sighted and unhelpful,' I said finally. 'She was not sleepwalking and I am not losing my mind. She knew stuff she doesn't normally know and forgot other stuff. Her *surname*, chief among them.' I moved to stand in front of him. 'Where did the paintings go?'

'I think *you're* being obtuse, and rather insensitive,' Renatus responded, though he didn't sound offended. Slowly, he was running his hands along what seemed to be a thick, invisible rope two metres above the ground, feeling for inconsistencies. 'Obviously, I swapped them.'

'Yes, I figured,' I answered coolly, 'and I can even read numbers, so I worked out that you got all the new ones around the time of the storm.'

'What a detective you're becoming,' he commented, without malice. 'A year later, actually. When I got control of the money I needed to replace every single piece.'

'Why? You don't even care about art.'

'You don't know that.'

'Oh, I know that.'

He dropped his hands from whatever spell he was working on and sighed again.

'I'm not saying that what you're telling me *didn't* happen,' he said, 'but I came straight in to you and that hallway and there was no residual magic there. You say you think she was someone else but if someone was sitting around a fire somewhere trying to puppeteer her – which, by the way, can't be done to anyone inside my walls – their trace would lie all around us. That's a messy sort of spell.'

He'd had his wand on him and had showed me the traces of magic in the hall where I'd spoken to Sterling. Broken magic and memory fragments, the sorts of things I tapped into all the time when scrying, lit up like we were shining a black light on blood. Most were old, faded. Nothing appeared recent or particularly concentrated.

'Aren't possessions done by, like, ghosts? Dead people?' I asked.

Renatus frowned and closed down emotionally, but not before I saw his eyes dart in the direction of the orchard.

'I'm not sure I believe in that,' he said, quite firmly, giving me the idea that he *chose* not to believe in that because he was uncomfortable with the concept. 'I'm talking about people with malicious or selfish intentions, reaching out with magic to control the actions of another.'

'Just sitting by a campfire and doing a spell and possessing someone, somewhere?'

'It's not that simple, but yes. Or Haunting.'

I bit my lip and looked away, feeling embarrassed although I'd not done anything wrong. My first breakthrough with scrying had come when Qasim had forcefully removed my emotional blocks and I'd exhausted my brain with practice to the point I'd pretty much torn through whatever veil existed there and tumbled down to the very extreme of the gift. Haunting was a scrier-specific ability, the top of my potential... and highly illegal. Renatus had told me later that I had to control it, and *never* do it again, because it was so incredibly dangerous. Had I touched anyone while I wandered among them, unseen and disembodied, I would have possessed them.

He was worried that if none of the other possibilities were ringing true, this option alone remained. He'd elected not to tell Sterling, he said, to avoid alarming her, but now he was out here, in the rain, checking the house's magical defences. Though a rarer gift, he, Qasim and I were not the only scriers around.

'Why would anyone want to possess Sterling Adams?' I wondered aloud, because while Sterling was a reasonably high-level Seer, she was not all that bright and not all that skilled in other areas of magic. Renatus shrugged and frowned at something only he could see, and reached out with one hand to nudge it with his fingers. A master clockmaker with his invisible clockworks.

'That's supposing she *was* possessed,' he mentioned, because there was no way of proving a Haunting, apparently, unlike the other possibilities. 'The White Elm exists to police that sort of behaviour, so it's very rare. We haven't had any cases of it as long as I've been on the council.'

Just because he hadn't received any reports of it didn't mean it wasn't happening, I knew. The council's sight had been seriously impaired by Lisandro's desertion. I tried to put that frightening prospect from my mind and tilted my umbrella to tip some of the water off.

'And the green in her eyes?' I checked. 'Is that common to Hauntings?'

'Not that I've heard. Trick of the light,' Renatus reasoned. He returned to squinting up into the rain and gently lacing his fingers between intricate webs of spells I couldn't see. 'There's nothing at all out of sorts here now, although that doesn't mean it wasn't disrupted for a while. It must settle after a few hours, giving you that window of opportunity to scry in your sleep. And *maybe* the window of opportunity someone needed to take hold of Sterling Adams,' he added, uneasily and grimly. I'd already told him everything I remembered of my dream, and he'd made a sudden connection – last night he'd done some maintenance work on the house's web of protection spells, the first time he'd altered them at all since we lost Aubrey and the Elm Stone. Both nights he'd not slept, and both nights I'd woken from visions of the 1950s.

On this night, Sterling had been utterly strange, maybe not her true self, and that scared me a good deal more. I knew the council was conferring on it. I knew I needed to leave it be, but what a weird, weird night.

'So you *do* have a spell up that stops us from dreaming,' I prompted Renatus, though I'd guessed this already. 'Which one is it?'

'Find it yourself,' he said, not nastily, and stood while I stared up hopelessly into the grey beyond my umbrella. Glen had worked with me on seeing energies when I adjusted my focus, but I couldn't get the focus necessary to see what Renatus had stitched together over the estate. I imagined, from what stray thoughts I gathered from his mind, a cage made of glass strands.

*Not far off*, he admitted, and waved a hand. Momentarily, lit pale greeny-blue, vague criss-crossed streaks shone above us, and then faded from my sight.

*A dream net*, I commented with wonder, and aloud asked, 'Why? What's so wrong with dreaming?'

'You of all people shouldn't have to ask that,' Renatus replied after a long moment. I knew he didn't want to discuss it when he redirected the conversation to what I'd scried. 'What were they all doing there together?'

'I think technically, they were celebrating New Years, but it looked more like our grandfathers were getting involved with some things that were over their heads.'

'Sounds about correct, considering my grandfather's surname,' Renatus commented. 'Who were the others?'

I paused, trying to remember.

*You won't regret this. Not for a really long time.*

The woman's words chilled me even now, but as soon as these words ran through my mind, a flood of little facts and details tumbled back to the fore.

'Andrew Hawke, someone Dubois, and Moira,' I said, grabbing the ends of my hair as the words left my mouth and I realised who one of these people must be. 'Hawke – like Kenneth Hawke? Asheleigh Hawke?' No coincidences, I reminded myself, and kept going. 'He was a Seer. He knew stuff and the others were just going to take his word for it and do something both our grandfathers had already decided they would regret.' I fought desperately through the fog of my memory but couldn't pull their conversation forward. 'I wish I could remember what they were going to do. I wish I could remember what Hawke told them. I wish I knew why I even had the stupid dream at all!'

'Stop trying to remember,' Renatus suggested, trying to calm my building frustration. 'The memory will return when you need it. And you will need it. Three of the men you saw went on to have children who were killed by Lisandro and grandchildren who survived him, for reasons he hasn't considered important enough to tell us.' He moved on to another spell to check. 'If Shell's grandfather was such an amazing Seer, it explains why Lisandro kept her alive in the first place. Too bad she turned out to have no talent, or so Aubrey led us to believe.'

We fell into an easy silence and after a while I found myself staring at the orchard. Many times I'd been drawn to Renatus's least favourite place but it had been a long time since I'd gone in. Life at Morrissey Estate had been so busy with normal and regular school-and-friend-stuff for the past few weeks, until last night's weirdness had interrupted that run. I'd not been irretrievably traumatised in some time now, and hadn't had any fights with Renatus, so I hadn't felt the need to escape into the depths of the apple orchard. That had to be a good thing.

Renatus noticed my gaze but didn't follow it. I could feel from him a conflict that was by now familiar; often there were topics he wanted to broach with me but also wanted to keep to himself. I kept away from his thoughts, waiting for him to bring it up without prompt. When he finally spoke, it was definitely not what I'd expected.

'It's Ana's birthday in two days,' he said, offhand. He kept at his task without looking at me. I felt his withdrawal as he contained the pain and sadness that went with this fact.

'I didn't know that,' I said eventually. I stayed quiet as I realised something else – Ana's birthday was the day Lisandro had attacked the Morrisseys and killed her and their parents. I counted back. In two days' time, it would be exactly eight years since Renatus had lost his entire family. What an awful time of year for him. No wonder he'd not wanted to talk about the paintings, if their replacement really was related to the storm. Had they been painful reminders of something too hurtful to dwell on? I didn't like to think about it; I assumed he liked it even less. 'It's mine in twenty-seven days.'

He still didn't look at me, but I sensed his surprise at my topic change. Normally I jumped at any mention of Ana and clung to the subject.

'I didn't know that,' he responded, immediately more open. 'That's less than four weeks away.' He appeared to contemplate this for a moment. 'It's a Sunday,' Renatus commented, dropping his hands again and looking down the hill towards the gate.

'No, it'll be a Saturday,' I corrected, because one knows these things about one's own upcoming birthdays.

'I mean *that*,' he said, pointing. I looked. A car had just pulled up outside.

'Mortals sometimes drive cars on Sundays,' I told him teasingly. 'They're even allowed.'

He started down the hill with me following behind him. He glanced once back at the house, presumably letting Fionnuala know that he was handling it and there was no need for her to come out and get wet.

The driver must have seen us coming because he or she stayed inside the car until we got near. It was an older vehicle, the shine long gone from its metallic paint, and the window wipers worked hard to clear the water from the front windscreen. There were quite a few little dings in the bonnet, I saw, and a scratch along the passenger door... where my cousin Kelly had ground past a lamp post while learning to drive.

'I know that car!' I exclaimed, breaking into a jog for the last fifteen metres. Renatus lengthened his stride to keep pace with me and laid a restraining hand on my arm when I reached the gate to stop me from opening it without being certain. The wipers stopped as the engine was disengaged and the driver's side door opened. An umbrella poked through the gap and immediately opened to cover my aunt, Leanne, as she stepped out.

'Aristea?' she asked, apparently surprised to see me despite having driven for over an hour to this obscure location and not knowing a single other person for miles. She shut the door, rounded the car bonnet and approached the gate. 'You're alright.'

'Of course I am,' I said, smiling. I pressed myself against the wrought iron bars of the gate, amazed by how good it felt to see her. Aunt Leanne was my father's sister. She had the goldy-blonde hair and light complexion of the Byrnes, like my father Darren and my two siblings. When my parents and brother had died, she'd taken Ange and me in, and even though we'd soon moved out again, she'd remained a constant (if sometimes annoying) support for us. Her daughter Kelly was my only cousin, and her husband Patrick, a schoolteacher, had home-schooled me through secondary education when my Empathic abilities got out of control. I looked past my aunt's concerned expression to the car. 'Where's everyone else?'

'Everyone else?' she asked, eyeing Renatus without enthusiasm, even slight suspicion.

'Uncle Patrick, Angela... Kelly?' I realised quickly that none of my special people had come with her. The car was empty. Aunt Leanne frowned at me as though this should have been evident.

'It's just me here,' she answered, 'to bring you home.'

The patter of the rain on our umbrellas filled the awkward silence that followed.

'What?' I laughed finally. 'Home?'

'This isn't a joke, young lady. Go and get your things; we're leaving.'

*Young lady.* Wow, that sounded so different from when Fionnuala said it. The awkward silence returned as I stared at Aunt Leanne, unable to connect what she was saying with my reality. I liked the Academy. I liked sharing a room with Hiroko. I liked learning about magic. I liked Renatus and, while I didn't like *everything* that came with it, I liked being his apprentice. Leaving was not an option. Renatus made an executive decision and stepped forward to touch the gate. It opened and he approached my aunt. Her eyes widened and she actually took a half-step back.

'I'm Renatus,' he said, offering a hand. 'I'm the headmaster here.' He was dripping wet, but that didn't completely undermine his commanding and authoritative presence. Cautiously, Aunt Leanne accepted his hand.

'You're on the White Elm,' she noted, her face and aura a rotating mix of emotions ranging from dislike and mistrust to awe and curiosity. 'You're a lot younger than I thought you would be.'

'Aunty!' I exclaimed, embarrassed by her forthrightness, even though this was exactly how I myself always spoke to Renatus.

'Leanne Nolan,' she added quickly, shaking Renatus's hand. Her eyes skirted all over him, as though trying to work him out. She was impressed on one hand, because he was the first White Elm she'd ever met (and she *loved* the White Elm) but at the same time displeased, because he was young, wet and insanely attractive, and therefore too much of a temptation to be a decent teacher to her niece. 'I'm Aristea's aunt. I'm here to collect her.'

'But why?' I burst out, rounding the open gate to join them beside the car. 'What's the matter?'

'We should discuss this inside, in the dry,' Renatus suggested, adding, *Get back inside the walls*, to me, but my aunt ignored him.

'Aristea, your sister and I haven't heard from you in a month,' she snapped at me. My heart sank with realisation as I counted back to the last time I'd written a letter. 'We didn't even know if you were alive. I've had enough of the worrying. It's time you came home.'

'I keep forgetting,' I admitted in a small voice, backing up through the gates as Renatus again directed me to do so. 'I've been really busy-'

'Yes, I'm sure there are excuses to be heard, but you are a part of this family and you have a responsibility to keep us informed,' Aunt Leanne said crossly. 'You're clearly not old enough to prioritise your responsibilities, as I suspected when you first signed up. Don't walk away from me, miss.'

I opened my mouth to protest; Renatus spoke instead.

'We can be overheard out here in the open,' he said. 'We need to move inside the walls where the spells on the property can protect our privacy. It seems we have a lot to discuss.'

Aunt Leanne put her free hand on her hip and frowned at him. Her confidence was shaky, though; her hand slipped down after only a second to hang loosely at her side.

'I don't know what we need to talk about,' she said, trying to maintain her bossy air but also put off by his obvious aura of power and self-assured manner. 'I am a great supporter of the White Elm and I believe in the things your council does, but I'm taking my niece home with me right now.'

'Respectfully, I'm not sure you're taking her anywhere, even after we've spoken at great length,' Renatus said smoothly, rendering my aunt speechless. 'If Aristea wants to leave with you, we may be able to arrange that, but otherwise I'm afraid you'll leave alone. You aren't Angela Byrne. Aristea's legal guardian is the only person I will release her to.'

'Did Ange tell you to come?' I asked her curiously. Aunt Leanne shifted her weight to the other foot and changed her umbrella to the other hand.

'I did speak with her,' she said elusively. 'She knows I'm here. She's worried about you. We all are, what with what we've been reading in the forums.'

'What forums?' I demanded. 'What have you been reading?'

'Kelly reads them, on her computer,' my aunt replied. 'So does Angela. It doesn't matter *what* forums, what matters is we're worried about you. Your sister worries. She's looking forward to seeing you again.'

'But she didn't send you to retrieve Aristea,' Renatus interpreted, 'and didn't come with you, leading me to believe that she doesn't wish to withdraw Aristea at this time.'

'She just doesn't want to be the bad guy,' Aunt Leanne insisted. 'Angela wants Aristea back every bit as much as I do.' She drew herself up a bit. 'We were happy to give Aristea this freedom, but she's our girl and we're no longer confident she's safe.'

'I am safe,' I insisted, at the same time Renatus said, firmly, 'She *is* safe.'

'Aunty, just come in out of the rain,' I pleaded with my aunt. I extended a hand, beckoning. I didn't like arguing with her, and I didn't like to think of my sister at home, alone and lonely and missing me. I wanted Aunt Leanne to see how great my life here was, so she could report back to Angela and ease her fears. 'Come in and meet some of my friends.'

'Aristea, get in the car,' Aunt Leanne ordered. 'I'll get your things myself.'

'Aunty-' I tried, thinking of the other kids who'd been withdrawn earlier in the year. I didn't want to be another one of them.

'Now, Aristea.'

'I'll write more, I swear.' I wanted to stay and see the four boys return. I wanted to be here when Hiroko and Garrett were reunited. I wanted to see Teresa recover and come back to work. I wanted to see Kendra hook Heath, even if I wasn't totally sold on him. I wanted to be here when Susannah's mysterious date, June twenty-sixth arrived, so I could decide whether or not to follow through with her secretive plans and find out what a rabbit's foot had to do with it. I glanced at Renatus and knew for sure that I would be going nowhere. More than any of that other stuff, I *had* to stay because I wanted to save him from his fate.

'I'm not arguing with you-'

'Neither am I,' I finished, speaking over her. 'I'm not arguing and I'm not going anywhere. I live here now. I'm part of something here. I'm important. And I'm happy.'

Aunt Leanne took a deep breath, clearly readying herself for another round with me. Renatus left her to return to my side within the walls of the house, briefly touching my shoulder. My aunt did not miss it and seemed to lose her puff. She looked between us, maybe only just realising that she was fighting a losing battle. I was sure I wouldn't like the next thing she had to say, but thankfully she never said it, because space contorted several metres behind her and Elijah appeared with Lord Gawain in tow. The shock of seeing two men – men she recognised from the White Elm's newsletter, no less – appear in mid-air seemed to put all of her other concerns out of her mind.

'Good morning,' Lord Gawain said with his usual cheer, quickly opening an umbrella and moving forward to greet my aunt. 'Welcome. My name is-'

'Lord Gawain,' my aunt finished, a little breathlessly, shaking his hand with both of hers. 'I know. I read the newsletter. I'm Leanne. Nolan,' she added as an afterthought.

'Leanne Nolan,' Elijah spoke up thoughtfully. 'I know your name. You write in to the newsletter, don't you?'

My aunt blushed delicately with pleasure at the recognition, and I recalled that Elijah used to be the one to read and answer the White Elm's mail.

'You must be Aristea's aunt,' the High Priest noted, looking between us critically. 'Yes; I see the similarities... The same forehead, hairline...' He shook his head. 'My apologies. We've barely met.'

'No harm done,' Aunt Leanne assured him. 'People have said more than once that I look more like my brother's girls than I do my own daughter.'

'Please, come inside for some tea and biscuits,' Lord Gawain encouraged pleasantly, gesturing for Aunt Leanne to precede him through the gates. 'It is always a delight to meet our members' families.'

'Your... members?' Aunt Leanne asked quizzically, glancing at me as she stepped onto the estate.

'Of course,' Lord Gawain said easily. He patted my shoulder as he passed me. 'Aristea is Renatus's apprentice, and Renatus is one of our most esteemed councillors. She is a member of the White Elm by proxy, and is on our waiting list to become a full councillor as soon as a place becomes available after her twentieth birthday.'

I knew my aunt had already known all this, but the words clearly resonated within her. She looked on me with renewed pride, now remembering what my being here represented for her family and eventual social standing, and when she next glanced at Renatus, it was with less suspicion and with more curious interest and respect.

'I hope my niece is behaving herself here,' Aunt Leanne said now to Lord Gawain, much more at ease as she walked with him and Elijah up to the house. Renatus and I dropped back behind them like naughty children. I'd had my silent issues with Lord Gawain and his pussy-footing ways but right then I wouldn't have swapped him or his timing for anything in the world.

My aunt stayed for about three hours. She spoke at length with Lord Gawain about dull socio-political topics that I could have slept through, and (once dry and redressed) Renatus impressed her by joining this conversation knowledgeably and eloquently. By the end of her stay she seemed to love him even more than she did me. He managed to make her completely forget why she'd even come.

'You know so much,' Aunt Leanne gushed, when Renatus finished explaining the reasons for the continued independence of Avalon from the governance of the White Elm.

'Renatus is very well-connected with many affiliated and non-affiliated groups and individuals,' Lord Gawain said, a nice way of saying that Renatus knew a lot of shady types. 'It is through their cooperation with him that the White Elm gains much of its intelligence. Because of a lot of the sensitivities we've spoken of today, many of these groups do not like to be seen to be dealing directly with the White Elm, so naturally, this is very delicate work. Aristea helps with this.'

Aunt Leanne regarded me again, becoming more steadily impressed by the minute.

'So... she's like an undercover spy?' she asked.

'Because we're scriers, it's mostly spying,' Renatus said, 'and research. For the most part, much less exciting than it sounds.'

*For the most part.* But for the least part, on that odd occasion, it was much, much more exciting than it sounded. He left out the bloodletting rituals, the shoulder I'd dislocated, the skin that had been burnt off my arm and neck... I, for my part, had neglected to pull my sleeve up and come clean about the tattoo on my wrist, and Renatus hadn't chosen to display his, either.

'They're diplomats,' Lord Gawain explained smoothly, and I choked on my next mouthful of tea. Beside me, Renatus cleared his throat lightly. My aunt, thankfully, did not detect our amusement.

I introduced Aunt Leanne to my friends; she was surprised, I could tell, by their diverse nationalities, and, apparently by the fact that Addison was a boy.

'Is he your *boyfriend*?' she asked me, teasingly, as I walked her back to her car that afternoon. I poked my tongue at her.

'Of course not,' I said. 'I don't have time for a boyfriend. He's just a very good friend.'

'And Renatus is out-of-bounds by decree of Fate?' It wasn't a question but her intonation went high on the last syllable, making it sound like it was. I knew she was just checking, being the mother I no longer had. 'He *is* a nice-looking man, it would be understandable...'

'Eww,' I confirmed. I stopped with her at the gate. Water squelched under my boots. 'He's my teacher. He looks after me. He listens to me. He shows me how to hone my skills to get the most out of myself.' I didn't tell her that he was part of me, that I loved him as I'd loved my brother, that I had made up my mind to murder someone for him. That was kind of personal. 'If we were anything else it would just be gross.'

'You know, you three girls are so different,' Aunt Leanne mused, reaching out from under her umbrella to underneath mine to rearrange the messy hair hanging over my cheeks. 'Kelly is just boy-crazy. Everything is boys, boys, boys. She won't be able to control herself when she meets your master.' We both smiled, because we knew Kelly, but I also smiled because I knew Renatus, and was pretty sure that if Emmanuelle Saint Clair wasn't good enough for him, Kelly Nolan certainly wouldn't be. My aunt continued, 'Kelly loves men; Angela hates them. And then there's you. You don't even seem to notice them. It's not a bad thing. It's refreshing to have one girl I don't need to worry about. And here I was today, coming to snatch you up because I thought you were the one I should be concerned for! I'm so glad I was wrong. It's funny, is all.'

She shook her head and hugged me tightly while I thought on her words. Was it weird that I was so apparently indifferent to the opposite sex? And what did she mean about Angela, hating men?

'Aunty,' I began, questions bubbling up, but she released me quickly and shushed me.

'I have to go, before I convince myself to take you away with me,' she interrupted. I could see that she was tearing up. I unlocked the gate and she kissed me one more time before letting herself out and shutting the gate behind her with a clang. 'What an amazing future you've carved out for yourself. I'm so very proud of you, of course, even if I didn't want you here to start with. Angela will be so impressed when I tell her about today. Just don't leave us hanging for that long ever again, young lady.'

'I won't,' I promised. 'Love you.'

'I love you, too, little darling,' Aunt Leanne said with an adoring smile, and then was back in her car and driving away into the rain.

# chapter seventeen

I kept my promise, wrote letters immediately that night to my aunt and sister, and made a silent pledge to begin a habit of writing my letters every Sunday night to send on Mondays. I knew I'd been a terrible sister and niece and I didn't want to slip into that category again.

Renatus got steadily more miserable and withdrawn over the next day until he was almost totally blocked from me by Tuesday morning. I didn't see him or even sense him on the property for the majority of the day, but when I asked Fionnuala where he would have gone, she looked surprised and said, 'The same place he always goes on this day.' She looked upwards sadly and continued gathering plates. I left my friends building houses from cards to go looking for my master, having suddenly understood what the housekeeper meant. How could I have forgotten? When I reached the top floor I went to the door of Ana's room and opened it very quietly.

Renatus was sitting on the floor with his back against the bed and a few piles of paper that looked very much like work beside him. His aura was cloaked in wards to prevent anyone, even me, from sensing his energy in the house, but now that he was caught, he let some of them down, and I could feel the deep, dark, grey well of misery he was drowning in. I kept myself right back from that, lest I fall in.

'No, I wouldn't rather do this in my office,' he said, pre-empting my thoughts. 'I tried having today off but sitting in here with nothing to do was too overwhelming.'

I didn't have anything to say to that, because sitting alone in a dead sibling's bedroom was in itself a bad idea, regardless of whether or not there was something to do. I hated that he did this to himself, year after year, knowing it would only make him feel worse. I squared my shoulders and fortified the type of wards I used to shut out other people's emotions (which could so quickly poison mine if I let them through), and then I shut the door and crossed the room. While he watched with surprise and mild interest, I threw myself onto the bed and wriggled over on my stomach to be able to see what he was reading over his shoulder.

'What are you doing?' he asked, apparently at a loss. I stretched for an envelope on the floor. It was just out of reach. Renatus moved it to where I could get it, and I snatched it up.

'This is *my* room, remember?' I reminded him as I got comfortable and tore open the letter. 'So I don't even know why you're in here, to be honest.'

Renatus didn't answer but his eyes and energy did soften, signs that if he were a normal person, he would be smiling.

I read the letter. It was addressed to the White Elm, and Renatus didn't try to stop me. The letterhead indicated it came from the medical examiner's office in the County of Dane, Wisconsin, USA, and the short letter itself told of a sorcerer found dead with no apparent cause of death. I summarised it for Renatus.

'That's Emmanuelle's domain,' he said, passing me a second envelope. 'I think she's on call today. She can get straight onto it.'

I started a "read" pile beside my elbow and got into the next one. A woman in Sydney was concerned about her son's spell-crafting and had enclosed a sample of his writings, in case it was bordering on illegal. Personally, I would not have alerted the council if I was worried about my loved one's hobby and its technical legality by sending them evidence of his potential law-breaking, but I knew it was the technically legal thing to do.

'Spell check,' I announced, smirking at the double meaning that was lost on Renatus. He reached back over his shoulder while he continued reading what was in his other hand and took what I handed him. After a moment he turned his attention to the son's handwritten spells, and I extended my hand again for another envelope. 'Next.'

'Why do people send us these?' he wondered aloud, voicing my own thoughts as he continued, 'It just puts her son on our radar for the future.' He grabbed a stack of envelopes and passed them back to me, and I got into them.

'Are the spells bad?'

Renatus shrugged; his shoulders rolled against the mattress and I felt the pull on the blankets beneath my elbows. 'So our laws say. Attempts at transformative magic. If the boy's an adult and tries out any of these spells he could be charged.'

'You don't agree?'

He shrugged again. 'No one's asking if I agree.'

'*I* am.'

'I think the White Elm does our society too much good to complain too loudly about the restrictions it places on magic,' he said carefully, 'but when it comes down to it, no, I don't agree with punishing sorcerers trying to transform into wolves by moonlight or change their hair colour with magic. From what I understand, the wolf change is excruciating – they pay their price – and everyone else playing with magic is just doing what our people have done for centuries. But luckily,' he added, stapling the evidence and letter to a blank form beside him and starting to fill it out, 'no one asks me.'

It had occurred to me before and did again now that Renatus was different from the rest of the council. Some of his views deviated quite widely from the set traditional values of the White Elm, and while a few of those he shared with others – one-can-be-worth-more-than-the-many Jadon, stand-by-your-word Emmanuelle, lies-that-serve-a-greater-purpose-need-not-be-revealed Qasim and now what-the-White-Elm-doesn't-know-about-magic-use-doesn't-hurt-them Oneida – I doubted there was anyone else who held as *many* disconnected views as he.

No one else, admittedly, lived with the traumas he did.

*Let's steer clear of those traumas,* Renatus suggested firmly, reaching into my mind and closing metaphorical books of thought before I could start reflecting on the history of this day. I sat up like I'd been hit with a shock. I didn't know he could *do* that, shut down my thoughts on a whim, decide what I thought about or didn't think about.

'Don't do that,' I said, voice steadier than I anticipated. He twisted in place to look back at me, surprised by my firm tone.

'Don't do what?'

'Make my choices for me. *I* make my choices. I choose what I think about.'

He stared at me, and I realised he hadn't known he was doing it. The same way I suppressed my own thoughts as they arose, the way anybody controls their unwanted thoughts, he'd felt the stirrings of my reflections in our increasingly shared mindspace and mistaken them for his.

We were starting to share opinions and now we could put a stop to one another's thoughts before they even came up. It was simultaneously fascinating and terrifying, because for how long could two people retain their individuality in a spiralling amalgamation like this? Right now, wards kept Renatus's crushing emotions from tainting mine. He was intense, emotionally overwhelming, and getting worse the longer he was paired with emotional me; would the wards always work, or would those powerful feelings one day soon begin to seep through and become part of me, too? What about our secrets? How long before those, locked up so tight, slipped silently across our connection and became his without my permission?

He would know.

I rejected the thought and my next words came out harsher than intended.

'Do you really come and sit in here and be deliberately miserable on this day every year?' I demanded, and he shut down. 'For eight years? Will you do it again next year?'

'Probably, if I'm still alive. What is it to you?' he contested.

*What is it to you?* If only I could say. 'It's depressing, for one. And it makes no sense. You gave this room to me. What would you have done today if I'd moved in properly, and moved everything around and hung posters on the walls and left my crap lying all over the place?' I paused for effect, giving him time to respond to this challenge. He was silent, seething. Hurt. 'If you want to feel closer to them, you need to go to them,' I said firmly, climbing off the bed. I knew he knew what I was talking about. His expression went stony. 'Don't be stubborn. I've visited my family's gravesites.'

'We've already established that you are both braver and better than I am,' he answered. Already on edge and now annoyed with his excuse, I kicked over the nearest pile of paper. He glared up at me. 'That's mature.'

'Says you,' I retorted, 'who thinks the best way to remember his family's loss is to sit on the floor and continue with his work as normal so he doesn't have to think about what today means.'

I turned and left the room, slamming the door shut behind me. I knew I'd been callous and already wished it back; the discomforting concept of losing control of my own mind kept me walking. His means of handling grief was *not* something I ever wanted any part in – would that be me, given another year connected to him? I strode almost to the staircase, my brisk footsteps the only sound echoing in the silence, before I heard the door open and close loudly. I didn't look back but knew Renatus was following, however reluctantly and unhappily.

I hadn't planned it, but now I was heading outside.

It was raining again, so I grabbed an umbrella at the door and continued out into the drizzle with Renatus thirty paces behind me. I walked all the way to the edge of the trees, to the spot where the trees thinned out and a distinct path became apparent. Every step closer I felt stronger, more attracted. I knew that Renatus felt the opposite, but when I looked back at him I saw the energy swirling around him, filling those sinkholes we shared.

I stopped there and let him catch up. We stood together at the mouth of the path, looking down its length of still silence towards the little gate at its end, for several minutes. I could hear Renatus breathing. It was the quick and uneven breathing of someone on the verge of panic, his body prepared for flight. This was his day of mourning and I'd just made it many times harder than it needed to be in a momentary overreaction and resultant spite. Of course he would reject any rising thoughts of Ana and the storm today, and of course it would be harder to tell whether those thoughts were his or mine in a muddled, tired and distraught brain. Remorse swelled in me. He was my protector and mentor and our pasts shared many of the same traumas, but it was easy to forget that despite this, those traumas had affected him differently from me and he was a deeply damaged human being.

The word "sorry" was forbidden between us, so I swallowed it. I didn't look at him. I didn't speak. Instead I tentatively took his hand in mine. His skin was always so cold. He barely seemed to notice me. His eyes were fixed on the gate, and beyond that, the looming shadows of gravestones.

'This is worse,' he said eventually, in a controlled voice. I felt another rush of guilt. I was a bad friend.

'Than the room?' I guessed.

'Not worse than the room. Worse than... before. It's worse, knowing what really happened. Lisandro could have picked any day. He chose Ana's birthday, *knowing* we always had a picnic outside. He'd attended every single one up to then. It was easier when I thought it was a stranger and that I'd already destroyed him.'

I squeezed his hand, my unexpected stress and anger of minutes before totally redirected.

'We'll get him,' I promised softly, keeping my thoughts to myself but completely certain right now that I'd made the right choice. Lisandro had done enough damage to his godson; Renatus didn't deserve the scars that would come from having to hunt and kill him. I could be tough. I could carry them instead.

'I want to believe that,' Renatus responded, confiding this uncertainty for the first time. 'He's got the upper hand. He has hostages we can't allow him to harm. He knows us better than we know him. He knows our allies but we don't know his. He holds all the cards.'

*Your war has been an uphill battle of uselessness since before it started. Lisandro fights for reasons you don't understand.*

*Wear shoes you can run in. And bring the rabbit's foot.*

The words of Seers murmured from the corners of my recent memory.

'Not all of them,' I said, dropping his hand to dig in my pockets. He hadn't noticed me take his hand but he looked down when I let go. I produced the little slip of paper Susannah had given me a month ago when she'd told me the news that had changed my future. I carried it with me most days, waiting for the opportunity to share it with him. Waiting for it to make sense. 'We have this.'

He took it and read it with an uncomprehending shrug.

'Susannah gave it to us as an apology gift after that circle,' I explained. 'She wouldn't say anything else except that we can make the future we want if we are in this place at this time.'

'Seers,' Renatus muttered darkly, but I saw the tiniest glimmer of hope in his eyes. He waved the note at me. 'How do you feel about this? You've held onto it long enough without bringing it up.'

'I was angry with her,' I admitted, 'but that doesn't mean she isn't right about it. I think we should wait until the night and make a decision then.'

'So you want to go,' Renatus interpreted. He gave the note back. 'Do you think the night of the twenty-sixth will roll around and you'll be able to think of anything else? You already made our decision.'

His words awoke fragments of my only partly remembered dream, and I suddenly recalled his grandfather saying something very similar.

'Alright, we're going,' I agreed. I gestured to the graveyard. 'Would you like to go closer?'

Renatus looked for a very long time before shaking his head slowly.

'No, not today,' he said, closing down his umbrella and handing it to me. The steady rain struck his dry hair and clothes but he didn't seem to notice. He closed his eyes and breathed deeply. I was glad to see the sickened look gone from his face. His breaths came evenly now. 'This is close enough for today.'

Grief affects everybody differently and everybody heals differently. I took the umbrellas and left him there to think, meditate, remember, be miserable or whatever else he was doing.

Sometimes Renatus irritated me but he certainly wasn't stupid, and as usual he proved to be correct in his prediction that Susannah's mysterious place, date and time would play more heavily on my mind as it grew nearer. Only a week later I found myself digging atlases out of dusty shelves in the library, wanting to get a better idea about the area of Scotland I'd apparently decided to visit and unable to stop thinking on what might happen there. Susannah had recommended running shoes, implying some degree of urgency, either chasing someone or running away from someone else, and then followed that with a random comment about rabbits' feet, which only made me feel more curious and unsettled. I took to running in the early mornings before breakfast, as I used to do with my sister when I lived at home. It did little to work off the anxiety but at least made me feel that I was preparing myself in some way for whatever the twenty-sixth would bring. What was Susannah sending us into?

Apparently Fionnuala stacked a bunch of different national news publications onto a coffee table in the front of the library each week, but they were snapped up swiftly, which explained why I had never noticed and might never have known except that Iseult read our local newspaper, told me all this and then reported that the unexpected good weather that greeted us through the dining room windows that breakfast was not to last. Rain was due to set in from Monday, so she and I insisted on the group spending the whole weekend outdoors. The others were less enthused, but as locals, Iseult and I knew what the weather forecaster meant by "set in". It meant there would be no more pleasant sunny walks through the grounds for a while, and that we would remember this outdoor opportunity with fondness in wet weeks to come. We'd been so lucky with the weather since arriving at the Academy on the first day of spring, with lots of fine days and only short spells of dreary rain. I dared to hope summer would mostly reflect this string of good luck, too.

On Saturday I was lying in the shade of an apple tree with a book I'd found in Renatus's memories of developing his own abilities (and then found for real in the library), entitled *The Scryer's Craft*, while my friends practised soccer skills behind me. I actually quite liked soccer, but allowing Heath to assimilate with our crowd and the innocent question of 'What would you like to do, Heath?' had elicited the excited response from Kendra that 'Heath plays club soccer! Soph and I love soccer,' and had so far meant three solid hours of what had started out as a game and had quickly become an intensive skills workshop, courtesy of our resident star player.

'Arrogant little fuck,' Addison commented mildly, collapsing on the grass beside me. I sat up to see that Heath was still schooling Sophia, Hiroko and Iseult. Kendra was standing by, beaming, oblivious to the pained looks of forced patience that passed between her friends as Heath kept correcting their form. 'Thinks he's the god of ball skills. "Nah, see, you gotta use the inner part o' your foot 'nd kinda *push* it forwar', see? Ya see, A'ison? An' it's *football*."' He mimicked Heath's British accent surprisingly well. He sighed, a contented sound that matched his tone but not his words. 'I hate English people.'

'I'm sure some are alright,' I ventured. I lodged my bookmark between my pages and nestled the sizeable hardback into the grass between us. 'Heath perhaps isn't the best specimen from which to base an opinion of the whole nation.'

'Alright, maybe not,' Addison gave in readily, 'so maybe it's Seers that are the problem.'

I opened my mouth to defend the class but closed it quickly. I knew a lot of Seers – Heath, Sterling, Xanthe, Khalida, Lord Gawain, Oneida, Susannah… Tian seemed nice but he'd also discouraged me from becoming Renatus's apprentice.

'I think Kendra's the only one I like,' I confessed.

'Be honest here: am I biased, or is Heath a total douche?'

I hesitated, eyeing Kendra's new conquest. He was undoubtedly trying to fit in, to a group of females that already possessed a dominant male, no less. He had no idea how little interest the rest of the group had in accepting him. He probably deserved pity, not spite. I couldn't muster it up.

'Maybe both?' I suggested. Addison theatrically threw himself back onto the cushy damp grass, muttering about the dew and the apparent inability of the Irish sun to evaporate correctly. I watched him a moment, reflecting on the last few weeks. 'I take it you're less cool with the situation than Kendra implied.'

Addison laughed without humour, not a usual sound for him.

'I'm not that cool with it at all. Why, what did she tell you?'

I hesitated again, not wanting to engage in gossip that may damage my newly re-established friendships, and thought my words through carefully. I ran my fingers through the grass around me and tugged a handful of wet green blades out of the ground.

'I got the impression that it was amicable. And until today, it's looked that way, too.'

'It *was* amicable,' he relinquished, staring straight up into the blue sky, 'until this dude came on the scene like four days later. Sort of undermined all her lame-arse reasoning.'

'What reasoning?' I asked, immediately regretting my nosiness. 'Sorry – not my business, I know.'

'She goes, "I need to talk to you, I've had a vision",' Addison barrelled on, ignoring my apology. 'She reckoned we needed to stop seeing each other and just be friends because she'd foreseen that I was meant for someone else. Reckoned she had to "let me go" so I could notice this other person.' He sat up and snorted with derision, mirroring me by beginning to yank grass out as well. 'And me, like a sucker, just took that. *Believed* that. Then, I'm introduced to Boots here,' he gestured vaguely in Heath's direction, 'and I suddenly realise what she was *actually* having visions of in that class.'

I filled the silence that followed by shredding into little pieces the grass I'd pulled up. I could feel Addison's ill-disguised hurt and, hearing his story, I could appreciate those feelings, but I really liked Kendra and, having only just won back her friendship, was loath to think too hard on any personal issues between this former couple that might colour my opinion of her.

'I'm not sniffing out sympathy or looking to cause trouble,' Addison finished, reading me. 'I'm just ranting. I'll get over it soon enough. But just to confirm,' he added, leaning in close, conspiratorial, 'you have to agree: I'm a way better catch, right? And don't refuse, my ego can't take the hit.'

'Your ego wouldn't even *feel* that hit,' I countered. 'It'd bounce right off. Wouldn't even leave a dent.'

'True,' he agreed, smiling and tearing more grass from the lawn. I spared him an objective glance. Being charming and funny amounted for the majority of Addison's appeal, but he was also a very good-looking lad, with a clean-shaven face of careful angles and long-lashed eyes. Social conditioning told me that he was one of the most attractive students enrolled at the academy, but so far that had had about as deep an impact on the course of our friendship as the dollish prettiness of Hiroko or the oddly elfin strikingness of Iseult or the way the stunning Prescott smile made the twins sparkle.

'According to Kendra, you'll be healthily distracted soon,' I said helpfully. He nodded, and we both watched as Heath and Kendra battled for the soccer ball, she laughing, he taking it way too seriously, trying to explain to her what she was doing wrong. A club footballer all his life, this game *was* his life. Discreetly, Sophia was ushering Iseult and Hiroko away from the pair, using the lapse in direct teaching to make their escape.

'That's the plan,' Addison agreed. He looked to me solemnly. 'Any minute now, word's going to get out that I'm single and fated to meet my one true love, and every girl in this place is going to be lining up. Right *there*,' he elaborated, pointing at an imaginary spot a few metres away, taking my chin in his hand and turning my face to ensure I was looking directly at it. 'I'm taking auditions. Even *you* could be the one for me,' he confided, flicking his eyebrows at me and letting me go. 'Pretty sure I couldn't handle you but who knows? Do you cook?'

'You're out of luck,' I apologised, unthreatened by his playful forthrightness. 'It'd be toast and scrambled eggs every night in the Byrne-James household.'

He shook his head, disgusted, and asked, 'Scrambled eggs and my name second in the hyphenation? The wedding's off.' I threw my handful of grass at him. We both grinned. He called out to Sophia, Hiroko and Iseult as they made their way to us, 'Which one of you cooks? Wait,' he realised, sitting bolt-upright. 'Soph – you apprenticed under the kitchen staff for detention, didn't you? Sorry, Aristea.' He patted my hand apologetically. 'I move on fast.'

His question drew Kendra and Heath's attention, and they jogged over, Heath dribbling the ball and kicking it lightly to the girls who had *almost* managed to get back to the safety of the tree. Hiroko, despite displaying the most limited skills of any of us, caught it – probably completely by accident – with her foot, and looked up at me with horror at the realisation that she was going to be drawn back in to Heath's tutelage.

'Try *pushing* the ball,' he said to Hiroko as he approached from the bottom of the hill, abandoning his conversation with Kendra in favour of schooling my friend in her dribbling ability. He headed off with her, not noticing her helpless glance at the rest of us. Sophia and Iseult abandoned her to her fate. 'Yeah, like tha'.'

'He's so good at this,' Kendra gushed, gazing after him as he walked Hiroko away from us again. Addison looked between the other girls.

'You're going to leave her to that?' he asked. Sophia shrugged.

'Sacrificial lamb. She's taking one for the team.'

'And we call ourselves her friend.' Addison shook his head sombrely and got up, brushing grass off his hands and jeans. He jerked his head at Sophia and started toward Heath and Hiroko, who were now well out of earshot because Hiroko had misjudged a kick and sent the ball far away. 'Try *pushing* the ball,' Addison mocked as he walked away from me, fake accent totally on fire, only just quiet enough to avoid being heard by Heath. Kendra gave him a don't-be-mean look and Iseult sat down beside me to leaf through my book.

Sophia obediently followed him and I heard her murmur, 'Yeah, like tha',' in the same mock accent. The pair grinned at each other and I knew that Addison had nothing to worry about. Once he came around he'd have no trouble replacing Kendra, and out of that failed relationship had come a pretty perfect friendship.

The next couple of days were relatively uneventful. The rain set in, as Iseult and the weather caster had predicted, and we were free of soccer. I still went running in the mornings, reminding myself that bad weather wouldn't have stopped Angela, and Angela didn't have a mysterious date with Fate looming on her calendar. Once Addison came with me, loving the idea of doing something active and out of the house. I knew he got cagey with being cooped up. He was fitter than I was and so tall that he had to work to keep a pace that I could keep up with. When we got back to the house he announced himself the winner, and furthermore declared "Irish rain-running" as his least favourite sport. He declined to run with me again until the rain stopped and challenged me to a surfing contest the next time I was casually in Australia.

All the while, as the days blended into one another, the twenty-sixth was creeping closer. And then, suddenly, the day was here.

'Send someone else,' Renatus was saying irritably when I arrived in his study that afternoon to go over our plan. He was standing behind his desk with a cluttered cardboard box open before him, filled with random old objects. Chalices. Music boxes. Candelabras. Gaudy jewellery. Combs. Cutlery. Books. Even a broken, grimy photo frame. Everything in the box looked dusty, unused, broken, unassuming, but the feeling of the box was yucky. Cursed objects, I assumed, sent to the White Elm for decontamination and spell reversal. Renatus's job had many facets but this was one task I'd never seen him do. I hoped he'd let me help, or at least watch. Then, if it was boring, I could up and leave him to it and find something more interesting to do, but if it was neat, I could learn the skills necessary, too. More likely, though, I thought as I entered the study and got closer to Renatus, it would be less than pleasant. Renatus was emanating a distinct sense of negativity, and I couldn't be sure whether it was caused by his leader's purpose for being here or the box of nightmarish treasures, or a joint effort by both factors.

'It has to be you,' Lord Gawain disagreed calmly from where he stood in the middle of the room. He cast me a quick smile as I walked silently past him. His persistent calm was inconsistent with Renatus's spiky reaction. Did that mean Lord Gawain was being unreasonable or that Renatus was overreacting? Both, again? 'You were the one invited.'

'Invited to what?' I asked, stopping where I could see them both. Lord Gawain opened his mouth to answer but Renatus got in first, pointing accusingly at me with an aggression I rarely found directed my way.

'You should have let me tear it to pieces,' he said tensely while I raised my hands helplessly. 'You shouldn't have interfered.'

'Interfered?'

Renatus scoffed, disbelieving, and gestured abruptly at his leader. 'Because of you, *he* found it.'

'What are you *talking* about?' I demanded, starting to feel annoyed. I could have been with my friends, laughing and joking, and instead, here I was, being dressed down for something nobody wanted to specify.

'The *pretty* invitation you rescued,' Renatus reminded me in the same tone as mine. It took a moment but then I remembered a conversation from weeks ago, the expensive flocked paper that I'd prevented him from tearing up. So what? He heard me. 'So what? So now apparently I'm *attending* this event, thanks to you.'

'You both are,' Lord Gawain corrected. He looked to me. 'It's an engagement party, but the theme is masquerade.'

'I don't care what the theme is,' Renatus replied coldly. 'I don't want to go.'

'You sound like a child,' I told him, still annoyed with his unbefitting bad mood. I asked Lord Gawain, 'Why are you sending us and not two people more... willing?'

'It was Renatus who was invited. The White Elm itself would not be welcome; it's not possible for me to send another pair in your place. They'd be turned away at the door. It's not our... usual crowd, let's say. Sean Raymond, the father of the groom, is hosting the party, and he has old connections with this family-'

'He doesn't *expect* me to be there,' Renatus chose now to remind his leader. 'I haven't accepted *any* invitation from these people in eight years. No one will notice if I don't attend.'

'So he'll be pleasantly surprised when you do,' Lord Gawain replied smoothly. 'And I already sent the R.S.V.P. card accepting the invitation because I knew you would be reluctant.' He indicated me, standing nearby. 'By this point the secret's out about Aristea, so there's no need to hide her anymore.'

'Doesn't mean I should show her off, either.'

'It mightn't hurt.'

Renatus scowled and looked away out his window as Lord Gawain handed the invitation back to me. I ran my fingers over the flocking of the emblem at the top.

'Why do you want us to go?' I asked. 'I hope there's a less degrading and undignified reason than "to show me off" like a new toy.'

'Lisandro will also be in attendance,' Lord Gawain said, and I lowered the invitation, heart clenching with cold. Too soon, too soon! Renatus turned back to the conversation incredulously.

'You might have *started* with that argument,' he said. 'Did you foresee it?'

'I did. Lisandro is coming out of hiding, finally, and re-joining society. *Your* society. If he's ready so are you. This is our chance.'

'I cannot confront him at Raymond's party,' Renatus said immediately. I frowned.

'Why not?'

'It's Raymond's party, Raymond's house,' Renatus told me, though this information didn't help clarify things for me. 'You don't bring violence into another man's house. We won't be able to *touch* Lisandro.'

'I understand that,' Lord Gawain agreed. 'There are rules and etiquette to be followed, and none on the council knows those better than you. You can walk among these people where the rest of us cannot. I hate to thrust you into the midst of people you'd rather avoid, Renatus, but your past life can be used to our advantage here. Just by attending. You do not need to engage Lisandro in a fight; not even in conversation. Your presence is all that is required.'

'For what?' I asked, sitting down on the arm of one of the chairs. I checked the invitation. This party was *this* weekend. I was going to come face to face with Lisandro again in only days. I was not ready. I wasn't ready to *look* at him, let alone kill him to save Renatus from having to do so.

'Balance.' Lord Gawain answered my question but addressed Renatus. 'The guest list includes almost two hundred influential, well-placed sorcerers who are already sympathetic to Lisandro, simply for the sake of not siding with the White Elm. The council has been their enemy in the past, but *you* are someone they can see themselves in and trust. Your return at the same time as Lisandro's will totally overshadow his reappearance, and prevent him from making any solid alliances this weekend. You, on the other hand, may be able to lay the foundation for several.' He spread his hands appealingly. 'I would not ask if it were not important.'

There it was, an appeal and not an order, but I knew by now that Renatus would comply. Not only could he not resist the opportunity to face Lisandro, he didn't like to disappoint his mentor, and wouldn't if he could help it, even if he had to argue and sulk first.

'We'll go,' Renatus gave in finally. He looked over at me. 'If you want?'

I hadn't realised I had a choice, but whether explicit or not, I saw now, Renatus always offered me an out to any situation we found ourselves in. The illusion of choice, at least, because I wasn't going to turn this down now that I knew the importance of the event.

'I don't have anything to wear,' I found myself saying, when I wanted to just say"yes". How sensible my answer sounded. It sounded thoughtful, like I'd considered how inappropriate it would be for me to turn up at a stranger's engagement party in jeans and lace-up boots, when really I wasn't thinking much at all. I was studiously trying to avoid thinking anything. If I let my mind wander I might start thinking about my plan to grow into a killer, which was not a nice train of thought and was also one I needed to keep private from my present company.

'We'll go,' Renatus said again to Lord Gawain. 'Just tell us what to do.'

'Nothing heroic,' Lord Gawain warned. 'You attend. You act civil. You mirror Lisandro – for every person he schmoozes with you make sure you're seen with three. You're White Elm and a Morrissey; he's an outlaw with no name and no lineage, and without *saying* it, don't let anyone forget that. Introduce Aristea. Make sure everyone knows you have an apprentice now, and when you leave, though you won't have been involved in any altercation with Lisandro, it's important that the party feels confident that if you had, you would have come out best.'

'So... you *do* want me to show off?' Renatus clarified.

'No more than usual.' Lord Gawain didn't smile here but I felt the amusement underneath his dry tone. 'These people respect money, status and strength. You're there to flaunt all three.'

'To undermine Lisandro's claim on their loyalty,' Renatus gathered. He lifted the cardboard box of broken yucky things and moved it onto the floor by the window. He straightened and said, 'We can do that.'

'What do I do?' I asked, because it wasn't clear. It sounded like I was going along to stand there in silence at my master's side and play the part of living doll. 'What do I say?'

'It's probably best you say very little,' Lord Gawain admitted, looking slightly uncomfortable. 'The less Raymond and the others learn about you the better, in all respects.'

So I was the doll. It seemed that, really, the task could be accomplished with Renatus and his trusty tattoo all without my help. It was hard not to feel offended by that notion.

*You'll be surprised by how many people will want to speak with you,* Renatus said, predicting my response before I could think it, though he didn't look at me to let Lord Gawain know that we were communicating. *There are people who won't be seen speaking with me but will make a point of talking to you. You won't be standing there with nothing to do. The difficulty will be in knowing what not to say rather than in trying to figure out what you should.*

'We have something to ask of you, too, while you're here,' Renatus mentioned now to Lord Gawain as he tidied the open books and papers on his desk that had been disturbed when he moved the cardboard box. His leader raised an eyebrow, curious. Renatus looked up from his busy work, expression unreadable, and said, 'Don't be surprised.'

Lord Gawain's intrigued expression faltered. This had been Renatus's code in the past for"we're going to do something you won't like, but we've got good reason so don't stress if you hear about it out of context". Lord Gawain, I could see, already didn't like it. He opened his mouth like he wanted to ask what my master had in mind, but then closed it. He knew he wouldn't want to know.

'It's related to Belarus,' he said finally, which sparked interest in both Renatus and I. 'Isn't it?'

'We don't know,' Renatus admitted. 'We're following a lead.'

'Mm-hmm.' Lord Gawain's unvoiced opinion was clear in his weary expression. 'Of course you are.'

'Hey.' My attention had been caught, totally redirected, and I crossed the study to the box of unsafe items Renatus had just set down. He quickly got between me and it to stop me touching things I didn't know how to protect myself from. I leaned past him to point at what I wanted. 'That. That rabbit's foot. Where did that come from?'

He looked back and lifted a hand; encased in a translucent bubble of magic, it floated free of the mess and up to our eye level. Renatus waited for me to explain, silent, acting like making objects fly was no big deal. He would never admit it, but Lord Gawain was so right – when it came to magic, he really was a show-off.

I didn't touch the bubble, just stared into it. The gross little foot was grimy and matted with age and lack of care, and hung from a single grubby, rusty key.

I couldn't believe it. It was Susannah's prophesised day, June twenty-sixth, and now I was looking at the last piece of her puzzle. *Bring the rabbit's foot.* I'd discounted it as an unhelpful metaphor for luck. I'd never expected that part was literal.

'What is it?' Lord Gawain asked curiously. I couldn't really explain. I looked up at Renatus.

'How long have you had this?'

# chapter eighteen

He'd had it for two and a half weeks, and this is how it came to be in his possession.

While Renatus moped in his sister's room, Emmanuelle was at her mother's house, alone, sitting at the dining table with all the printed data from the tests she'd commissioned spread out around her so she could see it all at once. It was meant to help her find a pattern within it, but so far did not. The blood results were normal, inconclusive.

She sighed and lifted her feet up onto the seat beside her, long crimson skirt falling over her knees. She'd grown up in this elegant little home in country France, outside Versailles, and most of her possessions were still here, but she had chosen to move out at twenty upon joining the White Elm. Her mother, Laure Saint Clair, had opposed the choice at the time, mostly out of fear of loneliness, but now Emmanuelle was glad she'd had the foresight to do it. Her apartment in Paris had been broken into only weeks ago by Jackson and nearly everything in the place had been destroyed or damaged. Emmanuelle hadn't cared for any of the broken things. Had he known of *this*, her heart's home and the home of everything she considered special, and come *here* to break and ruin in his single-minded search... Well, he still wouldn't have found what he was looking for, but the things broken would have actually mattered, and Emmanuelle would have had dozens more reasons to hate him.

Ugh – and she'd let him *touch her hand*. The memory made her shudder in self-disgust.

Deliberately, forcefully, she redirected her thoughts away from Jackson and back to the more current problem of Sterling Adams's blood test results. The girl's odd behaviour three nights earlier, coupled with the specific amnesia, were concerning to the Healer, and she wanted an explanation, but Renatus's worry outstripped even hers. 'Find me proof that this wasn't a possession,' he'd instructed her as soon as the girl was out of the office, and though she would normally have balked at him pulling rank on her, Sterling was her responsibility, and so far three separate blood tests run through the lab at the Royal London Hospital under order of Dr Miranda Rhode had shown her nothing out of the ordinary. All of her latest theories were ruled out. White blood cell count within normal range, so no infection. Vitamin B12 was sufficient. No signs of alcoholism, plus the students would have a good deal of difficulty obtaining it on Morrissey Estate.

In the first round of tests, she'd disproven the most worrisome and obvious causes of memory loss. There was no concussion, no sign of stroke or seizure, and the girl's blood sugar level was normal. Since then she'd danced around increasingly unlikely explanations. None were the answer Renatus wanted to hear.

*If it's not medical*, he said grimly, his mood already quite dark for reasons she'd guessed when she'd checked the calendar, *then there's another player out there we haven't considered, a scrier.*

A scrier who wanted to communicate with Aristea, apparently. Emmanuelle didn't send him through the thought. She knew it was one they already shared.

Instead she started to pack up, and asked him, *Anything to add to this afternoon's agenda?*

Renatus was responsible for reading and replying to the White Elm's mail. It had seemed a good task to give him to keep him busy when their world was living in its previous uneasy peacetime, but now he had an apprentice and stirrings of bad news were getting louder by the week. For the first time in decades, the role of Dark Keeper was becoming a genuinely busy one rather than purely an academic one. Soon that task would probably be moved back to someone else, Elijah or Glen perhaps, but in the meantime, it still fell to him to scour through the communications and allocate different requests to the appropriate councillors.

*Only one,* he answered her. *Medical examiner in Madison, Wisconsin. It just came in this morning.*

He read her the details and Emmanuelle headed through the house to her childhood bedroom to get ready for her afternoon. The house was small, perfect really for a single woman and her single daughter. Picture frames lined every available surface and plastered every wall. Embarrassingly, most featured Emmanuelle, at various events, life stages and fashion stages – another reason she'd opted against providing the White Elm with this address, lest they ask her to host a circle. Peter was the only councillor she'd ever invited here, and that had gone as expected, with many a 'Oh, weren't you cute?!' and 'Wow, there's more photos down this hall... and in here...?'

No amount of begging had ever convinced stubborn Laure to remove the pictures. She only continued to add to the collection. Even though Emmanuelle avoided cameras and had banned all of her friends from sharing pictures with Laure, the new picture frames always seemed to be filled quickly.

There was no particular system to Laure's display, something that had charmed Peter but would probably irk Renatus. The mismatched frames were level with the ceiling and floor but were not evenly spaced or in line with one another, and there was no semblance of chronology to their ordering. Pictures of baby Emmanuelle butted against photographs from her twenty-first birthday, a dress-fitting for a friend's wedding and her first day of school. Absolutely every event of her life was here, scattered and disordered but familiar and beautiful in its consistency – graduation, birthdays, holidays, the first day of every school year, first steps, horse riding, eating lunch in Paris, school plays, playful poses with friends both past and present... Even the first day of her current adult life was documented, the day of her initiation. There she was with her mother, smiling widely, white robes new and bright to match those teeth, totally ignorant of what she'd really signed up for, no idea what the man taking the photo would one day mean to her, no inkling that the pair behind her (never really noticed before now) were not to be trusted.

'*Imbécile*,' she muttered harshly to her younger self, '*à tourner le dos à eux*.' Such an idiot, to turn her back on them.

For there in the background, looking cheerful and rejuvenated by the double initiation, were Lisandro and Jackson, listening to someone off-camera. It seemed insane that they could be *right there*, right behind past Emmanuelle, and that nobody could just grab them and hold them accountable for what they'd since done. For what Lisandro had done *only hours later*. While others would revel in the good feeling of the initiation by partying, Lisandro would channel it all into a destructive spell to kill three people and leave two girls orphans.

And he would get away with it for more than five years.

Disgusted, Emmanuelle turned away from the pictures. How could they not have known? How could any of them not have worked it out? Renatus and Aristea – they should have seen this, like Elijah and Qasim had mentioned, but so too should have Qasim himself. Lord Gawain, Susannah and Tian were Seers and they should have been able to piece this together between them. And Emmanuelle... Emmanuelle should have known. She should have wondered where the council's attractive and charismatic Dark Keeper was during the initiation after-party. She should have thought through her irrational dislike of Renatus and realised it for a manipulation of Lisandro's. She should have trusted that boy earlier, listened to what he knew and sensed. She should have seen the changes in Peter when Lisandro first targeted him. Looking back, she couldn't recall a single clue, a single moment that he'd reached out to her, but that didn't make her feel any better.

A real friend should have known. Aristea Bryne and Sterling Adams had been friends for all of a month before they'd ceased contact, and *still*, Aristea had recognised in a single conversation when something was not right with Sterling. Peter was never possessed, but Emmanuelle was his closest friend on the council and they'd been close already for years when he defected. She *should* have seen it.

Five steps up the staircase she sat down. There, on the wall beside her, obscurely hidden at the eye level of cats, was a timber framed photograph taken two Christmases ago by Peter's fragile old grandmother. The elderly witch's dining room was warmly familiar to Emmanuelle. Peter's uncles, cousins and second-cousins populated the background, each wrapped in goofy woollen pullovers knitted by said grandmother, and in the foreground, comfortably sharing an armchair, were Emmanuelle and Peter themselves, frozen in time, laughing as they unwrapped their own monstrous knitwear.

Older, wiser Emmanuelle lightly touched the glass, barred from this precious moment by more than a panel of transparent material. Years and secrets separated her from that old self, and from Peter, and again she wondered how she could not have known. His arm was looped easily around her, meaningless, or so she'd thought. He'd adored her; she'd not known how much. She'd made a lot of mistakes, yes – Peter had made even more – but loving Peter was not one of them. Looking at this moment in time, she was sure of that. Whatever weakness Lisandro had exploited in him, whatever stupid promises he'd bought into and made, the rest of Peter – the friend who loved her in silence, the grandson – was worth being in love with.

Emmanuelle's many-ringed fingers looked full and well-adorned to others but to her they felt naked without the ring she'd found buried in her garden. Peter had deserted the White Elm for Lisandro but had changed his mind, returning the council's only publicly known weapon to her in the hour before his death. She'd wondered for months now: what had he Seen, what had he known, that made him do it?

Now she knew, or at least did in part. That list – the list he'd wrapped the ring in – with a dozen names, was a message to her. It had Renatus's name and Aristea's, and the names of members of their families. Peter had known about the storms and what Lisandro was doing. Maybe he'd worked out what Lisandro wanted the Elm Stone for and was trying to warn Emmanuelle.

'You were an idiot, too,' she told Peter through the glass, in English, because that's what they spoke to one another when he was alive. 'You should 'ave come to me. I would 'ave listened. I would 'ave saved you.'

Just as Jadon had listened to his traitorous friend Aubrey, Emmanuelle knew she would not have struck down or turned away Peter if he'd come to her before his death. Well, probably she would have struck him. But like Jadon, she wouldn't have followed protocol. She wouldn't have called Renatus in to kill or arrest him.

Not that it mattered now what she would have done if he'd come to her. He didn't, so she hadn't. Peter was dead, the Elm Stone had found its way to Lisandro and thanks to Aubrey's move in taking the four students, the White Elm's hands were tied in their attempts to get it back. Presumably Lisandro was with his camp, in Orsha, the one place they had pledged *absolutely* not to go and cause trouble, and also presumably, he'd taken ownership of the ring. After Renatus handed it over to secure Aristea, Emmanuelle's energy had pined for the Stone and its incredible potential for days. Then the feeling had abruptly stopped.

The ring had a new master.

All through May and now halfway through June, Emmanuelle had tensely anticipated Lisandro's retaliation, the beginning of this *real* war Lord Gawain had prophesised, but so far nothing had happened. Things had been painfully quiet, though the whispers of change still reached White Elm ears. Lisandro was still moving, still making connections, still forging ahead with his plans, whatever they were. It made Emmanuelle anxious.

Her afternoon was already well-organised with only one gap, and she checked her phone's world clock to confirm that the remaining appointment time would suit the time zone before leaving the house with her notepad, pen and small backpack slung over her shoulder. She looked more university student than travelling doctor.

Her first two stops were in France. She Displaced from Versailles to Vannes to confer with an oncologist who had written in requesting assistance with a persistent and unresponsive tumour in the brain of a small child. The four-year-old patient was small and frail, her body almost done fighting it, and the sorcerer who was her doctor had barely the energy left, between her and his other patients, to keep siphoning to her. These were the cases that broke Healers' hearts. Some complex ailments, like degenerative disease, autoimmune disease and cancers, fell outside the basic ability of Healers to simply "repair". Research by academics of magic had shown that with enough power, sorcery could indeed cure cancer, but those instances where it had been done were isolated, lengthy and mightily taxing on the Healer.

Less effective than a cure but much safer was siphoning, where a Healer transferred his or her own energy into the patient at the same time as a treatment, such as a drug or a bout of chemotherapy, was delivered. Too often these treatments dealt as heavy a blow to the delicate body of the patient as they did the actual illness, but with the extra energy and strength of their doctor the sick person had a much enhanced ability to weather the treatment, fight the sickness and heal their own system. Repeated throughout a patient's course of treatment, and sustainable, this approach was currently the leading method of Healers across the White

Elm's nation, and had been used to increasingly positive effect for the last several decades.

Dr Lefèvre had dark circles under his eyes and Emmanuelle knew he'd been pushing his limits, transferring more and more to the little girl in his care, to his own detriment. He talked her through the long, painful, miserable medical history of the child, and showed her the most recent brain scan.

No reduction in tumour size. The pair of them looked up silently at the tiny, undeserving victim of circumstance lying in the bed on the other side of the observation window, narrow chest rising and falling shallowly with each breath. She was dying.

'*Aidez-moi, s'il vous plaît,*' Lefèvre whispered desperately, and Emmanuelle nodded. It was her first call-in of the day and she really couldn't afford the energy this was going to cost, but no more could she leave here without having tried.

It took twenty minutes. It would have taken longer without Lefèvre in there with her, one hand clasped behind the patient's head, one hand each on the child's forehead. Eyes shut. Consciousness deep inside the brain. She followed his lead. The extra energy, meagre as it was becoming as her doctor wasted away from overuse, was not helping this child. The tumour was too strong. That could be addressed. Its long jellyfish-like tendrils wrapped around the brainstem could be painstakingly unpicked, careful not to rupture a single cell, and its blood supply could be redirected, preventing its further growth for the time being.

Emmanuelle withdrew when she sensed Dr Lefèvre do the same, but when she opened her eyes to a dizzying view of the ward at the Centre d'Oncologie she saw that he'd dropped into the chair beside the patient's bed and was shaking with exhaustion.

'Is it done?' he asked softly, eyes out of focus. They spoke in French.

'You did it,' she told him with a quick smile as she rounded the bed to check on him. Low temperature, rapid shallow breath, he was bordering on shock. The kind of strain this man was putting himself under for his patients had worn him terribly thin. She blinked through her own unexpected tiredness and went searching for a blanket to pack around him. 'The tumour is disconnected from the brain stem and the major arteries.'

He smiled thinly, relieved. 'This is perfect. For the first time, surgery is a viable option. I'll schedule another scan to confirm for the family and get her into surgery-'

'Not today,' Emmanuelle interrupted, tucking the ends of the blanket against him tightly. He was coming around, still weak but recovering his presence of mind, and now stared at her.

'The tumour is the size of a plum,' he reminded her blandly. 'It cannot stay. It's pressing on other areas of the brain. It needs to be removed.'

'Not today,' the Healer said again. She opened her backpack on the end of the sleeping child's hospital bed and dug inside it for what she always carried with her on council missions. 'The girl isn't strong enough for surgery yet and you aren't fit for it in this state, either. You both need time to recover. The tumour isn't going anywhere. Here,' she added, coming back to him and dropping four rough white quartz crystals into his hand. 'Take care of yourself and replenish your body. Then give her what you can to have her stable for the procedure.'

Lefèvre rolled the crystal points, each loaded with a similar-sized "shot" of pure energy, transferred and donated by Lord Gawain nightly as was his duty to his people, in his hand, thoughtful.

'Dr Saint Clair,' he began, then remembered her introduction, her correction, because she had no doctorate, and changed to, 'Emmanuelle, I don't know how to thank you.'

It was the same sentiment following her visit to a retirement home in Strasbourg, and her next trip to Djibouti, where a United States marine stationed at the naval base had reported a sudden lack of access to his natural powers as a Seer. She didn't need to sit with him, in a raucous bar off-base, for very long to identify the cause as trauma. Like Qasim had found with Renatus's apprentice, the marine's powers had ended up blocked behind a wall of self-preservation as a result of a horrible event. She did not ask what he'd seen or done, and did not probe his mind for it, but recommended extensive counselling. The alternative of forcefully dragging the ability through the pain was not something she'd ever advise, and was still irked to know Qasim had done this to Aristea without consulting with one of the White Elm's three Healers first.

This was all in a week's work for the White Elm's official Healer, but the most unique appointment of the day was the medical examiner in Madison. Dr Lund was surprised when a young French sorceress in leather leggings and a corseted waist introduced herself as White Elm, though she smartly recovered her poise and led Emmanuelle out the back to the unclaimed body she'd written in about.

'Forty-three-year-old male with no obvious cause of death,' the examiner recited as she pulled the body from its refrigerated cavity in the wall. The naked, pale and restitched cadaver lay still and clean on the tray, but the skin was heavily scarred and grotesquely disfigured by several prolonged periods of deliberate self-harm. Half of the scarring was white and pale pink, as much as ten years old; the other half was very recent, still open, still healing. There was nothing in between. 'You're here quicker than I expected but even still, more has come up since I wrote. He had no ID on him and no one came forward to claim him, so the police ran a check with his fingerprints.' She smiled wryly and looked down at the body. 'He was found on the train tracks about five minutes out from the station. Just dumped. I put his time of death at twenty to twenty-fours earlier. That means, altogether, this man's now been dead seven days.'

'The police search contradicted your findings,' Emmanuelle guessed, thinking on what Renatus had told her from Lund's letter. This must be the "new" information. The examiner nodded. She took the man's elbow and turned it in to reveal some of the unscarred skin on the back of the upper arm. Emmanuelle leaned close to see the unprofessional, now-vague tattoo of a ring there. A snake, swallowing its own tail.

'They said the tattoo was associated with a cult of crazies that killed themselves before the new millennium could start,' Dr Lund concurred. 'They said the prints belonged to a Paul Weston, born in the United Kingdom but immigrated here in the nineties, who was one of eight confirmed dead following this cult's ritual mass suicide in December 1999. Which makes my estimate of seven days *slightly* out.'

Emmanuelle smirked up at the older sorceress and straightened. She gestured at the cuts. 'How far back do these new injuries date?'

'The scars date to around the time of Mr Weston's official death. The new cuts are no more than a month old.'

Both women tapped their fingers thoughtfully on the edge of the metal drawer on which Weston rested. Emmanuelle was developing a timeline in her head. Around the time of his "death", Weston had regularly harmed himself – a typical indicator of a blood sorcerer trying to stay hidden from someone, as pagan sacrifice magic called for an offering of the self as payment for the magic of wards or cloaks. Then to all outward appearances, he'd "died", and he'd abandoned the practice, perhaps moving on with his new life. Up until now, that had worked for him. A few weeks ago, however, he'd gotten scared, and had resumed warding himself with his own blood. It had only served him for so long before something had caught up with him.

'What 'appened one month ago, I wonder?' Emmanuelle accepted the clipboard offered by Dr Lund and read through the autopsy notes. There was nothing at all to explain the man's death, or how he'd been living all these years. Emmanuelle suppressed a sigh and scratched her hairline, frustrated. First Sterling's bloods had turned up nothing.

Now Paul Weston's second death was just as unclear. It was a day for medical uncertainty, apparently. She handed the notes back. 'Did 'e 'ave anything with 'im when 'e was found? No ID, you've said, but anything else?'

Dr Lund retrieved a small box from inventory.

'Keys,' she said, unpacking it and presenting the items to the councillor. 'Pen. A handful of notes and coins, and two jacket pockets stuffed full of what the police initially thought was weed, but turned out to be a mixture of dried herbs they couldn't understand the purpose of.'

Emmanuelle examined the zip-lock bags. Gifted with an aptitude for wards, she'd never bothered learning the old witchy ways of cloaking oneself, which was probably good since she'd grown up to join the White Elm and the White Elm had banned their use, though she understood their effectiveness to be exceptional, especially over longer periods of time. Herbs were mixed with words, intention and blood (or other offering, such as fingernails or hair or even teeth, depending on the exact nature of the spell) to summon and capture wild magic. To someone not of that tradition, it sounded feral to Emmanuelle, and she assumed it took a certain level of desperation before it started to sound like a good idea.

She dropped the baggies back into the cardboard box. Blood magic took this case out of her field and into Renatus's, so she set about boxing it up for him. She put the money and pen back, too, and topped it off with the key. It was one single door key, with a dirty rabbit's foot keyring. *Charmante.* Charming. The teeth of the old key were rusty with dried blood, apparently the weapon of self-destruction.

Renatus's problem.

'Can I take these?' she asked, and Dr Lund said, 'Be my guest. What would you like me to do with the body?'

'I don't expect my colleagues will need to see it, but I will contact you tomorrow if that's alright. Will you sign it over to the state for cremation?'

'That's right. The police tracked down and got in touch with a family member in England or Scotland, but they wanted nothing to do with it. Turns out he was a scam artist, and I guess they were angry to realise he'd faked his death to avoid them. Still.' Dr Lund slid her hands into the pockets of her scrubs. 'After nearly six years, I think it's about time the guy got his funeral.'

*Mieux vaut tard que jamais.* 'Better late than never,' Emmanuelle agreed.

# chapter nineteen

Less than twenty seconds after arriving in Scotland that night I was thinking that we were wasting our time. The national park was massive. There were hills and woods and creeks and rocky slopes, but where we were standing, zero evidence of civilisation. Renatus teleported us to a random clearing in a wooded area of the park but we had no GPS technology to confirm whether it was where we needed to be.

But we had the rabbit's foot, whatever good that was destined to do for us, stashed safely in a sealed plastic bag in Renatus's inner jacket pocket.

'If we're going to find what Susannah sent us here for, it'll be wherever we are,' Renatus told me, walking a few paces away to examine a broken branch. The trees were growing dense and close together and the roots were starting to break free of the worn soil, giving a very uneven flooring to this already unwelcoming woodland. It was dark, it was cool, it was still, and the shuffly, unexpected sounds of hidden microfauna all around us set me on edge.

'This was a mistake,' I said, keeping my voice down and rubbing my arms as I followed my master from his broken tree branch to a patch of open soil, where he knelt down.

'Doubtful. Susannah is not in the practice of directing others into deliberately mistaken acts.'

I bit back a spiteful comment about Susannah's practices, though I'm sure Renatus still heard it. Instead I said, 'I'm sorry I dragged you out here. We're never going to find anything. There's nothing, no one. It's too big.'

'Big? That just makes it a better place to hide, if something *is* here.'

'Nothing's here,' I insisted as I tripped over an exposed tree root and came to stand behind him. 'Nothing but stupid trees.'

Renatus didn't answer except to tap my shin twice, a summons to my attention. He pointed at something in the dirt that I couldn't see in the dark. I crouched beside him, squinting and trying to focus on what he was showing me.

*It's too dark*, I complained, mostly to myself though with the knowledge that I'd directed the thought at Renatus as though it was his fault. I felt his gentle frustration with my lack of magical skill; stuff that seemed innately natural to him was mostly unknown to me.

*It's not too dark for you*, he disagreed, and took a moment to think explicitly about how he was able to see. He touched three fingertips to my temple and did something he'd only done a couple of times before, using *my* brain to perform a skill. Neurons fired and a new pathway of connections sparked across the scape of my brain as he taught it how to change its focus to incorporate information delivered by my magical senses. Everything around me went from black and slate and navy to take on a whole range of greys I hadn't known were there. Edges sharpened around unlit trees and rocks. Other features began to stand out. A hollow in a trunk; a shadow cast by my master's hand lowering from my face; a pair of nocturnal avian eyes blinking at me from the leaves of a tree at the extremes of my range of visibility; the glint of the silver ring I wore on my little finger, though there was no light to reflect. I could *see*. I was surrounded by sharp detail, clear as day though coloured with the shades of night.

I'd read about this.

*Weresight?* I asked Renatus, looking all around, marvelling in my new ability. It wasn't really new, and it wasn't really an ability. I was already capable of it, or else

304

Renatus wouldn't have been able to stimulate my brain to do it; it wasn't yet something I was *able* to do because if I turned it off, I probably wouldn't know how to make it come back. Renatus had shown my brain how to do it, once, but like any skill, the neural pathway needed to be solidified by dozens of repetitions. After the first time someone shows you how to read, or to play a guitar, you are not suddenly an adept reader or musician.

Of course, there's a reason for the natural pattern of learning.

*So they call it,* he answered, nudging my arm to bring my attention back. He pointed again at the soil. Now I could see what he had noticed a minute earlier. Drawn in the dirt, probably with a finger or a thin stick, was a complex and unfamiliar series of symbols arranged in a circle the size of a cushion. In the centre of the ring was a pile of sorts, maybe a handful of damp leaves or ashes. It was all mashed together and hard to discern its components, even with the improved vision.

'Someone thought what we thought,' Renatus said quietly, waving a hand through the air above the pile of materials to tap into the impressions. He didn't need to actually touch stuff to scry from traces left on things. Show-off. 'This park is a perfect place to hide something, or someone.' He nodded at the ceremonial design in the dirt. 'Someone doesn't want to be found.'

'What is it?' I asked, curious again.

'Protective spell.' Renatus directed me to touch one of the symbols gently and I got a flash of a stubby finger tracing this shape and a feeling of fear and desperation. 'Old magic. This particular arrangement of runes asks magic to keep someone safe and hidden. It's stopping us, or anyone else, from scrying this sorcerer to track him down. It's making him energetically invisible.'

'Like a ward?' I thought of the way Jackson had attacked Teresa's house under shrouds of magic.

'Similar, but not the same. A ward cloaks an area, or a *thing*, a person or an item. *This* is both simpler and more powerful. Crude, but effective. The herbs, ashes, blood and hair are bound together with magic to imbue the spell with the user's energy-' I sat back on my heels in disgust, realising that the little pile was damp with blood rather than dew '-and the spell is cast on magic itself. It's a general spell. It doesn't matter where the person goes. If you walk out from behind your ward you're vulnerable. Not this. But, like all magic, it eventually expires and needs to be recast.'

He swiped his hand quickly across the ring, erasing most of the symbols in the first sweep and knocking the pile of leaves and hair and blood out of the circle. A second sweep removed the last of the pictograms and we both stood.

'If he's smart he'll have laid three of those so it wouldn't matter if we found one, but I don't think we're dealing with a man abundant in time or resources,' Renatus said, looking around for footprints, broken twigs, any indication of where his quarry might have gone next. 'There was barely enough by way of ingredients there to conduct that spell.'

He started off to the left, having caught sight of something I hadn't. I followed.

'So… if that's the only one… you might have just undone the spell? Made him visible?' I clarified quietly. He shrugged an affirmative but didn't look back at me. I gathered that like much of magic (an inexact science, as Glen called it) it wasn't that perfectly simple and he didn't want to get hopes up. He slipped between trees ahead of me; I slid after him, more surefooted now that I had vision as keen as his. The ground began to slope away gently beneath our feet and as the minutes passed Renatus's pace also picked up. He stooped to touch his fingers to the ground and I spotted the footprint he'd found there. He circled an unassuming tree and hurriedly changed course, and when I took another look I saw a smeared red hand on the pale bark. It wasn't quite dry.

There really was someone here, in the wilderness, in the dark.

*Someone friendly?* I wondered with a shiver as I hovered my own hand over the print. It was too gross to touch. It was bigger than mine, but smeared, like someone paused to lean here and then pushed off this way, down the winding path. I glanced downhill at Renatus's determinedly trekking figure. His head was down, scouring the ground for more clues. I gathered from the mild frustration I got from him when I paid closer attention that he wasn't finding any.

He was *tracking*, I realised. It seemed such a wild, rangy skill for someone as domesticated, at least by outward appearances, as Renatus. There really wasn't that much I doubted he could do, but I'd assumed he was the indoorsy type. I wasn't aware he'd had experience hunting, though after some consideration of the traditional sort of upbringing he'd had, it shouldn't surprise me.

I'd hung back by the tree too long and Renatus had gained a lot of ground, so I started down after him, but my shoe slipped on some loose gravel and I stumbled. I lashed out with a hand to break my fall as I tottered forward on the slope, and my hand caught a thin young tree trunk and wrapped tightly around it.

*A man's hand wraps tightly around this tree's trunk... Loose stones, dislodged, underfoot, tumble down the slope... Desperation... A pause, an inhalation, an exhalation... Blue eyes in a rugged face, red wiry beard... A wild glance either side... He pushes away...*

I pushed away from the tree with a sharp breath, hurriedly getting my feet back under me as I backed away. The vision had come as suddenly as any but here in the dark, with so much uncertain, it left me hugely rattled.

'Renatus,' I called softly, looking around. He'd missed this clue. He was going the wrong way. Already he'd seen my vision in his own mind and was heading back up the slope to me, but we both heard the disturbance some twenty metres away as a frightened night bird took flight through the canopy of leaves overhead. We snapped our attention towards the sound to look.

And looking, and seeing, was enough to break the remainder of the spell Renatus had demolished.

The bird had been disturbed by the slinking figure of a bearded man, previously invisible to us, who now stood frozen mid-step. He was halfway up the hill, roughly level with Renatus but about as far from him as he was from me, forming a triangle. But he wasn't looking at me. It wasn't even clear that he knew I was there, at the edge of his peripheral vision and slightly uphill. He was looking at Renatus with the expression of someone who knows his game is up. Renatus looked back at him with the alert stillness of a dog that has spotted a rabbit.

*Bring the rabbit's foot.*

'White Elm,' Renatus called loudly, testing the waters. No one moved. I swallowed, recognising the man as the runaway from Lisandro's eastern European camp. 'I mean you no harm.'

The bearded stranger broke that stillness first. He turned tail and ran. Renatus wasted no time or breath calling him to stop. He took off after him.

I reacted just as instinctually. I knew there was no option of letting this man go unquestioned, not with what he might know. They were running across the slope, so I picked a direction – on reflection, not the one that I predicted would intersect with their path, but by the time I realised my failure to utilise math I was already in motion – and broke into a jog downhill. I dodged between trees and skirted around rocks. But it wasn't fast enough and I found my feet thumping the dusty hard ground more and more; I could see that at their unrelenting speed I was never going to meet up with them at a jog, and the slope pulled my legs into an ever-swifter cycle. The stranger changed directions and Renatus swung around a tree to follow. He was gaining. I wasn't. I jumped to clear a boulder and narrowly missed being taken out by an awkwardly angled branch that hung in my path. I chanced a glance over my shoulder and saw that the men had escaped my line of sight.

*Still in mine,* Renatus reported. *He keeps changing directions. Don't slow down – he could hook back towards you.*

Gravity wasn't about to let me slow down even if I wanted to. I was alone now, though the distant sounds of their chase occasionally reached me over the sound of my own pounding feet. I kept running and the woodland and the rocky ground kept flying ceaselessly back behind me. Susannah's suggestion in footwear had been appropriate.

Renatus's help in activating my weresight was both a blessing and curse as I ran. It sharpened as my heart beat harder and oxygen and adrenaline rushed my systems. *Everything* went into focus. On one hand it meant I was better informed on my surroundings – I could see details I normally wouldn't have been able to see, even squinting, and I could make decisions based on those details. I could see branches and duck below them. I could spot holes in oncoming ground and go around them. I could adjust my pace to suit less stable footing or awkwardly sloped patches that might have made me slip if I landed it on wrong. But for all this I could also see details I would rather *not* see, like spiders hanging in glistening silver lace webs between trees and the splintered, sun-bleached skeleton of a small woodland mammal in the split-second before my shoe landed with a *crunch* on its long-unfeeling tail. I winced and sprung away mid-step, throwing myself off-course and having to defend my face with my arms as I collided with too-detailed branches coated in too-veiny leaves. It was hard not to be distracted by such hyperawareness and the resultant oversensitivity. But I couldn't turn it off. If I worked out how and managed to return to my normal night vision, I'd be hardly better than blind. It was too dark.

*Where are you?*

I burst free of that branch and urgently shook off a too-bright beetle with two patterned shells over four soft, fluttery transparent wings and with six spiky little black legs that had been caught on my sleeve. It tumbled as it fell and it fell through a tangled spider web. When I saw the beetle strike a strand of web and I saw the predator hidden further along it twitch I yelped and bounded quickly in the opposite direction.

I ran until the ground dropped away and I hurriedly pulled up, but my speed almost sent me over. I dropped my weight back quickly. I fell and landed hard on my backside. My feet kept going but my body stayed where I landed, so I found myself sitting on the edge of a dry, rocky crevice in the landscape, once a creek no doubt, with my feet dangling above some ragged weeds drifting part in response to the breeze, part in response to the activity of small creatures crawling about at their base. I shoved myself upright and away, breathing hard. The dried-up creek was just over a metre deep but if I'd fallen in it I would have been considerably set back, and probably injured. With difficulty I dragged my gaze away from the sharply detailed every rock and every blade of grass in that crevice, and focused forwards, shaking my head hard. I was here because of Susannah's note. The bearded stranger, the crude bloody cloaking spell, the bloody handprint. I needed to get a grip. I needed to catch up with Renatus, and when I got to him I needed to not be jumping out of my skin over beetle legs.

*Did you pass a creek?* I asked him.

*A dry one,* he confirmed. *We jumped it.*

I made myself go still and look and listen. I made myself concentrate. The spiders, the leaves, the streaks in the bark of every single tree – yes, it was all there, but normally the absence of light at night filtered these out and kept me from paying undue attention to these irrelevant details. In the daytime I could see it all, though perhaps without the sharp contrast that the weresight brought out. Still. I could ignore leaves and patterns and bugs in the daytime. How?

I closed my eyes briefly. My heartbeat pounded in my chest the way my footsteps had pounded on the forest floor moments before. My blood hammered in my ears. I extended my awareness out, past myself, past the leaves and my immediate surroundings, until I found my companion.

*Three hundred metres west of you*, I answered, finding Renatus quickly and knowing innately where he was in relation to my own position. Given a map I couldn't have said where exactly in the park I was, but if he stopped and sat down and I set off, I would walk directly to him.

We didn't have the luxury of being able to test that claim right now. I took off running along the bank of the creek, careful to take in only the visual stimulus that helped me on my way towards Renatus and the bearded stranger he chased. The ground levelled out and I tried to even out my stride. I didn't have the speed, the necessary run-up space or the confidence to jump the creek as Renatus and the desperate stranger had, so every step took me further away from their position, further along the crevice as I looked for a narrower part or a natural bridge of fallen trees or something.

Worried that I was letting him down, I directed my attention to my master. The heightened visual sense seemed to have seeped into my other senses, too. I felt more aware of him than usual. I felt with certainty that he was running, not just because it made sense that he would be but more like as if I could *see* him. But I couldn't. I was well out of sight of him, too far away to hear or see, exactly, but I could *feel*. I just *knew* what he knew.

I focused on that instead of the spiderweb I now ducked right down to avoid, bolstered. The harder I concentrated on him, the more aware of Renatus's movements I became. I was sure I knew the moment he dug in his heels and changed directions after the zigzagging stranger. That certainty was followed immediately by a distinct sense of irritation from him – a feeling I could read and confirm.

I kept running, even as my lungs began to burn. I supposed that there had to be a trick to it, something that could be done to stop or delay exhaustion, because Renatus certainly knew it. He was still running, faster than I had ever run before. I felt his frustration as our target continued to run, dodging behind thick tree trunks. He was dying to use magic, to stun the man he chased, but with the trees everywhere and the speed at which they ran, there was almost no chance of getting the first shot right, and the stranger might assume that he was under attack when spells began bouncing off trees around him. So instead, the bearded man was twisting and weaving through the woods, with Renatus close behind, ever gaining.

Ahead I saw that the ground rose up on my side but not on the other. The creek was annoyingly consistent in width, always just too wide for me to feel safe about jumping it, but with the added height I thought I had a better chance of making it over. I determinedly drove my legs forward, heels down, powering up the incline to get the necessary run-up. I was useless on this side of the creek. I needed to get over to the other bank and stopping to scramble down into the crevice and up the other side was only going to give Renatus and the stranger a further thirty seconds on me.

The slope was short and my weresight pre-warned me of loose pebbles that might have interfered with my pace. At the edge I leapt clear of the bank and sailed over the dry creek and all those individually shaped rocks and lightly drifting blades of grass and whatever else was down there. I landed cleanly on the other side with room to spare and carried the momentum into a rolling next step, and then I was running again as if there'd never been an interruption.

*I think he's coming your way*, Renatus said to my thoughts as the rubble-strewn ground beneath my feet began to slope steadily downhill again. I hoped desperately that I would not fall as my stride lengthened uncontrollably to compensate.

I felt and knew that I was less than a minute away from them. I let some of my attention wander down the connection I shared with Renatus, trying to gauge where he was, and tried not to panic as my attention went further than it ever had before. Stones skittered beneath his pounding feet as he ran, sure-footed, through the thinning trees. Up ahead, dimly, I could see the heavy-set man from my vision of the escape from Belarus, staggering downhill. But he was not up ahead, not of me. I saw him only faintly, like a smudge on a window

I was looking through. A ghost, not really there, out of sync with his surroundings but nonetheless somehow still visible to me. *Through Renatus's eyes*. Through Renatus' ears, with his keen hearing, I heard the bearded man's laboured, wheezy breaths, and his gasps of pain as sturdy branches whipped his face and arms. I recalled him accidentally shutting down my thoughts; now here I was, hiding behind his eyes, seeing what he saw.

The hill steepened abruptly, for them, not for me, and the bearded man's exhausted legs just as suddenly gave out. He began to tumble violently down the rocky decline. Simultaneously, Renatus and I put on a burst of speed – he because he had almost reached the end of his hunt; me, because the bearded man's noisy fall and consequent shouts were now audible to my own ears.

*I'm not far*, I told Renatus. I felt his affirmation as he reached the bottom of the hill. I pulled my attention back to myself as the ground under my feet became looser. I was catching up. The trees were thinning, the hill was steepening, the landscape was changing as I neared their position. The world was still ultra-sharp in its hundreds of shades of black and navy and slate and grey and silver, but it didn't seem quite as overwhelming now that I had renewed my focus.

*We're coming straight for you*, Renatus said. *Wards. We'll flank him.*

I'd seen enough action adventure movies to know what this should look like. I powered up the wards I always wore now instinctively and cast another, the kind that would make me energetically invisible. Renatus would chase Lisandro's mutineer straight to me and I would come out of nowhere, blocking him.

I was too intensely focussed to realise that this was an utterly terrifying concept, since we had no idea what our runaway's abilities and intentions were. Everybody is more dangerous when they're cornered, too...

I was careening down the hill when I finally spotted them, coming full-pelt from my left. Renatus was hot on the stranger's tail, mere paces behind. At our current speeds we would all collide at right angles quite embarrassingly at a point about thirty metres ahead of me. The bearded mutineer was still apparently unaware of me but Renatus and I had noticed one another. Neither of us let off the pace.

Renatus was almost close enough to grab the bearded man when he swung violently aside, out of reach, and switched headings. This time when Renatus changed directions after him I saw it *and* sensed it, confirming that the supernatural knowledge of his movements a few minutes ago might have been true. But now they were both running straight up the hill. Straight at me.

I was warded and hence impossible to detect with energetic senses, but it only took two seconds for the stranger to notice the stones that were tumbling down the slope and to look up and see me bolting down at him. He'd had no idea Renatus wasn't alone, and the shock of seeing a second assailant pulled him up short and lost him his lead. A moment's indecision and then he abruptly turned to run to the right. He ran straight into a wall he couldn't see. A ward. Panicked, he spun on his heel to run back the other way but immediately stopped when he saw he was blocked by the now-slowing figure of Renatus. He turned; Renatus had built another ward, boxing him in.

Everybody is more dangerous when they are cornered. The bearded stranger was blocked by two solid energetic walls, Renatus and me closing in on him. He clutched momentarily at his chest, fingers slipping undetectably under the tattered lapels of his coat, and then he was brandishing a knife, desperate and defensive. A dirty knife, blade nicked with use and lack of care, recently sharpened, blood dried on the dull surface. My weresight picked up every detail available as I ran headlong into the situation, trying to slow myself.

'White Elm,' Renatus explained clearly, raising one hand wide and open to placate the runner. His other hand was slipping behind his back, under his jacket, presumably for his wand or another item of use. He took one step closer; meanwhile I took too many. Twelve metres, ten metres, seven... I stumbled on the loose ground as I struggled to regain control of my speed without losing balance.

'Stay back,' the stranger screamed at Renatus, slashing at him with the knife, forcing my master to erect a third magical wall, between them. The blade struck the ward with a *thwuck* and he drew back, turning on his heel like an angry animal as I burst onto the scene, only just now bringing my wild pace down to a clattering canter. There wasn't time or space to redirect myself so I had no choice but to run straight into the three-walled box of wards Renatus had built to restrain our stranger. Renatus threw me something just as I entered the trap and, amazingly, I caught it. It was cold in my hand but I adjusted my grip on it and brought it before me as I all but fell past the stranger and *finally* pulled myself to a complete stop just behind him.

He turned to keep me in his sights, and, breathless, I turned to make sure I was doing the same. I had only a second to acknowledge that now was the right time to be terrified – I had literally run straight into a magical trap in the middle of an unfamiliar forest and seemed to be facing off with a wild and armed stranger – but then over the stranger's shoulder I saw Renatus shift to block him from backing out of the artificial room he'd built for him.

The mutineer was right in front of me. Arm's length. One move and he could sink that knife he held, so scarily and richly detailed thanks to the weresight, straight into me. He was close enough that his heavy exhalations were warm on the skin of my arm, which I held defensively out in front of me.

I hoped his narrow, furious blue eyes did not notice the shock in *my* eyes when I saw that what I held was a small, jewelled knife.

# chapter twenty

'White Elm,' Renatus said again, and his voice made the mutineer twitch his head slightly towards him, but he did not take his eyes from me. 'Drop the weapon.'

'Like hell,' the bearded man snarled, still looking at me. Eyeing me bitterly, closely, like I was a *threat*. All because I'd come running in here like I knew what I was doing and I'd managed to catch a knife I shouldn't have and hold it properly.

*Don't give him an inch*, Renatus warned me, and I mentally acknowledged his words. I worked to keep my expression smooth, to not give away how fear gathered inside me as the adrenaline receded. My heart still thudded and my blood still rushed in my ears in the sudden stillness, and all around me the sights of the night glared harshly in overly exuberant focus, but I kept my breaths slow and deep and steady and through my nose.

'Drop the knife and I'll drop the wards,' Renatus offered. I didn't dare take my eyes from the dangerous man right in front of me but I could see, or perhaps I just could *feel*, that Renatus was flexing his fingers preparedly over his wand, settled as it was in his palm. Ready. 'I'm only here to talk.'

'I'm no' talkin' to you,' the stranger snapped, coughing once as he tried to catch his breath. No wonder he was hiding out in a big national forest in Scotland. I could tell from his thick accent that this was his homeland. He scoffed. 'White Elm.' He spoke to Renatus but still looked only at me. The overly sensitive weresight I'd discovered tonight took in every single detail of the face of the man before me. Knotty dark red hair, knotty beard with four scraps of leaf litter entangled in the bristly hairs. Clear blue eyes. Rough, fair skin, with a mole under the left eye, surrounded by a pattern of freckles. Asymmetrical eyebrows, a scar through one. Two lumps in the bridge of his uncomfortably large nose. 'Chasin' a man through the forest like tha' dun inspire trust, yeh know?'

'You didn't leave me much choice.' My master's response was cool. 'Drop the weapon and turn around. I have some questions.'

'I'm no' turnin' aroun',' the bearded stranger shouted back over his shoulder. He jabbed at me with his knife, more of a gesture than a threat. Terrified, I wanted to back up and cower against the wards Renatus had built, but for some reason I found myself stepping *up* to him, knife ready. My unexpected motion drove him to take a suspicious step back to keep the distance between us. He chanced a swift, angry look at Renatus. 'No' until she backs off.'

'Put your knife down and I will,' I retorted, hoping against hope he did as he was told so I could do the same. *Just do it, just do as he says…*

'Yeh can' hur' me,' the runner challenged now, sneering at me. 'Yeh said you're White Elm.'

'*I'm* White Elm,' Renatus corrected from behind him. '*She* isn't. She can do what she likes.'

Blue eyes bored into me savagely. Critically. Sizing me up. The Belarussian escapist was in his thirties, at least, and twice my weight, even after what looked like a good deal of recent weight loss. If he went me, I stood no chance.

'She gonna cut me?'

'Only if you cut her first,' Renatus answered smoothly, 'or if I give the order. This is my apprentice.' He paused for one loaded beat. 'It would be best if you cooperate.'

The man we'd just chased all through this stupid woodland looked from me to him and back. Reluctantly, slowly, he lowered his knife. I tried not to let my surprise register, and I kept my position, but I couldn't believe it. This man had lived in and escaped Belarus and, presumably, followed and served Lisandro. Who knew what he'd done and seen in his time of service there? He'd bled his own blood to create the magic needed to make his escape and to maintain his cover here. From the look of his dirty, tatty clothes – the same clothes I remembered seeing him in the night he jumped from the window of the hostel several nations to the east – I gathered he'd been in hiding ever since, roughing it for weeks now. And yet, and *yet*, he was afraid of *us*? Of *me*, no less? Renatus, obviously, was a man worthy of fear, even if the blue-eyed runner didn't know exactly which White Elm had caught him. He was fast and fit, which were easy qualities to associate with strength, and he was dressed all in black and armed with a wand he seemed confident with, and his aura was brimming with power most sorcerers had never before seen in a single person. Me, though: I was seventeen, a girl and I had never used a knife for any more malicious purpose than cutting up food.

But he didn't know that. And though apprenticeships were rare in our world, it seemed to be common knowledge that both parties involved received a spike in power following the initiation.

Renatus kept his end and the wards boxing me in with the stranger fell away. I tried not to sigh in relief.

'That's better,' the Dark Keeper said, taking a single step aside to put himself within the mutineer's range of vision. 'Now we can talk.'

'I ain' no snitch.'

'Of course you're not. Off the record. I won't even ask for your name. No one has to know.'

'I'm no' talkin' to yeh,' the man said, angry. 'Go to hell, the both of yeh.'

Renatus looked at me. He reached under his jacket, suspicious blue eyes watching his every move, and withdrew the plastic-bagged key. He showed it to the bearded stranger. The blue eyes went wide with shocked recognition.

'Where did yeh get that?' he asked, voice down near a whisper. He took half a subconscious step toward it and made himself stop with effort.

'It's familiar to you, then?' Renatus asked. The stranger choked on an incredulous laugh.

'Familiar? Tha's Paul's. How did yeh get it?'

'One of my colleagues retrieved it from Wisconsin.'

The Scot was still staring at the bagged rabbit's foot, but now blinked and turned his attention to Renatus, face falling a little.

'He's dead, i'n't he?'

Renatus nodded, and the blue eyes chanced closing momentarily in grief, trusting us to give him that moment of solitary pain.

'The medical examiner estimated around the third of this month.'

'Three weeks. Three *weeks*, and I di'n't even know.' The stranger struggled with that visibly for a few seconds, then swallowed the emotion that came with it. 'My fault. They would'na even known he wa' still alive.'

'What can you tell us about the people who killed Paul?' Renatus asked. He slipped the rabbit's foot away again, unnoticed.

'I go' nothin' to tell yeh,' the bearded stranger insisted wearily. He seemed to have lost some of his bluster. 'It's my life if I talk to yeh and I dun even know who the hell yeh are.'

'My name is-'

'No,' the blue-eyed stranger said sharply, turning and cutting my master off. He raised the knife again, sending a thrill of fear through me, but it was in place of pointing at him with a finger. Which, I noticed with another unpleasant feeling, this time a jolt to my stomach, was uncomfortably ironic, because he didn't *have* all of his fingers. The right hand, bearing the knife, was in typical five-fingered condition, but the left, dangling at his side, sported three scabby stubs, and was grubby with dried blood all over it from a cut he'd made on the back of his wrist sometime in the last two hours.

My weresight, still keen with my blood rushing through my veins, ensured I noticed every gruesome detail of the mangled hand.

'No,' the stranger said again, still pointing at Renatus. 'I dun wan' your name. I dun wan' *her* name,' he added angrily, turning his knifepoint to me. 'I dun wanna know anythin' I didn' come here knowin'. I know yeh know who I'm runnin' from, and I dun wanna give 'em any more reason to come lookin' for me. They already got Paul.'

Renatus inhaled slowly, and across our connection in his moment of silence I could tell he was re-evaluating his approach.

'Alright,' he agreed smoothly. 'I'll tell you only what you already know. *We* know you worked for Lisandro. We know you escaped his compound in Belarus.'

'An' now *I* know yeh lot knows about Belarus,' the older man snarled angrily. 'The less I know the better, alrigh'? They're lookin' for me, and it dun matter how long I hide: they'll fin' me eventually. An' then, the less I know, the quicker they'll be done with me, yeh hear?' He scowled. 'I dun need that drawn out, yeh know wha' I mean?'

Renatus nodded patiently. 'I think so. But I can protect you from Lisandro.'

The stranger lowered his knife and laughed at my master.

'From *Lisandro*?' he repeated, grinning a yellow smile of teeth not brushed in months. 'Lisandro isn' comin' for me. He's too importan' to come for small fry like me. He'll send someone else. Yeh even know who yeh lookin' for, White Elm?' He smirked, distinctive blue eyes narrowing to spiteful slits. I knew he was referencing the council's inability to recognise Aubrey as a spy within their ranks until too late. I turned the knife hilt in my palm, breathing carefully. This man was difficult but he was a potential treasure chest of information. He might have seen Garrett and the other boys. He might be able to share a weakness he knew of in the Belarus compound, or its protective wards. He might be able to tell us about plans Lisandro was working on.

I had to remind myself of these facts a couple of times. They were important but the stillness was dragging my attention off to other places around me. The tree nearest to us had lost a branch recently. Its torn bark still seeped beads of sap. Little insects scuttled around the sticky fluid.

'Why did you leave?' Renatus asked, cutting straight to the point. I blinked hard and listened to his voice. 'You went to lengths to send off that message to Paul before you made your break for freedom. You risked his safety by calling for him to catch you and help you Displace out of there.'

The stranger finally turned his whole attention to Renatus, apparently convinced that I was not going to jump on him and skin him or something equally macabre. He looked my master up and down, the same way he had me.

'Why did I get my stepbrother killed, yeh mean? Just to get away from Lisandro?'

Fascinating, the way Fate works. The letter I opened for Renatus had directed him to direct Emmanuelle to Wisconsin, where she'd found the rabbit's foot Susannah had told me I would need, so that hours before coming here tonight I'd notice it in Renatus's office among countless more interesting objects and Renatus would have it on him to change the tides of this conversation enough that we might get the information Susannah sent me here for in the first place.

Renatus shrugged idly. 'You must have been desperate to get away from him.'

The mutineer laughed once, unamused.

'Yeh ever met the guy, White Elm?' he asked, something of a soft challenge. Renatus blinked but his expression gave nothing away.

'I have.'

'Then yeh know why I left,' our runner answered coldly. 'Everythin' makes sense when yeh sign up. And then suddenly, it don'.'

'What do you mean?' I asked, forcing myself to take more of an active role in the conversation. To *focus*. He glanced mistrustfully at me. I swallowed shakily as my hyper-sensitive vision took note of a small sphere of blood that had gathered at the edge of his open wound on the back of his wrist and had begun to roll, slow and unheeded, down his thumb. He directed his answer to Renatus.

'Gettin' rid o' yeh lot, tha' makes a whole lotta sense,' he said snidely. 'Tha's wha' I was doin' there. Tha's wha' *hundreds* o' people are doin' there. But then tha's no' the only agenda. Then there's all the crazy shit. I didn' sign up for crazy shit, yeh know?'

The droplet of blood was insanely bright, glossy with detail I was certain it didn't normally possess, and it rolled onto the thumbnail, leaving a wet trail behind it. Now that I was looking at it I didn't dare look away – beside it was a single lonesome forefinger, and beside that were three rough stubs where the other three fingers used to be. And the scabs covering those were clearly different ages, varying in crustiness and moistness and state of infection, and I just *couldn't* look at those without throwing up all of my spiralling nerves.

'What's the crazy shit?' Renatus prompted. In my head I felt the nudge of his attention and I swallowed again, slightly relieved that I wouldn't have to actually *say* anything. Out loud, he said, 'Apprentice, check the area.'

He'd never called me "Apprentice" before, but the stranger had demanded no names. The interruption to my horrified reverie was welcomed. I turned abruptly away and strode off, inhaling slowly in relief. *Who cuts his own fingers off?!*

*Somebody desperate*, Renatus answered grimly as, aloud, I heard him repeat his question.

'The drownin',' the bearded stranger answered as I retreated. 'The supernatural weird shit. I'm no' into tha'…'

I walked far enough away that I couldn't hear their conversation and concentrated on my breaths, on reining in my hypersensitivity. I kept my eyes on the ground and deliberately ignored nearly every unique natural feature I noticed. I was upset with myself and my lack of self-control. This was the reason the world had boundaries, like time and distance and progress – natural barriers between amateurs like me and the overwhelming possibilities of magic. Like being put on a wild unbridled stallion after idly commenting that you liked horses, early exposure to magic too big for me, such as weresight and a few months ago, scrying, led inevitably to frightful effects. Overwhelmed me.

Led to the sort of circumstances where I found myself miserably wandering in the national park in the dark, shaky and unwell, berating myself for my uselessness. Hadn't I told myself I was going to get awesome, so I could take on Lisandro when the time came for Renatus to have to kill him? Wasn't using and *managing* the use of skills like weresight kind of necessary for getting awesome? Pretty sure having to walk out of interrogations because I felt queasy about some blood I couldn't stop staring at was *not* awesome and *not* very befitting of a Dark Keeper's apprentice.

I circled around Renatus's position, further and further out, pretending like I was doing something more useful than coming down from an overdose on magic. The slower my heartrate fell, the less crisp my surroundings appeared and the more I felt able to control what I was focussed on. Much like the state of concentration Glen had taught me for seeing auras and wards and spells, when I felt in charge of it I found I had a little bit of room for changing focus. The weresight could be dimmed slightly, retracted, like adjusting the lens of the eye to look at things that were closer or further away.

I was experimenting with the ability – Renatus's ability, to which he'd given me a one-night early-access-pass until I could build my skills up to being able to make it happen on my own – when I noticed an odd tingle, or itch, at the very edge of my consciousness.

Frustration.

I reached back for Renatus and found him where I'd left him, mildly frustrated with the roundabout way of avoiding facts that the blue-eyed stranger insisted on employing, but his frustration was familiar and near. The stranger was still playing at angry and confident, though more prevalent in his emotional profile was a simmering terror and impatience. He wanted Renatus to lose interest and go away, so he could go back into hiding.

Someone *else* was experiencing irritation. Someone else in this wide, dark, empty national forest. A sorcerer.

*How big is this forest?* I asked Renatus, starting in the direction I suspected the feeling was coming from. *How far does it go this way before it hits civilisation?*

Perhaps a bad-tempered sorcerer was driving along the road that skirted the edge of this forest. That could easily be the problem I could feel.

But, somehow, that seemed much too convenient an excuse.

*Miles.*

And the feeling was getting more distinct the quicker I walked. Like I was getting closer to it... and it was getting closer to me. A driver would have passed and gone on his way by now. This someone was in the forest, too. I couldn't imagine why anyone else would want to be out here tonight.

I walked for several minutes, quietly picking my way back up the hill in the direction I had come from. In my mind, the itch was getting stronger and more noticeable. It was a presence, unfamiliar but intense; it was the feeling of a powerful individual heading this way. I was safe, though. My wards were up, and they were good. Weresight and graceful acquisition of new top-shelf skills, I sucked at, but I was top of Emmanuelle's class for instruction in wards. Nobody would be able to sense me. However, if they heard or saw me, the invisibility would be lost and I'd be putting the barrier wards to the test.

The other presence, too, was cloaked energetically. I could not directly sense their energetic power. Renatus had no means of detecting the approach. But I was Empathic, and so what I *could* feel that the person could *not* cloak was their emotions.

The emotions are still linked to the person's energetic power. This person had unnaturally powerful emotions, which pulled in my attention and acted like a backdoor into the individual's otherwise perfectly shielded aura. And through the emotions, I could feel the incredible power of this person.

I was no match.

I stopped. Little pebbles dislodged by my shoes made a couple of half-hearted rolls down the slope before coming to rest in the dust. I initially started walking this way to establish whether or not I was right about the feeling, and I'd now confirmed I was. Someone was here. Someone stronger and probably more capable than me. What good reason could that person have for being out here? Either this was an ally of the runner or it was one of Lisandro's men, sent to assassinate him. Either way I was walking the wrong way. I silently turned and started back down towards Renatus. This was not my problem. This didn't have to be anybody's problem. I could sneak back to him without this person ever knowing I was here and we could all be on our way without any confrontation.

I carefully made my way through the trees, wanting more than anything to hurry but just as eager to stay hidden and alive. Behind me, the powerful being was gaining ground, heading straight for me. Why? How? They couldn't *see* me, detect me in any way. Unless... I felt a spark of fear in my heart when it occurred to me that I could not be the only Empath around. Renatus sensed my worried thoughts and I felt his concern.

*You're the first I've ever met,* he told me, which helped a fair bit. *Why? Is something wrong?*

*Somebody's coming,* I responded, starting down the rocky decline. I glanced over my shoulder to check that I was still safe. *You need to get ready to get us away from here.*

Renatus responded to that, some kind of question, but I did not comprehend it. My brain was frozen. I had just met a pair of unearthly-bright green eyes, staring at me through fifteen metres of forest.

I felt the woman's shock, because of course she had not felt my presence. But already I was running, weaving through the sparse trees, screaming to Renatus with my incoherent thoughts. I knew suddenly the instinct that had driven our stranger to fly from the sight of Renatus. That hyper-awareness I'd felt of him earlier made me sure that my master had broken away from his questioning of the stranger and had begun moving quickly in my direction. Concern emanated from him along our connection.

*They're behind me, and I'm heading straight for you,* I told him desperately, hoping to give him some bearing so he wouldn't charge ignorantly into the woods. *It's a woman; she's easily as powerful as you.*

I felt a rush of heat and darkness blast through the air above my head and into the tree trunk to my right. Shards of bark exploded all over me. My heart rate shot back up and I saw every single serrated edge of every single piece of wooden shrapnel that passed my face. I dodged through a pair of closely growing trees and felt another blast of dark magic scream past me. This woman wanted to hurt me.

I changed course a little and ran towards an area on the decline where the trees grew thicker. In the open I would make an easy target. In the thicket I lost the advantage of the weresight; I could still see every stark and unnecessary detail but now it was all the useless close stuff, and too many tree trunks obscured my view to see further ahead than my next three footfalls. Terrified, I yanked back on all of my energetic senses – my awareness of Renatus's position, the energy going into the weresight, which now shut off and plunged me into darkness – and concentrated them all behind me, trying to get a concept of where the enemy was.

I found her, an intense bundle of determination and thrilled excitement at this opportunity to chase me down, a bit further back now. I'd gained a bit of distance; I was faster, or maybe smaller and more agile, or maybe just more desperate. But I wasn't getting far enough away to kid myself into thinking I was safe, either.

The spells kept coming, blasting away branches. One struck my outermost ward and deflected off into a tree trunk. I pushed blindly through another clump of trees and half-screamed when I ran straight into somebody. I shoved automatically away before I recognised Renatus' familiar energy and the scream died in my throat, barely a yelp in the end, but I'd bounded back into the tangle of branches. I tried to undo the step and go back to Renatus, but a sharp pain in my scalp pulled me up short.

My hair was caught on one of the branches.

In the dark, panic spread through me without mercy. I grabbed at my long hair and yanked twice, hard, but it hurt and the ends didn't come free. Another blast of magic hit a nearby tree and Renatus retaliated without hesitation, flinging a ball of fire in the woman's direction. A tree burst into flame, illuminating the scene and pulling her up short, well out of our range of visibility. The first stranger's terror levels skyrocketed, and in the wave of heat from the fire and of unchecked emotion that radiated from him I lost all sense.

'Renatus!'

In one hand Renatus gripped the reluctant bearded man's left wrist, which twisted and writhed, desperate to get away. He held on tight but used his other to pull once on my hair. I cried out in response and he stopped.

'She's coming!' the mutineer exclaimed, pulling on his arm and shoving at Renatus urgently. My sense of the woman confirmed it. Beyond the fire, she was cautiously picking her way through the brambles toward us, keeping clear of the flames. 'Let me *go*. We have to go!' The bearded man turned his wrist this way and that. Renatus had to hold on. 'Yeh don' want this to escalate into a fight, White Elm! Yeh want to *go*.'

It seemed decent advice. Renatus was the best warrior the White Elm had to offer but the woman was shielded well and it was unwise to take on an opponent with no information available, especially with two liabilities like the stranger and me right here in striking distance.

'Get us out of here!' I shouted, begging. The woman was advancing, and I felt her spike of interest to note who Renatus had brought straight to her.

'I can't bring the whole damn tree!' Renatus snapped back at me, grabbing my wrist tightly and twisting the knife free of my grip. I'd forgotten I even had it. He had to pull on his reluctant companion. 'Hold *still*, would you?'

'Let me *go*!'

'I'm going to help you. Give me *three* seconds!'

'She's here to kill me!' the blue-eyed runner screamed, and he wildly threw his whole weight at Renatus. The resultant stumble back loosened my master's grip, and when the stranger twisted free and pulled back he had his own knife in his hand, freshly bloodied, and Renatus's hand was clamped over a tear in his shirt near his hip.

He was bleeding.

'*Renatus!*' I screamed, reaching for him but feeling myself torn back by the ripping sensation of hair pulled from my scalp.

The bearded mutineer backed away from us both, fending us off with his knife and his wild glare.

'Yeh stay away from me, White Elm!' he snarled at Renatus, and he turned and fled.

His terror did not go with him. It was already all over me, all through me, and the woman was still coming. Renatus came back to me without pause, apparently not so badly injured that he needed to keel over or react at all. He raised the jewelled knife above my head.

'No, *no*,' I shrieked, pushing him away and pulling so hard on my hair that tears pricked at my eyes. 'Don't cut it!'

It was stupid, beyond dumb, for even a second to value my long locks enough that it might cost us both our lives. Renatus's expression in that instant – incredulous, disbelieving – mirrored exactly how I felt with myself, and I felt so ridiculous that I opened my mouth to tell him not to listen to me, to do whatever he needed to do to free me so he could Displace us to freedom.

I didn't get to. He grabbed the branch that held me with both hands and snapped it. I felt its weight as it fell and tugged on my hair with the insistence of gravity. The woman's immense emotional profile was bearing down on us and in another split second she'd be within view, she would step past that tree, her face would be lit by wild flames, but in that moment of release from the tree I stepped desperately forward into Renatus's personal space. He wrapped an arm around me and took a hurried step back, and then we were gone from there.

Renatus stepped forcefully through the Fabric and into the physical world once again, dragging me with him. The split in between spaces closed and we both looked around. We were standing beside a rickety fence in a field, surrounded by sleeping cows.

Somewhere else. The woman was nowhere around, and in the tense seconds that followed, she didn't appear. Not a Displacer, then.

Silence.

Renatus dropped his arm from around my shoulders.

'*Don't cut it?*' he repeated derisively. I sighed, exhausted but relieved, and let my weight fall back onto the fence. I reached back and my fingers closed on the wood still tangled in my hair. I pulled it around to where I could see it.

Stupid, stupid. It was thinner than my wrist, thicker than my thumb. I probably could have snapped it myself if I hadn't been panicking like a child.

Like an amateur.

'Fucking Susannah,' Renatus cursed, striding away from me a few paces. 'Didn't mention any of that, I'm sure?'

Breathless, I shook my head. The chase in the forest was definitely the sort of terrifying misadventure my inbuilt excitement-o-meter classified at the Do Not Need extreme. I would never have gone with Renatus tonight if I'd known what the little scrap of paper with coordinates, a time and a date, today's date, was sending us into. It was all too much: the weresight, the stranger, the missing fingers, the woman, the knives...

My stomach roiled and I laid a cautious arm across my middle.

I looked up at Renatus anxiously. 'He cut you. Are you alright?'

He stopped his restless scowling and pacing to lift the hem of his shirt an inch or so. There was blood on his skin. My stomach clenched and abruptly settled as steel, and I pushed myself off the fence to nervously approach. Had this happened because I'd distracted my master at exactly the wrong moment?

'I should have been concentrating; shouldn't have let him get the knife back,' Renatus answered my unspoken question. 'I was wasting my time trying to make him come with us. He didn't want our help. This is nothing,' he added when I ignored everything he said and squinted in the dark at his side. He held the hem away until I'd had a chance to look and placate myself that it was only a scratch, maybe as long as a finger, across his waist. He dropped the shirt. 'Did you get a look at her?'

I straightened. 'No. I mean, sort of. Caucasian? Green eyes. But that's all I noticed.' Before I bailed.

I had been completely wrong. I was in no way awesome enough, brave enough or strong enough to pose any sort of opposition to Lisandro. I was a dumb kid, a silly little girl who couldn't handle improved night vision or get a good look at an opponent that would help Renatus in identifying her. I was the furthest thing from White Elm I could imagine.

I staunchly refused to let myself wonder how I was meant to save Renatus from his horrible self-destruction if I couldn't even do the sidekick thing properly.

'Age?' he asked, kept clear of my straying thoughts by my delicate question-free thinking.

'Adult.'

Raised eyebrow. 'Age?'

I shrugged helplessly. I wasn't the best judge of age, especially in adults. Didn't they get past twenty and suddenly just become "grown up", and lose the number tag? But even still, with this woman, even when I tried to picture her face, I had nothing for him. I hadn't gotten a good look at all.

'Older than you,' I said, though I wasn't sure by how much, exactly, 'and younger than Lord Gawain?'

Renatus nodded slowly and confirmed, reluctantly, 'Adult.'

# chapter twenty-one

Aristea's memory of the female assailant's face was blurred and unhelpful. Renatus touched on it in her head a dozen times over the next day, trying to identify features, or even the whole face. But the fact remained that in her panic, Aristea's brain simply hadn't processed all the details of the sight she'd beheld.

Green eyes, glowing bright in the unnatural contrast of the weresight she wasn't ready for, seemed to be the only feature she'd had time to acknowledge before intuition had driven her away.

Renatus didn't blame her, though he knew she was worried he did. She thought she'd let him down, repeatedly, from the unexpected overreaction to the too-early introduction to the weresight and the other abilities it opened to her, to the unconscious choice to run away from the woman before getting a decent look that could help him. She was keeping her distance, sulking in her room or hiding in the library or sitting against one of the trees in the orchard – all places where she knew he'd stay away. He didn't push it. He was glad she'd listened to the firm voice of her instincts and acted on them without thought. It seemed that they'd saved her life. The woman she'd briefly met in the forest had come after his apprentice without provocation and had fired on her without warning. Those blasts on their own wouldn't have killed Aristea but one strike would have hurt enough to bring her down, and then who knew what would have become of her?

'Not my problem,' Susannah said firmly without looking at him when he marched furiously into her classroom the early morning after. She sat at her desk with long brown hair drifting over her shoulder, brushing the pages of the book she was reading. There were no tangled branches snaring in *her* hair.

'It's about to *become* your fucking problem,' Renatus snarled at her, walking over and snapping her book shut. She pulled back so that her hand and hair didn't get caught, and looked up at him evenly. 'What *the hell* was that?'

'It was your choice to go,' she said coolly. She knew *exactly* what he was talking about and didn't pretend not to.

'On *your* advice,' he retorted angrily. The Seer sighed loudly and sat back in her seat.

'I didn't tell you to do anything.'

'Aristea could have been killed!'

Susannah glared at him, incredulous.

'How is that my fault, Renatus?' she demanded. 'Whose apprentice is she? Which of us took her out into the forest in the middle of the night and let her wander off?'

He could have hit her. He clenched his hands into furious fists at the twisted interpretation.

'Whose side are you on?' he asked, keeping his voice low so he didn't scream at her in frustration. *Goddamn Seers...* She cocked her head to the side as though intrigued by his question.

'Fate's,' she said, and he hated her even more for her stupid answer.

'You're meant to be on ours.'

'I'm not sure what gave you that impression.'

He pointed an angry finger in her face; she didn't even blink.

'You *sent* us into that forest, blind,' he accused, 'and you *knew* what would happen in there.'

333

'I knew that if you went in, at that time, on that date, you would find a crucial piece of information that could ultimately win our war,' Susannah confirmed coldly, 'but I didn't *send* you anywhere. You made your own decision, Renatus. Take some responsibility.' She shoved her seat back and stood. '*You* took your apprentice into a dangerous situation. *Again.* You're the one who barrels ahead into these things without question, without bothering with research or back-up because you're an overconfident little ass, and you think you're untouchable. Well, now you've got a weakness, and she's got a name. Grow up.'

Screw hitting her. He could have killed her. White rage flooded him, burned under his skin. He kept himself statue-still. The slightest motion could be the precursor to snapping her neck. *Bitch.*

She wasn't quite finished with him. 'Fate was generous enough to provide you with everything you needed to make last night a success. A date. A time. A location. A rabbit's foot. Fate even gave you an apprentice, for reasons I'll never fathom, since there doesn't seem to be a hope of her making it through your clumsy tutelage unscathed. Everything that happens happens for a reason and I'm not arrogant enough to pretend I know what all of those are, but by now you've got the clue you went there for-'

'Which is what, exactly?' Renatus demanded, calming himself by a tiny enough degree that he could offer a twitchy motion that should have been a shrug but was too constrained by his tenseness and determination not to rip Susannah to pieces to really look the part. 'I have no idea what we were meant to find. Nothing I learned from Lisandro's man was particularly compelling. Aristea didn't even get a look at the woman who attacked her. I think it's fair to say it was a complete waste of our time.'

'Not. My. Problem,' Susannah said again, taking care with each word. Her gaze was unapologetic. 'What you did or didn't notice is not my concern. If I pass on a message to you, I don't-'

'*No*. If you pass on a message to me, you pass it to *me*, not my seventeen-year-old apprentice.'

'She's eighteen next week, isn't she?' Susannah asked idly. She reached for her book, apparently done with this conversation, but Renatus was not. He slammed a palm down on the cover and her clear grey eyes flicked back up to his.

'Consider this me *taking responsibility*,' he hissed. 'You stay the hell away from her. No more notes with mysterious dates and places. She isn't one of Fate's little puppets for you to misdirect this way or that. She belongs to *me* and from now on if you need something from us you go through me.'

He shoved away from the desk and left the room, fuming, before he could say or do something he'd regret.

Searches of the woodland in the daytime with Elijah and even Oneida, who was keen to get involved with this first case of interest to her since her initiation, turned up nothing new. The woman, whoever she was, had left almost no trace. Oneida was impressed. She was a better tracker than Renatus and he trailed behind her silently as she retraced his steps of the night before, locating the ruined cloaking spell quicker than he had and pointing out droplets of blood on overturned leaves that he would never have noticed. The stranger's movements, despite his attempts to stay hidden, were not hard for her to follow, and she managed to identify the different paths he and Aristea had taken to go after their runner from the disturbed forest floor. The woman, though, had left minimal tracks. Once she started running after the apprentice, her feet stirred up the ground the same way Aristea's had, but leading up to position where they'd spotted each other through the trees there were few prints, and after a few minutes of backtracking along her presumed path uncertainly with no evidence of footsteps Elijah stopped and said, 'This is where she arrived. It's blocked.'

It was common practice for Lisandro's people to bury their Displacement by sealing it up, making it impossible for anyone, even a talented Displacer like Elijah, to follow them. Retracing their own tracks, more obvious in the leaves than the woman's, they followed her path all the way to where Renatus had broken his apprentice free of the tree's jealous grasp – *Don't cut it?! Seriously?* – and lost his hold on the stranger they'd supposedly come here to meet.

'She didn't stop,' Oneida murmured, crouched down over the leaves with her hand hovering just above them, fingers twitching slightly. 'She maybe considered it. There's a choice point here.' She looked up at Renatus. He didn't care about choice points, or anything else Seer-related, actually. The only reason Oneida wasn't lumped in with Susannah as *untrustworthy unreliable irresponsible lying Seer witch* was that she happened to be an excellent tracer, and because she wasn't the one who'd given his apprentice the stupid note and tried to dress him down for following her directions. 'She wasn't here looking for you. She was here for the escapist.' She stood and went back a number of paces, out of sight. Her next words were loud, projected for him to hear. 'How far away were you? When she was about here?'

Stupid question. He hadn't seen the woman at all, hadn't even sensed her, so how was he to know where he was in relation to her at any time? Oneida came back when he didn't answer.

'There was another choice point back there, behind a burnt-out tree. She stopped firing. When?'

'When...' He had to think. He'd seen the explosion of bark and wood, chips of tree fluttering everywhere and sending the stranger into a wild frenzy of terror. *Let me go. You don't want this escalate into a fight, White Elm.* 'When Aristea got tangled up in the tree.'

'So she didn't actually want to kill her,' Elijah interpreted, examining the scorch mark on the tree. Renatus shrugged.

'Or she was distracted by the tree that burst into flames right in front of her face.' Too bad he hadn't hit her.

Oneida spread her hands over the leaves and loose pebbles on the ground, as though they were little tiny friends who were all speaking to her at once and she needed to get her thoughts in order to be able to speak for them.

'She saw your apprentice stop, trapped, and stopped her attack,' she explained, stepping carefully forward. 'She saw you arrive, with her target. The altercation. The two of you escaped; your "stranger" kept running, downhill.' Oneida reverently followed the ghosts of decisions already made while Renatus threw a disdainful look at Elijah. Ever patient, the wiry New Zealander only smiled. The newest councillor broke into a jog and stopped. 'One of her spells struck him, here. She had the choice to finish him or take him in.'

Elijah and Renatus trudged down the hill after her.

'He didn't get far,' Renatus commented. Oneida shook her head in agreement, looking up at the sunlight streaming through the canopy. She was dressed more warmly than either of the men, coming as she did from a very warm climate while they were well-accustomed to low temperatures.

'She took him with her, alive,' Elijah said. He waved his hand through the space before him, sensing a sinkhole in the Fabric that the other two would need to concentrate very hard to identify. 'Blocked, again, from the other end.' He sighed and looked apologetically at Renatus. 'There's nothing I can do with a blocked Displacement.'

Frustration was becoming a constant friend to Renatus. The forest was devoid of clues. The boxes of missing persons files on his desk had yielded nothing regarding the man in the orchard. Aristea was still miserable with herself and avoiding him, and the weekend was drawing ever nearer, bringing that ridiculous masquerade party about much too quickly.

'Raymond won't notice if I'm not there,' he complained to Fionnuala as he walked with her up the staircase on the morning of the engagement. He'd intended, kind of, to tell her, but had managed to avoid doing so, and apparently Lord Gawain had contacted her of his own volition. She was delighted, and determined, that he would be going.

'You're absolutely right,' she agreed. 'He won't spare a thought for you. Unless you turn up. And you've grown so much,' she said fondly, smiling up at him. Once he was the one looking up at her, but he'd matched and then outgrown his childhood caretaker by the time he was twelve. 'They'll all be so surprised. And Mister Raymond – I would love to see his face when he sees you. He'll think he's seen a ghost.'

Renatus rolled his eyes. He didn't need the reminder that he looked incredibly similar to his father, with whom Sean Raymond's friendship with the Morrisseys had actually lay.

'Gearoid, engaged,' Fionnuala added disbelievingly, shaking her head. 'I remember that boy. Your families went to Portugal together for the day, do you remember?'

Renatus nodded once in acknowledgement. *To the beach.* He'd rarely been off the estate as a child. He hadn't cared much then. He liked it at home. But Ana had lived and breathed for those moments of freedom from her cage. She always cried at the end of the day and refused to go home, and Lisandro, the only one who could ever get her to do anything when she was like this, would have to work her around with promises of more excursions, more adventures, just not today.

Instead of fulfilling those promises he'd murdered her.

'I remember that he ate a whole spire off my sandcastle,' Renatus commented. He rounded the last curve of the staircase and started up the final flight, regulating his stride to keep pace with Fionnuala. She wasn't *old*, not yet, but he'd started noticing how slow she was sometimes. He remembered her being much livelier and more active when he was a child. 'He must have been only ten or eleven the last time I saw him. I doubt he remembers me, or particularly wants me at this party.'

'Mister Raymond invited you,' Fionnuala responded firmly. '*He* remembers you. And little *Teagan*. Not a little girl anymore, then. I think it's a lovely idea that you attend. And I should say, I think it's the most pleasant thing you've ever been asked to do in the name of this job of yours.'

She smiled again, and he forced a smile-like expression in return. She didn't know Lisandro would be there. Lord Gawain had left that fact out when he conscripted her to help talk her charge into going. Renatus hadn't brought it up, either.

They walked along the hallway of the top storey together.

'I already laid everything out for you on your bed,' she said when they neared his bedroom door. He opened it and leaned inside to look. Indeed, she'd saved him the trouble of staring resentfully into his closet and had prepared an outfit neatly for him. He felt a rush of gratitude. Her smile, already wide, softened, and she patted his hand. 'I know you don't enjoy this sort of thing, but I'm sure it will be very different from when you were a boy. And Miss Aristea will have a wonderful time.'

Renatus wasn't so sure. His apprentice had been sullen and anxious all weekend, which he was led to believe was a typical state for teenagers, but Aristea was generally a relatively bearable teen. She was still disappointed in herself about the challenges of the Friday night in the forest, and though she hadn't mentioned it, her mind kept spinning in circles over this afternoon's upcoming event.

She was worried.

'Is she ready to go?'

Fionnuala looked shocked by his question. As if expecting Aristea to be *ready* on-time was an unreasonable and left-of-field comment that clearly demonstrated his ignorance in how long it took to prepare a young lady for a party – did he not recall how long it used to take the staff to prepare his mother and sister for these sorts of events?

'No. Of course not.'

'*No?* There are three of you working on her, aren't there?'

'The girls are doing her hair now, in Miss-' Pause. Smooth correction. 'In her bedroom, Master Renatus. The rollers take a long time.'

Very smooth. So smooth it didn't even cause the rough jolt it used to. He eyed the closed door of his lost sister's bedroom and extended his senses inside. It was a place of deep emotional upset, the haunt of Ana Morrissey, and he'd left it exactly alone since she died. It was a virtual shrine to her memory. Not right now, though. The cool, lonesome stillness that characterised this room earlier in the month when he'd sat there by himself, soaking in misery and missing, was banished by the busy activity of the three young women preparing. The scene was like a warped reflection of times past.

'And you haven't even told me what colour tie you're going to wear,' his housekeeper reminded him with patience, because she loved to ensure things were done *right*, that her two young charges, appearing together at a society ball, should be properly matched. That they should look the part. That they should look beautiful together, because it was what others wanted to see.

Renatus rejected it, that whole damn world and its pretentious unspoken demands. The preoccupation with appearance, with what others thought. Like aesthetics and blood and position were the ultimate qualities, worthy of judgement, more valuable than independence or wit or capability or strength. This was one of the bars of Ana's cage – her inability to fight her society's forceful shaping of her into something beautiful, something passive, something useless, had kept her eternally frustrated, miserable, downtrodden. He'd seen it firsthand, the effects of this soft but constant pressure.

His and Aristea's worth was dependent on much more than what vapid strangers whispered behind gloved hands in an extravagant ballroom.

'She can wear whatever she wants. Her jeans, for all I care. But I've told her,' he was quick to add, seeing the look of dawning horror on his childhood nanny's face, 'that everything in the room is hers, including the wardrobe.'

Fionnuala smiled warmly and said nothing. Proud. Like there was something momentous about him giving his dead sister's last birthday present to Aristea.

He determinedly insisted to himself that it was no such big deal, and refused to feel any way about it at all. He'd already given her everything of Ana's. It... hadn't hurt as much as he'd expected it to.

Aristea was not like Ana. She did not take hours to get ready. What others thought of her had haunted Ana her whole life; Aristea's experiences upon first arriving at the house had already begun to lose their significance, and a strength of character Ana had never truly possessed had taken root. He was combing his hair back when there was a knock at *his* door. He waved the door open in response – much quicker than walking all the way over there to turn the handle – and Aristea was standing out in the hall. Dressed. Ready. Rollers out of her hair. Eyelids extravagantly decorated with golden paint.

'I told them I'm not the one getting engaged so I didn't need the three-hour Hollywood make-up treatment and the haunted family jewellery,' she said, drolly, gesturing vaguely with her bare wrists. She'd found the most modern and demure gown in the collection, apparently. It went to the floor, a necessity for such an event, with lace all the way up to her neck and capped sleeves.

Classy and classic and perfectly appropriate for a seventeen-year-old girl in a house full of adults.

'At least you're both in black,' Fionnuala couldn't help mentioning when Renatus came to the door, brushing imaginary lint from the front of his jacket and turning down the heavy collar he'd just finished standing up. She and her daughters were trailing behind the apprentice, hands full of the things they still felt she needed. Dana took Aristea's loose curls in her hands and piled them up over her head while her sister fitted a black lace mask onto Aristea's face and tied the ribbons. When Dana dropped the hair it fell over the bow, hiding it.

'They don't need to be matching,' Niamh said, standing back to admire her work. The over-the-top eye make-up made more sense now, showing through the mask. 'She's not his date.'

'And they already match,' Dana added, turning Aristea's hand over to show the tattoo. The black mark appeared stark and bold against her skin. She normally wore sleeves over it so it seemed very noticeable to Renatus today, out in the open. He knew it would not go unnoticed at Raymond's party, either.

'That's alright, we can hide that,' Fionnuala said kindly, offering Aristea a selection of gloves. Aristea shot Renatus a questioning look.

*Gloves?*

*Everybody else will be wearing them,* he answered, though he had no intention of bending with that convention. *So they can shake hands. Sorcerers, at least this kind, are funny about skin contact.*

For good reason. A sorcerer could do a great deal of damage to another if given the chance to make skin contact. Even telepathy was easier with touch. The practice of wearing gloves in public was a multi-faceted tradition, complex the same way everything else about these people needed to be complex. Wearing gloves was an unspoken assurance that harm was not intended at this time, but was also a protective measure, defending against unwarranted touch and ensuring the wearer did not leave prints or impressions on the things they touched. In Aristea's case it would stop her from tapping into every intense and uncomfortable trace left over Sean Raymond's ballroom. It signalled that the wearer respected the rules of the house they were visiting and appreciated their own vulnerability. It was a polite, submissive gesture.

Renatus would not be wearing gloves.

Aristea picked Fionnuala's least favourite pair of those offered, and he could tell from her momentary hesitation that she sensed the housekeeper's dissatisfaction with the choice.

She tugged the small lace gloves onto her hands and flexed her fingers in them.

'It doesn't cover your mark, dear,' Fionnuala pointed out, offering a long satin pair that would cover up to the elbows. Aristea blinked and looked up.

'I don't think I want to cover it,' she said, surprising the old nanny. Dana clutched her mother's arm supportively.

'It's different now, Ma,' she explained. 'Lots of girls get ink now.'

'She'll be the only one at Mister Raymond's party with *ink*,' Fionnuala argued weakly. Renatus nodded and stepped out of his room. That was the hope; that she would be noticed. That any guest he didn't get the chance to speak to at least saw the unfamiliar young woman with the mark on her wrist and wondered who in this whole grand building she belonged with.

She was the first White Elm apprentice since Qasim. It was gossip worth spreading.

'Renatus has a tattoo, too,' Niamh reminded her mother brightly. It didn't help. She took the extra gloves and turned back to Renatus. He'd known Niamh and Dana his whole life but, years older even than Ana, the age gap between the girls and himself had always been too big for much of a friendship to develop. She said, 'I've been practising this one. Ready?'

He nodded and let her get to work. She still had her paintbrush behind her ear. She tossed the gloves over her shoulder and grabbed the brush. The bristles never touched his skin. She worked quickly, sharp erratic strokes of the brush through the air over his face, around his eyes, over the brows, along the cheekbones, all the while channelling magic down the narrow wooden handle of the little paintbrush. Normally he'd never let anyone cast magic, even artistic, delicate magic, this close to his face, but he trusted Fionnuala's family and what she was drawing for him would be preferable over having to actually *wear* or *carry* a stupid mask.

343

Niamh pulled back and clicked her fingers experimentally. Renatus felt the tiny flicker of the spells initiating over his face. Aristea leaned in, amazed.

'My mask and make-up doesn't do that,' she said enviously. 'How come I can't have that?'

'You're a lady,' Fionnuala answered soothingly, and Aristea said nothing, but Renatus could tell from her thoughts that this answer was not really good enough to explain why she had a conventional, physical mask while he had a ghostly, smoky one constructed of magic.

Outside it was grey and looked ready to start raining again. Renatus flicked the collar of his jacket back up the way it was. The ground was soft and damp and even short distances were best Skipped to avoid muddying shoes. When Renatus closed the gate behind her, Aristea complained about the lack of waiting horse and carriage.

'Displacement is much quicker than any carriage they've yet managed to come up with,' he reminded her as they walked swiftly away from the house to where Displacement was possible. She glared at the ground, skirt hitched up in her hands to keep the hem clear of the grass.

'So far I don't believe it's *cleaner*.' She stopped. 'Renatus?' He looked back at her. 'Thank you for the dresses.'

His sister had worn dresses, only dresses, and had amassed quite a collection of them. Her twentieth birthday present had been a spectacular addition – twenty new ball gowns. She'd not lived to wear them. Aristea didn't look as comfortable in the finery. It made her look older, certainly, but her uncertain thoughts were as childlike as ever.

'I had no plans to wear them. I think you'll get more use out of her things than I will.'

'Probably. But the people at this party… They're…' She looked down at herself, trying to articulate her complex concerns. 'There are dresses in that room fancier than what my sister wore to her high school dance. The people at this party are going to be able to tell. I don't belong there. I'm a kid from a little beachside town.' *I'm no one.*

She didn't want to go. He didn't want to go. It was going to be hellish, sickening in its extravagance, and he was already deeply dreading the tedious dance of every falsified interaction he was to have for the rest of the day. The questions – *where have you been all this time?* The distrustful gazes – *he's White Elm now, you know.* The lingering lecherous glances of too-old men when they noticed Aristea – *whose daughter is that?* Polite faked interest in what people had been doing with their lives. Long winding conversations about nothing in particular with the other heads of the major families, seemingly pointless but actually strategic political interrogations intended to draw the facts out of opponents.

Everybody at this party was an opponent to every other guest. Friendship was an illusion the entire society simply liked to entertain, for convenience and elegance. The world seemed a nicer place when you were pretending to be friends with everybody.

'I'm not introducing you as a kid from a little beachside town so it won't be a problem,' Renatus answered eventually. 'You're Aristea Byrne, my apprentice, and she's not no one.' He paused, hesitating. He thought of the weresight, which she wasn't ready for. 'Listen. You don't have to go. I can go by myself, or I can try to convince Emmanuelle.' Though he didn't want to take Emmanuelle. It would be hard enough to hold back from confronting Lisandro if he really did appear; Em and her reckless anger would be only too happy to help.

Aristea thought about that for a very long moment. He overheard the thoughts she didn't lock away too fast for him to glean. She was getting private like that, hiding things. Uncertainties? Worries? He didn't know, and tried not to pry or be too concerned.

'No, you're right,' she said finally. 'I'm your apprentice. I should be where you are.'

'And it would be atrocious of you to send me to this forsaken party alone,' he reminded her, and she smiled.

Adequate distance away, Renatus offered her a hand. His mind was filling with the disquieted murmured voices of his colleagues, who all knew where he was going. They had varying feelings about it.

*Remember what you're there for*, Lady Miranda warned.

*I know what you said about the rules of these sorts of functions, but if* he *breaks them and you need back-up, I'm ready*, Jadon let him know, and Emmanuelle overheard and concurred.

*Watch Aristea's mouth*, Qasim said coolly. Renatus resisted the urge to retort to that. Aristea was impulsive, instinctively honest and increasingly opinionated. It wasn't bad advice.

*We won't be in communication with you unless you reach out for us first*, Lord Gawain said now. *You're there to develop trust. If anyone senses you speaking with us it could undermine the whole purpose of this afternoon. Be safe.*

Renatus felt an unexpected little flutter in his stomach as he slit the Fabric of space and pushed a wormhole through to Sean Raymond's estate. This was it. The long-awaited, long-dreaded return. There was no backing out once he stepped through. Then Aristea took his hand and let him pull her from the familiar into the unknown, and they were there, miles away from his home, standing outside a different pair of high iron gates.

'Locked out,' Aristea whispered, keeping hold of his hand a second longer than necessary as she looked around nervously. Even her soft voice fell flat in the stillness. Here, the low grey skies seeped into the world around them as soft, flowy fog, swallowing the crumbling stone fence, discolouring the forestry either side of them, fading out the long dirt road behind them back into town and totally obscuring the grand house Renatus knew to be beyond that gate.

It was the middle of summer, and it wasn't cold.

Renatus dropped her hand and went to the gate. He had a strong suspicion and wanted to test it out. He laid both of his hands on the gate, firm and flat, and waited.

After a second there was a loud click, and the gates swung slowly open of their own accord. Simultaneously, all around, the mists began rolling back and away, revealing the ambling fence line, the woodland it hid behind, the windy road behind them and the long double-storey home on the flat green land immediately before them.

The illusion of austerity deterred the unwelcome, and dissipated for the worthy and invited. Charming.

Aristea stepped closer to be at his side. She was nervous, he could tell, but her steady and deliberate breaths were controlled and her composure seemed complete. Outwardly she looked unfettered. He hoped he looked the same.

Weakness or uncertainty would not be tolerated, or treated forgivingly, in this world.

'You should consider a front lawn like this one,' Aristea said quietly as they stepped through the gates together and started down the straight, wide path to the big front doors. Raymond's home was much closer to the gate than Morrissey House was, and lacked the annoying winding uphill walk his own place demanded of any visitor.

'This front lawn is fine if you're hosting a party every weekend,' Renatus answered, just as quietly. 'Not so useful if you're trying to keep political terrorists out.'

'The mist effect could come in handy.'

At the majestic semi-circular feature that was in fact the front steps, a smartly dressed butler with a polished bronze mask came trotting out the doors. He bowed.

'Good afternoon,' he said smoothly, straightening to observe them as they walked up the steps. His expression was frozen in a practiced polite smile but behind that Renatus could almost hear the mental checklist he was going through. The pair looked the part. They'd found the house. The gates had let them in. 'Welcome to the house of Sean Raymond. Might I have your names?'

Renatus had been looking past the butler at the house. The front doors were tall, like at his own home, but had been recently replaced. He remembered heavy, plain hardwood planks with ornate iron hinges, knockers and locks. Now it was a lighter wood, both in colour and apparent weight, carved with story-like panels depicting the struggles of angels, monsters and men. A grand new face for a dynasty always clawing at the next rung on the social ladder.

The butler was waiting patiently and Aristea was keeping silent. Renatus resisted the urge to clear his throat.

'Renatus Morrissey.'

The butler didn't have, or need, a paper list to consult. His job consisted purely of knowing everything his masters required him to know and no doubt he was an expert at it. The guest list was probably burned into his brain, colour-coded to identify persons of special interest or concern. No surprise registered on his face. He simply nodded his head in welcome.

'Of course.' He didn't ask for Aristea's name. Consorts didn't need names. It wouldn't be on his list anyway, and in this world, if she had a name worth throwing around, she would have brought it up herself. 'Please follow me.'

He led them inside. The entryway was narrower than it looked from the outside, a structural fact of the house that Sean Raymond seemed to not have been able to yet get around in his relentless mission of improvement, and that opened up to a new feature – a large, open entry hall that spanned upwards all the way to the exposed wooden beams of the roof and the sparkling new chandelier that now hung among them. The second storey floor had been removed here to give this space the height and grandeur it now possessed. The walls were polished panels of wood.

And there were people in here. Not many, but a few, milling about a wide round table directly underneath the chandelier. The butler gestured over.

'Any weapons to check in, sir?' he asked. Renatus shook his head, noting the men casually removing knives and wands from under their jackets and the insides of their boots to add to the impressive collection laid out in the open on the tabletop. Aristea stared.

*These people come to a party armed like that?*

*They go about daily life armed like that,* Renatus confirmed.

'Miss?' Aristea looked sharply back at the butler and the patient, thin smile hanging steadily underneath the shine of his bronze mask. 'Anything to declare?' he prompted when she didn't respond. She blinked. Thoughts spun wildly past Renatus's in her head, skirting the edge of their shared connection. He could chase them, find out what had triggered that spurt of panic, but then she got herself under control. Shut something away. Blinked again, lifted her shoulders slightly.

'No.'

'Then you may enter the ballroom,' the butler said with a final respectful bow, intended to butter up guests and pander to their sense of self-importance, and he indicated in the direction of the open archway from which the sounds of music and voices wafted. Renatus nodded in answer before he could even think about it, falling easily back into the traditions drilled into him as a child, and guided Aristea away with a hand on her back. He felt the tiny surge of energy as she fortified her already perfect wards in preparation for the impending proximity to dozens and dozens of intense and powerful strangers and their intense and powerful emotions.

*There are no weapons allowed inside and strict customs preventing anyone from doing harm with magic at an event like this,* he reminded her. *Don't be afraid to be alone here if conversation separates us.*

Aristea nodded as their shoes made short, clear, echoing *click* sounds on the new floors on their way past the weapons table to the arched entry to the ballroom. The men there readjusting their dinner jackets watched the pair from the edges of their vision; Renatus wondered if Aristea could sense their curiosity.

*What can I talk about if that happens?* she asked. *Not the school. The White Elm?*

*I don't think anyone is going to ask you for the White Elm's secrets,* he answered. *I think they'll be careful with you — they don't know you, or what you do or don't know. No one will be so direct. Keep it light; keep away from topics you don't feel strong with. These people, they don't care what you've got to say, so if there's something you don't want to discuss, don't. They'll accept a subject change.*

*Avoid topics I don't feel strong with,* Aristea repeated, sarcasm colouring even her thoughts. *So... keep quiet?*

Renatus hesitated. It was hard to explain what he meant. *Talk... If they talk first. But don't tell anyone anything. It's an art. This is a good practice game.*

They reached the archway and the crowd inside the ballroom became apparent. Renatus slowed to give Aristea a moment if she needed it to gather herself. He pretended the pause wasn't for himself as well. It was an intimidating scene for anyone who wasn't sure they belonged there, whether it was because they were an alien in this world in a dress too beautiful to feel comfortable in, or because they were an estranged orphan of this world not sure if they were ready to return to it.

Too late now.

'Any last advice?' Aristea asked softly, brushing her thick dark curls back over her shoulder as they stepped through the arch into the party. She looked tall and quietly confident, whatever he knew about what was going on behind her mask, and falsely disinterested glances were already being cast her way. She would fit in just fine. She would be alright.

Renatus looked around at the faces, more than a hundred of them, some vaguely familiar, most disguised by masks or magic like his, and knew he was going to have to be, too. One man in a small knot nearby broke away and approached with a wide smile – one of the most genuine in the whole ballroom – and Renatus leaned down and aside to speak into Aristea's ear.

'Trust no one.'

# chapter twenty-two

The urge to smooth the fabric of my dress's fitted bodice or to tug on the hem of the gloves or to check my hair for flyaways was almost irresistible, but I managed. With immense effort.

*Anything to declare?* he'd asked. I'd almost lost control of my frightened thoughts for a moment there. Uh, you mean like "I'm shit-scared right now" or "I've been idly plotting to commit murder and today I'm going to come face-to-face with the man I intend to kill"? Renatus didn't seem to have noticed or overheard.

The ballroom was about the size of the one at Morrissey House but had different dimensions and a totally different feel. For one thing, it was *full* of people. The most people I'd ever seen in Renatus's ballroom was when all of the students and the White Elm had gathered there together for Peter's funeral. Sixty or so people. I was standing in a crowd of at least a hundred and fifty adults, all immaculately and classically dressed like they'd stepped off the set of movies about the Victorians, gangsters and flappers, the Hollywood golden age and pretty much any film I'd seen involving a bank heist where safety deposit boxes full of sparkling garish jewellery are obtained and briefly worn by the love interest or lead female. The women here wore enough jewellery between them to wipe the debt of a small nation. There were no tiaras or crowns, thankfully, but massive pendants the size of my fist and glinting chokers that encased the whole neck were less the exception than the rule. And the *rings*. They were everywhere, sparkling on every gloved hand, even the men's. Renatus was right, everyone was wearing gloves. Everyone except him, and the man now approaching us with a surprised smile and an air of comfortable, harmless confidence.

'I didn't believe it when I saw the R.S.V.P.,' he said, extending a hand as he neared, eyes set firmly on my master, taking him in. He exuded positive emotions and I unclenched my hands, trying to relax. Renatus was paranoid. Not everybody here had to necessarily be a bad guy, surely. I detected nothing untoward. Yet. That said, my guard was firmly up against most of what the people around me were feeling. All kinds of unpleasant motives could be worming their way through this room without me knowing right now.

'Mr Raymond,' Renatus acknowledged, bowing his head very slightly and accepting the hand when it was close enough. The older man clasped it inside both of his warmly, looking over Renatus's face, ignoring the spectacular spellcraft that was Niamh's mask. How it had escaped mention in the half hour of conversation with Fionnuala's daughters before Renatus arrived that Niamh was an *artist* of magic, I really couldn't figure. She'd *painted* a mask in the air over his face, and at a click of her fingers it had come to life – a visage of slate grey smoke, swirling and moving but contained to the shape she gave it. It was *the coolest thing I'd ever seen*, and everyone else was acting like it was nothing. I imagined having that kind of ability and couldn't reconcile that idea with the concept of not telling *everybody* about it: like, *Hi, I'm Aristea, I'm a witch and a White Elm apprentice, but more importantly, I can create incredible fashion accessories out of smoke with just a little make-up brush.*

Standing here, though, looking around the room, I was starting to see why maybe Niamh didn't think she was such a big deal. Renatus's mask was not the only corporeal accessory, nor was it the only evidence of complex and extravagant magic. Extending my senses cautiously, I felt the edges of many illusions – faces, masks, hair pieces, *hair...*

even the black-and-bronze artwork on the bare walls was only illusory, easily torn down after the event to be replaced with whatever suited the theme of the next one.

Mr Raymond held Renatus's hand for a beat longer than was probably expected, staring closely into his face, and then dropped it to lay one hand on my master's shoulder. He was older, around fifty, I supposed, and wore a more elaborate, finer version of the bronze mask his staff wore. It had no ribbon or elastic and seemed to remain in place against the suggestion of gravity quite of its own choosing. Behind the mask were two clear, light blue eyes; below it was a thick salt-and-pepper moustache and a wide smile of disbelief.

'It's like looking twenty years into the past,' he said. Behind him, the men he'd walked away from were watching with open curiosity. They all wore variations of the same pompous jackets with tails and shiny buttons. Renatus's attire looked basic and modern by comparison. 'You look like your father.'

Renatus made that expression he always made when he was supposed to be smiling, but I'd never seen him smile for real so for all I knew maybe that was his best attempt. 'Don't hold that against me.'

Raymond wasn't expecting that response, and laughed in surprise. He clapped Renatus's shoulder genially. So slight that it was probably impossible for most people to determine, the thinnest sliver of reserve fell away from the host's façade, and I realised that everything I was feeling from him from behind my safety net of wards and emotional blocks was what he chose to project. Like the paintings on the walls, Mr Raymond was *fake*, sharing only the airs he wanted us to see.

Renatus was right to advise I trust no one here. Nothing could be assumed.

'No promises, Morrissey,' Raymond joked, a sparkle in his eyes. Did he know Renatus didn't go by the name anymore? That he'd undergone a magical ritual to rid himself of it? Renatus didn't correct him. He was here to smooth the waters and make alliances, not raise questions. He half-turned, enough to encompass me in the conversation, and Raymond's light blue eyes moved from his face to mine. I almost felt them land on me.

'This is our host, Sean Raymond,' he filled in for the sake of politeness. 'Raymond, this is my apprentice, Aristea Byrne.'

Raymond didn't bother to hide his surprise but did try to make his glance at my bare wrist at least a little bit discreet.

'Apprentice,' he repeated, and the word sounded as ungainly in his mouth as it looked, like he'd prepped all the sounds for "wife" or "girlfriend" but then had to chop and change them without notice into the curveball Renatus threw. He recovered quickly and offered me his hand, palm up, clearly not a handshake. 'Full of surprises. Lovely to meet you, Miss Byrne.'

It should have seemed cheesy to put my hand in his and let him kiss the back of my glove, but in this beautiful room oozing with falseness and class it seemed appropriate. Raymond smiled up at me as he straightened, releasing my hand and gesturing back into the ballroom.

'Please,' he said, looking between us, 'allow me to introduce... *reintroduce*... some friends of mine.'

He led us eagerly to the three men he'd been speaking with when we arrived. They'd been murmuring amongst themselves, casting us looks varying from curious to suspicious to disbelieving, but when they saw their host returning with us they abandoned their secret dialogue and shifted, opening their circle to allow us to join. One, an overweight man with an elaborately embroidered velvet jacket and a chunky gold mask that stayed on by the same magic as Raymond's, was the first to acknowledge us. He parted his hands welcomingly and smiled at Renatus.

'Renatus Morrissey,' he said, shaking his head. 'Back from the dead.'

'Haven't been there yet,' my master responded smoothly, taking the man's silky green-gloved hand in his bare one when it was thrust at him. 'Uncle Thomas? Thomas

Shanahan.' The smile under the gold mask went wide and I felt the wave of pride and pleasure the man couldn't contain. Renatus turned to me. 'Mr Shanahan was first cousin to my mother.'

Thomas Shanahan. I recalled the name from the letter about arranged marriages I'd seen on Renatus's desk but I was surprised by this news. Renatus had told me he'd lost his whole family in Lisandro's storm and I'd heard Renatus referred to as "the last Morrissey". For some reason I'd never considered he might have extended family on his mother's side.

*Why didn't he take you in after she died?*

*He tried. Fionnuala, Lisandro and Gawain all said no.*

I assumed they'd had their reasons, especially if three people who, openly or privately, disliked each other managed to agree on this one point.

'Dear Luella,' Shanahan said regretfully. 'I hope you received my correspondence over the years. I never heard back from you directly.'

'I did.' Renatus never apologised for anything, even leaving a concerned uncle hanging for eight years. 'I have appreciated your kind words. These have been hard years.'

Understanding nods all around.

'Thomas Shanahan the Second is a guest of honour this afternoon,' Raymond told us, playing host and thoroughly enjoying himself. 'His daughter Teagan is the reason we're all here this afternoon. She was kind enough – or foolish enough – to accept Gearoid's proposal. Poor darling girl.'

There was a round of light laughter from the men gathered. Fake. Yet also, simultaneously, not. There was enjoyment to be had in making fun of Raymond's son.

'I don't remember Teagan as well as your other girls,' Renatus admitted, 'but if she's anything like Caitlin I'm sure she thought it through long and hard before she made a decision. From memory you father highly methodical daughters, Mr Shanahan.'

More laughter; but lighter this time, for apparently this was an inside joke. Thomas Shanahan nodded with a fond smile and turned to explain to the others.

'Pedantic might be the better word. My eldest, Caitlin, still writes out lists of pros and cons before deciding on *anything*. I'm sure she was a frustrating playdate for your sister on those occasions I sent her,' he added to Renatus, flicking his wide smile back to him. All eyes in the circle followed the smile to see how Renatus would react.

It was *mean*, but I was starting to get the hang of the game. Poke the bear, back off, repeat. No one was asking the kinds of questions nice, normal people asked. *I heard you ditched your name – is it alright if I use it or would you prefer I didn't? I'm so sorry about that tragic loss of your entire family in one day – would it be easier for you if we avoided that topic?* Instead they danced around the delicate, careful to step on only a single toe at a time.

'I think so,' Renatus answered, acting unaffected. 'Ana was impulsive. Lists weren't her thing. She was closer with Keely.'

He wasn't biting – that would only expose his deep wounds, and he was being careful to keep the locations of those to himself – but he was nipping back, apparently. The silent eyes of the circle moved back to Shanahan at Renatus's words. The ball was back in the other court. Shanahan was too slow to hit back.

'Yes, they were similar, weren't they? Must have been in the blood,' Shanahan theorised after a moment of stunned silence. It still blew me away that this portly man in the fanciest clothes I had ever seen on a man was a blood relative of Renatus. 'Goodness. Keely. That's a name I haven't heard in a long time,' he added with a deliberately dainty laugh and a wide smile that encompassed the rest of the circle, inviting the older men to laugh with him. They did, but I could tell they weren't fooled by his quick cover. 'I'm not sure I'd recognise her if I saw her today. She'd be all grown. It's not as though she died.'

356

An underhanded bite back. A nasty one, considering Luella Morrissey and her family were his family, too. I wanted to speak up and tell Shanahan to shut up and stop being horrible, but Renatus was the king of answering back.

'No,' he agreed. 'She just ran away from you, didn't she?'

A vague memory hit me, a name and a date on a missing person file: *Keely Shanahan. May.* Ana's "friend" – their *cousin*. *No coincidences*, he'd said as he came across that file while I asked about the invitation to this very event.

Renatus couldn't but I felt the dull pang of hurt inside Thomas Shanahan at that reminder. He'd been begging for it, really, but he'd bluffed with his cards one round too long and had lost the game. The other men narrowed their eyes in spiteful amusement. *Friends*, allegedly, except that they took abstract enjoyment in watching one another be ripped on. But they weren't gathered here to exploit one another. Renatus was the one they were testing out. Weakness not found, Sean Raymond quickly redirected, introducing the other two men in the circle – his cousin, Harold, and his "business partner", Robert Quinn.

'I knew your father well,' Quinn told Renatus as they shook hands. His gloves were a soft sort of suede.

'I'm afraid I don't remember you.'

'We had a professional friendship. We worked together a number of times.'

There was a miniscule pause in which the men waited for Renatus's reaction. They had to know he was White Elm, which was perhaps why they weren't openly discussing their "work" of trafficking black market items, trading secrets and extorting lesser sorcerers out of their money in exchange for the working of illegal magic.

'Of course,' Renatus agreed calmly. Like he was cool with casual illegal activity, which he pretty much was. 'He rarely conducted business outside of his study and so many of the faces he knew well are unfamiliar to me. My father was only just beginning to involve me in his work prior to his death. I'm sure he thought he had more time.' He turned the awkward silence back on them, and used the gap in conversation to introduce me. 'This is Aristea Byrne.'

'I hadn't heard,' Thomas Shanahan said graciously, having recovered from Renatus's flippant mention of what I had to infer was some kind of scandal involving the runaway daughter, and he flashed me a smile and reached for my hand. 'When's the wedding?'

'Aristea is my apprentice.'

These three reacted even less gracefully than Raymond had. Lips on the back of my hand, Shanahan froze, then pulled back and turned my wrist. Harold Raymond leaned across the circle to be able to stare at the tattoo, since Renatus's was covered by the black of his sleeve.

'I hadn't heard,' Shanahan said again, slower this time, opening his fingers and letting me take my hand back.

'Byrne,' Robert Quinn repeated. 'Are you related to the Belfast Byrnes?'

I shook my head, uncertain. 'I don't think so.' Wrong thing to say. I knew it immediately from the way their curiosity cooled several degrees. My uncertainty told them I didn't know my lineage. In this room, whatever I was wearing and whoever I'd arrived with, I wasn't anybody much without a lineage.

Renatus swooped in and saved me. 'She's from the Ó Grádaigh line.' Which I'd thought was kind of a secret. He reminded me, *Lisandro already knows so I don't suppose it's worth keeping secret anymore*, and I reluctantly acknowledged that it was probably never much of a secret at all.

And the curiosity ignited once again.

'Cassán Ó Grádaigh's work was genius,' Sean Raymond told me. 'You'd be hard pressed to find a guest here today who doesn't know his name.'

'His early books were very broad, quite fluffy,' Quinn said. 'Love and Fate and all that. His later work was where he got some focus.'

I only had one copy of one of his works, and I thought it was one of the early ones. I didn't know what was meant about the later books because I hadn't read any of them.

'Brilliant man,' Shanahan agreed, nodding at Renatus approvingly. 'I didn't know he'd had any offspring. Excellent find, Morrissey.'

I knew I wasn't meant to be talking unless spoken to or unless I had something to contribute, but it fell out anyway.

'I wasn't lost,' I said. 'I didn't need finding.'

Shanahan's smile froze again; the Raymonds and Quinn chuckled.

'My apologies,' the smile beneath the big gold mask demurred after a beat. 'I'm sure you didn't.'

Sean Raymond beckoned someone over and a bronze-masked staff member appeared at his elbow, Displaced directly into position.

'Sir?'

So polite, so respectful, so archaic. Renatus didn't have this old-timey master-servant relationship with his staff. I thought of Niamh, painting his face; Fionnuala, fussing over us both.

'Where are the drinks?' Raymond asked, and the skinny little servant bowed and disappeared. It was maybe five seconds before a different staff member materialised in his place with a tray of short glass tumblers and a couple of lovely crystal decanters filled with different levels of liquids, ranging from amber-gold to very dark brown. 'Ah. Much better.'

The servant removed his hands, clad in silky bronze gloves, from the tray, and it remained in place, floating determinedly. I'd seen examples of this type of magic from Renatus, but never so much at once. The careless way these people treated extremely cool magic was surreal. I tried not to look impressed. Absolutely everything impressed me. The servant poured the drinks and the men took the glasses.

'It feels strange to be serving something other than soda to Áindreas Morrissey's boy,' Raymond admitted, handing a glass across to Robert Quinn. 'What will it be? Whisky?' When Renatus nodded he smiled to himself and watched the server change decanters to pour a new glass. 'Your father's son.' He turned his smile on me. 'For the lady?'

I glanced helplessly at Renatus. "I'm seventeen" was probably not going to fly. Not only did they not need to know that, I considered the table in the entrance hall covered in knives and realised that like pretty much every other law in the country, the legal drinking age was probably not something these people recognised. "I don't really drink" didn't sound any better an excuse in my head than it would out loud, but I still had unpleasant memories of drinking my way through my uncle's spirits collection four years ago and I was nervous enough here without encouraging memories of alcohol poisoning to resurface.

'The same,' Renatus answered for me, and Sean Raymond offered a surprised look. But the look wasn't reflected in his emotional profile. He wasn't surprised that Renatus's apprentice would prefer hard liquor over some soft sparkly drink in a pretty glass. He didn't know I was seventeen. He didn't know anything about me at all bar what Renatus or I led him to believe.

It was a game, all of it, this whole party, this whole society.

*Just hold it*, Renatus advised as he passed me my tumbler. *The day I meet your sister, I have enough to justify without having to explain how you got drunk at a party under my supervision.*

I took the glass and swilled it around, watching the yellow-gold drink wash against the sides and over the cubes of ice in the middle. I lowered it and looked around at the rest of the partygoers. Most of the men had drinks in their hands like mine. Some of the women did, too, but more had champagne flutes or scooped glasses of a deep red wine.

Nobody had soft drink.

I wondered how much money had gone into providing the drinks for this event. Then I saw a staff member offering a tray of extravagant little entrées to some women nearby and I wondered how much the catering had set Raymond and Shanahan back. The sparkle of someone's ring caught my eye and I remembered the sheer impossibility of how much jewellery was amassed in this room. Then there were the clothes, from Thomas Shanahan's ridiculous pompous velvet jacket to my own borrowed lace number. How much *money* was in this room?

*You don't want to know,* Renatus confirmed.

'It's been a long time since the White Elm has had an apprentice, hasn't it?' Harold Raymond asked us when everyone had their drink and the servant had Displaced away. The other three looked interestedly up at Renatus. The topic of the White Elm had been brought up by force. Renatus nodded and took a sip of his drink.

'Thirty years, I think,' he said. 'They were as surprised as you are.'

'But they were okay with it?' Harold pushed. He had less tact and cleverness with his words than the other three, I noticed. He was more direct. 'At your age? And to bond you with a female pupil?'

'And knowing who your father was?' Robert Quinn added.

'They couldn't very well say no, could they?' Renatus said, and they all smirked appreciatively, buying the bluff. In fact, the council *could* say no. They almost had. But these men were eating out of Renatus's hand, happy to believe he had the White Elm twisted around his fingers like the strings of a marionette. It wasn't entirely an untrue perspective, but it definitely left some room for facts omitted.

'I don't think anyone would be more surprised with where you are today more than your father would be,' Quinn pressed now. 'He had some very strong feelings about the White Elm.'

His tone spelt out that Áindreas was not alone in his feelings. The others nodded and nursed their drinks. I moved my glass to the other hand. No one seemed to have noticed I wasn't drinking.

'Before his death I wouldn't have believed it myself,' Renatus admitted. 'The White Elm has been responsible for too many infringements on our society, on our liberties.' His words encouraged more nods. I looked down so no one would see my surprise. He never spoke ill about the council around me, but he'd indicated this perspective once or twice. I raised the glass and pretended to sip. I felt the cold whisky touch my top lip but I didn't let it in. When I lowered the glass, still nobody was paying me enough mind to notice. They were fixated on Renatus. 'In the years on my own I've come to understand my father's error. Rebellion is noble enough, but takes only two forms – the quiet type we have fought for generations, playing the roles of obedient subjects to a dominion we don't accept while continuing with our work in anxious secret, and the loud type that binds us all together in some mighty purposeful force but which ultimately topples not only the structures of oppression but also the composition of all that held us together in the first place. The way we were going, we were doomed to failure. The place to stand against an institution is *inside* it, where its direction can be steered.'

Raymond nodded approvingly. 'You seek to make changes?'

'They've already begun,' Renatus agreed, gesturing back at me. 'Apprenticeships were at risk of becoming pages in history books. As much as you, I want a world where magic is free to be passed from one sorcerer to the next without baggage checks, vaccinations and taxes. Aristea and I learn from one another with no interference from the council. Organically. The way it always was, before the council got caught up in the mission to sanitise magic.'

'That must be difficult for them to accept,' Quinn said.

'They're learning to,' I said, and their eyes turned on me with interest. 'Change doesn't happen overnight.'

Quinn nodded once, and I felt his feelings towards me warm by perhaps one degree. Progress, at least.

362

'There's no point in stamping our collective feet and saying we don't like it,' Renatus said. He motioned around the room, and we all looked around. Gazes that had been resting on us quickly darted elsewhere. 'Everyone here can say they hate the White Elm, they can damn me for joining, but the council is a fact of life. It's not going anywhere, so if it's going to stay around, it might as well be serving our interests.'

'How do they know our interests?' Raymond asked. 'Voicing them in the past has only found our friends and associates in trouble: an admission of guilt in the eyes of the White Elm's laws.'

'The council is dynamic,' I spoke up, remembering Anouk's history classes. 'The White Elm that introduced the majority of the laws you're talking about, in the late fifties, was made up of conservatives, old men who are all long dead. The council I know is diverse and open.' A fact popped to the front of my mind and I said it before I could lose confidence in its worthiness of mention: 'There are now two independents serving as members.'

My comment was not lost on my audience. I felt their intrigue even through my wards.

'We're going to see the control of magic move full-circle,' Renatus added. 'These are important times.'

'The White Elm mightn't be the government that oversees those times,' Shanahan mentioned, slyly. 'Magnus Moira is gathering speed, I hear. *All* independents.'

'I hate that name,' Raymond admitted, screwing up his mouth like it tasted bad. 'Flamboyant for a political party.'

Like anything was *flamboyant* compared with the decadence we were standing in. But I privately agreed.

'Still. Your godfather joined the White Elm with the same values you talk about,' Shanahan told Renatus, who listened without expression, 'and he saw fit to leave rather than attempt what you're saying.'

'He wants to see the White Elm uprooted, for lack of better term,' Harold Raymond said. 'His message is spreading.'

They all looked at Renatus for his rebuttal. Trial by fire, much?

*Brutal, isn't it?* he asked me mildly.

'Ripping down the establishment is all well and good to talk about but the people following Lisandro need a reality check,' I said flatly. 'The council does more than limit everyone's use of magic. Lisandro's promising free access to magic for all, no restrictions, but then who's going to manage its gross misuse? Who's going to investigate magical harms, prosecute our criminals to keep them out of the mortal systems and maintain our borders against the mortals? Who's going to negotiate new alliances with other colonies?' I was annoyed that most of this stuff, stuff my aunt had ranted about for years, even needed to be said, but apparently it did. Renatus let me go for it. 'Lisandro hasn't finished doing his homework. *Free magic for all* isn't a slogan our society can survive on.'

'We need more than a welfare system,' Renatus supported, and he got a few light chuckles out of his little audience. 'No, honestly: the White Elm has its flaws but it hasn't stood for centuries without cause. It works. It can take the battering of some very serious changes before it loses structural integrity. The biggest advantage a flawed government has over *no* government is that it can be improved.'

'And if it comes down?' Harold quipped. Renatus shrugged and finished his drink.

'We'd be out of work,' he answered, holding his empty glass in the air. The older men all laughed and the skinny servant appeared beside me. He bowed his head and took Renatus's glass.

'Refill, sir?'

'Not yet,' Renatus answered, and the skinny man vanished. My master turned back to Sean Raymond, who

364

smiled through the end of his laughter with a warm sparkle in his blue eyes. He liked Renatus. Apparently we'd survived that round. 'Where will I find Gearoid and Teagan? I want to congratulate them.'

Raymond looked disappointed to be losing his newest toy, but an elderly couple had arrived through the arch and was hovering behind us to greet him. He flashed them a quick smile to acknowledge their presence and pointed over into the throng of beautifully dressed party people.

'Gearoid is somewhere by the food,' he directed. He turned his hand to the big sweeping staircase at the back that led up to a sickeningly beautiful balcony level, from which the lifelike illusions of living, flowery vines hung in tattered curtains. 'Teagan and her friends are upstairs.' He grasped Renatus's hand again, a quick gesture halfway between possessive friendliness and a challenge. 'I can't tell you how good it is to see you here, Morrissey. We'll talk again soon. Delightful to meet you, Miss Byrne,' he added in a voice as polished as his mask, but he didn't try to kiss my hand again as Renatus took his own hand back and guided me away with a hand on my back. He acknowledged the other three men with a final nod, which they all returned. Shanahan and Quinn even raised their glasses to him and smiled as he left.

'So much nodding and bowing,' I whispered as we walked away. 'And kissing hands. I'm glad I'm wearing gloves.'

Renatus took my drink and took a sip as we entered the crowd of glittering human beings. Masks of every kind turned to us to watch our progress but no one stopped us.

'You're doing well,' he said. 'They liked you.'

'They liked you better,' I protested. He cast an almost playful look back at me as we slipped between two small circles of people.

'Didn't you hear Raymond? I'm a *Morrissey*,' he teased, and for the first time since getting here I smiled for real.

# chapter twenty-three

Gearoid Raymond was built like his father, with big shoulders, and was even working on his own thick moustache, but it looked like an imposter on his youthful face. Renatus had said Gearoid was younger than he was, and Renatus was twenty-two. When Gearoid kissed my hand, with much less grace than the older men had, I noticed the acne on his neck, mostly hidden under the collar of his jacket and which seemed blissfully absent on his bronze-masked face. I tentatively reached out my senses and pulled back at the first sliver of contact. He was wearing an illusion on his cheeks. But it didn't cover the gaps in the mask for his eyes, which were the colour of his father's minus the creases of age around them. He was young; maybe closer to my age than Renatus's.

As we mingled with this new crowd I revised the rules of engagement I'd so far surmised. The point of conversation seemed to be to antagonise your opponent into talking about things he'd rather not. The young men were notably less clever about the game than their fathers were, but they still played just as eagerly and with tools just as sharp. Renatus kept them on their feet. I started to get a concept of his strategy – stoke ego, remove rug from under feet, stoke ego, offend, stoke ego, shake hands and depart. Stoking these egos was easy. To start with all he needed to do was recognise them or their family name, and from there any demonstration of intimate knowledge of that person's history, even just a reference to their cousin or their house crest, served to the same effect.

It was a delicate game but I didn't mind watching it, and occasionally throwing my chips down. I didn't forget Renatus's warning against trust but Lisandro was still not here, and as I relaxed into the pattern of it all I let down some of the layers of the protection around me against the emotional atmosphere of the room. The partygoers were intense human beings, many of them quite powerful and competent, but their emotions were quite stable in the here and now. Gearoid seemed as intrigued by my master as his father was. He took charge of introducing anybody who came close enough, and I got the distinct impression that having a Morrissey, the *last* Morrissey, at his party was a source of great personal pride. The fact that he had a White Elm councillor in attendance might otherwise have been something of a disgrace, but Renatus's former surname seemed powerful enough here to make that White Elm label bearable.

To most people, anyway. The occasional tendril of poisonous malcontent drifted across the edges of my consciousness and it was hard not to glance in their direction where, invariably, I found myself meeting bitter eyes behind glamorous masks. Most of them looked away, muttering darkly to their companions.

When we came up the stairs after having sufficiently inflated Gearoid's ego, surprised him, insulted him and left him behind, reluctant to have to talk to other people, Teagan was easy to identity even without ever having met her before. She was the one surrounded by the other young women and dressed in the same green as her father.

If someone had tried to tell me Teagan Shanahan was any older than I was, I wouldn't have believed it. She was a bit shorter than me, though admittedly she'd already received her adult curves, and she had big innocent eyes behind her feathered green mask. Her dress was extravagant to the degree of her father's outfit, with a cape of golden feathers and a bodice embroidered with gemstones, but her rosy cheeks and spiralling blonde hair made her look like a beautiful child dressed in a doll's clothing.

Teagan didn't recognise Renatus straightaway, but she did double-glance him as he approached. Several of her friends did, too, and a girl in purple leaned conspicuously across to whisper in her ear.

*'Renatus!?'*

Teagan broke away from her friends to hurry over. Renatus slowed, unsure, but Teagan flung herself at him and hugged him tightly. When she released him she beamed up at him.

'I *told* Daddy you'd come back eventually,' she said knowledgeably, as convincing in her over-the-top outfit as a threadbare cardigan on a cold day. 'And here you are! For my party. Everyone,' she said, turning to smile at her crowd, 'this is my cousin, Renatus Morrissey.' Her introduction ignited a restless appreciative murmur, which she turned away from to look at me. Her smile stayed in place but her big innocent eyes cooled. 'Here with...?'

'His apprentice,' I said, taking charge of introducing myself. Being spoken for was for children. I offered Teagan my hand. Stunned, she took it. There was barely a shake, more of a squeeze of gloved fingers. Very posh. She dropped my hand and reached for my other one. I didn't give it to her – I wasn't here to do her bidding – but I did turn it over. 'Aristea Byrne.'

'Oh,' was all Teagan could say for a moment. Her smile widened even further. 'Well, then, welcome to the family!' And she hugged me, too, swirls of golden hair spilling over my shoulder. She looped one velvet-sleeved arm through mine and latched onto Renatus the same way. 'You *must* meet everybody!'

Teagan Shanahan was as false as her father, and that disappointed me deeply as she delightedly introduced all of her friends. She was a blood relation of Renatus's, and I wanted her to be lovely. She certainly seemed lovely, and she looked lovely, and everything she said was lovely, but was she lovely? She was like Sterling Adams, bouncy and cute and fun, but if Sterling Adams had been dropped in a vat of velvet and feathers and told that she was the best thing in the world. Spoilt to the core, Teagan talked about herself and her upcoming wedding and all the things her father and Mr Raymond were organising for it.

'Bless them,' she kept saying, 'they're so sweet.'

She proudly detailed to anyone who would listen (and everybody did, patiently) how Renatus's grandmother and her grandfather were siblings, which was how it was that she was connected with the Morrissey line. She said it almost challengingly, like, *so there,* in case anyone had ever questioned the connection in the absence of the Morrissey clan. She took extra care to mention that I was *not* Renatus's romantic other, and to find ways to include a comment about her friends' marital status as she introduced them, apparently determined that her first act as reunited distant cousin would be to find his perfect match among her guests. She was about the same with me. We were toys for her amusement.

'Brigid's brother just bought the house over the hill,' Teagan told me, clutching my hand possessively and pointing through the wall at some block of land I couldn't see or comprehend in this context. The girl in front of us, bright ginger hair piled atop her head in intricate braids, smiled coyly. 'He's *still* not married.'

Sean Raymond arrived at the top of the staircase and the girls and women parted to let him through.

'Morrissey, we're retiring to the parlour,' he invited, an unlit cigar already in the corner of his mouth and a glass of whisky in each hand. 'Would you join us? I was just telling Eddie Driscoll about you. I know he'd love the chance to speak with you.'

'Certainly,' Renatus agreed, accepting the drink and disengaging from the fawning attentions of Teagan's friends, much to their disappointment. I didn't miss the omission of my name from the invitation. Renatus had been accepted into the old boys' club of his father's friends.

*Don't leave me alone with these people,* I said pitifully as he passed me and as Teagan seized my hand again and dragged me away to meet someone else.

*Don't let them marry you off before I get back,* was his advice in return, and then he was gone.

The girls were actually more bearable without him there. They dropped out of the flighty, flirtatious role they'd all been collectively sharing in and returned to some state similar to reality. The showing off turned into gossiping.

'I didn't know the White Elm accepted apprentices,' Teagan said to me, all seriousness. She took the moment to add to her many listeners, 'He's White Elm, Renatus.' She turned back to me. 'However did you get a position like that?'

'It's... a long story,' I said, carefully. The White Elm's school at Morrissey House was not common knowledge.

'When did you meet?'

'March.'

'This March?' Brigid clarified. I nodded.

'And you're already marked?' another of Teagan's friends demanded. 'But that's so soon!'

Teagan shook her head knowingly.

'Sometimes you just know,' she said, smiling at me like we were on the same page. 'Like me and Gearoid. Daddy had been telling me about Mr Raymond's son for *so long,* and I knew I was supposed to marry him, but when he asked me over for dinner earlier in the year I just *knew.* I couldn't wait until I could kiss him whenever I wanted,' she added with a giggle. The girls around me all smiled with false adoration and I felt like I'd fallen into a movie about killer robots disguising themselves as humans, just biding their time. *What. The.* 'Fate found a way to put us in each other's path,' Teagan said, probably the deepest thing I'd yet heard spill from her beautifully shaped, beautifully painted lips. 'Was it the same for you and my cousin?'

'Uh,' I said with all the smoothness of a seventeen-year-old at a party who thinks about killer robots instead of where to get her next glass of whisky, 'aye, I guess, except I don't want to kiss him.'

That was apparently the right thing to say because my audience burst into laughter. Teagan hugged me again around my shoulders. Her feathers tickled my skin.

'Aristea Byrne, you are absolutely adorable,' she informed me affectionately. 'You are most definitely welcome in this family.'

By the time I prised myself away some forty minutes later I was immensely grateful for my life. My sister, cousin and girlfriends were nothing on the scale of Teagan Shanahan and her crowd. Even the catty girls at school would meet their match in this room. Teagan and the others were intense in a different way from their male counterparts, but hard work all the same. All that pretending to be interested in one another's lives. All that smiling instead of rolling eyes. I knew I wasn't the only one. I could *feel* their dislike for one another and their simultaneous determination to be liked by everyone around them. How exhausting.

*Didn't agree to marry anyone's brother*, I told Renatus as I walked down the staircase, looking around the main level of the ballroom. There were more people here by now, but even when I sent my witch senses out across the room I knew that Lisandro had still not arrived. Maybe for the best. This party was hard enough without him turning up and sending me into a tailspin.

I was not ready to *look* at him, let alone kill him.

*I've turned down two offers already.*

I smirked. *You're the mysterious stranger. Fresh meat.*

*It isn't me Quinn wants to marry his son to*, Renatus replied. I stopped on the last step.

*Me?* Once the surprise subsided I expected to feel flattered, but I just felt offended. Robert Quinn had barely acknowledged me when we'd met. Now he thought he could sidestep having to actually speak to me and go straight to Renatus to organise my future for me? *You don't speak for me.*

It came out wrong, but Renatus knew what I meant. *That's what I said.*

He withdrew, distracted by physical conversation, and I hopped down off the last step. A pair of middle-aged women, skinny and gaunt, glanced at me over their glasses of Irish cream. Their hands, deep in black satin gloves, were encrusted with so many rings I couldn't tell if they wore wedding bands. Were they here with their husbands? Had their fathers chosen their partners for them the way Teagan's dad had chosen Gearoid? The way Quinn was trying to arrange with Renatus for *me*?

Down on this level I was accosted less, but I still found my gaze catching on the deliberate eyes of others and found myself pulled into brief conversation with older strangers, mostly women and couples. It was less threatening at least, talking with small groups, but it was mostly the same pattern on repeat.

'You're Renatus's apprentice.'

'Yes. Aristea Byrne.'

And then either a semi-friendly introduction and three minutes of light discussion about the beauty of the ballroom, or a suspicious nod and a 'Good day to you'. Invariably they soon walked away. I knew I'd never remember their names, and with the masks I had no chance at all of remembering these faces.

I wandered over to the long table, piled high with lavish foods I had no name for. I picked something that started with some kind of cracker and ended with some type of brown paste, and tasted it experimentally.

'Official verdict?' someone asked from behind me while my mouth was full. I turned, trying to catch any crumbs. There was nobody there, just empty space, at least according to my eyes. I chewed quickly and swallowed. I knew that voice, though I couldn't place it.

372

'Not terrible,' I answered, feeling foolish for speaking to thin air, but if I had accepted anything today it was that my grasp and understanding of magic left a lot to be desired, that it was all a great big game, and being surprised by random acts of magical weirdness was simply a time-wasting activity designed to impede the enjoyment process. I narrowed the focus of my eyes. That "thin air" shimmered and wavered, and the vague outline of a man slowly shifted into being.

I was rewarded for my willingness to participate in the sport. A hand in a fingerless leather glove appeared before me, disjointed from any apparent arm or body, and seemed to *unzip* the air in a downward motion. The illusion of invisibility fell away, as did the ward hiding the person's energy from me and everyone else, and then standing in front of me was Declan O'Malley.

'Not terrible is good enough for me,' he said, reaching for one of the same hors d'oeuvres I'd started on. He stuffed one into his mouth and made a sound of appreciation. 'Mm...' He swallowed and dusted his hands off. He smiled widely at me. 'Sorry, I was starving, and Raymond always puts on such ostentatious spreads, I never know what's safe to eat. Forgive me. Where are my manners?' He bowed, low and theatrical. 'Miss Aristea, it's my absolute pleasure to see you again.'

'Hi,' I answered, not sure how to manage a graceful curtsy in this dress with its mermaid-like skirt and pretty sure Renatus would be furious if he came back and saw me deferring in any way to his least favourite informant. 'I didn't know you'd be here.'

'Neither did I,' he said cheerfully, straightening slowly and taking care to rove his eyes from the hem of my dress on the floor all the way up my body to my face, 'but now I'm glad I am. I didn't have the slightest inkling *you* would be here. Or my charming cousin,' he added, still smiling easily, looking around. His expression fell; it was part of his ruse, part of his game, I knew, but after the exhausting games of everybody else I found myself appreciative of his relatively harmless theatrics in comparison. 'Dear me, has he left you alone with these animals?'

'I think he's smoking cigars and playing cards with all the mafia bosses,' I said.

'Typical,' Declan sighed. 'A lovely young thing like you shouldn't be standing by herself at a party like this. Any creep could come onto you.' He shuddered and I grinned. I liked Declan. Renatus openly despised him and they were far from nice to each other, but Declan's playful flattery and infectious banter had won me over the first time I met him. He was in no way going to get anywhere with me, of course – he was completely too old and too dodgy – but I liked being around him. Even now, standing beside him at the table, I felt more comfortable and safe than I had since arriving. I'd been on my toes all day, careful with my words. Renatus would say I needed to do the same with Declan O'Malley, but this was one case in which I was quite sure Renatus was just biased. Declan was alright. Now he was hovering his hand thoughtfully over the plate of crackers, looking to select the best one of the dozens of identical entrées. He flashed me another appreciative smile. 'You do look ravishing, by the way.'

'You look nice, too,' I offered, and he smiled what I hoped was an honest smile at the food as he finally chose one. He actually did look much nicer than the previous occasions I'd seen him on, but then, I was sure I did, too, all dressed up. Declan's coat was slim-cut and long, hanging behind his knees, and his mask was one of the traditional Roman theatre character masks. I recognised it from a play my brother was in when he was in high school. *Il dottore*. The doctor.

'I did spend a long time on my hair,' he admitted, running a hand back over it, all glossy black and smoothed down, 'but I forgot to weigh myself down with diamonds. I could float away!' He rubbed his hands together. When he parted them, his fingers were encrusted with big chunky rings, glinting in the half-light of the ballroom. He twisted his hands on his wrists and cuffs of silver chains and diamonds appeared. He held his hands out between us to admire. 'Much better. You forgot your diamonds, too?'

'I didn't want jewellery,' I confessed, glancing around. I was the only person in the whole room without it. 'Now I feel like I shouldn't have been so obstinate.'

'Not to worry,' Declan said brightly, stepping closer to me. I resisted the instinct to pull back. He nodded in the direction of my ear. 'Move your hair. Renatus will know if I've touched you.'

Surprised, I obliged, pushing the big round curls of my hair out of the way. Declan extended a hand like he was going to stroke my earlobe but he didn't touch me. A new weight settled there, pulling lightly on my lobe. He did the same on the other side when I moved my hair back over my shoulder. He drew back and with a complicated-looking flick of his hands produced a compact mirror. He opened it so I could look at my reflection.

He'd strung big diamond earrings from my ears, sparkling princess-cuts with a comet's tail of littler diamonds hanging at different lengths on dainty silver chains.

'Something different,' he said, pleased with himself. 'Classic but not traditional. Like someone else I know.' He grinned his biggest grin and the mirror disappeared at his whim. His missing tooth was spectacularly obvious. I couldn't help smiling back.

'Are these real?'

'Could be.'

'If you can make diamonds materialise out of nothing,' I said thoughtfully, 'why did you care for the money Renatus paid you the first time I met you?'

'He didn't pay me with money, sweetheart,' Declan said with a wink. I tightened my smile patiently at the playful insinuation.

'There were coins in the bag.'

'It wasn't the coins that were of value,' he said. 'Money is such a limited currency. Falls out of your pocket. Gets recalled every so many years to change into something else.

And you get to the border and they want to swap it for some other set, some different amount. Useless.'

'What did he pay you with, then?' I asked. I uncertainly touched the stone in my earring. Solid. I could detect no illusion.

'The only currency I trade in,' Declan answered. 'Secrets and stories.'

I wasn't sure what this meant in relation to the money, but on deeper consideration I remembered the coin I'd found behind my ear at his place and the impressions left on it of Teresa's horrible mistreatment at Jackson's hands. Money moved through so many hands. I wondered if it all kept traces, little stories, as it went from hand to hand.

'Thanks,' I said, gesturing at the earrings. 'Now I might stand more of a chance of fitting in here.'

'Oh, you stand no chance,' Declan shot me down casually, waving idly in the air. A member of Raymond's staff Displaced right beside us. Declan placed his order for 'whatever you've got' and I asked for a cider, thinking it was probably my safest bet. The servant left and Declan continued. 'So you're a pretty thing with a tortured past. That's about all you've got going for you. Where's your spoilt demanding demeanour? Where's your nasty spiteful desire to skin your family and friends with only words and wash yourself in their tears? How many mortifying scandals have you been involved in? You've got nothing, baby.'

He accepted his drink from the tray of the returned staff member. I grinned at him but I still grabbed my glass before he could. The first time we met Declan, Renatus had told me not to accept food or drink from him. He'd recommended I not even talk to him if I could help it, and he'd expressly forbidden physical contact. I didn't fully understand Declan, what he stood for or what he was capable of, but I did know that the only other person Renatus had tried to keep from touching me was Lisandro himself, and for all his paranoia Renatus was also much more knowledgeable about absolutely everything than I was. I heeded his warnings.

Declan was more likeable than anybody else in this whole room and I wanted to talk to him, but I wasn't about to let him handle my drink.

His smile widened and I felt his slippery presence withdraw quickly from my mind. I'd lowered my wards slowly over the course of the afternoon and into the evening; apparently too far. I channelled energy into them, plugging the gaps.

'You stay out,' I warned, sipping my drink, 'or we're done talking.'

'I can't leave you standing here all alone,' Declan protested. 'You'll look awkward and lonely. The vultures will be at you.'

'It's a risk I'm willing to take.'

He sighed heavily. 'Alright. But you'll have to do your part. Keep up those walls. Otherwise it's too tempting to let myself into that pretty head.'

'Alright,' I agreed, countering, 'but you have to try harder, too. Just because I might let barriers slip a little doesn't mean you should take advantage of that. You could just ignore the urge to pry. Self-discipline, I think they call it.'

Big playful smile. Honest enjoyment that I would discuss his indiscretions head-on rather than tiptoe around it. 'I haven't heard of it.'

'Yes, well,' I said coolly, 'that's hardly my problem. You'll have to give it a go. Holes in wards are not invitations to poke around in someone's head. It's unethical *and* illegal.'

'Oh?' Declan's eyes danced behind his mask. 'Does everyone else here know that?'

I stopped talking. I looked anxiously around. A few glances clung to me or turned away. Was that Declan's way of suggesting that he wasn't the only one listening to my thoughts? Was I walking around leaking state secrets out of my head through lax wards?

Declan relaxed and turned away to admire the crowd, apparently letting me off answering.

'I'll stay out,' he acquiesced finally, surprising me. 'I'd rather stand beside you and have everyone wonder what I'm doing talking with Renatus Morrissey's hot new apprentice than stand all by myself. But you have to understand. When you're not paying attention, your head is just an Egyptian throne room full of potential treasures and jewels, and you're expecting me – *me* – to just stand at the door.' He offered me another smile, this one kind and affectionate. 'How am I meant to get dirt on you?'

I really did have the weirdest relationships in my life.

'Do you have secrets and stories about the people here?' I asked, gesturing around with my glass. Declan looked mildly about at some of the faces nearby. The song had changed and some people were moving out onto the dance floor.

'Most of them, yes.'

'Can you tell them to me?'

He raised his eyebrows above his mask. 'In exchange for what? Secrets are expensive.'

'For free,' I answered. 'Because I asked nicely.'

Declan finished his drink in one knocked-back mouthful. He put it down on the table. A bronze-masked servant appeared to remove it, casting him a distasteful look for littering the beautiful arrangement.

'For sure,' he said cheerfully. 'But not for free.' He bowed again and offered me his hand. 'Dance?'

'You're not touching me,' I said flatly. I handed my finished cider glass to the servant.

'Miss Aristea, you offend me,' Declan said, feigning hurt. 'Who said anything about touching? I swear on my life that I will not touch you. Do you really think I would overstep the bounds set out by my dear cousin?' he added reasonably.

Uh, yes. I didn't think Renatus's wishes were particularly high up Declan's list of priorities. But he seemed determined to win me as a dancing partner.

'Cecily Donovan,' he whispered, still bowed over in front of me, eyes angled towards a woman passing on my left. I glanced uneasily at the woman. Her mask was scaly and red, and her hair was twisted into long snakes with what looked like real snake fangs and ruby pins woven into the ends to give the effect of snake heads. 'Poor thing. Lost her sixth husband last month.'

'*Sixth*?' I demanded in a soft hiss, leaning closer to Declan when he continued. I wasn't good with ages but Cecily Donovan wasn't at all old enough to have been married six times and to have enjoyed any decent amount of time with any of her life partners.

'Terrible accident, I heard. Cut himself sleeping and bled out in their marital bed. Needless to say, even entitlement to all his money wasn't enough to fill the hole left behind in her heart.'

I stared after Cecily Donovan's elegant form, draped in clinging silks, and leaned down to whisper in Declan's ear.

'Are you saying she *murdered* her husband?'

He looked up at me, apparently shocked. 'What? No! I would never say such a thing. All *I'm* saying is she has had terrible luck with husbands and remarkably *good* luck with money. The world is full of coincidences, isn't it?'

I swallowed and straightened up. One of the first big lessons I'd learnt about magic was that there were *no* coincidences. I gestured reluctantly for Declan to stand up and I started towards the dancefloor. In two long strides he was in step with me.

'It must be hard on her at this painful time,' he continued, still talking low, playing at mournful. 'But good on her, coming out to celebrate for Gearoid and Teagan even in her time of loss. Such a generous soul. So *loving*.' He slipped ahead of me to pass between two women much too old for him. One wore a dead fox over her shoulders, and Declan's uncovered fingers trailed lightly along the tips of the fur. The way he briefly closed his eyes let me know he was tapping into impressions left there. Like me, he was a scrier, but unlike me he had absolutely no fear of trace energies. When the owner of the fox shawl glanced back he was looking the other way and she ignored him. He was just as quick with the other lady. He touched the massive bangle on her wrist with such swiftness that she didn't even notice.

I squeezed through the same gap after him. He grinned back at me and moved more out into the open. Couples were dancing here but there didn't seem to be a uniform expectation of what that looked like. Some pairs danced slow and close, romantic, ignoring the tempo of the music altogether. The majority seemed to be caught up in a sort of waltz, but one young couple was unabashedly making out in the middle of the floor, swaying and grinding roughly in tune to the song. Everyone else just danced around them. Declan backed to a spot away from the others and idly watched the couple while he waited for me to catch up. They were too involved in one another to notice his unembarrassed stare.

'Ah, young love,' he said appreciatively when I got close enough to hear. 'So flighty and sweet, so hard to stay out of. I think he fell desperately in love at the last big party, and the one before that, too. I hear that Roslyn Driscoll's new baby looks *just like him*. Weird, right? Now,' he said, changing tact with grace from slippery storyteller to professional instructor, 'first we bow.' He did, and I did, too. When I was upright he had one hand out like a traffic policeman. I did the same, 'Wrong hand,' swapped hands, and he repositioned his hand in front of mine, palms facing each other. Softly, I could feel the pressure of his wards against mine. 'One full circle,' he coached, criss-crossing his feet easily, like he did this all the time, and I circled the other way, starting to worry. I was sure to fall over my feet or the hem of my dress in front of everyone. I'd never learned how to dance and this was probably not the "safe" classroom situation I would have chosen, given time to think about it. Why hadn't I thought about it?

'I'm going to make a fool of myself,' I said now, anxiously, stopping when Declan did. He swapped hands and so did I. Still no physical contact. He gestured to the other side and led me in another reluctant circle. 'I'm going to fall over. Everyone will judge me.'

'Nonsense. You're aligned with the White Elm, your master's a Morrissey and you're dancing with that sleazy O'Malley. Everyone's already judging you. They're not going to wait for you to fall over, silly thing,' he explained kindly. We stopped where we'd started. 'You spin. I walk around you.'

'I look ridiculous,' I complained, but did as I was told. When I stopped he was standing behind me.

'Hands out at your sides. Not that high. It's not a stick-up. Good. Normally we're meant to hold hands at this point, but, you know.' Amiably Declan mirrored my hands with his. Still not touching. 'Three big steps to the right, pause, then three back.'

He paid no attention at all to the music, which was good because I didn't yet have a working knowledge of the moves and there was no way I'd be able to keep up with any rhythm he pointed out. He took me slowly through the steps with only words, never attempting to touch me or breach my wards again. He interspersed dance instruction with sly comments about the people around us. I had to work to keep my jaw from dropping open constantly. I didn't know any of these people but *the scandals* and *the gossip*. Who'd stepped out on whom, with whom. Whose children were already betrothed. Who didn't speak with whom and whose grandson had been written out of the will for marrying a mortal when he'd been promised to Robert Quinn's sister.

'Marrying for love. Some people are just so selfish,' Declan lamented as we circled one another again. It was my third run through the age-old moves and I was starting to feel more like a lady from *Pride and Prejudice* than a clumsy, leggy foal. 'As you can imagine, it was quite the scandal.'

'Obviously,' I concurred, amused. I saw a large, now-familiar form re-enter the ballroom from a shadowy little door hidden behind a curtain. 'And Shanahan? What's his story?'

'Oh, where do I start?' Declan turned and I did too, without prompt this time. I was getting it, slowly. 'The time his daughter blew up at him at her older sister's wedding and stormed out *in front of everybody*, never to be seen or heard from again, or the time he turned up at Morrissey House after his cousin died claiming custody of the estate and the money, and Renatus if he had to take the kid on to get at it?'

The first tale had sounded perfectly enticing until I heard the offer of the second.

'Shanahan wanted the *money*?' I repeated, unsure I'd heard right. These people had money dripping off them. They weren't seriously concerned with getting *more*?

'He had his lawyer in tow and had all necessary documentation to prove he was the closest living relative,' Declan confirmed. He slipped his hand into an inside pocket of his jacket and withdrew a little scrap of notepaper. 'Or so I heard. And by *heard*, I mean I was in the games room – does he still have a games room? – with much-cuter-back-then young Renatus, and we overheard the whole thing. *Huge* row with Lisandro in that front entryway. I'd never heard Lisandro shout like that. I'd never heard him so angry. Phew,' Declan whistled at the memory, flicking his note like a fan. He circled me as I spun slowly, lost in thought. He spoke so casually about the man who'd killed my parents, my brother. The others here mentioned him flippantly, too, but in relation to politics. This was different. Personal. This was Declan's own memory. 'Lisandro was not going to let anyone get what belonged to his boy. He sent Shanahan and his pedigree charts on his way. He put the housekeeper, what was her name... Fionnuala. He froze all the accounts, put her in charge of the money until Renatus was sixteen and arranged with Gawain to have him sent to Avalon. Shanahan made a few little attempts to stop him but Lisandro was the godparent – the legal guardian. Renatus was lucky.'

'*Renatus was lucky*?' I stopped spinning. 'You want me to believe Lisandro did something right by Renatus? Ever?'

Declan stopped, too. 'You can believe whatever you like. This is just the way I remember it.'

'You remember it like he was some kind of champion for Renatus in his time of need,' I said coldly. 'Renatus doesn't remember it that way.'

'Renatus was biased,' Declan pointed out, folding the piece of paper deftly in half, 'and recently traumatised. And fifteen.'

'So?'

'So, maybe his version of events from that time is a little skew-whiff. Maybe he was a bit hard on the man, in that case at least.'

'Tell me the other story,' I said staunchly. 'I don't like this one.'

'Alright, just give me a moment,' Declan said agreeably, blowing on the little card. It lifted off from his palm and took flight across the ballroom. A few people glanced at it lazily. I watched it fly like a bird to land on the shoulder of Cecily Donovan. Declan immediately lost interest in it. He bowed low and waited for me to do the same so we could begin the dance over.

'What's in the note?' I asked.

'Words,' he answered unhelpfully. He launched into his story. 'So Shanahan's got three daughters, right? Two older girls, a bunch of fat sons, and then sweet little Teagan. The eldest one-'

'Caitlin,' I filled in, and he nodded in respect to my show of knowledge.

'Caitlin does as she's expected. She marries who she's told to marry because it helps Daddy secure an alliance with the Murphies and they control all the ports and they're the kings of document forgery – keep that in mind, sweetheart, if you ever need a fake I.D. – and there's this big beautiful wedding over at Reilly Murphy's farm. Keely, the second daughter, what they call the "black sheep" of a family, ruins the whole affair by confronting her father at the reception about his arrangement for *her* marriage, which she takes it upon herself to feel all self-righteous and disrespected about.'

'Naturally.'

'I know, right? So,' Declan went on, dipping easily into mode of entertainer, 'she's screaming "you don't have the right to sell me like a farmyard animal" and he's telling her to be quiet and then her *sister* gets in on it and tells her she's ruining *everything* and then the sisters are clawing at each other and it's all very messy. And Teagan's, I don't know, ten or something, so she's crying. Delightful occasion. And Keely *slaps* Caitlin and walks out, and that's the last anybody saw of her.'

'I've seen her file from the White Elm's Archives. Renatus said she just disappeared.'

'Completely. And that's difficult,' he reminded me seriously. 'There are ways to shield yourself from being found but for ten years? It's a feat. Someone was paying attention to her daddy's lessons.'

'You think Thomas Shanahan taught his daughter the skills she needed to go into hiding?' I asked. Declan scoffed.

'I *know* that's who taught her. The same person who taught *me*, though I envy Keely's talent for it. He should have spotted that talent and promoted her to principal heir over her stupid brothers instead of trying to marry her out of the family. Shanahan pretends like he doesn't care anymore but he hasn't given up on finding her. There were rumours at first, a couple of potential sightings over in the States. No one ever found any trace of her there, though.'

'That's awful,' I said, sidestepping along with him. 'But I don't blame her. I think it's medieval. Which society creep was her father trying to marry her off to?'

Declan grinned as he stepped around me. 'Me.'

I stopped again. '*You*?'

'I know. I can understand why she felt she was getting a raw deal when her sister got the Murphy boy.'

I let that information process. I kept forgetting that Declan O'Malley was part of this crazy magical underworld, too, not separate from it just because I'd met him separately from the rest of them.

'I... I'm sorry.' I really was. 'I don't suppose you like telling that story,' I said, apologetic now for even asking. I felt rotten. Declan was meant to have married this Keely, and here I was tactlessly raging about the institution of arranged marriage and supporting her choice without any real understanding of the situation, ignoring the hurt she must have caused.

He shrugged.

'It was just an arrangement, a betrothal. We were too young to start the courting process. I barely knew her. Probably for the best.'

'I guess,' I said dully. 'I still feel terrible. I'm sorry, I have no tact whatsoever.'

'One of your most attractive qualities, I assure you,' Declan promised smoothly. 'Let's call it "refreshing".'

I groaned. He pointed over my shoulder.

'Refreshing is a good word. People use it all the time in a positive context. O'Callaghan, for instance, uses it at least three times per conversation when discussing his son's political allegiances. Benny O'Callaghan left, oh, maybe two months ago, and he's making his father very proud with all his letters about his new job. *He's so disciplined now*, he says, *he's got principles*. It's... refreshing... apparently.'

'I'm sure I'll only end up with my foot in my mouth again if I invite you to elaborate.'

'I'm sure, too. Benny joined Magnus Moira.'

I'd taken the first couple of steps into beginning the dance but his words stopped me so fast I swayed in place.

'I don't think we're dancing anymore, Declan,' I said weakly. 'People openly admit to that? That's like an open rebellion.'

'His son; her brothers...' Declan ticked off the guest list, pointing out the family members of Lisandro's army. I had to force myself not to look. I hadn't realised it was so prevalent, so open. I was surrounded, totally surrounded by sympathisers of Lisandro's cause. My companion must have seen the spark of terror on my face at this prospect. 'It's not uite as out-there as I make it sound but I'm in the business knowing who's doing what. What's the White Elm going to do? Wherever they go, they stay hidden, and you can't go around prosecuting the families left behind so you'll never track them all down.'

'But they can't be happy when their friends and children and whatever disappear to follow a psycho and his flimsy promises,' I protested. Declan cocked his head to the side.

'Can't they? In my experience they've been smugly delighted. Very proud. Lisandro says "free magic for all",' he explained patiently when I just stared at him, 'and these people rally. You don't know. You don't know what it's like to have free rein forever and then to have a power like the White Elm take it away. Someone like Lisandro rises out of the woodwork promising to change it back? You think anyone's asking to see the fine print after fifty years in the Dark Ages?'

'The White Elm is pulling itself together about this issue,' I insisted. 'Renatus was just talking-'

'Jimmy Ellis,' Declan interrupted me, pointing to a short old man with a too-young partner on each arm, 'had his offices searched four times by the White Elm in the last six years. They never found anything, but they keep raiding him because they think he's trafficking organs.'

'*Is* he?'

'Yes, of course he is,' Declan answered impatiently as my heart skipped a beat in horror. What kind of party was this?! How did Renatus justify bringing me into this crowd? 'But that's not the point. There's a market here for that kind of product. There's a huge branch of magic that requires human blood and flesh – *my* branch of magic, *our* branch of magic – and merchants like him ensure practitioners receive their supply so they don't have to go out and find it themselves, you understand? You used to be able to get it from the Tresaighs but the council put a stop to that and now Ellis has almost total control of the market. The White Elm says no sacrificial magic, and take a look around. A room full of malcontent and mistrust. Purge the pond and all you can ever catch is ninety-nine percent, which just gives the most insidious weeds room to spread. You create a vacuum, an imbalance. People get desperate.'

'Desperate?'

'Families that held the power in these circles sixty years ago aren't even around anymore.' Declan delicately turned one of the rings on his hand, straightening it. 'Did you meet any other O'Malleys this evening, Miss Aristea?'

I shook my head slowly, horrified by the implication. Was he suggesting…?

'The White Elm's laws are a stranglehold on this community's way of life. It's not a question of whether what they're doing is right or wrong – we can probably all agree it's mostly wrong. But not all of it is, and when the laws are making the situation worse instead of better we have a problem. The Raymonds, the O'Callaghans, the Murphies, everybody. Me. This is our magic. This is our culture. Renatus learned the new way but we're not all prodigies capable of rewiring our brains. How are these people meant to get along without the ingredients they need to weave the magic they've been learning for generations?'

'Can't they use other tools?' I asked, feeling small. I'd never learnt anything about the kind of magic he was talking about, but I briefly flashed on the bloody pile of herbs and scribbles in the dust in the Scottish national forest the other night, and of three moist, scabbed stubs where fingers used to be.

'There are other ways to do some of what they do, but less efficient and less trustworthy. White Elm says we've got to use the "clean" stuff. But that's *their* magic, the kind they can trace and control. Nobody wants to be controlled, Miss Aristea.'

'You're talking about this like it's okay,' I said, shaking my head. 'We're talking about trafficking human organs, and using them in magic. It's not okay. That's why the White Elm condemns it.'

'Oh, they don't use it? Blood magic?' Declan's surprised tone tricked me into saying, 'No, they don't.' He was quick, and jumped on my mistake, asking, 'How'd they get that mark on your arm, then?'

I slowly looked down at my wrist, at the black symbol stark against my skin.

'I'm not in the practice of taking sides,' Declan said, knowing he'd made his point clear. 'I'm only pointing out the inconvenience the White Elm has dealt this community. It's good Renatus is here, and I'm sure a lot of people here are listening because he's one of them, but he's been gone a long time and generations of suspicion with authority are not wiped clear in one conversation. Lisandro has been talking through other mouths all year, murmuring things these people like to hear. Revolutionary things. *Refreshing* things.'

'And you think people are listening?' I asked, looking around again. Few faces were looking back at me but I reflected on the first thought I'd had on walking in here. These were not friendly faces. Cold, pointed, sharp, heartless, beautiful...

'Sweet Miss Aristea, I *know* people are listening,' Declan corrected. 'You tell people what they want to hear and they'll hear it. Like you. *Sweet* Aristea. *Darling thing.* You hear all that, don't you?'

I blinked, stomach twisting. 'Excuse me?'

'Don't get thinking I don't mean what I say, but flattery and lies will get you everywhere,' Declan said easily, insensitive to the wounds his words struck at my insides. 'Lisandro's got his angle and his audience and he's running with it. Why wouldn't he? He's a genius.'

'Lisandro is a murderer,' I hissed, angry, hurt by the idea that he'd been flirting with me for no discernible reason except to upset me, apparently. What were we dancing for if he didn't even like me? 'Do you know what he *did*?'

''Murderer' is rather unambiguous.'

I stared at him. I felt offended by his careless perspective on the White Elm's enemy and all things disgusting and underhanded, his insistence on playing devil's advocate and offering the absent Lisandro the benefit of a doubt he didn't deserve, and I felt angry with myself for expecting Declan to be any different. He wasn't a friend. He wasn't mine, he wasn't Renatus's. But the hurt and the anger manifested themselves as a distinct sense of injustice with Declan's obvious ignorance, and I could hear the echoes of Renatus's voice in my head saying *He's our informant, not the other way around* as I blurted in a strained whisper, 'He killed my family.'

My wards were up as dense and high as they went but I still felt Declan's slow surprise as the same reaction registered just as slowly behind his theatrical mask.

'Oh,' was all he said at first. Then, '*Oh.*' He looked up at something over my shoulder and a strange expression passed over his almost-attractive features. 'Well, in that case, little darling, you keep those wards up nice and strong, alright? Take care of yourself.' He didn't touch me but he positioned his hands either side of my face like he was going to hold my cheeks, and he kissed the air over each side. 'Thanks for the dance.'

He was already backing away and I frowned, confused by the sudden change in demeanour. Without thinking I reached to catch his arm, to stop him leaving. He whipped his hand away from me before we could touch.

'Wait-'

'I like my head where it is,' he said firmly, which made me think Renatus must have returned. I looked around but couldn't see him. Uneasily I became aware of how long it had been since I last saw him or even heard from him, but before I could think to reach for him my eyes snagged on a pair just now walking through the archway.

My stomach dropped at least an inch.

'Declan,' I whispered, terrified. Lisandro was *here*. Unmasked. Ungloved. Dressed to impress in a tailored crimson suit and shimmery cream-coloured tie, a sharp-looking ensemble that was at least twenty years more modern than anything worn by any other man in the ballroom. His long black hair was unsecured – I'd only ever seen it pulled back into a ponytail – and fell to his waist, silky and straight.

The last time I'd seen him, he'd tried to kill me.

He had a partner. Her hair was the same as his, black and long and free; her elaborate dress and decadent butterfly mask matched the crimson and cream of his suit.

They were shaking hands with Sean Raymond.

'Declan,' I whispered again, but the spot he'd occupied was empty. He'd left me. I couldn't believe it. *Jerk*.

Probably a dance like the one I'd been part of was meant to circulate around the same patch of floor but I'd managed to work my way almost to the edge of the dancefloor closest to the arched entryway. So I was standing all alone when Lisandro's date, resplendent in her finery, turned her head and caught my gaze.

The instinct to run hit me as strongly as it did the first time I saw her, two nights ago in Scotland. I spun on my borrowed heels and started back across the dancefloor, snatching at the long skirt of my dress when my toe caught the hem and almost sent me sprawling, sliding past a still-waltzing couple into an open area of polished floor, not sure where I would go-

She Displaced directly in front of me and I slid to an immediate stop, breathless after only a few steps at speed.

'You're in a hurry,' she noted while my heart tried to smash its way out of my ribcage. I stayed completely still, caught in her otherworldly-bright green stare. I couldn't look away. Instead I spread my witch senses out either side of me as far as they would go, using the feedback to determine the floorplan. People everywhere. A few watching this interaction with interest. Most ignoring it. Power, energy, magic *everywhere*, but shockingly centred on this woman in front of me. I tentatively touched her aura with the very edges of my awareness and quickly pulled away.

She was the most powerful being I'd ever encountered. She was stronger than Lisandro. She was stronger than Renatus. I hadn't known *anybody* was stronger than Renatus.

The thought of him had me clawing for him in my head, but he wasn't there. My desperate calls for his help bounced back to me. Blocked. Aubrey had done that before. Who was doing it now?

Lisandro's date was still watching me. Her bright eyes were curious behind her big extravagant mask. I didn't know what to say.

'That's a lovely dress,' I managed finally, because "your date is the killer of my family" sounded over-the-top in my head as a first contact. She looked down in surprise.

It was easily the best dress in the room, now that I was close enough to see the detail. The dress itself was a heavy cream, fitted exquisitely to her womanly physique, corseted bodice giving her a neat, narrow waist above smoothly rounded hips and then enough taffeta in the piles and piles of skirts to make at least seven smaller dresses. The silhouette was enviable but what made hers the best dress at the party was the effect of a hundred or so *living* butterflies scattered across the fabric's surface. Varying in size, all of them deep red with eye-like markings, the insects occasionally fluttered to a new position on the dress. The underside of the wings was dark, maybe brown; the effect of the red disappearing whenever a butterfly lazily closed its wings or more hurriedly fluttered them in flight was like a sparkle or twinkling light. There was a cluster on her puffed sleeve and another at her hip, and one vain creature now took this opportunity to snatch the limelight and fly from her chest to land on her hair, settling happily like a bobby pin.

Every single butterfly was real and alive. No illusion detectable.

'Thank you,' the woman said, bringing her eyes back up to me, trapping me again. 'Aristea, isn't it?'

I wasn't about to introduce myself to her. 'We've met.'

The "proper" thing to do would have been to play along but I wasn't part of this world and I wasn't part of this big stupid game. I wasn't going to pretend she hadn't chased me down and attacked me. That made her pause and re-evaluate.

'Only briefly,' she acknowledged finally. Her accent was unusual. I detected hints of wide American vowels and Eastern European intonations – been travelling with Lisandro, love? – and underneath it all, that rhythm, that softness, she was definitely Irish. 'The circumstances were not ideal.'

You don't say. It was my turn to take a moment to consider her. She was about my height, maybe a little shorter, though it was hard to determine while we both wore heels. She had a slight frame and narrow shoulders but carried a healthy weight on her, curves that drew attention from both men and women around us. She was heavier than any of the gaunt, twiggy ladies I could see in my peripheral vision but she was certainly more attractive for it. She was older than me, a proper adult. Thirty? I could never tell. Her mask was too big to see much past, so detailed it was distracting. Again, I wasn't going to get any decent facial information for Renatus to work with.

I tried again to get his attention. He was nowhere on my radar and I couldn't hear his voice in my head. I was cut off. I was alone. I was terrified. Had he left without me?

The woman had covered nearly her entire face, even her nose and cheeks, with her mask, and only her eyes and mouth were visible. Her lips were painted deep wine red, dark against pale skin. They were exaggerated in definition, the shape an artist might employ when drawing a "perfect" face. I couldn't see much of her but I was quite sure Lisandro's date was stunningly beautiful.

Her magic was incredibly intense, like Renatus on steroids. How was that even possible? The scale went to ten. Renatus was a ten. What was the point of the scale if it didn't account for someone like this woman, and *how* had she gone under the White Elm's nose for three decades unnoticed before turning up at Sean Raymond's party? Why hadn't the council tried to conscript *her*?

'And today, once again, you tried to run away from me,' she went on in my extended silence. 'Do I frighten you?'

I couldn't answer that truthfully so instead I said, 'Why are you talking to me?'

'You're all alone,' she answered, and I couldn't tell whether that was an implied threat, 'and you're the only other person here that feels as out-of-place as I do.'

The admission threw me and I didn't know what to make of it. 'You don't look out-of-place.'

'Neither do you. Looks are so deceiving.'

I didn't like her. I didn't like her one little bit, and I wanted to be far away from her. My wards and emotional barriers kept most of her at bay but whenever I lowered them to feel about for Renatus I felt yucky waves radiating out from her. She was *bad*, something about her was *wrong*, and I wanted to be away from her.

'Who are you?' I asked. Something brushed my shoulder and I turned my head quickly, startled. A little folded-up note was sitting there. I snatched at it, desperate, just as a too-familiar but still unexpected voice answered me smoothly.

'Aristea, I see you've met my wife,' Lisandro said as he came around me, Raymond moving around my other side, encircling me like pack predators and sending a shudder down my spine. I kept perfectly still, note clutched in my hand. His *wife*?! She curtseyed elegantly.

'Nastassja,' she provided, and extended her left hand. I wasn't sure what to do with it so I left it hanging expectantly between us. Her elbow-length silk gloves were deep dark garnet to match her butterflies, her mask and her *husband's* suit. Only one finger had a ring, a wedding band set with a ring of high, sparkly, oversized diamonds around a flattish, dull black stone.

Etched with an ancient symbol of a tree.

And the incredible power that emanated from her? It centred *here*, on this hand, not unlike the way Emmanuelle's had when she was its bearer, but not exactly the same. I couldn't explain how it was different except to say this woman wasn't *just* wearing it.

I pulled my painfully sharp attention from the woman, Nastassja, up to look at Lisandro. He stood *right there* beside me, watching my reaction, unafraid of consequences, unconcerned of conflict. He'd tried to kill me, he'd hurt me and stolen me and tormented me with the threat of being struck by lightning out of nothing better than spite. He'd done it to get a ring – *this* ring, though it looked very different now – and to distract Renatus long enough to make his own escape. All weapons were of course checked in at the table in the entryway but I knew firsthand that he didn't need any of those to inflict damage, to me or anyone else.

He was the most dangerous entity I could imagine. And I'd thought I could *take him*?

I was nobody. Just a dumb girl. No wonder he didn't look worried about standing so close to me. I was no threat.

'Pleasure,' I said coldly, 'but I don't want to talk to either of you.'

I turned to stalk away but Sean Raymond raised a hand like he was going to rest it on my shoulder and guide me back, essentially blocking me before I got even a quarter turn. I shied away from his ungloved touch, stuck in conversation.

'Miss Byrne,' he said, slightly reproachfully, 'I'm sure you did not mean that.'

'I'm sure I did,' I snapped. I wrenched my arm away when I tried again to leave and he tried again to prevent me. 'Don't *touch* me.'

'It's alright, Mr Raymond,' Lisandro leapt in slickly when our host's eyes widened at my rudeness. 'She's my godson's apprentice. She's got Morrissey blood now. They were all like that, don't you remember?'

'Of course,' Raymond agreed, too easily calmed, and he smiled at me indulgently. Iseult's words came back to me about the Crafters' ability to adjust the emotional atmosphere of a space. To make people agreeable to their opinions. 'Yes,

Áindreas was always one to have his true opinions heard, wasn't he?'

'And Renatus is the same,' Lisandro added. I clenched my hands in anger. The little note was still in my palm.

'Shut up,' I said angrily, pointing at Lisandro with one hand while I hurriedly opened the note with the clumsy fingers of the other. 'Don't you dare talk about Renatus.'

'He's my godson,' Lisandro said, feigning confused hurt. Raymond frowned at me, buying the act. 'I love him.'

It took me weeks to reflect on this day and realise I detected no accompanying flicker of magic to denote a lie. I was distracted by the note I unfolded.

*Whoops. Diamonds don't suit you after all.*

That was it? I'd guessed the sender, even though I couldn't see him anywhere. I'd expected something more helpful. *Diamonds don't suit you...*

Diamonds! I dropped the note and grabbed at my ears. Declan's lovely earrings still hung from my lobes. Why was I wearing his jewellery *on my person* when I wouldn't let him feed me or touch me? I yanked them out without unfastening the stoppers at the back, causing myself pain and discomfort. But as the little stoppers fell to the ground and the posts came free of my skin I felt a huge burden lift from me. I threw the earrings to the polished floors and the diamonds clattered prettily before dematerialising in a snap.

*Renatus!* Immediately my connection with my master was back in full, and as I looked from the floor to Lisandro I felt his concerned presence in my mind, looking through my eyes. He ripped away instantly and I distinctly knew he was in action, on his way from wherever he was.

'...seem unaware of the protocols and customs we observe here,' Raymond was telling me, a little sternly. I turned on him, furious.

'You can shove your protocols and customs,' I snarled. I pointed again at Lisandro, and he looked determinedly at me. We'd gathered an audience. 'This man-'

'Aristea!'

Two voices called my name at once, and we all looked from side to side. Renatus had shoved aside the curtain to the secret passageway, or whatever was behind there, and was jogging this way. Coming down the staircase was Teagan Shanahan.

Nastassja looked from one to the other and pursed her dark, shapely lips. My wards were thick but she was intense and I felt the spike of anxiety from her like a sword through my armour. She met my eyes for just a moment when she saw I'd noticed.

'Excuse me,' she murmured, and turned quickly away. She'd already torn a hole in the Fabric so when her foot landed, she and her butterflies were somewhere else. Displaced.

'Renatus,' Lisandro exclaimed brightly, undeterred by the abandonment of his wife. 'What an unexpected delight to see you.'

My master was emanating hatred and rage as he approached and even with his tightened mouth the only outward clue of his true feelings, I fully expected him to attack, but instead he shocked me by answering, 'I can't begin to tell you what a pleasure it is to see you, godfather.'

His response was so nonsensical that I turned to watch Teagan shoulder gracefully through the crowd on my other side. She smiled, distinctive lips curving gorgeously.

They all converged on us at the same time. Renatus *accepted Lisandro's handshake* in front of *everybody* and Teagan grabbed my arm excitedly and prattled off something about Brigid's brother asking after me. I just stared at her. I watched her mouth move, spouting rubbish. Sterling to the tenth power.

I looked at Renatus, *finally* here, and watched *his* mouth move as he told Lisandro it had been too long, as he *laughed*, still without actually smiling, at something Lisandro said. I looked around and saw dozens and dozens of eyes on them, on all of us, silently gauging the situation. Approving. All other mouths were still.

None of those lips had that same shape.

*Keely Shanahan. May.*

I shook Teagan off helplessly, so confused. What I'd anticipated to be an explosive moment had collapsed into a hallucinogenic fall down an unexpected rabbit hole and nothing was the way I'd expected.

'Renatus-' I began. He cut me off.

*Don't.* 'Aristea, I'm glad you finally had this chance to meet in person,' he said aloud, voice slippery and smooth like Lisandro's, like Nastassja's, like Raymond's, like everybody's. 'Our opinions and methods might differ but Lisandro's time on the White Elm was one of my greatest influences. I wouldn't be where I am today without him.'

I blinked. Numb.

'You're too modest,' Lisandro admonished placidly. 'You were always going to go far, son. You always knew more than you should.'

A ring of scattered laughter lit up around us and Renatus's eyes narrowed only by the slightest degree. He was *playing*.

'I value your belief in me,' he said, and a few people nearby smiled. 'It's given me strength.' He glanced at me when I silently demanded to know what was going on. *Not now.* 'I never would have believed it possible to serve as an agent of the White Elm while maintaining the integrity of who I am, but your years on the council while I grew up showed me it could be done.'

It was Lisandro's turn to squint a little. Annoyed? That Renatus was reminding the crowd that *he*, too, had served the council?

'I am humbled to hear it,' Lisandro answered. 'For you to be changed by the influence of those you work for would break my heart. Speaking of,' he said, breaking off gracefully, 'my Nastassja seems to have departed the conversation. I'm afraid I must do the same.'

Short and sweet. Necessary pleasantries exchanged and completed.

'We will speak again soon,' Renatus assured him as they both bowed politely. My master turned me around with a firm guiding hand between my shoulder blades and all but pushed me back to the table laden with food. Away from Lisandro. Away from the crowd.

'What just happened?' I hissed when we were far enough away. I tried to look back over my shoulder but he deliberately blocked me and kept walking. 'You let him *shake your hand.*'

'It's a game,' Renatus hissed back. 'Haven't you been paying attention?'

'You didn't mention the boys,' I said. 'You didn't tell anyone what he's *done.*'

*It's not the place,* Renatus answered when a pair of older men walked right by us.

*He's a murderer! What's the right place to say so?*

*Not here. Not today.* Renatus walked me to the table and dropped his hand. He chose something to eat, all casual. I couldn't believe it.

'He's right there,' I reminded him, keeping my voice low as I looked pointedly over his shoulder. Lisandro was mingling, slowly making his way to the back of the ballroom to that curtain. 'He killed our-'

'Aristea,' Renatus interrupted quietly. 'No. Not here. It'll blow up in our faces.' His eyes flickered aside as someone else neared us, and he continued speaking in my head. *These people don't care about our personal issues with Lisandro and that's not the message we're here to spread. Besides,* and he bit into his cracker, *it makes us look petty for bringing it up, and weak for not having been able to do anything to stop him. So we keep it to ourselves.*

'Okay,' I whispered, realising what else I needed to tell him, what he couldn't have been close enough to notice, 'but *her* – Nastassja – she's-'

'The one who chased you, I know.'

'No, not just that. She's-'

*Stop.* But I didn't need Renatus's reminder because I cut myself off. An elderly gentleman weighed down with jewels tottered past on his way to the food and cast us a vague smile. I inhaled slowly, calming myself as best I knew how.

I was having trouble accepting the current circumstances as being my life. I meekly took another hors d'oeuvre and ate it.

*Where were you?* I asked eventually. *I couldn't find you anywhere.*

*With Raymond and the others, initially, in his parlour. It's shielded to hide the people inside.* He winced uncomfortably before sharing the next part. *Then on my way out Cecily Donovan cornered me.*

That didn't altogether surprise me, considering Declan's note, and I didn't ask for details.

'What about you?' Renatus asked, taking some grapes. 'I didn't hear from you until you were already talking to Lisandro.' *Did you freeze up?*

I cringed, wishing I could give an answer different to the truth. I supposed it wasn't much worse than allowing oneself to be accosted by a black widow seductress.

'Declan,' I admitted reluctantly. Renatus hadn't anticipated my answer and inhaled his next mouthful. He coughed hard to get the piece of grape flesh out of his windpipe. He opened his mouth to demand what I meant, but an older couple draped in long necklaces and in matching white masks sidled up beside him and introduced themselves, redirecting his attention.

*We'll talk about this later,* he told me irritably as he kissed the woman's hand. I nodded slightly.

*We've got a lot to talk about later,* I agreed.

We stayed for hours, well into the evening. Nastassja did not reappear. Lisandro did. When he left he looked around for us and farewelled Renatus with a friendly salute. We waited another twenty minutes. Renatus dropped me back at the house.

'There might be something of an alliance to be made here with the Raymonds,' he told me, and he went back. I walked up the winding path to his house, thinking that for someone who didn't want to go in the first place he was oddly reluctant to leave that world.

# chapter twenty-four

Ten years inside someone else's head resulted in a relationship simultaneously intimate and lukewarm, similar to that shared between siblings. When you knew someone that well, when there were no barriers between your deepest shames and your warmest memories, pretences were unnecessary and one of the truest forms of the self was revealed. The same way a sibling knows when you stopped wetting the bed and how red your face went the first time you were caught stealing money from your mother's handbag, Glen knew all there was to know about Anouk, and she must have known all there was to know about him, too. And exactly like a brother's perspective on his sister, the embarrassments and shames and secrets were too tightly entwined with his knowledge of every other dull and routine event of her everyday life that he failed to be as curious about her secrets as he might have been of others'.

Ten years connected so intimately to someone else developed an unfathomably deep bond but also had a wearing effect on personal identity. Glen rarely reflected on it because it wasn't something he could control, and any changes to his personality since Anouk's initiation had happened so slowly he'd not noticed, but on nights like tonight he knew it was a fact of his life.

He was sitting at Anouk's desk, in Anouk's classroom at Morrissey House, poring over Anouk's unfinished notes, adding footnotes and amendments as Anouk thought of them. She'd merely realised, while working in the Archives, that she'd left Oneida's minutes of the last circle on her desk, incomplete, and Glen had gone to work on them. She hadn't asked. It didn't work like that; it wasn't entirely conscious, though to say it was *unconscious* implied a degree of unwillingness that didn't apply. The acting out of each other's thoughts happened all the time. They frequently cooked the same meal at the same time – because they lived in different time zones this meant oats or pancakes for lunch for Anouk and various afternoon and evening meals for Glen's breakfast. They worked on each other's council projects. Anouk had turned up once at Glen's ex-wife's house to collect his daughter for his weekend visitation. Their minds were two creeping vines planted too close to one another, now densely twisted together into one strong tree they would never have been without each other. What one thought or wanted impacted the other and for the sake of simplicity and comfort they worked as a single unit spread across two bodies.

The data stream was constant. Anouk reflected idly on the document and Glen read it silently to her and she noticed the areas she had planned to work on, and he made the notes in the margins. Likewise she read the labels of the boxes and files on the shelf in front of her and Glen commented on what he received from her.

*You've got 1976 and 1975 around the wrong way.*

*That whole paragraph about the suspicious magic in Mexico. It's not under investigation, it's* pending *investigation.*

Glen neatly crossed out "under" and rewrote "pending" above it. He remembered the mention of it at the last circle. There wasn't enough evidence to warrant a full White Elm investigation into the claims at this time. There were only thirteen of them – twelve at present, with Teresa on leave – and they were already spread so thinly without delving immediately into every single report they received. It had been added to Qasim's list of incidents to follow up on, but

402

his list at the end of each circle was long and it was sometimes days before he got to the end of it. Had he found anything worrying enough to investigate he would have brought it back to the collective council attention and as yet Glen had heard nothing about this particular report out of Mexico and so could assume there was no current investigation into the claims.

*It was a civilian claim, anyway,* Anouk agreed with him when he thought the same thing. They eventually looked into every report they received of magical misuse but those that came from more credible sources, such as White Elm citizens working in medical or law enforcement roles in mortal society, tended to be taken more seriously than angry letters from disgruntled seniors trying to spite their neighbours.

The house was always full of dynamic minds, some better shielded than others, and so Glen didn't particularly notice Aristea approaching the door.

'Anouk? Oh.'

He looked up in response, and she hesitated, momentarily confused, wondering if she'd chosen the wrong door.

'No, right door,' he said kindly, putting Anouk's pen down. 'Can I pass on a message for you?'

Aristea took a moment to gather herself together and in that moment Glen quickly examined her energy. Her aura was spiky, unsettled, in direct opposition with her unruffled appearance in a sleek, demure evening dress. He knew from Renatus's update upon his brief withdrawal that they'd encountered Lisandro at the party they'd attended. It had not dissolved into conflict and the mission was successful. Renatus had even returned to further schmooze and cement some of the connections he'd made today. Personally Glen wasn't convinced of the wisdom of sending a seventeen-year-old girl into a situation like the one Lord Gawain had put the pair in today, but it wasn't his call and he was aware from the council leader's thoughts that there were gains to be made in strengthening Renatus's connection with his past.

*I knew it was a mistake,* Anouk commented bitterly while Glen considered the obvious energetic impact on the apprentice. Ten years wore down the identity and drew them closely together but Anouk and Glen were still discernible as two separate people. Anouk was much more vocal about her views than he ever was, and felt more strongly about them, too. She liked to be right. Glen didn't. Being right meant being right about some frightening fears and concerns, and he would be happier to be proven wrong in a lot of cases. His pride could take it.

*At least Renatus took her out of it,* Glen reminded Anouk, always trying to find the brighter side. At least the girl wasn't still there.

'Aye, yes, I need her help,' Aristea said finally. A lace mask with long black ribbons hung loose in her hand and even marginally aged with make-up her bare face bore the obvious traits of youthful worry. 'Can you tell her I want to look at some old records?'

Anouk was immediately curious when she overheard Glen's thoughts.

*You can bring her here, if she'll come,* she said. Glen had already started clearing off the desk and collecting up the documents Anouk had wanted to work on.

'She's at the Archives now,' he told the apprentice. 'I can take you to her if you would like.'

Aristea paused again. It was impossible not to overhear her wondering. *Am I allowed to go off-campus with other people? What will Renatus say? Will he even notice?*

'Alright,' the girl agreed. She put her hands out. 'Can I carry anything for you?'

Glen smiled and gave her a thin folder of paperwork Anouk had left here. She was a sweet girl, really, a child no matter what Renatus or Lord Gawain thought. Dressed up and only a few short years off turning twenty and being wholly responsible for her own actions, she looked like an adult, but her eagerness to be helpful, her enthusiasm in class activities and her trusting nature were all indicators of her true inexperience with life. She was so young, and the pressures of working with the White Elm were constantly overwhelming her.

Poor girl.

Renatus was a distant cloud on the horizon of Glen's telepathic awareness as he left the house with Aristea and let her out of the gate. She was hesitant in leaving – she'd never left without her master, and she was the innocent type of teen that hadn't hit her disobedient phase yet. Though maybe it was starting. She closed the gate behind them and locked it with her own key. Renatus, miles away in deep conversation with people the White Elm would *love* to have just cause for locking up, did not notice. He didn't check in with Glen or tell him to put her back or ask him to keep her close. Aristea's telepathic link with Renatus was closer than that even of the White Elm but she seemed not to have told him where she was going.

Glen was under strict instruction from Lord Gawain to maintain radio silence with Renatus to avoid compromising his situation.

*We can't tell him,* Anouk reasoned. *If she chooses not to, it's hardly our fault.*

*If he takes issue with it he can take it up with her,* Glen agreed, and Displaced with Aristea. A split second later they were across the sea walking over a dark, windswept grassy plain. Several large, shapeless mounds stood out at random on the gentle rises of the field. The near-distant sound of a car on a country road reached them but was well out of sight. Aristea looked around as she trailed after his swift pace, questions firing in her head.

'Stonehenge is fifteen minutes back that way,' Glen said to help orientate her, pointing the way they'd come from. She kicked off her shoes, snatched them up in one hand, lifted her skirt carelessly and hurried after him.

'*Stonehenge?*' she repeated. 'England?'

'We have guardianship of it, but the local Druids mostly manage its care. The mortals are very good, too. Most everyone likes to help to look after things as old and unique as the Stonehenge.'

*Is it going to let her in?* Glen asked now. He'd never known of anyone other than White Elm being admitted to the Archives.

*Fate accepts her at our circles,* Anouk said, which Glen thought was not really an answer, so she added, *We'll find out, I suppose.*

'I've never seen it,' Aristea admitted wistfully, still looking back into the night behind her. Then she looked back at her teacher. 'What *are* we doing here?'

'Stonehenge isn't the only structure of interest out here,' Glen explained. He didn't let off the pace. He gestured at the mounds all around them. 'Do you know what these are?'

Aristea considered for a moment, reflecting on things she'd read. She'd once worked at an occult bookstore, Glen knew from her often-unprotected thoughts, and it seemed that half of the knowledge she brought with her to her current employment was collated in her time there.

'They're, like, tombs, aren't they?' she asked finally, uncertainly. Glen nodded.

'They are,' he agreed. 'The honoured dead of our Bronze Age ancestors were buried in this manner. I know one is the resting place of Merlin. The rest, Anouk could probably tell you.' Glen came to a stop at the foot of one of these mounds. It looked just like the others. 'This is the only one that does not contain human remains.'

Aristea looked doubtfully at the rounded rise of grass and dirt, unimpressed. That would change. Glen raised a hand carefully, feeling for the gentle magnetic pull that would alert him he'd found the invisible, undetectable door. It took more than ten seconds. Then the air around his hand lit up palely, like someone was shining a low-power torchlight behind his hand, creating that soft silhouetted glow, which grew and brightened and stretched away from him with increasing speed until it hit the extremes of its form. A free-standing white door of pure light waited before him, harsh enough to make both Glen and Aristea squint and turn their eyes away.

His hand was on the knocker. He knocked three times and withdrew his hand.

It didn't have a doorknob because doorknobs were for doors that people chose to open. This door chose when to open and who for. It didn't appear to have hinges, either, but after a moment's consideration it swung open, revealing a dimly lit passageway that simply could not have been physically *here* because walking around behind the door would show that there was nothing but air, and then grass-covered dirt.

Glen turned back to Renatus's apprentice. She'd probably never seen anything like this.

'It's very safe,' he assured her, but she'd already stepped determinedly forward to his side.

'I'm fine,' she said. 'You have no idea what I've seen in the last few hours.'

He gestured onward and she held her dress out of the way of her feet as she walked through the door. The light reached for her, pulled on her, and she was stuck momentarily in the doorway, held in place. Then it released her and she was through. Accepted.

'What was that?' she asked anxiously as Glen followed, unimpeded. The door closed behind them and the light that formed it began to sink, running down the wall like water to pool at the floor. The shape of the door ran away with it.

'The Archives are very secretive, and the door is very selective on who it lets through.'

*She's in.*

*I'm over at the back but I'll come and meet you.*

The chamber – four dirt walls, dirt floor, dirt ceiling, no doors – looked empty and barren, with only two lonely candles burning in sconces on the walls. Glen raised a hand. The flames responded and also rose, burning brighter and fiercer. Their circles of light grew, too, and kept growing until in the middle of the room they finally touched on the dark, dirty floor; and then there was a deep well in the floor where the light of the two candles had met, and a tight spiralling staircase down to a subterranean level.

'I've seen more magic today than the rest of my life combined,' Aristea confessed as she followed after Glen down the stairs.

The chamber below the surface was massive, segmented into a series of rooms and alcoves. Ancient wooden beams framed walls of compacted dirt, supported the low dusty hardwood ceiling and formed hundreds and hundreds of wide, strong shelves. Anything not of earth was very old wood, giving the candlelit space a rustic, claustrophobic, enclosed feel. Glen had been here numerous times, usually with Anouk or under influence of Anouk's thoughts. As the council's Historian, she shared the role of maintaining this Archive with the Scribe. Much as Valeroan Anouk had been many years ago, Oneida was still something of an outsider, an independent taking position on the White Elm, and from Glen's understanding, the newest councillor had not yet begun coming here on her own. He imagined she felt unwelcome. Anouk had that effect on many.

She said nothing of it but she did cast a mildly irritated look at him as she emerged from one of the many antechambers that led off the stairway room. He didn't have any private thoughts.

'Glen said you wanted to see me,' Anouk said directly to Aristea as the girl stepped off the staircase. Their faces were only illuminated by the lantern hanging in Anouk's hand, but even in the poor light Aristea looked around curiously.

'Yes,' she said, trying to bring her focus back despite her fascinating surroundings. 'I wanted to ask you about someone who went missing. Renatus and I have been working through missing person reports and there was one I wanted to see again. He said you got the files from the Archives.' Her straying attention caught sight of shelves in an adjoining chamber and she leaned aside to look better. 'From here. I wondered if you could get that file back out for me, and anything else relevant to it.'

Anouk was as fascinated by Aristea's request as the girl was with the Archives. Glen was more intrigued by the circumstances by which Aristea had even learned of the chamber's existence.

*What have she and Renatus been looking for?*

*Potential suspects. Renatus thinks Lisandro might have been enlisting supporters from as early as the nineties.*

'What year was the case?' Anouk asked aloud. 'I gave you several years' worth of files.'

Aristea blinked, certain.

'I don't remember the year, but it was in the first lot you gave us, 1996-2000.'

*Four years' worth of files and she wants to dig out one needle from that haystack?* Anouk asked Glen sarcastically.

'Do you remember any details from the document that would help Anouk locate it?' Glen asked, smoothing the waters. Aristea was trying. He wasn't sure what, but he could tell she thought she was on to something and she was trying to utilise the resources available to her to solve it. She nodded quickly.

'A girl,' she said, putting her mask and shoes down on the bottom step of the staircase. 'Keely Shanahan.'

*Shanahan. I know that name. But not a missing person case.* Anouk didn't recall it but Glen did.

*Renatus's cousin,* he said. *She ran away. The father didn't tell us for three weeks and then was furious when we couldn't find her. The trail was dead cold.*

'All of the missing person files are kept this way,' Anouk told Aristea crisply, turning and walking away with her lantern under one of the low-hanging beams that separated the chambers. Glen and Aristea followed her glow past rows and rows and rows of journals, boxes, folders and tightly bound scrolls.

*Do you remember the outcome?* Anouk asked as they walked. Glen shook his head.

*We couldn't find a trace of her. We assumed she must have died, but Qasim never received a vision to confirm it. We couldn't close the case.*

*And this was a cousin of Renatus? He didn't want to investigate it himself?*

*He wasn't a councillor then,* Glen clarified. *It was around the time you were initiated. The Shanahans were directly linked with the Morrisseys, the Murphies, the Franklins and the Tresaighs – we wanted to find their daughter. We wanted their allegiance.*

'There must be so many memories here,' Aristea mused softly as they walked. Glen overheard her gratefully acknowledging the gloves she was wearing. A moment's stray along that thought path revealed a fear of trace visions. Interesting. 'How old is this place?'

'The first White Elm council won it from an enemy clan,' Anouk answered. 'There are no records from before that.'

*But we couldn't find the Shanahan girl,* Anouk guessed. *Shanahan... I don't remember the case, but perhaps when I see the file it will jog my memory.* She stopped, several rooms and turns away from where they'd started. Glen caught Aristea wondering how they could get back. Indeed, it was like a maze down here. Glen relied on Anouk's intimate knowledge of the place and her natural tongue of Russian to get around it. He needed to, because no section was labelled or signed, though many of the boxes and shelves were – in Russian.

'It should be here,' the Russian sorceress said, gesturing at a wall of shelving stacked with cardboard boxes, all odd colours and sizes. Glen pulled the topmost box free and placed it on the dusty ground for Aristea to pore through. She was looking at the opposite shelf.

'What are those?'

'Homicides,' Anouk answered brusquely. *No focus whatsoever, these young people.* 'Glen said your missing person was never found dead, so she won't be in there.'

'No, I know,' Aristea said, slowly kneeling beside the box Glen had gotten down for her, 'but... can I request those? To go through with Renatus, I mean?'

Both Glen and Anouk stared at the girl. She kept her thoughts and reasons very close on this matter, with only single words slipping to the Telepaths. *Stranger... faked...?* She worked hard to redirect her thoughts.

'You need to make a written application to take files from this vault,' Anouk said finally. 'And I'll consider it.'

Aristea nodded, letting it go, and turned her attention to the box. She opened the lid, already doubtful.

'The box was more of a greyish cardboard,' she explained, leafing through some of the documents in the box to confirm her suspicion. 'These are too recent.'

Both Anouk and Glen dislodged another box each, this time choosing grey-coloured ones. By the light of Anouk's lantern, Glen helped Aristea sift through their contents. Anouk put the first box back.

'Why didn't you ask Renatus to bring you here?' she asked, glancing down at the apprentice kneeling on the floor. The girl didn't look up.

'He's still at Sean Raymond's big party,' she answered, though it wasn't quite an answer.

'You didn't tell him you were leaving the estate,' Glen added. He lifted a handful of documents free of the box and sorted through them. 'He doesn't know you're here.' Each stapled document consisted of at least a cover sheet for ease of reference and a photograph at the back, but many also included receipts, letters, photocopied passports and other evidence pertinent to the investigation. Some included interview transcripts or typed reports from either White Elm investigators – Qasim or Jackson, mostly, at the time of these disappearances – or mortal detectives.

Aristea still didn't look up from the box. 'I'll tell him later. He's busy and I don't want to distract him. This is the right box,' she added, digging more eagerly through the paper. Anouk stopped looking among the shelves for more boxes.

'What's your interest in this case?' she asked finally, though Glen knew she'd been itching to ask for some time.

'I'm not sure,' Aristea admitted. 'I'm probably wrong. I thought I *saw* her at Raymond's party.'

Anouk didn't need to give Glen a look. *You said this case was ten years old. How does she know what a girl ten years missing looks like?*

'What made you think it was Keely Shanahan?' Glen asked, always more patient than his counterpart. 'She's been missing a long time.'

'I'm probably wrong,' Aristea said again. She pulled a sheet free and checked its photograph. Wrong one. She put it back and kept looking. 'It was Teagan Shanahan's engagement party – Keely's sister. She was wearing a mask.' She shrugged, uncomfortable and losing confidence in her theory as the file she was looking for continued to evade her.

'Even if the person you saw was the missing Shanahan girl,' Anouk said, dryly, 'what is *your* connection?'

Aristea finally looked up.

'I think she's the woman who chased me on Friday night,' she said, 'and I think she was wearing the Elm Stone.'

For the next two seconds Glen stared at the girl kneeling opposite him in disbelief. In his mind, his voice and Anouk's fired back and forth at the speed of synapses.

*Lisandro had the Elm Stone.*

*Now this woman has it. Whoever she is.*

*Keely Shanahan? But she's been missing for ten years. How could she stay hidden for so long?*

*If Lisandro's had her all this time…*

*The Shanahans are strong in magic. It's not surprising he would want to ally himself with one. A Shanahan with the Elm Stone, though. She'll be powerful.*

*That backs up Aristea's claims from Friday, if we assume this is the same person.*

*Why did he give her the ring? And why has she allied herself with him at all?*

*Maybe it's in the file.*

Almost no time had passed when Anouk snapped her fingers. A thick set of stapled pages tore free of the pile in the box and flew into her waiting hands. She could have done it all along, had it in an instant. She just wasn't interested enough until now.

'What I saw of her face looked like Teagan Shanahan, but older,' Aristea said as Anouk flipped through the pages. Glen stood and leaned over his colleague's shoulder as she found the aged sepia photograph attached to the back of the file. It was a posed portrait shot of a very pretty teenage girl, a little younger than Aristea, with long dark hair and big bright eyes. The lack of colour in the picture made it impossible to determine their colour, but it seemed obvious from the contrast with the pupil that they were either blue or green.

'Is this the person you saw?' Anouk asked, offering Aristea the file as the apprentice got to her feet. She looked at the picture for a long time.

'She looks exactly like Teagan, except for the darker hair,' the girl said, touching the photo with her lace-gloved fingertip. 'She has the same mouth, and jawline.' She traced the relevant features, thinking on the face she saw tonight. Glen saw it in her thoughts and was struck by the likeness. She lifted the edge of the picture and twisted, hinging it on the staple to read a handwritten note on the back. *Keely Shanahan, 1995.* 'She looks a bit like Ana Morrissey, but don't tell Renatus I said that. He'll flip.'

'They were blood relatives,' Glen reminded them. 'It's not surprising they would look similar.'

'But Keely was younger,' Aristea said, taking the file from Anouk without asking and flicking through the pages. *More and more like him,* Anouk couldn't help commenting, though without malice, Glen noticed. Slowly, she was warming to the Dark Keeper's apprentice. 'Born 1980... If she ran away in '96 then she was pretty young to be out on her own. And to stay hidden.'

'That's what we thought,' Glen agreed. 'We assumed foul play but we couldn't get anything out of the family apart from that one picture and the date they last saw her. They wouldn't give us access to their home to look for traces – not that they probably hadn't had the O'Malleys or the Morrisseys come through and do that for them, they were well-connected enough – and they wouldn't let us interview their other children.'

'How could she stay hidden for so long?' Anouk wondered aloud, sceptically.

Aristea was on a roll.

'Declan O'Malley told me her dad taught them both techniques for disappearing themselves,' she said, though she couldn't explain any further. 'Who filled in the profile?' Aristea had found a form completed in elegant script. She impulsively put her finger in her mouth and bit down; she pulled with her teeth and tugged the glove off. Fingertips free, she brushed them across the page. Her eyelids flickered slightly on her next blink but that was the only sign she had tapped into one of the impressions left by circumstance on the page. 'Her mother. That's where she got the dark hair from, and the green eyes, though her mum's don't look that bright. Her eyes are *so* green.'

*Quite the little detective,* Anouk mentioned.

*Earning her keep,* Glen agreed. 'Anything to suggest why Lisandro would entrust her with the Elm Stone?'

*Maybe Keely Shanahan employed him,* Anouk offered. *Maybe she bought the Stone?*

*She's a runaway. Where would she get the money or the equivalent resources?*

*Allies, then. Part of some promise or arrangement?*

'Not in here,' Aristea said, still reading. It would be vague, Glen knew. The family had wanted their daughter back but not at the expense of having to actually work with the White Elm. 'This information's too old.'

'Did you *see* the Stone?' Anouk pressed, and the apprentice nodded. She looked up.

'She was wearing it over her glove,' she described. 'But it's not the same as when Emmanuelle had it. They've changed the setting. It's in a new ring. A wedding ring.'

*How is it that Renatus isn't here telling us all of this?* Anouk demanded. *Did he say any of this to you?* 'A wedding ring?'

*No. This is the first I've heard of it.* 'Did you happen to find out who her partner is?'

'Lisandro introduced her as his wife,' Aristea explained quickly, with the hurried tone of someone bearing too much knowledge and in need of an outlet. Anouk smiled and shook her head.

*No. Lisandro would not be married.* 'I don't think that is likely.'

*He wouldn't want to have to choose just one.* 'Are you sure you didn't mishear?' Glen checked.

'It's what he said,' Aristea insisted. 'They made a point of talking to me, and they were very eager to make sure I saw the ring. She was *so* powerful,' the girl added, and Glen saw the way her aura rippled at its edges with hardly contained fear. 'Stronger than Renatus. Stronger than anyone I've ever seen.'

*Why didn't he mention any of this when he checked in an hour ago?* 'Is Renatus there with them now?' Glen asked sharply, touching base with the other minds connected to his. Renatus was distant but still present, like Teresa. Others felt his attention and sent enquiring thoughts. He opened up his recent experiences to them to show what was being uncovered through Aristea's search for answers. Aristea shook her head.

'They left. Nastassja – *Keely* – left before Renatus really saw her.'

Lord Gawain, Elijah and Jadon were the quickest to take on board what Glen was showing them.

*The Elm Stone?! Does Renatus know? Is he in position to take it back?*

*Lisandro gave it away?*

*I've never heard of her. Who?*

'She's wearing the Elm Stone,' Glen reasoned. 'Maybe she's not as confident flaunting it in front of a councillor?'

415

'Maybe,' Aristea agreed. 'I hadn't thought of that. I thought, if she really was Keely Shanahan, she might have worried Renatus and Teagan would recognise her. They were both walking over at the same time. On a side note,' she burst out, looking up at the two councillors, 'am I the only person who didn't know Renatus still had family?'

'Thomas Shanahan,' Anouk realised, and Glen saw the string of associated memories flare to life in her mind through their open connection. 'He wanted custody of Renatus after the Morrissey storm.' She looked around, thinking about other files she had stored safely away here. 'He made multiple applications. He even tried to get to him through the mortal courts system. I have copies...' She trailed off, lost in thought, and wandered away purposefully into the dark stacks.

'Lisandro was adamantly against it,' Glen continued when Aristea turned her expectant, intrigued gaze on him instead. 'He sent Renatus away to Avalon while they sorted it all out. Lord Gawain had to infiltrate the local legal system to keep his applications from progressing too far. The situation was complicated enough without the mortals getting involved, developing an interest in this kid and this property. It took so long that Lord Gawain ended up relocating his whole law career to Northern Ireland.'

'Shanahan kept making the same claims for him,' Anouk called back to them through the gloom, vaguely. 'He had children and said Renatus should be raised with his relatives. But he'd managed to *misplace* one of his own children, without ever reporting it to mortal authorities. I think Jackson leaked a copy of the file you've got to the mortals. It wasn't me,' she made sure to add, and Glen knew that Anouk would never have put her neck so far out into the ethics of confidentiality for the sake of Lisandro's Morrissey godson, 'but it definitely found its way into their hands. They went after the Shanahans instead. Lord Gawain was on damage control for weeks, trying to weed that investigation out before we made an enemy out of them. But,' she conceded, returning to Glen and Aristea with another box, 'we stopped hearing from him.' *Playing dirty won out.* 'These were civil applications made in 1998. The copies will be in here somewhere.'

Aristea closed up the missing person file she was reading.

'Thank you,' she said. Anouk eyed her thoughtfully. Glen overheard every one of those thoughts.

'What are you hoping to find?' she asked after a moment. Aristea knelt again and packed up the box she'd emptied, leaving out the file she needed. She paused, cardboard lid in her hands. She pressed it slowly on top of the box and asked, hesitantly, 'Do you believe in coincidences?'

'No,' Glen and Anouk said at once.

'No, well, me neither,' Aristea agreed, putting the box back on the shelf with its brothers. 'Ten years ago the Shanahans lost a green-eyed daughter. A green-eyed woman chased me in the forest and accosted me at this dumb party wearing the White Elm's ring. Teagan Shanahan's engagement party. And they look just alike,' Aristea reiterated, reopening the file on the floor beside her to look again at the photograph. 'I want to know why Keely Shanahan ran away, how she came across Lisandro and why she would come back for her sister's party if she didn't want her sister to see her. I want to know how someone can go from *this*,' she held the photograph to the lantern to better see the placid expression on the youthful face, 'to being the kind of person Lisandro sends after mutineers.'

It was an appropriately reflective answer for Anouk, and she hefted the cardboard box she held higher onto her bony hip. It was much heavier and fuller than the missing person files, Glen thought, and Anouk heard.

*Citizens don't lose people quite as often as they make formal requests for things they think they're entitled to, so, yes,* she said at the same time as, 'We can take the box and look through it together in my classroom. It's too dark here to do any proper research. And *I* don't need to apply to take a box out of here.'

'Thank you,' Aristea said again, truly grateful for the veiled offer of assistance, as Glen took the box. 'I'll be careful, I promise. I won't lose anything and I'll put it back in the same order I find it. I won't mess up your system.'

'You'll be the only one minding my system once the rest of the council arrives,' Anouk said. She collected the lantern from the floor. 'This is the Elm Stone, after all.'

# chapter twenty-five

Renatus was unhappy.

'You went off the estate *without me?*' he demanded as he slammed the door of Qasim's classroom shut, locking me in with him. Anouk, Glen and a few other councillors were gathered in hers to go over the materials my querying had turned up and to talk out the facts from the assumptions I'd made. Lord Gawain had decided against recalling Renatus from the party for fear of compromising whatever connections he was working on, but just after midnight Renatus had checked in of his own accord and seen what the rest of the council were thinking about. I didn't know what time he would have eventually returned home otherwise.

'I went with Glen,' I said again, defensively. 'I would have gone with you but you weren't here.'

'I'm responsible for you,' Renatus reminded me. Bad temper rolled off him like curls of smoke. 'I'm supposed to know where you are-'

'No one was stopping you from checking on me,' I snapped. 'You could have looked at any time and known where I was.'

'I shouldn't have *needed* to check where you were because you should have been *where I left you,*' Renatus bit back. He gestured irritably at the walls, apparently implying the greater surrounds of the estate. 'What's the use of having a fortress if the people you want to protect don't stay inside it?'

'I wasn't in danger,' I argued. 'I was with Glen and Anouk.'

'Have you not been here these last four months?' he asked incredulously. 'Did the fact that our council *can be compromised* escape your notice?'

'Glen and Anouk aren't spies for Lisandro,' I said, rolling my eyes. He rolled his, too, exasperated with me, and I was reminded that we were both very young people saddled with some very big responsibilities. Right now, we didn't seem mature enough for those responsibilities.

'Neither were Aubrey, Peter or Jackson, until we found out,' he said coldly. Hostile. 'You're *my* apprentice. Your sister gave me permission to train you and I answer to her if something happens to you. Glen and Anouk,' he added, pointing at the wall, behind which they were working, 'no, they're not spies for Lisandro, but if they fail to protect you from an attack-'

'We weren't being attacked,' I butted in, but he kept talking.

'-I'm the one Emmanuelle will drag over the coals. I'm the one who has to tell your sister if you're hurt, and I don't want that to be the theme of the first time I meet your family.'

I had further arguments but I swallowed them down with difficulty. He was the adult, barely, but I was the Empath, and I knew that his anger was fuelled by worry for me and pent-up frustration from the events at Raymond's, and I was being a bitch. I was tired, and proud, and upset by the trapped feeling of having to talk to Lisandro at the party without rescue and annoyed with myself for accepting Declan's stupid earrings, preventing Renatus from realising I was in trouble, and overwhelmed by the entire mystery of Nastassja, the Elm Stone and the Shanahans. Renatus didn't know any of that because I hadn't thought to tell him, and that wasn't his fault.

'Fine,' I said shortly, folding my arms over the front of my dress. I hadn't had time to get changed. 'I won't go off the property without you again.'

He hesitated, surprised by the win.

'Good. Thank you.'

'I was angry with you for leaving me alone at the party,' I added, more of an accusatory comment than an admission, but I tried to keep the vindictive bite out of my voice. 'I didn't know where *you* were. And I don't want to know about Cecily Donovan,' I said quickly before he could remind me she'd cornered him on his way out of the parlour. I remembered telling him that Xanthe had suspected me of kissing Sophia and I understood his confronted reaction now. I wasn't upset; I just really preferred not to know. Ugh. Boy thoughts.

'I got away in time but I didn't know what she wanted with me,' Renatus admitted. 'I thought she was married. Apparently not.'

'She *was* married. Six times. She murdered her husbands and took their money. You're lucky I interrupted before you got sucked into being the seventh.'

'How do you know all that?'

'Declan told me.'

Our argument had fizzled out into something civil and almost friendly, but now Renatus flared back up.

'Why were you talking to him at all?' he asked. He came over and grabbed my hands, turning them over and holding them out like he was looking for something written on my skin somewhere. 'Did he touch you?'

I wrenched my hands back. 'No. I didn't let him. But he still managed to get blocks on me so I couldn't talk to you.'

'How?' Renatus demanded. I pursed my lips, reluctant to tell him, because I knew he'd be mad with my numerous blatant acts of ignorance.

'It doesn't matter. I won't let it happen again.'

'It shouldn't have happened-'

'There are more important things to talk about,' I interrupted. 'I'm sick of this day and I want to go to bed so can we please prioritise the topic of conversation?'

Renatus struggled with his frustration for a moment but got it under control.

'Alright,' he agreed tensely. 'The Archives. The *ring*. Are you *sure* that's what you saw?'

I nodded, inhaling slowly to regain control of my own emotions.

'I know what I saw,' I agreed coolly. I tapped my forehead with a finger. 'You can look, if you like. Go for your life.'

'I will. And the woman? You're sure she's the same one who came after you in Scotland?'

'I didn't see her face on Friday night but she had the same eyes, and I got the same *feeling* from her. Like I needed to get as far away from her as possible.'

It was a tangible sense that I could remember clearly even now. I never wanted to encounter Nastassja again in my life. She made me feel yucky.

'And how did you draw the conclusion that she might be Keely Shanahan?' Renatus pushed. 'You never knew her. I didn't know you knew anything about the Shanahans at all.'

'I didn't,' I said instead of saying *I didn't; thanks for neglecting to mention that whole extended family of yours, by the way.* 'Declan told me about her.'

Even the mention of his informant's name made him tense up, but he didn't lash out at me this time.

'He mentioned her and the next woman you saw with a mask on you assume is her?'

'No, *you* mentioned her, then he mentioned her, and then a terrifying woman in a mask and the Elm Stone on her ring finger turned up with Lisandro and forced me into a very unwelcome conversation, and what I saw of her face looked like Teagan. I was stuck talking to that girl a lot longer than you were and I spent most of that time staring at her mouth and trying to decipher the rubbish pouring out of it. I think that qualifies me to say they had similar features. And stop attacking me about Declan,' I added irritably. 'He's a bastard for blocking us off to each other but he also got a message to

422

me to warn me how I was being blocked, once he realised the position he'd left me in.'

'What you saw of their features, you mean,' Renatus reiterated, totally discounting the comment about Declan. 'Because they were wearing masks.'

We were not getting along that well tonight.

'Yes, they were wearing masks,' I said touchily, losing patience immediately. 'Nastassja *in a mask* looked extremely similar to Teagan *in a mask*.'

'Nastassja?'

'That's what she called herself. Lisandro's wife. Keely.'

'His wife,' Renatus repeated. 'I just can't believe that.'

'Anouk and Glen didn't believe it either. They thought I must have heard wrong.'

'Well, they're right, you must have,' he told me firmly, and I narrowed my eyes to glare at him.

'I *didn't* hear him wrong,' I said, very coldly. 'He said "I see you've met my wife" and she said her name was Nastassja, but I shouldn't have heard him *at all* because *you* shouldn't have *left* me alone to be caught like that. I shouldn't have even *been* there. Declan told me what those people do, Renatus. You took me to a party full of crazy people who murder their husbands and buy organs off each other to do black magic and you left me *alone*.'

'I didn't want to go!' he protested.

'You didn't want to leave,' I countered. He sighed heavily.

'I wasn't about to waste an opportunity to form new connections,' he said. 'Lisandro-'

'He killed my parents,' I reminded him, and my voice was meant to sound angry but it came out a little cracked. Renatus fell silent. 'He killed my brother. He killed your whole *immediate* family. He tried to kill me last time I saw him. And tonight I had to *talk* to him and watch you shake his hand.'

Renatus considered this for a long moment. 'I came back as soon as I knew he was there. I would have been back sooner if I'd heard from you.'

My fault. Don't need to rub it in. 'I wouldn't have gone if I'd known I'd have to talk to him.'

'I wouldn't have taken you if I'd known that would upset you so much.'

That was meant to be a nice thing to say but it only upset me further and I demanded, 'So you knew we'd have to talk to him?' But though my anger was directed at him, it wasn't really at him. I was so disappointed in myself. *I wouldn't have taken you if I'd known that would upset you so much.* Seeing Lisandro in person shouldn't unsettle me as deeply as it had. I should be stronger than this. I should be able to hold it together. I'd entertained some insane plan of killing Lisandro but that clearly wasn't going to happen because I was pathetic.

Renatus answered, carefully, 'I knew it was a possibility. I should have been clear on that with you,' and I shot back some smartarse response that I didn't really mean because I *knew* he was trying to apologise, in his own way, and that was so good of him, and everything was just so unfair.

He worried about me when I wasn't where he expected me to be. He came flying back to my side when he realised I was stuck with Lisandro. He gave me plenty of opportunities to escape this stupid party before we ever went and I ignored him each time. He had tried to get out of it himself because he knew he wasn't like those people, and having now been among them I could wholeheartedly concur. He was so much better. I was arguing with him and an observer right now mightn't have guessed it, but I really appreciated him. He always came through for me. He looked after me.

But Susannah was going to be right. Renatus was going to have to kill Lisandro himself and according to her, it was going to unravel him.

And it was my fault because I wasn't strong enough to avoid it.

My nastiness, whatever I said, inflamed the dispute again and Renatus started angrily telling me that this was the job, but he didn't finish because I burst into tears. His argument crashed uncomfortably.

'Aristea,' he sighed, prepared to apologise. I quickly raised my hands like I was fending him off.

'No,' I choked. 'This isn't your fault. None of it's your fault. You...' haven't done anything wrong. Yet. 'I don't...'

'Aristea, what's wrong?' he asked, voice very firm, leaving me no room to talk around the issue or avoid the truth. I swallowed painfully and wiped tears off my face with the back of my hand.

'I...'

All the things I thought were upsetting me were mere smokescreens for what was eating at me inside. A secret. A lie. I wasn't used to keeping secrets and it had been killing me for months. The party, Nastassja, Lisandro, Declan, the Archives – it was all distressing, this whole day, but none compared with the distress of knowing I was going to fail the person who had never once failed me.

I was going to have to tell him.

'I can't tell you,' I managed, breathing deep through my tears, trying to pull myself together. I almost had it when new sobs wrenched on my body and drew my shoulders forward, and I covered my face to hide the fresh tears. Lisandro, Mum, Dad, Aidan, the horrible horrible truth of their deaths, and all the pain I'd refused to feel before now, and on top of all that, the worst: I wanted it avenged, I was a bad person, I knew Renatus would try to avenge it for me, and I *couldn't* let him... but I wasn't going to be able to stop him. 'It isn't... *Don't* hug me,' I warned when he stepped closer. Skin contact voided most telepathic wards and my internal debate would be immediately apparent to him. Thus far I'd managed to keep the secret hidden by not thinking about it, and by not giving him any reason to go digging for it. 'I don't even know why I'm crying.'

In the air around us we both felt the flicker of my lie. I knew why I was crying.

'You've been hiding something,' Renatus knew. 'Come out and say it.'

But I couldn't. It could make things worse.

But I couldn't keep it to myself anymore, either.

'I... I have to tell you-'

The door opened. I'd been too focussed on Renatus and myself to sense the approach of anyone else. Qasim and Emmanuelle stood in the doorway.

I went quiet. My blurry range of vision encompassed the three White Elm councillors I had the deepest respect and admiration for. They were healers and spies, yes, but also front-line warriors, fearless and resourceful and confident. My dreams of joining the council one day centred around growing into someone like one of them. Knowledgeable. Wise. Respectable. An expert at my craft.

Good at keeping massive secrets when it was the right thing to do.

I thought of Renatus, hiding his greatest shames from Fionnuala and Lord Gawain, not for his own selfish protection but for theirs, because he knew it would crush them to know what he'd done.

I thought of Qasim, learning of this and everything else in Renatus's past during a Trial by One, and keeping it to himself because he knew it wouldn't affect the outcome but that it might undermine what faith the White Elm still had in their Dark Keeper, rendering him useless in the upcoming struggles against Lisandro.

I thought of Emmanuelle, tricking Lisandro *and* us into thinking she was a double agent and offering him the Elm Stone, because she was trying to edge me out of the conflict zone.

Sometimes keeping secrets was the right thing to do, and these three people were prime role models of that fact.

'Aristea, are you alright?' my supervisor asked, concern radiating into the room, as Qasim's quick gaze took tearful

426

me in and then turned accusingly on Renatus, who frowned at them.

'We're talking,' he said pointedly. 'Knock.'

'No, I'm fine,' I insisted, rubbing my eyes, smearing the gold paint. 'I'll be okay. I'm just too tired.'

'Go to bed, then,' Qasim said in his short voice, grating on me. To Renatus he said, 'We need to see you next door.'

'Thirty seconds,' my master said in the same tone. Qasim walked away. Emmanuelle hesitated, but shot me a supportive look that told me she really would be right next door if I wanted her, before she left too. The door stayed open. Renatus turned back to me, expectant. I took a deep breath. I'd dug a hole to bury myself in consequences and honesty but now I wasn't sure I was ready.

'It's alright,' I said. 'I changed my mind.' Back. 'I don't need to talk about it.'

'No, you do,' Renatus disagreed. In my mind I felt his presence, his thoughts, and I felt him begin to sift through everything he found. 'I need to know. If you're keeping something from me-'

'She looks like Ana,' I blurted out the instant it came to me. Renatus withdrew immediately, surprised. I pushed on, taking advantage while I could. 'Nastassja. Keely. Whoever she is. Not the same, but similar. Lisandro is *sick*, Renatus. I knew it from the last time we saw him, with what he did to me just to hurt you, and what he did to both our families. But he murdered your sister,' I reminded him, more heartlessly than I normally would have, except I was desperate, 'and eight years later he turns up at the same party as you *married* to her lookalike cousin? With the ring he blackmailed out of *you* as her wedding band? This is all some huge bad joke and it's on you. This is all to hurt you. He told those people there today that he loves you but he's a psychopath.' I met Renatus's wide violet eyes. 'How are we supposed to contend with a psychopath? He's going to kill us. For sport.'

This was a true fear of mine and Renatus bought it completely as the sole reason for my little breakdown. He gathered up his own emotional disturbances and tucked them away, prepared to be the adult, the mentor and protector, once again.

'I'm not going to let him kill you,' he said. 'I'm not going to let him kill me. I'm not going to let him hurt me. Keely,' he paused when the hold he had on his feelings on the matter shook slightly, 'and Ana *did* look similar. But if finding Shanahan's daughter and parading her at parties to remind me of my sister is Lisandro's idea of a threatening move on the game board, he wasted his turn. I buried my sister. No magic in this world or any other can bring back the dead, and he's going to know that better than anyone when I get my shot at him.'

I swallowed and nodded, keeping my thoughts well back from where he could overhear them. He fully intended to kill Lisandro when he got the chance. It was his job. He wasn't to know that I was quietly calculating other possibilities. If I couldn't do it and I didn't want it to be him, either... surely there had to be a loophole, whatever Susannah said.

I would find it.

Renatus leaned closer to me so our eyes would be level and so I could see the resolve in his.

'Yes, he's a psychopath,' he said. 'Yes, he's trying to unsettle me. He wants me off my game because he knows I'm coming after him. But he doesn't scare me. He's not perfect. He's cocky. He didn't count on you connecting the dots and recognising Keely or he never would have brought her out into the open. Now we're streaks ahead of where he thinks we are. We're going to beat him,' he added, an assurance.

I nodded again, slower. He was right. He had to be. I finished locking my thoughts firmly away and hurriedly wiped my eyes and nose.

'Alright. Okay. You can hug me now.'

He straightened up and he never smiled, but his eyes softened in that way they did when he was meant to be smiling.

'I think you'll manage.'

428

I slept well that night, right through the wake-up bell at seven the next day and into the first break, missing Glen's lesson. He was dismissive when I ran into the dining hall, untied shoelaces clattering and hair not yet brushed, apologising and offering to make up the lesson later. He said there was no need. He understood I'd had a late night and a big day.

Hiroko, Iseult and the twins listened in fascination as I described the splendour of Raymond's party that afternoon. The summer sun was out and Dana had pointed out a pile of picnic blankets she'd dug out of a closet somewhere and left beside the front doors. We helped ourselves and spread them across the still-damp lawn outside. We were lying there with our notepads open, sunning ourselves and sketching glorious dresses, both those I described and those imagined.

It was a huge improvement on yesterday.

'They did a great job with your hair,' Kendra commented enviously, reaching over with her pencil to lift one of my big, soft, slept-in curls. 'I can't get curls to stay longer than an hour or so in mine.'

'Hers is already wavy,' Sophia reminded her sister. She closed one eye critically at the sketch on Hiroko's page. 'More of a sweetheart line, I think.' She turned her pencil over and erased the neckline of their combined creation. Hiroko obediently redrew it.

'This one woman had real live butterflies all over her dress,' I said, neglecting to mention her significance. 'How would she do that?'

'Were they stitched on?' Kendra asked, and both Sophia and Hiroko looked up at me in horror at the idea. I shook my head.

'No, they were just sitting there by choice. They flew around a little bit.'

'Animal magnetism,' Iseult said as she shaded in the waist of her dress. 'Black magic. You can't make choices for other living things – nature won't allow it. So you'd need to circumvent nature if you wanted to enforce your will on a swarm of insects like that and make them stay with you. The White Elm banned animal magic in 1958.'

I thought a lot about that over the next few days as I drifted in and out of the White Elm's investigation into the Shanahans' missing daughter. The blatant disregard for magical law, and for the ethical reasons the laws were introduced in the first place, went directly against the grain of my principles. I was not one for blindly following the current and I was not one for accepting authority on its word, and I certainly couldn't pretend I'd never broken the rules before, but I was not one for self-congratulating shows of personal power, either. I had started off very willing to sympathise with the Keely Shanahan Declan had described, the headstrong second-born daughter who chose her freedom over bowing to the institution. The Keely Shanahan calling herself Nastassja garnered no such respect. She attacked me in the dark and gave chase, unprovoked. She cornered me at Raymond's and forced me into conversation despite knowing I didn't want to talk. She hid from her family and vilified her own sister at her wedding for her choices despite wanting the liberty to be allowed to do the same. She twisted the will of lesser minds, a hundred little butterflies, to serve her own vanity, and though she'd looked glorious, I couldn't stop wondering what species they were and how many precious days they had to live. How much of their short lives had she taken for her gown and what had she done with them when she changed out of the dress? I hoped she'd set them free.

My birthday crept closer but I didn't mention it to anybody. On the Friday before, I received cards and presents from my aunt and sister.

'You can open them now,' Kendra insisted once we'd gotten the demands of 'When's your birthday?' out of the way. 'We won't tell anyone.'

'You're meant to wait until your real birthday,' Sophia countered, and I was inclined to agree. I stashed them under my bed and pretended not to desperately want to tear them open.

# chapter twenty-six

From Aunt Leanne it was mostly "practical" things – a scarf she'd knitted but which she presumably expected me to wait months to wear since it was the height of summer, a pencil case, an expensive stationery set, a lovely new journal – and from Angela I'd received a gift with a card that read, *Emmanuelle has my number. Get her to let you call me, and open your present while we talk. I want to hear your reaction when you open it.*

The idea of hearing my sister's voice while I opened my presents made my chest tighten a little. From her last letter, I knew she was away in Dublin with our cousin Kelly this week, and I hated that I wasn't there with them.

'What is it?' Hiroko whispered, shuffling closer. It was Saturday morning and Xanthe and Sterling were still asleep, breathing softly on their side of the room. I'd cast my first silence ward to ensure they stayed that way in case my whispers got out of hand with excitement. It was *my birthday*. Hiroko had noticed me awake and sneaked over to join me on my bed, newspaper-wrapped gift clenched in her arm.

I shook the unopened box from my sister. 'Don't know. She wants me to wait.'

'Until she can see you. This is nice. So, wait,' Hiroko advised, pushing the box off my lap onto the covers and placing her gift in my hands instead. 'Open this while you wait.'

I carefully unpicked the tape so I could unwrap the newspaper with as little rumpling noise as possible.

The present within was a glass jar, cleaned out and with the brassy lid screwed back into place. It contained an assortment of natural litter – dried petals, leaves, pebbles – about a fifth filled.

'Okay, this does not *appear* exciting,' Hiroko admitted, taking the jar and turning it over. Rather than obey gravity and slide to the new bottom of the jar the paraphernalia inside scattered about like it was suspended in water. I watched in awe as the contents drifted about, spinning and swirling in what was clearly *not* water. Even the little stones behaved like they weighed the same as the feathers and flowers.

For all the exposure to cool magic I had, cool magic, especially when performed by my friends, never ceased to impress me, and Hiroko was the queen among my friends for stumbling across very cool magic and learning it.

'Did you make me a magical snow globe?' I asked, amazed. She smiled, pleased with my reaction.

'I am sorry, I could not find any. It is too hot for snow,' she answered, and we grinned at each other.

The snow globe went to live on my desk, where I knew I would get a good deal of use out of it as a procrastination tool against having to study, and I put Aunt Leanne's gifts there, too. Angela's pink-wrapped gift remained unopened and I reluctantly left it in my bedside table with my grandfather's book (still unread), to have my shower and go eat my breakfast.

In the dining hall I was jumped by Kendra and Sophia, who literally leapt on me and hugged me tightly. Unable to resist, Addison swung his long arms around the three of us and squeezed, yelling, 'Happy birthday!' while we squealed in protest at the pressure. They dragged me over to where Iseult was already sitting, already eating, and presented me with the stapled pages of the next chapter of our humorous co-written tale of Roki, this time detailing the adventures of her sidekick Risi. Upon receipt of the book I lost all interest in lining up for food, much too excited to know what my crazy friends had written.

'Read it now,' Sophia begged, pushing Addison into the seat beside me so she could lean on his shoulder and see. The others squeezed in close, too, and listened as I cleared my throat and began to read.

It did not disappoint. It was hard to read fluently because I kept having to stop for my own outbursts of laughter and to be heard over the laughter of my friends. The other students in the hall looked at us curiously but I didn't care. Risi, the cartoon-fiction version of me, was a superhero in training, undergoing all sorts of secret night-time missions she had to keep secret from her friends, usually with hilarious consequences, and I absolutely loved this depiction of the way my friends saw me. Each person had written different passages, just as we had all done with the first Roki story, and I loved that I could hear their voices in their writing style. Cheeky Addison; subtle Sophia; clear-cut Iseult; big-picture Hiroko; witty Kendra.

Roki had just discovered Risi's true identity in a painful act of clumsy disguise and we were roaring with tearful laughter when Fionnuala and Niamh placed plates of chocolate pancakes in front of us all.

'Happy birthday, Miss Aristea,' Fionnuala said warmly, leaning down to kiss my hair. Her daughter shot me an equally affectionate smile.

'Thank you,' I said, taken aback. I hadn't known she knew what day it was. I'd hardly mentioned it, despite my inner scorching desire for time to accelerate to get to this day. My friends echoed me.

'No, you are all most welcome.'

We ate our breakfasts and finished the story. Sophia and Addison groaned when it was done.

'We should have written more pages!' they complained. Addison narrowed his eyes and turned to Iseult. 'How far away's your birthday? When do we get more?'

'We can have more whenever we want,' Kendra said reasonably. 'We're the writers.'

'The Roki series are *birthday books*,' Addison said in the same voice. 'That means we have to wait for the next birthday. And you selfish women,' he added, gesturing at Kendra, Sophia, Hiroko and I, 'all went and put your birthdays all in a row, didn't you, so now we have to wait until *next year* for mine and Iseult's.'

'We should have spread them out more,' Kendra said sorrowfully, looking around at the rest of our group until her eyes settled on her sister. 'Especially us. What were we thinking, putting them on the same day?'

'Or we should have kept Sterling and Xanthe,' Addison chanced, smirking a little when we all frowned or shifted awkwardly in our seats. 'I bet they have birthdays.'

'Sterling and Xanthe are younger than us,' Hiroko provided. 'Their birthdays are still to come.'

'Yeah, see?' Addison rounded on Sophia. 'If you hadn't been so intolerant of her views on female friendship and equality, and if you'd just let it slide when she called your sister a tramp and just left her alone to be a nasty piece of work, we'd still be friends with Xanthe, and probably Sterling, too.'

'I have come to terms with this loss,' Hiroko said calmly, making us all laugh again.

'I think Lien Hua's birthday is coming up,' Sophia said brightly. 'We could befriend her. She's nice.'

*Qasim found our mutineer*, Renatus informed me, and I smiled at my friends and put my fork down. The wonderful part of my day was over and reality was back.

In his study he was in conversation with a well-dressed, middle-aged stranger in a brown suit. They had paperwork spread over the desk and Renatus was signing wherever the man told him to. I walked in and stopped in front of the desk, looking with interest at what they were doing as I waited.

'Aristea, this is Martin Sullivan, a lawyer for the firm my father dealt with,' Renatus said, gesturing with the end of his pen at the man standing beside him. The man looked up at me and smiled politely. I smiled back. 'Mr Sullivan, Aristea Byrne.'

'Your heir,' the man interpreted, leaning across to shake my hand. I hadn't been referred to in that way before, but I detected his lack of magic. A non-witch. "This is my apprentice in sorcery" was not the ideal introduction to those outside our society, so "heir" would do, I supposed. 'Pleased to meet you. Happy birthday.'

'Aristea, sign this,' Renatus said, waving me over to the desk without answering Mr Sullivan. He handed me one of the pens from the neat line at the top corner of the desk, and slid a document over to me. The paragraphs were heavy blocks of black type, and a brief skim of the legal jargon made my head swim.

'What is it?' I asked, but I already had the pen to paper, already printing my name where the stickers told me to and scratching my signature beside it. Already dating it.

'This is for insurance,' he said simply. 'You're eighteen, an adult by mortal standards.'

'Excellent,' Mr Sullivan said when I straightened. He seemed unfazed by the "mortal" comment. Maybe he knew. He had a witch for a client, after all. Maybe several. 'And if you don't mind, sign here...' He flicked through to other pages to present other places that needed a signature, and looked at me like he expected me to ask more, but I didn't. It wasn't like Renatus wanted me to sign my life away – hadn't I already, when I underwent my initiation? I just wanted a complication-free birthday. When I signed the last page, the lawyer took the document with a flourish. He leafed through it to check every page, then smiled at us both. 'Well. Everything seems to be in order.'

'How soon can you move that through?' Renatus asked. 'I know what your offices are like.'

'I'll make copies of this today, just in case, and make the necessary changes when the banks open Monday. You can rest assured it's in effect immediately.'

I waited for the door to close. I didn't care much for that exchange and had little interest. Renatus would have told me if he'd particularly wanted me to know.

'You said you found the man from the forest?'

'Qasim did. Nailed to a tree.'

'To a *tree*?' I repeated. 'Is he dead?' I hoped so. I thought of the clear blue eyes in the rugged, dirty, bearded face and though my only interaction with him had been negative and I hadn't even known his name, it rocked me a little to know that eyes I looked into only a week ago were now dim and empty.

'Yes, thankfully,' Renatus said, putting his maps away in the smoky-glass cabinets behind his desk. 'Qasim is at the scene now and I'm about to leave to meet him.'

'I'll have to change my shoes,' I said, looking down. Strappy summer sandals weren't going to cut it out in the field.

'You don't have to come,' he answered. 'He's been there a few days. It's going to look and smell terrible. Qasim and I can handle the sweep for evidence without you and believe me, it's the last place you want to be for your birthday.' I'd mentioned it once, more than a month ago, but since then I'd kept it to myself. I really didn't think he'd remember. He placed a long, thin box on the desktop between us and I leaned forward on my toes, curious. 'This is for you.'

I didn't move, even though I was dying to open the box. 'You shouldn't have gotten me a present.'

'Let's say I wanted to,' he replied. He gestured at the gift. 'I'm needed elsewhere. Open it.'

I didn't have any better arguments so I stepped up to the desk and put my hands on the box. It was some sort of textured cardboard and very dark green. I put my hands on the sides and pulled up. The lid came off without effort. Inside was a pair of thin silver swords.

'Sai,' Renatus told me as I lifted one out of the box. It was weighty and solid. The main blade was more of a post, rounded and safe to touch, roughly the length of my forearm.

Its tip was sharpened to a point. The handle was wrapped with black leather and silver cord, leaving the pommel exposed. But most distinctive about the weapons were the prongs that struck out either side of the central blade from the top of the handle. They looked like tridents. Altogether sleek and aesthetically pleasing, the Sai were a very unique weapon. I'd seen them on the odd occasion in movies and I knew they were used in pairs and could look extremely impressive in action.

'They're beautiful,' I said, admiring the one I held. The metal was polished and glinted like silver. 'Where did you get these?'

'I know someone,' was all he said in reply. 'Do you like them?'

'Aye, yes,' I said. 'Thank you. Can I hang them in my room?' Can I drill holes in the walls of your centuries-old mansion?

'No. You're going to learn how to use them.'

That pulled my attention from my new toys over to my master. 'Use them? But... I can't use swords.' I'm a kid, I'm useless, I only caught that knife last week by fluke and I really didn't know what to do with it once I caught it. I certainly couldn't use a pair of beautiful ancient knives in synchronism to combat an opponent.

'Tian will teach you,' Renatus assured me. He took the second one out of the box and held the handle. I copied his grip with the first knife. 'He tells me it is a very difficult weapon to begin your training with because of the coordination required, but he is confident you will pick it up.'

'I don't know that I should have a weapon,' I said uncertainly. 'I don't know if I want to hurt anybody.'

Whatever I'd said about killing Lisandro was all bluster. I was soft.

Renatus stepped away from the desk, rounding it to be more in the open. He shifted his fingers and the knife swung in his hand, flipping around in a graceful arc to point down along his arm. A second flick and he had it pointing forward again. It was so quick I didn't catch how he did it, but it looked flashy. I wanted to be able to do that.

'They're mostly a defensive weapon,' he explained. 'They're hard enough and strong enough that nothing's going to break them if you use them to block another blade, and these outer prongs,' he extended the knife to show me the parts he was referring to, 'are for both blocking and disarming.' He slid the knife against the one I held as if they were clashing in slow motion. He twisted his wrist suddenly; the Sai was caught in the jaws of its brother and wrenched out of my slack grip. Renatus caught the handle and disentangled them. He swung them around his fingers with another of those easy-looking flicks and offered me both knives handle-first. I took them.

'You make it look easy,' I accused, but I was very impressed and excited to start playing with them. I flexed my fingers over the handles, eager to try swinging them but sure I would only drop them. I would wait until I was alone. I pointed both knives forward experimentally and remembered the sharp tips. 'If they're defensive...?'

'Mostly defensive,' Renatus said again, going back to the desk to pack up the empty box. 'Sometimes defending isn't enough.' He stopped, then stood back from the box, holding the lid clear. 'Perhaps you should keep them in the box rather than walk through the house with them.'

It was a wise suggestion. I placed the knives gently back inside the box and accepted it from Renatus when he handed it to me. Their combined weight was quite heavy, especially given the narrow profile of the box. I smiled at him.

'Thank you,' I said again, trying to convey how much I meant it. 'I love them.'

'Good.' Renatus walked with me to the door and out into the hall. 'Enjoy your birthday.'

He didn't go back into his study. He left through the invisible portal in the wall beside the door, and I headed back to my room to store my new gift.

I was sitting on my bed, indulging in a few minutes of solitude before re-joining my friends downstairs, playing with my new knives – my very own knives! – when I dropped them with a clang onto my bedcovers for the eighth time and decided I should wait until I was taught properly how to use them. I put my Sai under my bed and reached for my shoes. I'd kicked off my sandals in order to clamber onto the bed in the first place, but one had skittered away somewhere, probably behind Hiroko's bed, so I grabbed boots instead. Socks were easier to locate than the missing sandal. I really needed to clean my part of this room.

But not today. It was my birthday.

It was a Saturday and most of the White Elm only visited the estate to plan or conduct lessons, or to work on other projects with other councillors. On my way down the stairs my hand drifted on the bannister, sending me a brief impression of Anouk carting a heavy cardboard box, resting her hand momentarily to catch her breath. My interest piqued, I went back up the last flight and went instinctively to her classroom. I had time. My friends didn't know how long I was going to be, and I wasn't arrogant enough to believe they needed me in order to be entertained.

The wall of Anouk's classroom had become a bulletin board of clues and connections. Photos and post-it notes were scattered about with twine strung between them. It was messier than if Renatus were in charge of it, but every day I dropped in here it was fuller, with new handwritten Russian notes pinned to the pictures or strings. There was clearly a system to Anouk's (and Glen's – he was often in here instead, or as well) madness, and she was making ground with it. She had cancelled her lessons this week and worked exclusively on this wall. Today she was in here alone, thin blonde hair wispy after days unbrushed and eyes dark and drawn with tiredness. I wondered how long she'd been-

'Is that a formal invitation?' she asked coolly, not even looking back at me as she strung a new line of cord between two photos. I made myself smile reluctantly as I walked into the room. Anouk and I had had our issues but from my observations of her interactions with other people, her abrupt manner was nothing personal against me. She was a Telepath and most of her communicating took place in her head. Perhaps her people skills hadn't fully developed as a result. And her dislike of Renatus was definitely not something to take offence to. Hardly anyone liked Renatus.

'I've been working on keeping my thoughts to myself,' I told her, determined that I would not bite. 'Have I gotten any better?'

She turned to look at me. She was the skinniest person I had ever known, hips and collarbone starkly visible, but her long limbs and narrow frame indicated that this was simply the shape her genes were programmed to give her.

'Yes, you have,' she said after a moment, relenting. She was the one who had gotten on my case in the first place about the dangers of thinking in questions and how it invited Telepaths to listen to other thoughts, no matter how well-warded I thought I was.

'You've done so much,' I commented, trying to maintain the moment of friendliness, looking at her wall and putting my box down on a table. She turned back to it.

'This should have been done months ago,' she admitted. Her Russian accent was rolling and smooth and made me wish I spoke in a more exotic way than I did. 'But beside Lisandro and Jackson, we didn't have any names to follow up on. The connection you made between Lisandro and Shanahan has cast new light on our investigation. The boxes you and Renatus were working through,' she gestured behind her at the classroom desks, which were littered with open case boxes, 'were filled with Shanahan family clients. They were right under our noses: we just didn't know what to look for. All of these people,' she said, pointing to the photos she'd pulled off the back of the missing person files and pinned to the wall, 'had loose connections with Thomas Shanahan. He made them "disappear" and they went to work for Lisandro.' She paused. 'I think it's what he promised Aubrey.'

I looked at her. I hadn't heard her, or anyone else on the council, mention their former brother in some time.

'So these people,' I clarified, hopping up to sit on a desk, turning my attention back to the wall, 'are in some way dissatisfied with their lives, and they get in touch with Thomas Shanahan. He does *something* to make them hard to find, because that's what he does, and Lisandro takes them under his wing and they pay out their debt in service to him.'

'Presumably he has some system in place of payment to Shanahan,' Anouk agreed. 'We haven't yet determined what that is. Regardless, it seems that those who refuse to pay with time in service ultimately pay with their lives, like your Scottish mutineer and his stepbrother Paul.'

'Do you think Thomas Shanahan knows Lisandro has married his missing daughter?' I asked. Anouk's mouth twisted, unwilling to take a stab at that one.

'We can't be sure. If they're working together, even distantly, it stands to reason that Shanahan would know, but the fact that she attended the party and avoided people who might recognise her, including her own sister, implies that he mightn't. It would be like Lisandro to dangle a secret like that over his ally. Perhaps Keely's success in hiding from her father inspired Lisandro to make the deal he did with the family. We don't have all the information so we don't know.' She yawned. 'At least now we have a few dozen new places to start.' She blinked, exhausted. 'Tomorrow. I'm done.'

She put her packet of pushpins down and I slid off the desktop obediently. But I didn't feel my feet hit the ground. My attention went somewhere else, unbidden.

*Long hands sweep loose black hair into a ponytail...* 'They'll *try to stop you.'... Dark muscled arms fold together... Doubt...* 'Good. I'm counting on it.'... A smile in bronze-brown eyes...* *Fingers button up a light summer coat...* 'Where is it?'... 'Prague. *Bunch of kids out in the street being vocal in support of* *democracy.'...* 'Dead kids always make the news.'...

I inhaled deeply and shakily as I snapped back to my own body, Anouk's classroom, Morrissey House. Anouk had a hand on my shoulder and I had a hand on the desk, knuckles white, keeping me upright. I had no memory of grabbing it.

'What was that?' Anouk demanded. 'What did you see?'

*Did you see that?* Renatus asked at the same time. I nodded, even though he couldn't see me. Thoughts rampaged unchecked around my head. Lisandro. Jackson. Where were they? What was Lisandro going to do in Prague? What did Jackson mean by "dead kids always make the news"?

'Calm down, you're a sieve,' Anouk said reproachfully. She took me by the shoulders and made me face her. Telepaths found their task easier with eye and skin contact. I didn't try to stop her, but she didn't need to look in my mind because Renatus and Qasim must have shared the vision with the rest of the council. Anouk dropped her gaze to concentrate on what she saw.

*Qasim says there's a street party of young activists in the middle of Prague right now.*

'He's going to kill them,' Anouk murmured, still not looking directly at me.

'What are we going to do?' I asked both Renatus and Anouk. The Russian Historian tilted her head like she was listening, and I assumed she was in conversation with my master. Neither spoke to me for a very long moment and my anxiety only built higher in that time.

*What are we going to do?* I repeated, directing my question at Renatus. Anouk lifted her eyes to mine and I felt her presence in my mind as she *melded* herself into my dialogue with Renatus. No one had ever done that before but she wasn't an ordinary Telepath. No one on the council was an ordinary anything. She said, *He knows we'll come. He said so,* and I heard her as clearly as if she'd spoken aloud, but her lips didn't move.

It wasn't until days later that it struck me how far her opinion of me had come if she felt I deserved a part in their conversation.

Renatus agreed. *We shouldn't do anything. Any vision we receive from Lisandro is deliberate.*

*Jackson said there will be dead kids on the news,* I said, distressed. Both councillors hesitated at that reminder.

*Nationals,* Renatus confirmed reluctantly. *They're our citizens.*

*We can't do anything,* Anouk insisted. *He's baiting us.*

*Qasim can see at least two dozen civilians at this gathering. Aged between seventeen and twenty-five. What does it say about us if we let Lisandro attack and kill thirty of our citizens and we do nothing to stop him?*

My age. Renatus's age. The "kids" Jackson wanted to see dead on the news weren't children, but they were only our age.

*We can't do nothing,* I said, scared for the young strangers in the Czech Republic. I didn't know them but the idea of allowing Lisandro or anyone else to hurt people – anyone – was incomprehensible. He'd hurt enough people. These were twenty or thirty people *my age* who were other people's sons, daughters, siblings... We couldn't do nothing.

*He's "counting on" us trying to stop him,* Anouk reminded us. Still she stood before me, staring into my eyes, and neither of us moved. *He knows we'll come, and he'll have a reason for trying to draw us out. We can't give him that opportunity.*

*It's a trap,* Renatus agreed. *We can't go.*

*We can't afford not to,* Anouk countered grimly, and the pair of them both changed their tune.

*No, you're right,* Renatus said with the same feeling. *Bring Aristea. She'll be able to sense him first if he tries to sneak up on us under wards or illusions. I'll get you out of there at the first sign of trouble,* he promised me as Anouk broke eye contact and lifted her leg to feel for something in her boot, like she was adjusting a sock. She jerked her head toward the door and I followed her meekly. My stomach was roiling with displeasure at the change in my circumstances. I was meant to be eating cake. I wasn't meant to be facing my family's murderer and the catalyst for Renatus's eventual downfall for the second time in a week. He didn't hear those thoughts because I took care not to think them, but he must have known I didn't want to go because he said, *We won't stay around. We'll break up the party and send everyone on their way. If Lisandro does turn up, we'll Displace them all out of the conflict zone and I won't take you back there. Elijah and Qasim are staying here with the body in case Lisandro is trying to draw us away from the scene, but they'll be ready to come join us if we need them.*

I nodded again, thinking it sounded very sensible. It fit Lisandro's past pattern of behaviour to make these sorts of appearances right when he wanted to distract the council from something else he was up to. He'd sent Jackson to break into Emmanuelle's house to look for the Elm Stone while he had the White Elm's attention concentrated on himself. He'd sent Aubrey around the world planting false evidence of councillors trespassing on their independent neighbouring nations while he allowed snippets of his otherwise-shielded conversation with Renatus to slip through to Qasim. Telling us to look to Prague was as good as saying 'I'm up to something even worse somewhere else' but that didn't mean we could ignore what he was doing in Prague.

Passing the dining hall, I wanted to break away from Anouk, whose pace was quick and sharp, and run back in to my friends and ask who wanted to take those picnic blankets outside to lie on the lawn and look for shapes in the clouds passing overheard. I thought that sounded like a perfect way to spend a birthday afternoon. But I kept up with my teacher and left the house. The students hanging about outside enjoying the sunshine ignored us, or pretended to.

*I'm nearby. I'll Displace there when you do,* Renatus said. *Everyone is standing by, on alert.*

'Get those wards up,' Anouk reminded me brusquely as we stepped out the gate and locked it behind us. 'Close your head down. I don't want to hear anything out of you.'

I didn't take offence to her words or her manner. She was totally right to be as forward as she was. It was imperative. There wasn't time to be nice or encouraging about it, to make suggestions. It was just *do it*, and I hurried to build my physical wards up as densely as I could and to get control over my panicky thoughts. I needed an uncurious mind with no questions dangling out like ropes of Rapunzel's hair, and I needed shields that would protect my body and mind without blocking my Empathy from sensing everything that was happening beyond me. I wasn't useful if I was so well-protected that I was energetically blind, like at Raymond's.

When we were far enough away from the house to make the Displacement across four countries, Anouk turned to face me.

'Ready?'

*Ready*? Renatus asked at the same time.

'I think so,' I told them both. She didn't wait for me to change my mind. She took my wrist and pulled me after her as she tore a hole in the Fabric and stepped through to someplace else.

We arrived in the shadows of a narrow alley, a favourite of Displacement spots, and Anouk dragged me out into the sunshine of the small square. I halted, breathless. Prague was two time zones over from where I'd lived my whole life and at almost the same latitude, so it didn't surprise me when the temperature was similar and the sky above was the same blue as the sky above Northern Ireland this morning.

The sky *line*, though. I had never seen anything so spectacular. The medieval buildings around me rose like golden castles, spires and towers all reaching into the heavens. Tourists milled in and around stores set into buildings so old yet still so serviceable. And before us, dominating my vision, a fourteenth century arch bridge stood proud, unmoved by the attentions of the many cameras pointed at it. Through the abutments I saw the wide footbridge itself and gaped at the statues of saints that lined it.

Anouk was unimpressed, and took me back into the alley. 'We're not close enough.'

'Where exactly are we?' Because I was happy to stay right here and stare at the unexpected architectural beauty I was confronted with.

'Not where we want to be,' Anouk said. We fell into the shadows of a repurposed building, now a souvenir shop with a glorious view of the bridge and the river it spanned. 'Charles Bridge.'

We Displaced again.

Where we landed was relatively *eh*, an empty ladies' room, but once we stepped outside back into the lovely sunlight I was again surrounded by splendour. This city had my enraptured attention unlike anything at Raymond's party.

Anouk looked about for only a moment, taking in relevant things like the lack of interested onlookers and the lack of apparent danger, before setting out. I remembered why we were here. What a dampener reality can be. I jogged after her, trying not to radiate fear. Trying to appreciate that I was in the Czech Republic for my birthday and that *that* was pretty cool.

*I'm three streets over, east*, Renatus said tensely. *I found the rally. It's on the next block to the north. Tourist hotspot.*

'This is a very bad idea,' Anouk said now as she walked swiftly, and I was surprised to hear concern in her voice. She was scared? 'He knows we are coming. This is what he wants.'

I didn't know what to say. I was already afraid. The fact that *she* was afraid, too, only supported the claim fear already had on my heart. I'd hardly seen Anouk in action but I was pretty sure she was perfectly competent, like the rest of the council. Her uncertainty meant there were sufficient grounds to be terrified.

We turned onto the main street, squeezing between shoppers and tourists, and saw Renatus coming our way. I was relieved to see him and his tense but sure demeanour. He wasn't afraid of Lisandro. He wasn't afraid of anything much.

446

*Everything's going to be fine*, he assured me again.

'What are they all doing?' Anouk asked him as they fell into step together and led the way across the busy road and down a quieter side street. They kept a brisk pace and I stayed close behind them.

There were still people everywhere. Non-witches. Mortals. Going about their normal business.

'Dancing. Drinking. They're speaking out about their opposition to war. Emmanuelle's at home on her computer,' he added, glancing back at me to include me in this part he had no connection to, 'and she says this group has been talking in *forums* for some time, discussing views, young people from this country and some of the neighbouring ones, and this is the first time they've met in person. Does that make sense to you?'

Anouk glanced back as well, and I remembered that she was from a fortified medieval community in central Russia. Neither of them had a clue what Emmanuelle was talking about.

'They've been networking, communicating online,' I explained. 'The same way you two talk telepathically when you're not physically together. It's the mortal version.'

The two councillors looked at each other to confirm that the other had gained the same understanding, and they didn't ask for clarification.

'Is their stance anti-council?' Anouk asked Renatus, and he shook his head.

'No. Emmanuelle says they seem relatively objective, and they exclude *haters* from their discussions.' Again Renatus looked at me, like I was the encyclopaedia of digital dialogue. 'Their main interest is in democratic processes.'

Their concern about this further darkened the scenario for me. I thought of Renatus's reaction to the show of democracy in his office, when Lord Gawain had allowed Garrett's parents and those of his missing friends to vote on what to do next. Surely it was *what* they were voting on that day that Renatus had a problem with, not the concept of voting itself. I wondered whether he even differentiated the two.

We heard the party before we saw it. I took a deep breath and worked to feel a little calmer. Lisandro wasn't here, not yet. Young people, European sorcerers my own age, were getting political together on the internet and organising street parties with excellent bouncy dance music – in total disregard for likely wrath of local authorities – to meet one another and demonstrate their views. Maybe Anouk and Renatus felt threatened by those views but I didn't really understand what they were, beyond "not anti-council". Things weren't so bad. I reminded myself that once we made contact with these young activists and evacuated them, we'd be perfectly safe.

'What an awful noise,' Anouk commented darkly as we turned the next corner into a more open street. I failed to comment. The music was absolutely pumping and I was surprised that none of the businesses that lined the street were out complaining. I didn't mind it at all.

We came into sight of the rally and the source of the noise was immediately apparent. Among the scattered throng of idling tourists and under the shade of a large tree, a huge boom box sat atop the roof of an old car parked perpendicular to the street, blaring a very modern track. As many as thirty young sorcerers crowded around the car, dancing and drinking, some alcohol, some just bottled water. One or two were shaking spray cans; they weren't alone. I saw that many of the non-witches around were bearing spray cans or permanent markers, and many people were writing on the high wall beside the footpath. We stopped a fair distance away.

'Delightful,' Anouk muttered. 'Let's do a quick survey and get them out of here.'

'Wait,' I said, and they did. I pointed at the wall. 'It's so…'

'Colourful,' Renatus agreed. In a place of old-world beige and sandy-gold prettiness, the wall was a sight. Every square centimetre of it looked to be graffitied and decorated in the brightest colours, and nobody adding to the decoration looked ashamed or worried about being caught out. 'It's the Lennon Wall. Poetic place for these people to meet to promote peace.'

'They're *violating* the peace,' Anouk argued. 'Asking for trouble. Public self-expression like this is so egotistic.'

Renatus glanced at me. *A healthy social opinion.* Anouk overheard and frowned but said nothing. She and Renatus moved away from me, going wide to circle the group. No one paid them any mind – we were too well-warded to give anyone any indication of our energy signatures. Feeling brave in this knowledge, I stepped forward, drawn by my curiosity. This was what normal eighteen-year-old witches did on weekends. They threw street parties and got drunk and bathed in the utter joy of being young and opinionated.

*Stay there,* Renatus warned. *Keep your back to that wall so he can't get behind you. Keep us in your sights.*

I obediently backed up so that my shoulders pressed against the window of the building behind me. It was good advice.

The song ended and a young man, not much older than me, disentangled himself from the crowd to climb atop the car. The others raised their voices and bottles to him; even many of the non-witches about glanced over in interest or gentle amusement. Someone called out his name, Jaroslav, and passed him up a paper cup with the base ripped off, a makeshift megaphone. He laughed and graciously used it, pointing into the group at someone else.

'She won't get up here with me, but three cheers for Marcy for organising this!' he shouted in richly accented English through the cup, and they all did as he said, laughing and converging on a girl who covered her face with her hands, embarrassed to be put on the spot. 'All the way from Johannesburg, South Africa! Her blog and the forums she manages are the reason we all found each other and have the space we do to share our views. She's the only one here who's actually *met* the *whole* White Elm council – *studied* under them, even.'

'Only for a little while!' the girl called back nervously in a slightly strangled voice, the kind of voice that doesn't like to be pushed for volume. Her accent was different again. Jaroslav brushed her nervousness aside.

'It doesn't matter. We're lucky to have your insight. I want to thank everyone for coming, and especially those who brought friends,' he said to the rest of his audience, rich voice projecting well even when he tossed the ruined cup back to its creator. 'Talking online and following Marcy's blog has been a fantastic start to our movement and it's brought us all together but it's when our message spreads that we'll start to see real social change.'

People clapped. I pulled my fascinated gaze away from him to share an uneasy look with Renatus, by now directly to my right, well behind the crowd, mixing with the non-witch tourists.

*Let's hear them out*, he said, but I knew he didn't feel comfortable with what we'd heard so far. A *movement* the council had known nothing about? Someone with "insight"?

'The more people we have singing our tune the harder we'll be to ignore,' Jaroslav went on, and a few girls whistled in appreciation. 'We've all heard Seers whispering about a war endorsed by the White Elm; we've been visited in our sleep by emissaries of Lisandro, trying to conscript to an army. Has anybody asked *us* what *we* want? *No*, because democracy is good enough for mortal society but not good enough for ours. What does Lisandro tell us? *Free magic for all.*' The teenagers and young adults in Jaroslav's audience raised their bottles and yelled the catchphrase back at him in a medley of disjointed voices. He got louder to be heard over them. 'And what does the White Elm tell us? *Follow, and we will lead.*'

Again the crowd yelled it back, emotion pouring out of them and swelling in their voices, their auras, their proximity. I stepped forward, caught up in the uncertain excitement. Far away from me now, I saw Renatus and Anouk share an uncomfortable cringe at the youthful exuberance of the activists. Jaroslav kept going, shoving his mop of thick brown hair back off his face, raising his voice along with the level of enthusiasm from his new friends.

'And what do *we* say?' he asked, and with them in chorus he yelled, '*Peace, Freedom, Choice.*'

Peace, freedom, choice. *Choice.* I glanced at a middle-aged American couple who were watching on with mild interest when the wife asked, 'Noble. What's he on about?'

The husband shrugged and I swallowed, thinking of what Renatus had said this group's website promoted.

These people wanted a free vote on who ran their nation. I'd been so focussed on my future within the White Elm, surrounded by a family of council supporters, living in their midst, seeing the admirable acts of its members, that it had totally escaped me that not everyone saw what I saw. To many, it would be easy to resent the council. They were never voted into power. They rose to it hundreds of years ago and held on, for better or worse, an authoritarian regime.

I was an apprentice to what others – *these* others – saw as a dictatorship.

Jaroslav was talking again.

'It's not fair that thousands will be caught up in conflict we never agreed to. This city can tell a hundred stories of war, but none of it speaks as loudly as *this* one monument.' He gestured at the wall, where tourists still wrote their names amid countless layered works of street art, messages of love and inspiring song lyrics. Some had stopped to watch him, lacking context but intrigued by his passion. 'Give us the right to elect our own government. Vote on laws before they're passed. Uprisings like Lisandro's won't threaten our very society if there's a fair democratic system in place. Peace, freedom and choice is the only way forward.' He raised a hand in salute to the man depicted in art on the wall; the music volume and clamour of agreeable voices started to increase. 'We aren't the first to proclaim it and be heard.'

The music was pumping again and everyone was dancing energetically. Someone bumped into me and I noticed how deep into the crowd I'd wandered while I listened to Jaroslav's stirring speech. I watched him move fluidly with the music atop his car stage. He and his new international friends looked like my school friends – big kids, not activists. Yet here they were, proving that youth was no barrier to political opinion, coming together to draw strength from their shared dream of peaceful people power.

I was part of the regime they were arguing against but I didn't feel uncomfortable the way my master and teacher, at the edges of the square, did.

My wards were still tight around me but they only hid my energy. I was fully visible.

'Aristea?' The voice was right beside me but I barely heard it over the music. I looked around and spread my senses out to find a vaguely familiar soul. I was looking through a pair of glasses I kind-of recognised. The owner was a girl my own age with wide surprised eyes and an open jaw. She grabbed my forearms excitedly before I could think to stop her. '*Aristea?!* It *is* you!'

'*Marcy?!*' I yelled back, and was still hardly audible. I tried to recall her surname but couldn't. Marcy! She'd roomed with Kendra and Sophia for the first few weeks of our time at Morrissey House, and all I'd learned about her was that she was South African, wore glasses and liked healing.

Now I guess I could add "wrote blogs about the council", "travelled to Europe to meet friends" and "organised support rallies over the internet" to that list. She'd been pulled out of the Academy by her parents.

'Gosh, you're *here!*' she shrieked, and laughed delightedly. She dragged me over to the car and tugged on the leg of Jaroslav's loose jeans. When he glanced down, his eyes met mine and he smiled, a welcoming smile. He knelt to listen to Marcy as we moved closer and he said something, but over that noise I had no hope of hearing either of them and I didn't imagine they heard each other, either. He must have realised this, because he extended a hand. I probably should have but I didn't hesitate in taking it and letting him pull me onto the car roof with him. A few girls shot me disgruntled looks. I didn't see them but I certainly felt them.

*Where are you?* Renatus had noticed I wasn't where he left me. *What are you doing?*

Still holding my hand and still smiling, Jaroslav leaned close to my ear to be heard.

'What did she say?' he asked loudly. 'What's your name? Who are you here with?'

'Aristea,' I answered just as loudly into his ear, 'and I'm here with the White Elm.'

He kept smiling for a second; when my words registered, I felt and saw everything about him pause. His smile froze, his hand went rigid on mine. His dark eyes slowly moved to my wrist, and, cautiously, he used his thumb to slide my sleeve up a little, just enough to see a point of the marking I bore there. He inhaled audibly, even over the music.

'You really are,' he breathed, his mouth making obvious enough movements that I could read the statement. 'Hold on, I need to get this.'

With his spare hand he pulled a mobile phone from his pocket and I thought he was going to answer a call, but instead he held it at arm's length and turned its screen away, simultaneously leaning closer to me. I kept my eyes on the phone, stupidly wondering what he hoped to achieve by holding it so far away (did he have spells up that were preventing him from getting good reception?) and then the flash went off and I understood.

'No, don't,' I argued, pulling my hand free, but the photo was already taken. In the edge of my vision I saw Renatus and Anouk moving closer to the group.

*Get off that car*, Renatus ordered. *You're out in the open.*

'This picture will be worth a fortune, seriously,' Jaroslav told me, showing me the screen. I reluctantly looked and was glad to see I hadn't blinked. 'Everyone is talking about you.

When news about you broke, Marcy blogged that she'd *met you* before. Everybody wants to know what you look like.'

'What news?' I demanded, feeling unsettled. The White Elm had gone to great pains to keep their business secret, yet someone was posting this stuff on the *internet*?! My *name* was out there, being shared and discussed as if people knew anything about me. It had taken Lisandro weeks to learn of my existence – now the whole world knew?

'You know Marcy?' he yelled as the music rose to a crescendo. I gathered he hadn't heard my question. He pointed into the crowd. 'Marcy Pretoria?'

I glanced down at her and saw that she'd lost interest in me, though some of the friends she'd shouted into the ears of were grinning up at me. Marcy was pulling on the hand of an older girl who looked like she might have been her sister and was pointing excitedly at Anouk. The sisters pushed through the group to reach the councillor and I saw Anouk's expression of surprise as Marcy threw her arms around her in a hug. I remembered that Anouk was Kendra and Sophia's supervisor, and had therefore been Marcy's too.

'Kind of. What news?' I yelled again. Jaroslav heard me this time and laughed.

*Get down!*

*Give me a second.*

*No! Get down now!*

'What news?' Jaroslav repeated incredulously. 'The White Elm getting an apprentice. You. You have no idea how excited everyone is to know the council is moving forwards again.'

'You don't even like the council,' I protested. He stared.

'What? No, the White Elm's fine,' he disagreed, 'as an institution of magic preservation. Collecting the great among us and making them greater – no one's done that better, anywhere. But governance should be decided by the people, not by the authority. Wait,' he said urgently when I gave in to Renatus's badgering and tried to climb down from the car roof. Jaroslav held onto me so I couldn't jump. 'Where are you going?'

The song changed and the crowd screamed in appreciation of the new track, and I looked around anxiously as yuck feelings started to weave among all the good ones around me. Lisandro wanted us here. He hadn't yet appeared. Every second that passed was a second we would regret wasting when he arrived and we hadn't yet dispersed this crowd.

Or the tourists. The locals. Forty or more innocent mortals, photographing the wall, adding to it, walking along the street on their way somewhere else...

'Jaroslav, listen,' I implored, leaning close again so he'd hear me. 'You need to send these people home.'

'Why?' he asked. He frowned. 'We have a right to speak our minds.'

I felt Renatus's discomfort and glanced back at him, beginning to push through the crowd. He ignored the young women trying to engage him in dancing.

*I don't like this,* he said. *Let's go.*

*They listen to him. He can tell them to go home.*

*It's getting too late for that. I'll get you out first and come back for them. Quick; come on.*

'Jaroslav, this is great, but you're all in danger,' I insisted, desperate to break up this party before we left. I would feel awful if Renatus walked away from them for the twenty seconds it would take to evacuate me and something happened to them that he or I could have prevented. I kicked the boom box. It fell onto its side but continued playing. I felt someone's disappointment. Those icky feelings were getting stronger. Something was brewing. 'This is too open, too public. Go home and write a blog.'

'Change doesn't happen in blogs, Aristea.' He gestured around, ignoring my aggression towards his music. 'We're bringing it to the streets.'

'Any other day, that'd be fine. But get these people off the street before-'

The boom box exploded. Instinctively I threw a small ward up before me, protecting myself and Jaroslav from the chips of plastic and metal that flew forth. The crowd screamed and dropped their bottles, tourists emptied their hands of cameras and drawing tools to cover their heads and faces, and in the abrupt silence that followed, a voice carried over the crowd.

'I can't stand that song.'

My stomach bottomed out and I turned quickly in the same direction everyone else did. An unfamiliar young man was standing right where I'd started, leaning against the window of a closed-up shop, grinning easily. He had his brown hair gelled flat to the side over his high forehead. Magic swirled in his aura; a sorcerer, like us, but he wore a hooded cloak inappropriate for the season and the gorgeous day.

A crimson cloak.

Renatus and Anouk didn't move. A few tourists straightened, gaping at the site of the explosion, backing away, reaching for mobile phones. I heard the whisper that ripped through them, ignorant of the existence of magic: *bomb, it was a bomb.*

'Bomb? What an excellent idea,' the newcomer proclaimed loudly, grinning, sending the whispers up a notch, sending the same worry through the crowd of witches around Jaroslav and I. He started toward us; the crowd got noisier, more restless.

'Who are you?' Renatus demanded. The crimson cloaked stranger just grinned and shrugged, still advancing without haste.

'Don't be *afraid*,' he called over to us, accent distinctly Irish, 'but I've brought something to liven up this party. A gift from Lisandro.'

There was nothing in his hand until he performed an underarm throw, and a silvery tennis ball-sized object flew from his fingertips. The activists gasped and ducked but it didn't strike them. It caught itself in the air at about my eyelevel, raised up as I was by the car. It hung there in the centre of the square, glistening. A little disco ball.

It was such a ridiculously harmless thing to throw at us that we were all adequately distracted staring at it and *something* energetically weird happened all around us.

There was a shriek. A tourist dropped her camera and ran, then froze. Out of every alley and side street that led into view of the Lennon Wall, a man in a hood now emerged, each bearing a long, sharp knife. The people around me noticed at the same time I did and I felt the collective surge of fear, a good portion of it mine.

The disco ball swelled to the size of a basketball.

'Get *down*!' Renatus shouted at me, shoving past two men his own age to reach me. I jumped down from the car, pulling Jaroslav behind me, stretching out my hand for my master's. He grabbed me and yanked, and I followed, stepping after him, prepared for the change in flooring under my boots from road to springy grass.

It didn't happen. We didn't go anywhere.

'What happened?' I cried, my fear spiking. Was it me, or did that disco ball just get bigger? I looked around wildly – the armed men were bearing down, slowly, and the crowd around me was shouting and screaming in a flurry of languages, milling uncertainly about, tightening up, drawing closer and closer to the car and the wall. We were being encircled, no path of escape left uncovered. This was an ambush.

'*Je jich tu tolik,*' Jaroslav, beside me, exclaimed worriedly. I didn't know what he said.

'We can't Displace!' Renatus yelled over the noise, and I felt his worry like a stab in my heart. *He's pulled the Fabric too tight over this area and we're stuck inside it, like a bubble.* 'We've got to get outside the perimeter.'

'They're armed!' someone at the edge of the group shouted, terrified. Beside him, a woman in a suit and big sunglasses, looking like she was on a lunch break from some nearby office, was trying to make a call on her mobile phone with shaky hands.

'*Nemůžu se jim dovolat!*' she exclaimed in a panic, shaking her phone as though that would help it connect through the thick field of magic that had settled over us. '*Zavolejte někdo policii!*'

Police, yes, I thought, desperate. I didn't speak Czech but *that* I recognised.

'They're coming!' someone else cried shrilly. 'There's so many!'

She was right. I looked around and counted at least twelve hooded assailants, all of them moving straight for us, none bothering to hide their knives. I faintly recalled my new knives, shiny and unhelpful underneath my bed.

'*Hej!* What do we do?' Jaroslav demanded of me, tugging on my hand. I looked at Renatus, whose attention was fixed on the grinning ring leader.

'White Elm,' he shouted. 'Stop where you are.'

His willingness to take charge and engage in direct interaction with the man responsible for this frightening situation calmed the crowd a little, enough that they huddled together and went quiet to hear what happened next. The disco ball, which by now was the approximate size of a watermelon, quivered but briefly ceased its continuous growth.

The oncoming crimson-cloaked men did stop, wavering in place like they were hesitating. When I touched them with the edge of my senses I was confronted by the depth of their unwillingness. Unwillingness to what? Stop? Be here? Their leader lifted his chin and laughed.

'For you? I don't think so.' He gestured onwards. Slowly, almost reluctantly, and not all at once, the men circling us continued in their advance. 'We heard there was a soapbox here and we've got a message to spread, too.'

'Stop, or we'll be forced to act,' Anouk warned. Again, some of the assailants wavered. She and Renatus revealed their wands, holding them high enough to be seen. 'You're in breach of the Statute of the Privatisation of Magic from Mortals.'

*Who's coming?* I asked, looking around for our backup.

*The perimeter's huge,* Renatus said. *Elijah and Qasim are at the bridge. They're on foot from there.*

We were alone. Renatus and Anouk were grossly outnumbered and help was minutes away.

'Haven't you seen the movies, White Elm? Mortals *love* magic. Look at them, they're loving it.' The Irish ring leader, the only one with his face exposed, smiled maniacally at the crowd around us. Sorcerers and non-witches alike, nobody was enjoying this. 'Should we show them some more?'

He nodded at the nearest of his troops and they all raised their knives, blades glowing. The threatening act sent a shudder of terror through the crowd I stood in that almost choked me with its thickness, and the silvery ball hanging over us grew suddenly to the circumference of an exercise ball.

'Get down!' Renatus shouted again, pushing me against the car for cover, and most of the people around us did as they were told. He and Anouk were on the same page and they both fired shots of glowing white magic from their wands. Both hit their marks, striking an oncoming attacker in the chest, and both men sunk to the asphalt without noise or protest. Renatus was quick enough with his next shot to take out a second, but after that the attackers adapted their wards to deflect this spell. The apparent turning of tables demoralised the terrified activists and their refreshed fear coincided with a surge in the size of Lisandro's disco ball.

*Don't be afraid…*

I could hear the echo of Irish's words as clearly as I saw the easy smile on his distant face. He made no move to come after us. He just watched with apparent enjoyment as his men closed in on us. I had no idea what they would do to us when they got close enough to use those knives. I had no idea what they were doing here – attacking sorcerers and mortals in the streets in broad daylight in the name of Lisandro, whose mission of late had been to win people over. It made no sense. All I knew was I was petrified.

It hit me.

'It's what he wants!' I shouted, shoving away from the cover of the car to allow my voice to carry. Renatus pushed me back; I caught his arm so he couldn't get a grip on me. 'Everybody needs to calm down! We're feeding him.'

I didn't know how he was doing it, but I was the only one who could sense the connection between our emotions and the growth of the ball, and I knew I was right. Renatus and Anouk paused in their cycling through of different ineffective spells to look up at the silvery disco ball.

'It's a bomb,' Anouk realised, and her words made everything worse. Alarm shot through the group as her statement was restated again and again in frightened whispers. *Je to bomba, it's another bomb...*

'Nobody panic,' Renatus called loudly. 'It won't explode if we stay calm.'

Many people did not seem to understand, or were too panicky, until Jaroslav loudly reiterated, '*Řekl, ať zůstaneme v klidu.*'

The crowd wanted him to be right and I felt the deliberate energetic lull of everybody desperately trying to remain anxiously calm. The non-witches were in a state of disbelief. All eyes clung to the ball hanging ominously over us. It maintained its dimensions.

'You don't know that,' Irish called back, playfully, and the words created doubt and the doubt reopened the fear, and the ball swelled just a tiny bit in response. His next words he shouted, a manic roar: 'Long live Magnus Moira!'

It was enough to send the group into unsalvageable panic. What had been a motionless pack of obedient activists huddled at the White Elm's feet, protected, became a bubbling mess of people, all absolutely terrified, all on their feet and moving. They had nowhere to go; they shoved past each other to get away from one edge of the crowd to find themselves at another, facing a different hooded stranger, eventually backing themselves against the bright wall of peace. All they achieved by standing was to block the councillors' clear shots at the oncoming threats.

'Calm down!' Anouk shouted across the group. 'Stay together!'

'*Držte se u sebe,*' Jaroslav translated immediately, waving someone over. The girl who'd given him the paper cup megaphone squeezed through the crowd to get to him.

'Stay together!' Renatus repeated, casting a ward to halt the progress of the three men closest to him. They had to stop, walled off, but one of the younger members of the crowd burst free at the other edge and made for a gap between two of the hooded assailants. He was too slow and a gloved hand caught the collar of his shirt.

It was so fast. The hunting knife glided across the boy's neck without any resistance and blood sprayed across the road and the people nearest. The boy's shock and fear, and the attacker's deep revulsion, ripped through me and then so did the reaction of the crowd. They utterly dissolved.

'Don't look! Don't panic!' Renatus tried to say, trying to push more people between himself and the wall to defend them, but the crowd was too big for just him and Anouk, and none of them heeded his advice. They – we – all watched as the hooded man dropped the boy's shivering body onto the road to bleed out and die, and continued to advance, hot blood dripping from the blade of his weapon.

The bomb, fuelled by our fears, was now even bigger than a washing machine, and its silvery surface bubbled menacingly like it was struggling to contain its ugly innards.

'Don't panic! Don't-' Renatus cut himself off when one of the hooded men broke through his ward and seized a girl by the arm. He blasted the attacker with some crackly black magic I was sure he wasn't meant to use. It was effective: the assailant was flung back onto the pavement, writhing and screaming, clawing at his clothing like it was on fire.

'Renatus!' Anouk shouted, and their eyes met over the surrounded crowd for only a fraction of an instant. He sneered, an unexpectedly explicit show of expression for him, and he looked one last time at the bomb. Cracks had formed in its silver surface and something black and awful glowed within, urging to get out. He grabbed my shoulders and turned me around.

'Go. Run. Run!' He shouted the last instruction to us all and began shoving people after me. I rounded the bonnet of the old car and took off, Jaroslav still holding my hand tightly. Two men in hoods barred my way, so close now that they could slash and kill me or any of the others. In desperation I threw a ward at them. It behaved like a wrecking ball and knocked them clean over with audible winded puffs. I leapt over the legs of one and took advantage of the gap left in their semi-circle, racing out into the relative safety of the street.

I felt their horror and shame, as sharp as their blades. It made me stagger with confusion.

I glanced back after a few strides to see where Renatus was, and was surprised to see I was leading the majority of the young activists, tourists and locals out of danger. Renatus and Anouk were directing everyone after me and fending off those hooded attackers who didn't follow me.

Half of Irish's remaining men, Lisandro's men, Magnus Moira, supposedly, had broken formation to come after me and my little band, so I only paused long enough for Renatus to yell, 'Don't wait! Go!' before turning on my heel and running away with those who were beginning to overtake me. We streamed around parked cars and dodged around lamp posts and street signs, leaving the inspiring colours of the Lennon Wall far behind. Distantly I felt an edge to my awareness up ahead, two hundred metres or so, beyond the square, out of sight, and gathered I must be sensing the barrier of the no-Displacement zone.

My awareness of Renatus became less and less as I ran, and I knew he wasn't keeping up.

'Don't stop!' I shouted even as I did. I swung around to watch the action I'd left behind. Renatus and Anouk had taken care of the men who had stayed to concentrate on them and were coming after me, finally, with the remaining few of the young activists. Renatus led, blasting at the backs of the men who still chased me.

Jaroslav pulled my hand and I shook him off when I saw how near the fastest hooded stranger was. I didn't have my wand so I aimed my palm at him and channelled my magic through. My ward hit him like a net and he went down and stayed there, pinned.

Afraid, ashamed.

'He said not to wait,' Jaroslav reminded me urgently, but he stayed at my side. I wondered why. Did he think he was safer with me than further away from the threat? The others, I saw, had slowed or stopped, too, and were sticking close to me.

Renatus was catching up now.

'Run!' he ordered, and again I turned and obeyed. The crowd followed my example and ran with me, my herd. Their petrified energy ran through and with mine, simultaneously terrible and thrilling.

We hadn't even cleared the square. The moment the bomb went off was undeniable in its stomach-wrenching awfulness, and I put on a burst of speed, overtaking a few girls, but all at once I also knew it was worthless. Lisandro's Irish psychopath wasn't going to let us *outrun* his weapon, and if it was a weapon he was bothering with, it was lethal.

I stopped for a third time and raised my hand above my head, drawing as much magic as I knew how to hold at once and streaming it along my arm and out of me. A pearly whitish stream of magic shot into the air, ten, twenty metres, and mushroomed outwards and down, encasing me and those around me inside its umbrella-shaped safety net. I turned my head to look for Renatus as the ward fell quickly earthward.

I could have swallowed my own tongue the way air whipped down my throat. The disco ball had imploded and a black shock wave was rippling down the street after us, flooding the square right to the walls. One of the hooded men I'd knocked down was up on his feet but when the black flowed over him he dropped back to the asphalt, life blinking immediately out.

Renatus was not inside the perimeter of my ward! It hadn't touched down yet but when it did he was going to be on the outside. Panicking, I scraped for more magic, more power, and sent it surging into the ward. The overdose of energy in my body made my nerves tingle and burn – hadn't Jadon warned us about the risk of burnouts? – but I kept it up, desperate. The ward glowed and grew outward by a few metres. Just enough.

Renatus dropped to the road and rolled underneath the edge of the ward as it touched ground and went solid. *Safe.* Thank heavens.

Two hands slammed into the transparent glassy wall of my dome and my relief shattered. Outside, the black shockwave tore through the bodies of the four people I'd failed to include in my protective mushroom and struck the ward. The crowd I'd shielded jumped in fright at the *thud* of a deadweight human being falling against the outer wall of the ward and the crackly sound of the black wave of fear rippling over the dome, unable to get through. It washed harmlessly over us and most eyes tracked its progress as it weakened in colour and resolve.

The square was exactly as it was before, the stunning medieval surrounds undamaged.

I held the ward in place for a good ten seconds longer. The others maybe thought I was just being sure. But my undivided attention was on the motionless shapes on the outside of my ward, and in particular the one lying at the base of my dome.

The one whose hands had struck the ward, banging, desperate, demanding entry.

The one who was just a half-second behind Renatus.

The one who brought me here.

*Anouk.*

I felt absolutely nothing as I dropped my hand. The ward dispersed and the vacuum of power in my body left me utterly numb. Renatus was on his knees from rolling to safety and he was staring too at his colleague. I was too overwhelmed from the consistent levels of everyone's terror over the past minute to register the shock he felt.

Her eyes were still open, still ringed with the dark circles of tiredness. Her mouth was open, halfway through saying something she was never going to finish. Her wispy blonde hair was strewn across her face and neck. There was no blood, no wound, no evidence at all of injury, but like the three people behind her she was definitely dead.

Gone. Like that.

I'd cast a ward to save everybody but I hadn't made it big enough. I'd locked her out to die.

One of the overwhelmed non-witches near me burst into tears and in the distance, I heard sirens. But my attention was at the other end of the street, where, in my emotionally vulnerable state, I felt someone's sorrowful satisfaction. *Satisfaction*. I *knew* automatically, and magic only works when those around believe in it. I looked and adjusted my focus with no effort at all, and I saw the glimmer of another ward flickering.

Lisandro stood at the window I'd started off beside, a little observant figure hidden in invisibility wards we'd normally be well and truly onto if we weren't distracted by explosions of terror, and for a moment he regarded the devastation he'd caused. The men he'd brought with him were all dead. Even Irish, the ring leader he'd sent to appear to orchestrate this on his behalf. Most of the people he'd come here to terrorise were still alive, still crowded behind me. I had no idea what he'd come here to achieve – this whole attack was so counter to his goals. I thought of him last week, schmoozing with rich society witches. How was this going to look when word got out? It didn't make any sense.

Anouk was *dead*, and Lisandro had made it my fault, and nobody else could see that he was here.

I had no energy but no one had told my limbs. I broke into a run. Renatus snapped out of his reverie and stood to grab me.

'Where-'

'It's him!'

And then Renatus knew, too. But he didn't let me go.

'No, it wasn't your-'

'Get *off*!' I snarled, trying to struggle free of his grip, but he was stronger and wouldn't let go. I reacted without thinking. A ward erupted between us and threw us apart. It was weak because I was weak, but it got me loose – and still looked plenty supernatural to the poor non-witches all around me – and I bolted back down the street, stumbling when my legs remembered that their energy had been drained to power that overambitious spell.

Renatus came after me. Lisandro noticed, must have realised his disguise had failed, but just watched us. Calm. Interested. I still couldn't understand what had driven him to do what he'd just done, how this could possibly serve any sort of purpose, but I couldn't care. I just wanted to get to him and to *hurt* him, to catch him and kill him for the horror he'd just put me through and the horrors he'd done to me in the past. To my family, and Renatus's. For the things he was yet to do; for the death he was meant to have at Renatus's hand, which would undo him. This was unforgiveable.

A silvery ward was about to materialise in front of me; I saw it in Renatus's thoughts a microsecond before he cast it, and grabbed that thought and broke it. He'd lost the thought, couldn't cast without the intention. He tried to think it again. Again I stamped it out.

Controlling his thoughts, manipulating his choices, doing exactly what I had no right to do.

*Stop! You can't do anything. He'll kill you; just stop!* Renatus was shouting at me, either aloud or in my head or maybe both, but I couldn't oblige. I was motivated by something other than my head or my heart, something hot and bitter and opaque. Hatred? I hadn't known it could fill me so completely that I couldn't control my own actions, but I didn't feel the need to retake control. It seemed to know what it was doing.

Lisandro waited until I was almost at the car Jaroslav had pulled me atop less than three minutes ago before he turned away and began to walk down the alley we'd arrived from, back toward the bridge. Where was Qasim, where was Elijah? I pushed off the bonnet, half wishing I could stop there and rest, lean against it, and half wishing I had the magic and the knowledge to ignite the old car and send it flying through the air in Lisandro's direction. I was granted neither wish and Lisandro continued walking, purposefully but without breaking into even a jog.

His apathy was infuriating.

'Lisandro!' I screamed, leaping over the dead bodies of the Irish ring leader and one of the other hooded men. All of them, dead. Thrown away. Had they known they were coming here to die for his entertainment? And the boy – I steered clear of his still-bleeding form. Who was he? Did his parents know he was here today, meeting friends from the internet forums and losing his life to political extremists?

'Aristea, stop!' Renatus demanded, and if I was paying attention I would have recognised that he was terrified. He wanted to Displace, to jump ahead of me and catch me, but he was still restricted by Lisandro's spell over the city block. 'You can't change anything!' *You'll only get hurt. Please. It wasn't your fault.*

But he didn't understand. *You didn't just kill someone.* Lisandro disappeared from sight but when I lowered my wards I could still sense him, just ahead, just around that corner, just down that alleyway…

I came at the corner so quickly that I had to catch the bricks with my hand and swing myself into the turn.

*SLAM!*

The attack was to all of my senses – a blinding flash in my vision, an ear-shattering scream, an excruciating pain tearing across my face, plus I was sure I'd been knocked to the ground. I didn't know. I had no awareness of anything but the blindness, the incessant scream that would prove to be mine and the agony.

I was sure I had my hands on my face, over my eye, but that couldn't be right because my hands were slick with hot blood, and then there were hands closing over my wrists trying to pull my hands away, and there were overwhelming feelings of horror twisting with mine, and there was a voice saying my name over and over but the screaming was still ringing in my ears and I was in *so much pain*, and I was already in darkness so when the option to slip away came I took it. It seemed the right thing to do.

# epilogue

*1961 – Salem*

The schoolyard was a dismal, barren place, but the children who ran out to it from their classrooms brought their excitement, laughter and smiles all the same and soon it was lively and noisy, all colour and motion.

Cassán spotted Mánus against the fence, head resting on the railings, eyes forlorn and reluctantly observant as he watched the playing children. Though he was still, he radiated conflict.

'Áine wants children,' he said as Cassán approached. He didn't pull his gaze away from the schoolyard. 'I don't know how to explain to her that Morrisseys only have one. I'm not sure I understand it myself.' He fell silent, conflicted emotions tumbling over themselves inside him. Cassán reached his side and leaned against the fence also. 'I should make it happen soon, I suppose. I don't even know if I'll be *capable* of fathering a child, afterward.'

Cassán hadn't considered this. He had just last month given in to his desire to return to Greece, and there on the beautiful isolated little island where he'd left her a year before was Anthea, every bit the wild and glorious goddess he remembered. The spark that had attracted them initially was still there and they'd married before all of her family and friends in a ceremony full of fun, laughter, colour, motion... not unlike the scene in the playground on the other side of the fence. He'd brought his new wife back with him to Ireland to begin their life together, and to begin with, all had been wonderful. He wrote his books and she arranged and decorated her new home. He studied with his group and she cooked fabulous meals her mother had taught her and everyone enjoyed them.

Now, six weeks into marriage, Cassán was starting to realise things he should have considered earlier. Anthea's English was stilted and unclear, and though she was trying hard to learn, she was still not fluent enough to manage community life on her own. She was stuck at the house unless he was home to accompany her into town, which he increasingly was not, and despite having invited many couples living nearby to come for tea and despite all of these occasions being quite pleasant and polite, none had yet asked Cassán and Anthea over in return. The neighbours were snobbish and conservative – they did not want to befriend the new immigrant next door. Anthea had no friends here, and Cassán was also starting to suspect that his whirlwind arrival and then return to her idyllic Grecian island had given her an impression of him as something of a gypsy adventurer. He wished that were the case. He wished he had the time to take her to see the world the way she seemed to think he would. He loved her and he wanted her to be happy, so it stung his conscience to think he might have misled her or dropped her into an expectedly miserable existence.

If it so happened that his pursuit of knowledge of magic, Fate and human existence meant they could not have a family, how would that affect her?

'Does Anthea want children?' Mánus asked, shifting his eyes to his friend without moving his head from the fence. 'Those Greeks have big families, don't they?'

'I imagine she will,' Cassán answered. 'I haven't asked.' He paused, feeling rotten. 'I should ask.'

A playful squeal drew their attention to a pair of girls chasing each other around the swing set. Children didn't have these burdens, these responsibilities to others, to weigh

470

them down. They didn't need to balance their own desires with those of the people they loved. They simply had their innocence and their right to its preservation, which allowed them to live free of the weariness of the rest of the world.

Which made them a source of power that could not be found anywhere else.

Mánus pointed through the fence at the fireman's pole. 'That's the one.'

Cassán didn't want to look but knew he'd have to face this truth one way or another. A small boy, six or seven years old, was waiting patiently for the children at the base of the pole to move out of the way so he could slide down. He was grinning, two teeth missing from his set of little whites, and his mousy hair was neatly cut but messy with boisterous play. The men were too far away to hear what was said but they watched as the child gestured to the other children, directing them away. When the way was clear he locked his legs around the post and slid deftly down to the dirt below, and then disappeared into the throng of speedy little bodies.

'How do you know?' Cassán asked, waiting for the mousy head to reappear, for the blue overalls to be visible between the dashes of other colours.

'Andrew.'

Cassán looked away, incensed. Of all his friends, Andrew Hawke was the one he could most do without. His overconfidence and immorality fell in direct opposition to the way Cassán conducted himself.

Or so he liked to tell himself.

'Eternal life looks a whole lot less appealing, knowing *he's* going to be there for it,' he commented darkly. Truth be told, he would probably prefer eternity without Moira Dawes, too, and her self-motivated, oft-cruel manipulations; likewise, Eugene Dubois's invasive carelessness for a hundred more years was not an exciting prospect. In three short years the five lives had become so inextricably entwined that the possibility of a future without them seemed laughable. Bitterly so. What had begun as enthusiasm and impassioned rebellion against the White Elm's restrictions had become all-consuming, costly. Beaded with resentment. They'd spent too many days together, grating on one another's nerves, five personalities too big to share one common goal but by now too deep in the manifestations of their work to know how to back out. Mánus kept watching the schoolyard.

'He's just a mortal,' he said vaguely, apparently not having heard Cassán at all. 'The mother's a widow and he's the only child she'll ever have. She'll live to eighty-three and wonder every day what became of him.' As Cassán turned back, the little boy in question reappeared, climbing the play structure again to have another go at the fireman's pole. Tenacious things, children were. 'She patched a tear in those overalls last week and she calls him Bunny. He dropped his sandwich at lunchtime and his teacher gave him hers.' Mánus shook his head slowly, uncertainty spiralling around him in slow curves. 'People care about this boy, Cassán.'

'I know.' Cassán's response was soft, because he'd been avoiding thinking the same thing. He swallowed. 'That's... why it works.'

'And there's no other way? No other way to power the spell?'

'I wish there was.'

Mánus was not typically expressive but now he sneered in frustrated disgust and shoved away from the fence. He stalked away and Cassán sighed, taking a moment's regretful, reflective pause before following.

'We don't have to do it,' he called after the Morrissey heir as they traipsed down the hill to the road. Mánus ignored him, kept his pace. 'You and I are free to make our own choices.'

'Are we?' the other scoffed without a glance back. 'Three years of *freedom* hasn't left me feeling particularly *free*. Dubois in my head, Hawke dictating my next step, Dawes in my shadow, *you* fishing for a conscience.' He shot an angry look back now and Cassán staggered in his footing, taken aback by the claim. Mánus kept going. 'What makes you think you'll find it in me? What makes you ask what I'll do before making your own mind up? I'm not any better than the rest of them.'

It was a good question, and not one Cassán had expected.

'You're the only one who cares who patched those overalls,' he said, trying to ignore the swelling of positive feelings behind him as the schoolchildren started a new game. For one of them, that positivity could soon be turned on its head. He tried not to think about it. 'You're the only one who wonders.'

'I'm not,' Mánus retorted, stopping at the road and looking about for cars. Cassán caught up and they crossed together. 'You're here, too.'

'We don't have to do it,' Cassán said again, quieter this time now that they were in step. 'Forever is a long time to live with something like this.'

'It's too late for that,' Mánus disagreed. They walked down the road, heading for town. They could Skip the distance but neither was all too eager to reach their destination. 'The others have seen the spell. They're going to do it, whether you and I are involved or not. It's done. We can't save that boy.'

Cassán hesitated. 'We could stop them, somehow.'

'Somehow? The only way you'll do that now is if you kill them.' His friend, the one member of their "book club" he would actually, genuinely consider something close to an actual *friend*, cast him a condescending look. 'Are you going to kill them, Ó Grádaigh?'

Cassán shrugged uncomfortably. 'Wouldn't be the worst thing I've considered doing. And relative to what we're planning-'

'Don't,' Mánus warned, pointing an unhappy finger in his face as they walked ever onward. 'You'll put ideas in my head that I really don't need.'

They turned a corner, into the wind, and shrugged their coats higher to shield their necks from the cold. The new street was busier than the last, pedestrians window shopping in little boutiques, the deli, a fruit grocer, a bookshop. A previous incarnation of Cassán would have stopped to go inside, browsed the shelves, chatted up the clerk to see whether he could get his work among their titles. Today's Cassán kept walking. Hardly spared the bookshop a glance. His early books were out of print; his latest work was in blatant opposition to the White Elm's 1958 restrictions on magical knowledge. He'd published under a pseudonym to avoid the charges that would come with it, but everyone who knew what they were reading knew it was his. Bookshops weren't the right medium for spreading his word anymore – too public, too open. Now the work found its audience through other means, through the slippery hands of the magical society's underbelly.

'I don't know what else to think of,' Cassán admitted. 'I feel helpless. Like this spell, this future, everything that's happened in the last three years... the man I've become, the things I want, the things I'm willing to do, it feels like it's all sneaked up on me, outside my control.'

'Unbidden,' Mánus agreed. 'But it isn't. It's the product of our choices. It's the product of who we let into our lives, into our minds. We brought this upon ourselves. We *invited* this turmoil we're feeling.'

'Then what are we supposed to do?' Cassán demanded miserably. 'Just live with the consequences of our actions?'

'It's no worse than what we deserve.' Mánus sidestepped to allow a mother with a pram the space to pass him. 'We live with it, we get on with things, we father children with our beautiful wives, and we pray our descendants grow into better people than us. What the *hell*?' he interrupted himself, outraged. They had reached their destination, a poky little café halfway along the main street. The doors and bay window were closed tight against the icy wind, and a handmade paper sign was taped onto the glass of the door.

*Mánus & Moira*
*Welcome the enlightened*
*To join their new coven*

*10 o'clock Tuesday*

'This was *her* stupid idea, not mine,' the scrier snarled, reaching for the sign to rip it down, but Cassán pushed his hand away before he could.

'I know, I know,' he murmured, looking around to see if anyone was watching, 'but we need anchors. In *case* the spell backfires. You know that.'

Already, inside the warm café, he could sense the intrigue and excitement of four sorcerers, each of them beguiled by Moira's charm and manipulation of their energetic surroundings. Tearing down the sign ran the risk of a potential gullible soul walking right past instead of taking interest and stepping inside.

They needed five. Five souls to tether their lives to, just in case their massive spell drained them too much. Instead, it would drain on the anchors. In all likelihood, nobody would die, and the anchors would just feel exceptionally tired the next day.

Well. Nobody but Bunny.

'Fine, but I don't want my name attached to this,' Mánus said staunchly, angry. 'I'm planning to live through this spell and my family line has to live with any reputation I gather. *Mánus and Moira welcome the enlightened,*' he scoffed, affronted by her nerve, insinuating a partnership or intimacy by using his name with hers like it belonged there. 'Imagine if Áine saw this?'

'I can't say I expect to see her to turn up, considering the obscurity of where we are.' Cassán dug in his coat pocket for a pen. It had long run out of ink; carrying it was a habit from when he used to sign books. Now he channelled a little burst of magic through the instrument, the Crafter's touch, and he ran it swiftly over the sign without touching the nib to paper.

It was a party trick, no effort, not worth boasting, but was so effective in impressing non-Crafters. The ampersand shifted, the ink lifting clear of the porous paper and inserting itself between the *a* and *n*.

'Who is this guy Magnus?' Cassán asked, pocketing the pen and pulling open the door for his friend. 'Apparently he and Moira are starting a new coven.'

Mánus never smiled, but Cassán felt the wry appreciation that overtook the anger.

'*Magnus Moira welcome the enlightened*,' he read, as though seeing the sign for the first time. He shrugged and stepped inside. 'Terrible name for a coven. It won't last.'

THE END

## Acknowledgements

Another book done, and so many wonderful, creative and generous souls to acknowledge, because no such project is managed in total isolation.

Thanks first to Sabrina, fairy godmother, editor and assistant publisher, for the way you make all of this happen, from bookings to much-needed deadlines to ordering paper butterflies online. I appreciate your part in my journey so very much.

Thanks to Laura-Jane for the incredible cover artwork and for continuing to magically intuit what I mean by various gestures and incoherent descriptions. We're getting better at this! Thanks to the butterfly who kept very still while I took that photo outside a cheesecake shop.

The Elm Stone Saga has achieved great momentum this year and that is in no small part due to the generosity and support of the wonderful bookstores that have welcomed my books onto their shelves. Thank you to all of my vendors but special thanks to Michael and Karen at Books@Stones for your warmth and for reinvigorating my confidence in approaching stores, to Phil at Dymocks for taking a chance on me, and to David at Hedleys for providing the venue for my first international book event, in my childhood bookshop. I am so grateful to you all, and nothing ever beats the feeling of seeing my books on the shelves of your beautiful stores.

The rest of the credit for Aristea's success really goes to you, the person reading this, and everyone like you who took a chance on an indie author at a signing or a convention. Thank you. Huge thanks to my many imaginary (internet) friends from around the world for supporting me from so far away, and for taking that same chance based on a shared love of *Dexter* or *The X-Files*. Thank you to anyone who has ever messaged me, stopped me in a walkway or sent a handwritten note to tell me how much you like my writing. You cannot imagine how gracious I am for your praise and how lovely it feels to know what you think.

While writing Unbidden, I wanted to give it its own identity, and I concentrated on the guiding question of *What makes this book different from Chosen or Scarred?* I knew this story needed a wider scope, to start looking at places, people and times outside of Aristea's previous experience – and outside of mine. Thank you to the real-life Jaroslav Košut for skipping class to show me your beautiful city of Prague, and for the Czech translations, and for the use of your name. I hope I've done it all justice! Thank you Kirsten Lund for all the support you've given the Elm Stone Saga since its beginnings, for the many discussions of the ways American English differs from Australian, for organising the French translations (thanks Jessica Klang!) and for letting me borrow your name for my medical examiner. I hope you like her. Thanks to Mum, Dad and Brigid Kudzius for your insight and feedback on the draft. One pair of eyes is never enough, and your perspectives are all so unique and much valued.

Life this last year has been busy, juggling the writing of this book with both work and university studies. Thank you to the people at work who make this feel possible. Thank you to my beautiful children, past and present, for your encouragement of me following my dreams, and thank you to your fabulous and supportive parents for your enthusiasm for my writing. Thanks to my amazing P/1/2 team for being the most generous, funny, thoughtful and inspiring people I have ever had the privilege of knowing, let alone calling friends, and for the way you keep me buoyed when I'm drowning in my own self-created stress. Thanks for supporting my writing so wholeheartedly, and for finally starting to share books and DVDs with me now that I'm writing more frequently. Thanks to my principal James for giving me this year to focus on this side of my life. Most thanks of course go to my awesome teaching partner/work wife, for keeping me sane, for making me laugh and for putting things in perspective.

Lifelong thanks to the many inspiring teachers who shaped me and encouraged me through my childhood and into adulthood, who never let me believe I couldn't do this and who gave me the space to be creative. Thank you for ensuring I grew to be literate in a world where literacy is both strength and privilege, for giving me the powers to create my own literature and for giving me the skills to empower and inspire another generation with the magic of words. Thank you to my lecturer and peers at USQ for your part in guiding my learning in the publishing process and making me a more informed author.

Thank you to my wonderful friends for sticking with me no matter how many weeks go by in hermit-mode and for supporting this dream of mine. Thank you to my amazing family for encouraging me and for helping me to prioritise my goals. The biggest thanks of all are reserved for my parents and husband, for being quietly proud of me, for working around the chaos that is me with a deadline, for knowing when to push and when not to, for reminding me I can manage, for enjoying the books and for all the love I could ever ask for. Like a spell, your belief in me is what makes this all possible.

CPSIA information can be obtained at www.ICGtesting.com
Printed in the USA
LVOW07s1700081016

507970LV00001B/16/P